DOCTOR WHO

THE SHADOW IN THE GLASS
JUSTIN RICHARDS & STEPHEN COLE

BBC

Published by BBC Worldwide Ltd
Woodlands, 80 Wood Lane
London W12 0TT

First published 2001
Copyright © Justin Richards and Stephen Cole 2001
The moral right of the authors has been asserted

Original series broadcast on the BBC
Format © BBC 1963
Doctor Who and TARDIS are trademarks of the BBC

ISBN 0 563 53838 4
Imaging by Black Sheep, copyright © BBC 2001

Printed and bound in Great Britain by Mackays of
Chatham
Cover printed by Belmont Press Ltd, Northampton

For Gary Russell
Without whom this book would quite simply not exist

'...I asked Hitler, "for whom should we fight on now?" And to that Hitler said in a monotone, "The Coming Man"...'

Heinz Linge (Hitler's Valet)

Schwerpunkt

Grey clouds striped the white sky like dirt that wouldn't shift. The sun had barely been up an hour but Flight Lieutenant Carl Smithson had been watching the heavens for most of the night as they lashed down wind and rain on the airfield, and for what? Not a sign of anything untoward, although the endless, regular drumming of the rain against the cracked glass of the camp windows had been cranking up the tension he felt hour after hour. He should've spent the night listening to the rain in bed, nuzzled up against Mary in Turelhampton. The rain sounded comforting outside when you were tucked up and warm. Here, standing by the glass, it sounded like machine gun fire.

Terrible weather for May. And it had brought with it strange sightings. Lights in the night. Not Luftwaffe, so the CO said – these lights weren't acting like planes, they were just hovering, a vivid red, burning… stuck in the sky over Sword Beach near Caen, like an omen warning the allied forces away. Smithson had overheard the AOC talking about Hitler's V weapons. The CO had told him there was probably nothing to worry about, but even so…

482 Squadron was due to fly this morning, and Smithson didn't want strange, hovering red lights up there with him.

He needed some fresh air, and so walked outside, his slipper soles slapping down on the wet asphalt. He stared stupidly up into the watery white sky. The airfield was quiet, deserted for now. Anyone watching from above would see him as tiny and insignificant, a speck on the ground.

The sirens howled, obliterating any other sound. The order to scramble had come just an hour or so after Smithson had finally called it a night and tried to get some sleep. Now, running for his plane, the frantic activity of the airfield ran jerkily in his vision like the silent movies he'd loved so much as a child. Props turning.

Mechanics dashing to and fro. The men of 482 squadron clambering in to their Hurricanes. Neddy, the CO, giving him the thumbs up.

Smithson was glad for his plane, for the comforting familiarity of every dial, of every spring in the seat as he wormed into the cockpit. Everyone sung the Spitfire's praises, which had largely replaced the Hurricanes as fighters. But Hurricanes had brought down more Luftwaffe planes in 1940 than all other British aircraft combined, and still nothing could turn in the air like one, even four years on.

Smithson felt the ground drop away as his plane took to the air, falling in with his squadron, following the steersman's vectors. He put on his mask, braked right for the coast, and far below him were the dummy camps at Trowhaven Patton had set up to bamboozle the Krauts. Fake tanks and trucks and troop housing and even dummy landing craft in the estuaries and rivers. All tying up the German 15th at the Pas de Calais very nicely, playing Hitler the giddy kipper. Fortress Europe would come tumbling down at Normandy next month. It *had* to. Nothing could stop that fall.

But what was Hitler sending at them now?

'It's coming in high, Red Leader,' squawked control, tinny-voiced in his cockpit. 'Vector three one zero, unidentified object at 40,000 feet. Falling slowly. On present trajectory you'll meet it shortly. Over.'

Neddy's voice: 'Will comply. Fan out, boys. All units report sightings, over.'

The hard Dorset coast had given up to the Channel's grey waters. Smithson broke away from the Hurricanes flanking him, rising to 30,000 feet. Then something struck him in the eyes, so brightly he flinched, the annoying catch of sudden sunlight reflected on metal.

The familiar fear gripped him; of running into the enemy one more time and running out of luck.

Then he saw properly what it was, and nothing was familiar. He tried to speak but his saliva had turned to sticky paste.

'I see it, Skip,' Smithson said thickly, even so, surprised by how

8

calm his own voice sounded in his ears. 'It's not a plane. It's…
cylindrical by the look of it. Keeps spinning, it's like it's…'

'Joining you, Smithson, over,' Neddy reported.

Steersman was keeping matter of fact, unfazed by the situation.
'Intercept, Red Leader, over.'

Smithson barely heard. He'd been watching the skies all night
for this thing, knowing it was up there. Up there waiting for *him*.
And here it was, and he was first to find it. This was destiny, or
fate, what all the papers and the pulp romances talked about
when someone died before their time with some queer twist in
their tale: fate was just death dressed up, and now it was coming
for him.

'Two red lights,' Smithson announced, transfixed as he drew
closer, raised his altitude to 33,000 feet. 'They're holding still, even
while the thing's spinning… they're a *blazing* red. It's like no
colour I've seen… over.'

'Engage bandit,' came Neddy's voice. 'Head on, three sections.
We're bringing it down. Over.'

There was another flash of light from the silver cylinder
hanging in the bleached out sky. Smithson realised that the metal
was surrounded by something else, something like glass.

You could break glass.

It was a simple realisation but in this strange meeting it acted
to focus Smithson's attention back to the job in hand. 'Roger that,
CO,' he said, flanked once more by his fellows. He upped his
speed to match theirs, passing 300 miles per hour, climbing
higher, to 36,000 feet, nearing the ceiling. He felt his plane
tremble with the acceleration.

Now it came into his crosshairs. The thing was still just hanging
in the sky. It wasn't moving, wasn't firing. Should he chance it?
Smithson knew the boffins said the Hurricanes lacked the vertical
performance and the horsepower to weight ratio to keep on
target when chasing their prey. Well, that was all right. Like Neddy
said, you just had to kill on the first try.

Smithson found he was closest to the thing, and now
spearheading the assault. Red machine eyes – and that's what they

were like, eyes burning into anyone that dared approach – glowed at him through the strange opaque glass structure surrounding the object. It was almost like crystal. But the unidentified craft was still taking no evasive action. It hung as small and insignificant up here in the scrubbed-clean sky as Smithson had been, back down on the airfield. But there was something about it, its unnatural shape, the way those lights were moving…

But you could break glass. And bugger fate.

Smithson's Hurricane went in with all eight machine guns firing 120 rounds per second. Those planes flanking him did the same.

The spinning cylinder's glass cocoon shattered. A moment later the cylinder itself dropped from the sky, as if the glass had been holding it up. The red lights burnt out, extinguished swiftly by the blustering winds and the rain.

Terrible weather for May.

'Downed it, Steersman,' he heard Neddy report, 'repeat, unidentified bandit brought down.'

'It's changing course,' squawked an unfamiliar voice over the headset, a Yank accent. Smithson couldn't have heard right: 'Upward of 500 miles per hour…'

Then Control came back on. 'Bandit heading inland. Losing altitude. Pursue and intercept. Trowhaven base must be protected, repeat, must be protected at all costs. Over.'

'Wilco that. Over.'

Smithson fell in with the rest of his squadron, banking and diving, giving chase. The other voice must be some USAF bigwig. If the dummy camps were blown apart then the Allied campaign of misinformation would go the same way. Deliverance Day would go west.

And yet, even straining at full speed, the squadron couldn't keep pace with the bandit, sparking and tumbling from the sky. It was like trying to outrun a missile, but in reverse. Smithson didn't stop to consider the irony, racing through the patchy cloud, watching shifting sea become stolid land again. They were too late, it couldn't be caught, but it was coming in low now, it was over…

Smithson felt his heart stop beating, the blood freeze in his veins.

When the end came for the thing it seemed to halt in mid-flight and drop like a stone from the sky. There was no explosion, but having banked and turned, Smithson could see a plume of smoke rising from the outskirts of a village. The thing had come down on Turelhampton.

Bugger fate, he'd said. And now the damned thing could've come down right on Mary's sweet dark head.

After an hour finishing the sortie, of checking the skies for any more of the things, the atmosphere back at the airfield was jubilant following 482's apparent victory over their strange quarry. But after a quick conflab with Neddy, Smithson left the celebrations and charged straight to old Arnold's office. He rapped hard on the old oak door, and stepped through smartly without pause.

Wing Commander Arnold, inscrutable as ever, wasn't fazed by the intrusion. 'Chain of command, Smithson,' he remonstrated mildly, but seemed oddly subdued.. He almost seemed to welcome the intrusion.

'The bandit came down on Turelhampton,' Smithson blurted out.

Arnold nodded but said nothing.

'Any casualties?'

'Limited, according to first reports,' Arnold said eventually. 'But Trowhaven's integrity remains unbreached.'

Smithson nodded and half-smiled. 'I have… Please, sir, I… *know* someone… in Turelhampton. Could you tell me…?'

Arnold considered, then gave a watery smile. 'Don't have names, Smithson. But…' He paused, rose stiffly to his feet. 'Well, you must go along at once. Perhaps you can help out with the evacuation, stop Dogson's boys making too much of a mess, you know what they're like.'

Smithson stared. 'Evacuation? But –'

'105th division is already moving in to clear the area. The object came down in one piece. We… we have to be sure it is not a risk to civilians. You understand?'

Smithson could see papers on Arnold's desk. Official-looking papers with the ink barely dried: a graph with a steep curve then a sudden falling off. A memo from Ground Control, and some instructions on USAF paper.

'Get yourself down there, Smithson,' Arnold repeated, and Smithson, a little calmer now, noticed now just how pale-faced he was.

Smithson had to abandon his car, since the road to Turelhampton was blocked by convoys of army vehicles trundling towards it or by supply trucks scraping past, loaded with civilians, rumbling out. Making his way on foot, feeling sick to his stomach, he scanned the bewildered, bemused or excited people clustered in the trucks for Mary's face.

'Carl! Here, here!'

Fate may have been tempted but it hadn't struck. Mary was safe and sound in the second such truck passing by, and he shouted when he saw her, flooded with relief. He ran along the road to keep up with her.

'Did you see it!' she called excitedly.

Smithson bit his tongue. 'Don't know what you're talking about, love,' he called.

'That thing, the glowing thing… fell like… like an enormous oil drum or something, out of the sky.'

A belligerent-looking old man was observing Smithson's fast jog to keep level with the van. 'Was it you that brought the thing crashing down on our heads?'

'We brought it down over the water,' Smithson said defensively, before realising he should've kept his mouth shut. How rattled was he?

'So how did it come down here?' the old man demanded.

Even if Smithson had been able to talk about it, he shivered to realise he didn't have an answer.

'Why are they taking us away?' asked Mary.

'I don't know,' Smithson admitted.

'Don't know or won't tell us?' huffed the old man.

Mary rolled her eyes and grinned at Smithson. He saw that all this was quite an adventure for her. 'They're saying we have to stay at Crookhampton. "Arrangements will be made", very hush hush. Seems we won't be going back for a while.'

'Why?' the old man grumbled. 'Why should that be?'

Smithson glanced over his shoulder at another army truck, a dark green shadow against the cornfields, pressing on to the village. The smoke still hung above the crash site like a thick swarm of bees.

Smithson suppressed another shudder, looked back at Mary and forced a cheery smile. 'Well, you'll be closer to the base, anyway. Not as far to walk in blackout. That's something, isn't it?'

The old man was harder to mollify than Mary. 'What was that bloody thing, anyway?' he shouted.

The truck picked up speed, and started to pull away. Smithson stopped running, panting hard as he waved to Mary. Soon she had blurred to become one more featureless face among the dozens in the vehicle.

Behind him, in the distance, came the calls and shouts of Dogson's men on their Army business, and strangulated roars as more trucks and staff cars bedded in. It looked as though the 105th would be keeping busy.

He thought again of Arnold's pale, distracted, face, of the red lights that had burned so coldly through the thick glass and metal in the bald white sky. He decided that Mary was right; that she wouldn't be returning to Turelhampton for a while.

That night, Smithson was back by the dorm window in the early hours, staring uneasily up into the blackness. He was wondering what else might be up in the sky, and what might come looking.

Chapter One

The air was alive with noise and bullets, and Ilya Petrova had just killed a child.

Acrid smoke drifted aimlessly across the ground as he knelt to turn over the body of the sniper who had shot three of his unit. He found himself looking into the face of a boy no more than twelve. His head barely filled the dark metal helmet. He looked as if he was asleep, and for the briefest of eternities the noise and the bullets froze in the air around Ilya. He thought of the blood and the waste and the killing still to come. He thought of his own son, Sacha. Then a dull detonation chewed the side out of a nearby block of offices and he blinked back the moisture in his eyes and stood up.

The Russians had taken Tempelhof airport that morning. Now they were inside the inner ring of the city – the Zitadelle – and closing on the area their generals had designated as 'Sector Nine' where the government buildings were. Each unit wanted to be the first to reach the Reichschancellery; each soldier was desperate to be the one to find the Fuhrer, dead or alive. Whoever did find Hitler, it was said, would be proclaimed a Hero of the Soviet Union.

And so they inched closer and closer to victory. It was like Stalingrad, Ilya reflected not for the first time. It was not so cold, and they were attacking not defending. But the Germans would fight to the death – even the children, he thought numbly. The attacking Russians had learned more from Stalingrad than the German defenders. They were making progress, slow and costly but steady. It would be over in days rather than months or weeks.

But for the moment time seemed to have slowed. The repetition, the constant process of clearing building after street after building, made it seem to Ilya as if he had spent his whole life in the torn and ragged city of Berlin.

They moved forward again, stooping close to the ground,

scuttling towards the next building. It had been an apartment block, now it was a half-standing disjointed structure ready to collapse into rubble. Vlad's flame-thrower charred the broken bones of the infrastructure where they stuck out awkwardly from the twisted framework. If there were screams, they were lost in the sound and fury of the flames. When Vlad stopped, small pockets of fire still burned along the broken walls and in puddles of orange and yellow scattered across the broken ground.

Cautiously, watching and listening constantly for any tell-tale sign of life – of enemy life – the group edged through the shattered remains of the building. Each soldier covered his fellows. At once they watched each others' backs while looking out for themselves. You had to trust completely in your comrades, and in nothing and no one else.

There was no sign of life. The only sound that came from within the building was the crack and drip of falling masonry where it had been dislodged by the flames or disturbed by their movement. A blackened body lay face up in a corner of what had been a bedroom. It was impossible to tell whether it had been male or female. A bundle of charred rags was clutched to its chest. It had been dead for some days, the face all but eaten away by the rats and the stench fighting with the cordite and phosphor from outside.

The door to the basement seemed untouched by the devastation around it. The wall beside the frame was pitted and scarred, yet the wooden frame and the door itself seemed unblemished. A splash of mud – or old blood – clouded one panel.

They had congregated in the area, as if sensing this was a focal point. Captain Yazov nodded to Vlad to use the flame-thrower.

His name was not really Vlad. But none of them could pronounce, or remember, his real name. The Russian army was a cosmopolitan grouping of disparate races drawn together from within the Soviet Union. 'Vlad' was Mongolian, and he spoke no Russian. And because none of the Russians spoke Mongolian, all communications were handled by sign language. Some of the units had interpreters, but not this one. Vlad had the flame-thrower as he was least likely accidentally to harm anyone in his own unit with it – it was used when and if, and only when and if Captain Yazov gave the signal. That much at least Vlad and his comrades understood between them.

The burst of oily flame engulfed the door, pummelling it with a smoky fist. When Vlad stepped aside, the doorway was a blackened hole in the wall. The smoke cleared to reveal a flight of concrete steps leading down into darkness.

Yazov had a torch, shining it along the juddering barrel of his rifle as he led the way. He stopped so abruptly at the bottom of the steps, that Ilya almost cannoned into him. Then slowly, carefully, incredulously, they stepped forward into the room. Yazov swept the torch beam over the scene that awaited them before sharing an astonished glance with Ilya.

For once, Vlad seemed to understand when Yazov shouted and gesticulated at him. He sprayed a stream of liquid fire into a corner of the basement room, igniting a pile of boxes, books, paper and other detritus. By the smoky light, Ilya stood beside his captain and gazed at the bodies.

There were seven in all. Each was dressed immaculately in the uniform of a soldier of the Third Reich. Six of the corpses were lying face up in a rough circle, feet towards the centre. In the middle lay a seventh body. It seemed identical to the others, lying face up, dressed in German army uniform. Except that this man wore gloves.

The gloves, Ilya noted with surprise in the drifting light, were bright green.

When he looked closer, he noticed other oddities. Apart from the fact that the whole scenario seemed bizarre. A gasp from Yazov beside him indicated that the Captain had spotted it too.

'They are…' Yazov turned to Ilya, as if for confirmation. 'They are Oriental. All of them.'

Ilya nodded. Trust Yazov to spot that before noticing the real surprise. 'I know,' he said. To his left he was aware of Vlad stooping beside one of the bodies, his silhouette made stumpy and grotesque by the metal cylinders on his back that fed the flame-thrower. His shadow flickered on the floor beside him like a malevolent imp. He looked up at Ilya, and it was apparent in his eyes that he had seen it too. His hand strayed towards the thin fragments of glass on the floor. They caught the firelight, seeming to jump and blink. The Mongolian changed his mind, pulled back his hand and straightened up.

'They have all taken poison,' Ilya told Yazov slowly. The fire was dying now. 'Look at how the teeth are clenched, the lips drawn back.'

Yazov frowned and stared into the gloom.

'Suicide,' Ilya said. 'Each and every one of them has bitten into a cyanide capsule.' To make the point he stepped forwards and ground the shards of glass into the concrete floor with the toe of his boot.

'But why?' Yazov demanded, as if he thought Ilya might know. 'Why would...' he paused to count them. 'Why would seven Chinese poison themselves?'

'And why lie in a circle to do it?' Ilya asked. He decided not to mention the gloves.

Vlad was shaking his head. 'Not Chinese,' he managed to say, his accent guttural and thick, the words strained and clumsy.

'You're right,' Ilya agreed. 'Japanese more like.'

Again Vlad was shaking his head. When he spoke it was a rush of words that meant nothing to Ilya. After several moments, Vlad was quiet, thoughtful. He gestured for Ilya to crouch with him beside the nearest body and pointed at the face. 'Not Chinese,' he said again.

'What's the idiot trying to tell us?' Yazov demanded.

'That they're not Chinese,' Ilya said. He shrugged. 'Or Japanese either, I think.'

Vlad was nodding now. His teeth shone in the fading flicker of the firelight. He seemed pleased to have found the word in the depths of his meagre vocabulary. 'Tibet,' he said indistinctly. 'Men of Tibet.'

There was no door to close behind them as they left the basement and moved to the next street. By the end of the day,

Yazov was dead and his unit had other things to worry about. But what they had found in the basement continued to haunt Ilya's imagination. That and the sleeping face of a young boy, his head too small for his helmet.

Chapter Two

TRANSCRIPT FROM THE LAST DAYS OF HITLER?
WRITTEN AND DIRECTED BY CLAIRE ALDWYCH
ORIGINALLY BROADCAST ON THE CONSPIRACY CHANNEL,
AUGUST 12TH 1997

Footage of Eva Braun happy, playing, walking with Hitler.

It was the arrival of Eva Braun that signalled the end for most of the people in the Berlin Bunker. Hitler had gathered together his closest and most trusted advisors. But even they could tell that he was cracking under the strain – the end was rapidly approaching.

When Eva Braun forsook safety and arrived at the Bunker on April 15th 1945, it was a sign, a portent of the approaching end. Despite Hitler's insistence, she refused to leave him. The Fuhrer was touched.

But behind Eva's back, many of the others in the Bunker christened her 'The Angel of Death.'

Close on picture of Eva's smiling face.

The Russians were already approaching the capital of the Third Reich.

What happened in those last days within the confines of the Fuhrer-Bunker is unclear. There are conflicting accounts, or no accounts at all. People came and went for the next few days – until Berlin was effectively sealed off by the Russians.

Russian troops closing on the outskirts of Berlin.

On April 20th Hitler celebrated his fifty-sixth birthday. This was the last day he saw the sunlight, the last day he left the Bunker alive. Probably.

Footage of Hitler inspecting the Hitler Youth in Berlin.

As can be seen from this final film of the Fuhrer inspecting members of the Hitler Youth Brigade as they prepared to defend their capital city, the strain was taking its toll. Gone was the exuberance and confidence. The man we see here looks closer to seventy-six than fifty-six. Propaganda Minister Joseph Goebbels had already ordered that the Fuhrer was only to be photographed and filmed from certain angles to hide his increasing infirmity.

Montage of photos of the Bunker - interior and exterior.

Yet he refused to admit the obvious, the inevitable, even to himself. He continued to order military operations and troop movements that at best made no sense, at worst were impossible. Many if not most of the army units he had marked on his map-table no longer existed. Those that did were in no fit state to follow his grand orders.

Close-up of Himmler.

Hitler's birthday party, held in the Bunker itself, was a sombre affair - more like a wake. Significantly, Heinrich Himmler - the Reichsfuhrer and formerly Hitler's closest and most trusted ally - left the Bunker afterwards. He never returned. Instead he opened secret negotiations with the Allies and sued for peace. When Hitler discovered this, on April 28th, he declared Himmler a traitor and executed Hermann Fegelein, one of Himmler's closest aides who had tried to leave the Bunker without permission.

Wedding photo of Hermann and Gretl Fegelein.

Fegelein was married to Eva Braun's sister, Gretl.

One of the most enigmatic figures of the Third Reich, Himmler is best remembered for being head of the SS. He was also a keen devotee of the occult, seeing himself as a latter-day King Arthur, gathering his SS knights around him as they sought for the Holy Grail.

This was a man who on the one hand could see the end coming earlier and more clearly than his colleagues. He ordered the death camps closed in September 1944 – an order that was ignored. Yet when he tried to slip away and evade capture by the Allies, it was disguised in the uniform of a sergeant-major of the Gestapo. He was captured and recognised almost at once, committing suicide to cheat Nuremberg of yet another war criminal.

Close on Himmler's dead body.

Ironically, in matters of the occult, Hitler was a realist. He had little faith or belief in the supernatural, which makes it easy to dismiss as rumour and falsehood the claims that in those last days secret occult ceremonies were held on the lower level of the Bunker. Hitler would hardly have countenanced such a thing even while Himmler was there. After his departure on 20th April, surely such extreme clutching at straws was impossible.

Archive footage of Hitler at rally.

The reality of the situation seems to have hit home to the Fuhrer on April 22nd when the Russian forces at last entered the city of Berlin. When he received the reports, Hitler was distraught. According to some sources, he actually suffered a nervous breakdown. Certainly, this was the point at which he saw his own destiny.

Close on Hitler's face.

'All is lost,' he said. And it became apparent to those in the Bunker that Hitler would never leave it. Having resisted all suggestions that he should leave Berlin for Southern Germany, he now made no secret of his intention to commit suicide rather than surrender or witness defeat.

Film of Eva playing in fountain.

21

It was also clear that Eva was determined to share his fate. She was a happy, bubbly slim blonde woman, then in her early thirties. She had few admirers among the higher-ranking Nazis, and her only real friend in Hitler's inner circle was Albert Speer. She refused his offers of help and rescue.

Shot of Hitler, Eva and Speer.

Speer, the only man with the integrity to plead guilty at Nuremburg, finally left the Bunker on April 24th. The next day the Russians took the main airport of Berlin and started to advance on the inner city.

Footage of the Russian advance through war-torn Berlin.
Dubbed on sound effects.

Over the following week, Hitler grew increasingly paranoid. His left arm shook almost uncontrollably and he had to hold it still with his right. He had declared Goering a traitor, largely egged on by his personal secretary Martin Bormann. As we have seen, he also denounced Himmler. Only Bormann and Goebbels remained close and loyal.

Pictures of Bormann and Goebbels.

Goebbels, on Hitler's instructions, had even moved his wife and their six children into the Bunker. None of them would ever leave it.

Just after midnight on April 29th, Hitler married Eva Braun in a civil ceremony. To say it was hurried is no exaggeration. Geobbels was sent out into the burning streets to find an official to conduct the ceremony.

Image of marriage certificate. Close in on signatures.

Eva signed her name 'Eva B' before scratching out the 'B' and finishing 'Eva Hitler'. The Fuhrer's own shaky signature betrays his deteriorating physical condition.

Film of Hitler in full rant at Nuremburg Rally.

After the marriage, Hitler dictated his final 'Will and Political Testament' to his secretary. If she was expecting the level of rhetoric and political insight of his early writings, she was disappointed. It is a rambling, unfocused document. Feeling betrayed by the army which had failed to relieve Berlin despite his orders, and having never forgiven the Luftwaffe for losing the Battle of Britain, Hitler named the highest ranking naval commander, Admiral Donitz, as his successor. Typically, he blamed a Jewish conspiracy for starting the war in the first place.

Goebbels family portrait.

The following afternoon, Joseph and Magda Goebbels held a party in the Bunker for their six children. Surely this celebration organised by parents who would murder their own children in the next few days must have been one of the most bizarre events in those final surreal days.

Now, with evidence newly released from Russian archives, it is possible at last to reconstruct what happened on the fateful day of April 30th 1945 in the Bunker beneath the Berlin Reichschancellery.

Long shot of the Reichschancellery, closing in on the garden and the Bunker's exit.

In the morning, Eva Hitler went outside, to take a last look at the sun, she said. She stood in the garden of the Reichschancellery, and must have been able to hear the sound of the advancing Russians and of their artillery fire.

After lunch, Hitler and Eva said formal farewells in the main corridor of the Bunker.

Artist's impression of the main corridor.

It did not take long, and the Fuhrer made no great pronouncements or rousing speeches. In fact, witnesses recall little if anything of what was said. Hitler placed his valet, Heinz Linge, in charge of subsequent events and gave him strict instructions. When Hitler and his wife retired to their room, Linge was to ensure that nobody disturbed them for a full ten minutes.

Move 'along' the corridor towards the door to Hitler's rooms.
Hold on the door.

It was actually Hitler's adjutant, Otto Gunsche who guarded the door. But even he was unable to keep Magda Goebbels, who had missed the farewells, from forcing her way past for a few final words with the man she had secretly loved for so long. Perhaps she tried to persuade Hitler to flee rather than die, certainly by this stage she must have decided that if her Fuhrer died she and her family must follow his example. When she emerged, she was sobbing and shaking.

Animated shadows on the door to signify the various figures –
grotesque, misshapen silhouettes.

Arthur Axmann, head of the Hitler Youth, was however turned away by Gunsche and waited with the others in the corridor.

Some say they heard a shot, despite the fact that the door into Hitler's rooms was bomb-proof and airtight. Whatever the case, when they finally entered, Linge and the others found the bodies of Hitler and Eva on the sofa.

Despite having a pistol, Eva had taken cyanide and died almost instantly. She was sitting, we are told, serene and composed with her legs drawn up under her.

Hitler we now know, also took cyanide. And from the recently released Russian evidence, it appears that he also shot himself as he bit into the capsule.

Photo of Linge.

There has been speculation that Linge administered a *coup de grâce* to his Fuhrer. But this is based on one witness's interpretation of a single comment of Linge's.

Close-up of Hitler.

Whether it was a bullet that did the work, or the cyanide he had so carefully tested on his beloved Alsatian dog Blondi several days earlier, Adolf Hitler, Fuhrer of the Third Reich was dead.

Footage of Hitler playing with Blondi. Freeze-frame and defocus.

The bodies were taken into the garden of the Reichschancellery, doused with petrol reserved specifically for the purpose, and burned beyond recognition.

Autopsy pictures of the blackened corpses.

That, at least, is the accepted version of events, but it leaves many questions unanswered. Why were the Russians so slow to admit Hitler was dead? Why were there so many apparent sightings of the Fuhrer after his 'death'? Why, if Hitler shot himself in his living quarters, was there blood on the bed in the next room...?

Chapter Three

Alan Watson was losing her attention; he could see her eyes darting about, perhaps looking for her husband. She was still smiling and nodding, but he knew he must be boring her. All around them uniformed men and posh-frocked wives were talking and laughing animatedly in groups. Watson badly wished he was in one of them himself; his awkward, rambling narration of his post-wartime life was boring himself, never mind this poor girl.

'I was sorry to leave the pre-fab,' he continued stoically, 'but since Mags went, well… didn't need so much space. Got a bedsit, now. You know.'

The girl wasn't even looking at him now.

He swallowed. 'Shame about old Dogson, he'd have loved to be here. Bedders ever mention old –?'

She smiled at him abruptly; a polite, prim smile. 'I'm sorry, I have to just… would you excuse me?'

Watson nodded and smiled apologetically. 'Of course you must, of course…' The girl – he realised he didn't know her name, she was just Bedders' wife – walked over to the buffet table and added a pork pie to her plate before joining the periphery of a sizeable group where Bedders was holding court. Flash beggar. They'd both been just the same serving as privates under old Dogson, but it seemed life had smiled since on Bedders: pretty young wife, good job… He was living up in London. Little semi in Wembley; you could see the twin towers from his back yard, so he said.

Watson swigged his glass of warm beer and glanced up at the bright bunting hanging over the stage in the church hall, the hand-drawn banner catching in the October sunlight: DOGSON'S BOYS – TENTH ANNIVERSARY. He'd been looking forward to this day for months: the regiment's first reunion since breaking up in '45, the chance to catch up with old mates, to feel the old

26

camaraderie. Just to feel that he belonged to something again, that there was more to life than taking fares on the buses all day before falling asleep in a chair by the wireless.

Yeah, he'd been looking forward to a good old natter about the old days, but now he was here he couldn't help feeling cheated. The lads had been happy enough to talk about those times at first – most of them, anyway – but they all seemed to have so much else to talk about. Watson had drifted between groups, trying to join in, but it seemed they'd always disperse about him, leaving him alone again.

People drifting away; it seemed to sum up the last ten years of his life.

Just as Watson was about to make his third trip over to the buffet table to consider who he might buttonhole next, he noticed a tall, imposing figure strolling directly towards him.

'Watson!' the man called. 'Alan Watson!' His smile was as smart and straight as the cut of his dark, well-tailored suit, but no laughter lines scored the skin around his deep-set brown eyes. In fact, there was barely a mark on the classically heroic, square-jawed face. Even his fair, almost-white hair was slicked back in its old familiar style. He was one of those lucky sorts that never seemed to age a day.

'Sergeant Henderson,' Watson muttered in disbelief, happy yet also worried to be singled out for attention from the officer class. Old Spinney had christened Henderson the Dorset Darling, and the name had stuck with the lads. They'd always been joking back then. Watson felt automatically for the keepsake in his jacket pocket. His lucky charm, got him through D-Day. Got Spinney seconded to guard duty in Turelhampton. Shame Spinney wasn't here… not surprising though.

Henderson's fixed smile never wavered as he made his way nimbly through the noisy crowd to join him. He even seemed to talk through it. 'Please, Alan, we're not in the army now. You must call me George.'

The thought of doing so unnerved Watson still further. 'You're looking well,' he said.

'You too, old man, you too. Good to see you here. Hear you're on the buses these days.'

'Fare cop,' Watson joked weakly – his usual joke.

Henderson nodded genially, looked about him. 'No Spinney about? You two used to be inseparable.'

'We lost touch, sir. Since his troubles.'

Henderson's smile dropped a little and Watson instinctively knew that their small talk was now out the way.

'Noisy here, isn't it,' Henderson said. 'Tell you what, why don't we find somewhere a little quieter, have a chinwag.'

'Outside?' Watson suggested.

'No...' Henderson indicated to a door by the little stage, which was standing ajar. 'Tell you what, my coat's hanging up through there. I've got a little flask of something in it. Let's have a nip, shall we? Drink to old times, eh?'

A fresh wave of laughter from Bedders' own adoring army rattled out brutally in the hall, and Watson found he wasn't resisting as Henderson steered him over to the doorway and ushered him through.

It was a lot quieter behind the stage, and shrouded in darkness. Watson could hear splashes and the clinking of china from the kitchens in the adjoining area; a comforting sound, it reminded him of Mags, elbow deep in suds doing the pots.

Henderson flicked on a light switch and in the brilliance of the bare bulb above them Watson saw the man's hand was ringless, which surprised him. 'Not married, then, sir?'

Henderson shook his head, reached into his coat and offered Watson a hip flask.

Watson relaxed a little as the whisky splashed into his dry mouth. It was good stuff, too. 'Only we all reckoned you were the marrying sort. Never short of a sweetheart as I recall.'

Henderson's dark eyes betrayed a flash of annoyance at such triviality. He took Watson's arm firmly. 'Listen, Watson, there's something I'm interested in. Something I'd like to talk to you about.' Henderson pulled him closer to the shadow of the heavy stage curtain. 'The night we were all told never to discuss.'

'Never have discussed it, neither, Sarge,' Watson said immediately.

Henderson smiled again, coldly. 'Is that a fact?'

'Who'd believe me?' He let out a short, self-pitying laugh; one that couldn't have been more different from Bedders' confident roar. But Bedders hadn't been sent in to look inside the thing. He hadn't seen what Watson had.

'Spinney would've understood, of course…' Henderson went on.

'We lost touch. Missing out on the action in Normandy to guard the old place, it messed him up, I think.'

'I stayed behind myself,' Henderson pointed out mildly.

Watson looked away, embarrassed, pretending to be fascinated by a display cabinet on the bare wall to his right. Notices and old photographs were pinned up behind the glass, and his misshapen portly silhouette was slouched on the magnolia beside them, squaring up dismally to Henderson's slim physique. He looked back to Henderson. Why couldn't his body have stayed firm and slim like the Dorset Darling's?

'I know you did, Sarge,' Watson wheedled. 'Orders is orders, right? But Spinney always reckoned his place was with the lads… I mean, a lot of good boys died in France while he was back here shoring up dry stone walls… I think he felt guilty.'

Henderson pursed his lips. 'Boys like poor Gerrard Lassiter… I don't suppose he ever had much *chance* to talk about it.'

Watson took another sullen swig from the flask and said nothing. Something caught his eye, some movement behind Henderson in the shadows of the stage curtain, some breeze perhaps catching the fabric.

Henderson took a step closer, and Watson's attention shifted back to his unlined face. 'May, wasn't it,' Henderson said quietly. 'That's when she came down.'

'May 17th. Still see it lying there, in that bloody great hole in the ground…'

Henderson looked at him coolly. 'You saw more than that, though, didn't you, Alan?'

'Sarge?'

'You went inside the object.'

'Did I, Sarge? Well, well.'

Watson wondered at his own bravado, and blamed it on a good few pints with a whisky chaser. But why should he be worried? It was all so long ago, so far behind… a lightning flash of excitement and intrigue in his dull grey life. He'd been thinking about it more and more since Mags had gone away. It felt good to talk about it now, and even better to be one up on Sergeant Bloody-Dorset-Darling. That was a first.

'I might've seen a few things that night,' Watson went on cagily. Well, why not? They weren't in the army any more – what could Henderson possibly do to him now?

'I believe you may have seen them and *taken* them, Alan.'

'Taken them?' Again Watson thought he glimpsed a moment's movement to his right, but there was nothing, only their shadows. 'Don't know about that. We had orders not to touch…'

'I checked with old Dogson before.' Henderson took another step closer. 'Before his accident.' He gave Watson an encouraging, confidential smile, but his voice had a new edge to it now. 'I was assigned to the supervision of that vessel from the night of its arrival in Turelhampton. When it came down after dawn, Dogson assigned the three of you to guard it short term. Just you three. Alan Watson. Gerrard Lassiter. Peter Spinney.'

'Suppose we must've been the first inside that thing, sure… there was stuff lying about the place. Broken stuff.' Watson shook his head, remembering. 'I mean, you must've seen it yourself –'

There was the sound of breaking glass from the kitchens. Henderson lowered his voice but his expression suggested he'd rather be raising it. 'What components did you take?'

'Weren't no components,' Watson protested. Then, deciding he'd rather just be out with it and get back to boring the guests in the other room, he pulled the keepsake from his jacket pocket.

'It's just this.'

Henderson's eyes lit up brighter than the bulb at the sight of the small shiny disc in Watson's hand. It wasn't glass and it wasn't crystal; it was something else, opaque, warm, and always glowing a faint, soft red, as if an ember was trapped inside, burning on forever.

'Everywhere I go, *it* goes. It saw me through France, and safely back home again. Reckon it's my good luck charm.' He frowned, thought of the empty room he'd be returning to tonight. 'Used to be, anyway.'

'Used to be,' Henderson echoed softly, still staring at the disc. Then his eyes snapped up to meet Watson's. 'How much do you want for it.'

'It's not for sale. Priceless, this is.'

'I'll give you thirty pounds.'

Watson stared at him. 'You what?'

'Fifty pounds.'

'It's *not for sale.*'

'A hundred, then. Cash.'

Watson stared at him, took in his cold expression, saw Henderson meant business. He looked away, caught off-guard by talk of such a sum.

And saw there was another shadow on the wall under the cabinet, small and misshapen, beside his own.

Beside Henderson's.

As he stared the shadow seemed to fade, to shift back into Henderson's silhouette. A trick of the light, the curtain moving? Henderson was standing rigid, still staring straight at him.

Watson's armpits were soaked with sweat. This wasn't funny anymore. He closed his fist around the disc, moved to push past Henderson, and found his arm seized tight.

'I *will* have that component, Watson.'

'Sorry, Sarge. Finders keepers, and it's not for sale. Let's go back inside, eh?'

'The disc is not your property.'

'Well then, I *can't* sell it, can I?' He struggled half-heartedly to break Henderson's grip. He considered shouting for help, but to do so seemed absurd. Call out to the old dears in the kitchen? Get them to drag his old sergeant off him?

But while he was squirming as much with embarrassment as to pull free from the bony fingers pinching his arm, he saw movement to his right again.

Saw that it was *reflected* movement, in the glass of the display case.

There was a horned figure, small and squat, flickering out of Henderson's shadow. An imp. Its eyes were a smoky red, like the stubborn glow caught in the disc clasped tight in his hand.

Terrified, Watson turned back to Henderson. There was no sign of the creature there, it was only an image in the glass, a shift in the shadows.

But he could see it on the wall, closing, reaching inside his shadow's fist for the disc. And it wasn't stopping there.

Henderson reached casually for the light switch and flicked it off.

Watson wanted to scream for help, to scream in terror as the imp stamped around inside his body, screwing things up and wringing them out, but like a nightmare no noise would come. In the dark, as he jerked and shook in silence, the clinking and splashing of the crockery, the conversation and laughter in the hall, it all sounded just as loud. But it was an impossible distance away. How? Just a few minutes ago he'd been out there himself.

Talking about the last ten years of his life.

Chapter Four

When she had first come here she was nineteen, idealistic, naïve and didn't believe in ghosts. But now she knew better.

Over ten years ago, but the memory of it still made her tremble with fear. It returned to her whenever she brought someone new, walking with them from the airstrip to the main entrance. It returned to her in moments of loneliness and in the dark. It returned to her whenever she went into the Ceremonial Chamber. And it haunted her dreams.

She had seen the ghosts so many times since that she was no longer scared of them. Only of the memory of that first encounter.

She paused by the doorway and turned to watch the Englishman struggling through the snow to reach her. And despite the thermal lining of her jacket and despite the warmth that glowed out from the doorway, she shivered.

It was a week before they stopped following her about. Hanne Neumann was the new girl, barely nineteen and just out of college. Her idealism was sound, tested on the throat of an informer in the damp Munich basement of her uncle's house. But once they let you into the Redoubt they needed to trust your tongue and discretion as much as your knife and your loyalty.

Hanne did not mind that. She knew she could be trusted. She *believed* as much as they did – more. She derived a thrill of satisfaction from their attention, from their testing. She felt the same frisson every morning when she pulled on the black uniform, when she looked at herself in the full-length mirror in her tiny room, when she pretended not to notice how they all looked at her as she passed them in the corridor. As she imagined they whispered to each other: 'Is that her? ... Is it true? ... Her own father?'

They stopped watching her eventually, though she knew they

still didn't trust her. So she decided to see the chamber for herself.

She felt the same rush of adrenaline, the same shudder of fear-tinged excitement as she let herself out of her room and walked quietly along the corridor. It was an effort to keep the heels of her boots from clacking on the stone floor. An effort not to pause at every third step and listen to hear if anyone was there in the darkness with her.

She did pause outside the door she had never been permitted to open. Just for a few seconds. Then she turned the handle, knowing in her heart of hearts that it would be locked and she would return to her room and honour and trust and confidence and curiosity would all in some strange way be satisfied.

The heavy wooden door swung open soundlessly. It led into a small, dark room. There was another door at the back of the room, and she opened this too. With a slight gasp of surprise, Hanne stepped into the chamber and closed the door behind her.

All the rooms she had seen here, with the exception of the dining hall, were small and cramped. This room was much larger, with a high vaulted ceiling. The damp stone walls receded into the shadowed distance. The room was circular, perhaps thirty feet across. It was lit by candles. Black candles. There were hundreds of them.

Tiny flickers of light shone from plinths and stands arranged in concentric circles round the room. They gave the place an almost religious aura.

Through the candles there were paths left clear leading to the centre of the circles – five paths. A pentagram of darkness in the eerie light. At the ends of the paths, the walls seemed to recede into the night-blackness, leading out into the world.

Slowly, deliberately, silently, Hanne made her way along an aisle of candles towards the centre. The flames shook and quivered as she passed, her uniform dark against their straining light – a little touch of blackness in the night.

There was a plinth in the very centre of the circles. Plain, wooden, with a green cloth covering it. On top of the cloth was a small stand, and resting on that was a perfect glass sphere. Like a crystal ball. Candle flames curled round its sides, elongated and magnified, dancing together within the glass. Hanne reached out to touch it, to pick it up. The sphere would fit snugly in the palm of her hand. She could imagine its cool smoothness nestling there. But her nerves got the better of her curiosity and she drew back her hand before it reached the glass.

For several moments she stood in the dead centre of the room, with the crystal. Then a sound from the corridor outside jolted her back to reality. Her eyes flickered towards the door, then round the shadowy room, looking for a place to hide. As the door handle started to turn, she ran, tip-toed and silent, along a line of darkness towards the shadows at the other end. A candle snuffed out behind her, a thin black wisp of smoke trailing in her wake. She did not notice.

It was the first time she witnessed the Ceremony. The first of many, alone and cold concealed in the darkness at the edge of the chamber, her back pressed against the damp stone wall. The icy floor ate through the soles of her boots as she stood there and watched.

They entered the room in a procession, ordered and silent save for the sound of their feet on the floor. Their faces were shrouded in the hoods of their dark robes as they filed between the candles and took up positions equally round the circle. Six figures, watching as the seventh, their leader, walked slowly and purposefully to the centre of the room and stood behind the glass sphere on the table.

Then a final figure entered, quietly taking his place just inside the door, watching with a fierce intensity that Hanne could see flickering by the candlelight in his ice-blue eyes. She caught her breath, knowing at once who it was, fearing those eyes would swing round and fix on her. The blood was rushing in her ears, and she could make out little of what the man by the sphere said as he reached up with his gloved – green-gloved – hands and pulled back the hood of his robes. The other figures did the same.

She knew them all. Not by name, but she had seen them in the dining area. They tended to sit together and keep themselves to themselves. Nobody seemed willing to talk about them, to say who they were or why they were here. And Hanne knew better than to ask for information that was not offered. When they were referred to it was simply as 'the Tibetans.' But whether they were really from Tibet or in fact from some other Eastern country, Hanne did not know.

As the ceremony progressed, as the leader stared deep into the crystal ball and chanted, as it seemed to Hanne that she could see a misty light swirling in the very heart of the glass despite her distance from it and the poor light, she became aware that she was not alone. Slowly, carefully, she looked round, her eyes peering into the darkness and gloom beside her at the back of the room.

But there was nothing. A breeze, perhaps. A tremor of anxiety or even fear. There was nobody, nothing there.

Or was there?

As she looked closer, straining to see into the blackness she realised that what she had taken for a jutting section of wall, a buttress or pillar perhaps, was actually separate. She shuffled slightly closer, trying to make out the shape and form in the gloom.

It was a cabinet, upright and smooth. Like a coffin stood on end. It widened towards the top and what light there was seemed to fall into its inky surface. It was smooth and shiny, reminding her of the glass sphere. The faint sputtering light of a nearby candle glowed and spat in its surface, an imperfect reflection.

She breathed a quiet sigh of relief, and turned back to watch the ceremony. But as she turned, her eyes swept briefly over the man by the door, still watching intently. And she froze, blood chilled.

The candle light had cast a flickering, distorted shadow upon the wall behind him. His image was magnified, so that it seemed to look down on the whole chamber. His ears were just visible at the side of the massive shadow-head. The collars of the greatcoat he wore against the cold and the damp stabbed up alongside his widened neck.

But that was not what caused Hanne's blood to run cold. The

man stood alone, there was nobody else anywhere near him. Yet, on the wall, standing beside his shadow was another image flickering in the dull light. A shorter figure, hunched as if about to spring forward into what light there was. The back was humped, the head perfectly round and smooth. Except for the stubs of what might be short horns protruding from the forehead.

Hanne held her breath, searching the area in front of the shadow desperately for something that might be casting it – some odd shape, a jutting part of the wall... Anything.

But there was nothing. Was she mistaken? She screwed up her eyes, hardly daring to look back. But even through her lidded eyes, the image was still there – the figure. And as she peered at it, it moved, turned. Towards her. And as the horns disappeared into the black silhouette, a hooked nose was briefly visible. Then the shadow was facing directly at her. As if watching her. As if it could see her in the darkness they shared.

She was transfixed, unable to move. For how long the effect lasted, she had no idea. She had never felt fear, not real fear like this, before. Excitement, anticipation, the cold leaden lump of anxiety in her stomach... But not raw fear that froze her rigid and swept away all concept of time and place.

When she finally blinked and shook her head and felt the feeling return to her limbs, the room was again empty. The ceremony was over and done. The shadow was gone, as if it had never been there. And her teeth began to chatter even as the sweat prickled under her arms.

She ran from the room, not caring about the noise of her boots on the stone floor, not caring if she closed the door behind her. Not caring if she was caught.

Over ten years ago. And now she took the shadows, the reflected glimpses of the ghost, or whatever it was, for granted. As they all did.

Hanne Neumann wondered how Maskell, the Englishman with his money and his stiff upper lip, would react when and if he caught sight of the ghost. Would he dismiss it, as any rational man would? Or would he accept it, as Hanne did now, as just one more thing for which there was no explanation either forthcoming or necessary? It would be interesting to witness his fear.

She smiled at him as they stepped together into the warmth. She closed the door on the blowing snow outside and led him along the access corridor.

'He wants to see you at once,' she said. 'We leave for England in an hour, and he wants to go over the details of the meeting before then. You can rest on the flight back.'

'An hour?' He was surprised. 'I thought I'd at least have a day to recover from the journey. All this way, just to go back again.'

'He has many things on his mind as the time grows nearer. He wanted time to discuss the English side of things on the flights back.'

'An *hour*?' he repeated, incredulously.

She did not look back as she led him deeper underground. Her voice was level, devoid of emotion as she said: 'Of course, if you are unhappy with that you must discuss it with him yourself.' But she was smiling as she heard his frightened intake of breath at the very thought. She quickened her pace, knowing that his old, frozen legs would struggle and ache to keep up.

Chapter Five

She shivered with cold, checking the clip mic was fixed in place with numb fingers. Then she squinted into the bright light pointing at her face. 'Are you turning over?'

'Hang on, hang on… nearly…' The soft northern whisper was disembodied in the dark behind the glare. 'Give me some level again, will you?'

'Sure.' She took a deep breath and felt her face tighten into her habitual "TV expression", authoritative yet slightly concerned. 'This is Claire Aldwych, single white female, 29 years old, feeling fifty, reporting from some Dorset shithole in the middle of the night for "So *They* Say" on the Conspiracy Channel. Cold. Fed up. Tired. Tired of pratting around breaking cordons and risking arrest, churning out the same old "same old" just to cater for the paranoid fantasies of delusional males.'

'OK,' the voice behind the light said. 'Got that, cheers.'

Claire ignored him. 'Tired of making do with so-called teams with no researcher. No Production Manager. Just me and some ginger goateed doesn't-know-any-better student acting as runner-cum-cameraman-cum-sound engineer-cum-sparks…'

'Up to speed,' reported the voice sourly.

'You want conspiracy?' Claire found she couldn't stop now. 'I've got a good one for you. It's called trying to get a job with Terrestrial. "You're too niche." "Face doesn't fit." "Cable doesn't count." "Never mind love, UK Style need a researcher for *Anne Diamond's TV Week*, why don't you apply?" It's all bollocks!'

'Up to speed, I'm running.'

Claire scowled into the brightness. She felt just the same as she had aged eight, shoved on to a stage at drama school by her failed actress mother, squinting into the spotlight. There through necessity. Having to perform and not allowed to leave until she did. Her mum had always been so determined to see her dumb ambitions achieved through her only daughter, never mind that Claire had less talent for drama than she did and none of the drive.

It had taken ten years and a fortune in wasted fees to convince her mother she was never going to be picking up awards for her definitive Cordelia or even starring alongside Robson Green in a Sunday night serial. All that faked emotion and clichéd characterisation and luvviness didn't interest her. It wasn't *real*. It was what happened in the real world, the way you could interpret it from *behind* the camera that held her interest – choosing a subject, choosing a shot. Documenting events. Pulling it all together in the edit: juxtaposition, bias, manipulating your audience...

The voice sounded distinctly nervous now. 'How about you pick it up before every squaddie in the place comes looking?'

Claire sighed. She knew she shouldn't have a go at Simon, her 'crew'. She'd be doing the same in his position, giving heart and soul to any old crap – young, hungry for it, eager to get on. Satellite and cable had seemed such an opportunity at the start, and the Con Channel just a short step on the road to awards, acclaim and the big league. She'd got on well, they liked her there. Kept pushing the work her way, kept her in the industry, kept a roof over her head. But they were getting tighter and tighter with staff and overheads. Each time she did one of these stupid, scaled-down shoots she told herself it would be the last. Tell the CC where to stick it. Burn your boats, that'll force you to make something *real* work for you, something big and decent.

And yet with each stupid assignment they sent her way, there was the nagging, superstitious thought... Suppose there was something in it. Suppose this was the one. The Big One. The one that would blow some major scandal wide open and get picked up by terrestrial, finally make her hot property instead of lost property. Stuck in the shivering cold, trespassing in a restricted area...

There through necessity.

Claire picked it up.

40

'There is no indication that the papers concerning the militarisation of Turelhampton will be de-restricted, despite their being well over fifty years old.' Her voice was calm now, commanding, in control. 'Nor is there any sign of the village being demilitarised. Still, each night and day, an army platoon patrols these deserted, decaying streets, keeping the outside world in the dark. And still nobody knows exactly why.'

She held her grave expression for a few moments longer, then stuck out her tongue and crossed her eyes. 'All right, Simon, wrap it.'

'We cut to what's-his-face then, do we?'

'That's it. Cue Peter Spinney. Eyewitness account. If the poor sod doesn't croak before we can film him.' The bright light cut out, leaving Claire entirely blinded while her eyes tried to adjust. 'He'll give us some old spiel, and we can use it as wildtrack. I got some good stuff from that old crow they evacuated at the time, too, Mary Smithson?' She paused, stamped her feet and rubbed her arms. 'We'd better get some footage of the crater to run beneath it.'

'We've got footage from the plane, isn't that enough?' Simon was packing away the portable lighting as quietly as he could. They'd got in through the cordon without much difficulty – the dozen or so guards must be so bored on this posting as to be practically catatonic, but Simon didn't seem too pleased at the thought of pushing their luck further.

'I want to mix from that to close ups. Really wow them.' She switched on her torch and peered into the gloom. It was a typically freezing cold April night, but what little spring had sprung had turned the trees green and the hedgerows overgrown – affording them plenty of places to hide.

She hoped nothing else was hiding here.

Simon must be reading her mind. 'This place spooks me.'

'Don't worry. Just some silent footage. Make it nice and creepy.' She shuddered. 'Shouldn't be too hard.'

Simon passed her the DV camera while he hefted the huge tatty holdall bulging with cables, the DAT and the lighting. Then they made their way cautiously through the silent village, by torch- and moonlight, sticking to the grassy areas as much as they could. Several times they saw bored squaddies stalking the streets, quietly talking and laughing. Claire nodded in grim satisfaction. What trouble could soldiers be expecting here?

After a couple of wrong turns she and Simon found their way to the crater site. It was huge, like an enormous burrow, long and cylindrical, gouged out of the earth.

'Like being on the moon, isn't it?' Claire whistled through her teeth, and brought up the DV to view it through the lens. 'Bet that made a bang.'

'What the hell was it, do you think?' Simon wondered fearfully, starting to tug out the collapsible lighting rig from the holdall.

She hit record, and shone her torch down into the dark hollow. A bright flash signalled back at her in return, light on metal. 'I think you mean what *is* it. There's something down there. Under the tarpaulin.'

'What? But it came down in '45, they can't just have left it there!'

'*Something's* there,' Claire insisted. She edged closer to the lip of the crater, ready to scramble down.

Then she heard the footsteps approaching. Running footsteps.

From Simon's frantic swearing, he'd heard them too. 'They're on to us,' he whispered, his eyes wide and terrified in the gloom.

'On to *you*, you mean,' she told him.

Simon's goateed jaw sagged open.

'I'll take the DV. You take the flak.' He started to protest but she slapped her free hand over his mouth. 'It's OK. Cover story, remember? You're just a film student on a recce, right? No camera. They'll send you off with a slapped wrist. You're not worth the paperwork.'

'But –'

'I'll wait for you outside with the car, OK?'

Leaving Simon with a mouth open as wide as the crater, Claire tried to keep her cool as she crept away into the night, back to the break in the cordon. This was the last time she'd be doing crap like this. This was definitely the last time.

She reached the village perimeter without incident. Through to the other side she ran like hell for the car, and waited for Simon to make his way there.

An hour later she was still waiting, her eyes prickling with tiredness. She closed them.

When she opened them again, dawn was white like snow through the huffed-up windows of the car, and Simon still wasn't back.

The corporal's voice squawked excitedly into George Henderson's ear. 'We told him, sir, the story about the testing ground. Unexploded bombs. Live ammunition. He bought it. Just a film student, sir.' It was clear that the corporal was actually quite pleased to have this unexpected distraction to deal with. 'But we've held on to him, like, scared him enough that he won't be back. No danger.'

'No danger?' George Henderson fought to stay calm, gripping the phone so tightly his fingernails glowed white. 'There was someone with him, you idiot. Someone with a camera.'

A pause. 'No, sir, he was on his own, he didn't have no camera.'

Henderson took a deep breath and shut his eyes. 'Take it from me, Corporal, he had an accomplice, and that accomplice has taken footage of the crater site. Get the truth out of your prisoner.'

'He's not really our *prisoner*, sir –'

'You're holding him aren't you? Put the frighteners on him!' Henderson roared down the phone. 'I want those tapes found and impounded.'

'But how can we impound it if it's not on site, sir?' the corporal protested awkwardly. 'Got no powers to do that, have we? I mean, we –'

'All right, Corporal.' Henderson bellowed, fuming. 'All right. I'll deal with that side of things.'

Henderson slammed down the phone in its cradle, then rose stiffly to his feet and stalked over to the window. After so many years in the same office, he knew every detail of what he would see in the early morning light. The same old view of the MOD car park with the green tongue of the lawns beyond. While ministers, underlings, secretaries had all come and gone around him, and the political climate had cyclically frozen and thawed time and time again, his own work had gone on unimpaired. Looking out through the window you'd think nothing had really changed at all. Such constancy soothed him, lent him patience in the long task.

Twin pinpricks of faint, ghostly red looked back at him from the glass.

Henderson crossed back to his desk and buzzed for his secretary.

'Red line, Thompson, scrambled,' he ordered. 'Get me UNIT.'

Claire sat on her bed with the duvet wrapped about her, hugging her knees. She thought wistfully of the few uncomfortable, stiff-necked hours she'd slept in the car. Right now she couldn't imagine ever sleeping again.

She'd assumed Simon was so spooked at his encounter he'd taken off back to London on his own. That he'd call, get in touch. But he hadn't. His home phone was just ringing and ringing, his mobile was switched off.

The real spooking had yet to begin.

Claire wished she'd stayed in the car and waited. No, she wished she'd stayed in Simon's place and let the troops take her camera. Take the tape. Destroy it.

She wouldn't have seen those… *things*, then.

The DV tape still lay where she'd thrown it away, in the corner of her bedroom. Although it was daylight outside, she'd closed all the curtains and switched on all the lights. The radio was blaring out self-indulgent tripe from a prattling DJ, and Richard and Judy were hosting a silent phone-in on cheating lovers. Claire just sat rocking herself back and forth, wishing she could feel warm. She should get out of here. Go to her mother's, maybe. Jesus, she *was* desperate.

The doorbell rang.

Simon. At long bloody last. Claire leapt from the bed in her pale blue pyjamas and rushed for the door. She knew she must look a state, panda-eyed from crying, pale face streaked with make-up and her dyed plum-red hair pushed back in an untidy ponytail, but at least Simon would see she the state she was in and know she hadn't run out on him lightly...

She flung open the door to find a tall, dark-haired soldier on her doorstep in immaculate uniform, and immediately made to close it again. He swiftly placed a gleaming black boot over the threshold.

'Miss Aldwych? My name is Captain Palmer.'

Claire looked down at the floor. 'I don't care if you're Captain Scarlet,' she said quietly. 'Would you please take your foot away?'

'I'm with UNIT.'

Now she looked up, not sure whether to take comfort from this visit or be still more afraid. 'United Nations Intelligence Taskforce?'

'That's right. I'd like to talk to you about Turelhampton.'

'Nothing to say,' Claire snapped. 'I'm off the story.'

Palmer shook his head. 'Miss Aldwych, we know you were in Turelhampton last night.'

'Yes. And since I played back my footage, believe me, I am *off* the story. How did you find me?'

'Your friend Simon? He told the MOD troops your name.'

'Is he OK?'

'Of course.'

'Thank God.' She paused, reflected. 'The loud-mouthed little git.'

Palmer gave a small, tight smile. 'We'd have tracked you down regardless. We've had your address on file for a long time.' He gave her a stern military stare. 'Your secret history of the Nunton complex raised a few eyebrows, Miss Aldwych...'

'Wish it had done the same for the viewing figures.' Claire gave up, walked away back into her bedroom. 'All right, all right,' she called. 'You've come for the tape, I suppose? Well, you can have it.'

Palmer was clearly caught off-guard. 'I... That is...'

She retrieved it from the corner and held it out to him. 'Go on, take it. Take it away and do whatever your quasi-secret military organisation does in situations like this and sort it all out.'

Palmer frowned at her. Claire decided he looked like an old Action Man, well-proportioned with neat, unremarkable features; one of the dark-haired ones her brother had coveted so badly in the 1970s. Palmer's eyes were piercing eagle-eye blue, and she wondered if his peaked cap hid a little black lever that moved them back and forth. Right now she'd believe anything. Damn the bloody Con Channel, it had finally turned her as paranoid as the rest.

'Please?' she added, thrusting the tape a little further out towards him.

Palmer paused, bemused. She doubted this had been what he'd expected. 'You'll appreciate I must verify the tape for myself?'

She went back into her bedroom, bidding him follow, loaded it into the camera for him with shaking hands, and flicked the telly on to the AV channel. 'Enjoy,' she told him. 'I'll be in the other room.'

A few minutes later, Claire heard her own voice start up from the bedroom. Palmer had worked out rewind and play. Clearly he had hidden depths for a military man.

She turned the kitchen radio on as loud as it would go, drowning herself out.

Half an hour later, Captain Palmer emerged from her bedroom, grave-faced, holding the little tape.

Claire turned off the radio's racket. She found she felt a little calmer now someone else had seen the tape. Someone in authority. She could just forget all about it now UNIT were involved. She could just...

Palmer was looking at her, and she guessed not just because she was a girl in her pyjamas.

'You're going to ask me to go with you, aren't you?' she said quietly.

'My orders are to destroy this tape.' Palmer paused. 'But before I carry them out, there's someone I think should see this. And since you were an eyewitness –'

'I was there, but I wasn't an eyewitness,' Claire said shakily, scrutinising his reaction. 'Those... *things* weren't there when I was shooting, the place was empty. But... but the camera picked them up, somehow.'

Palmer didn't even flinch. She didn't know if that should make her feel better or worse.

'Miss Aldwych, you really must come with me. It could be important.'

A nagging little voice not yet cowed by the events of the day started up inside her head. It *could* be important. It could be the Big One.

Claire sighed and nodded. 'Give me five minutes.' She crossed to her bedroom and paused in the doorway. 'Captain Palmer...' She swallowed nervously. 'What do they look like to you?'

Palmer didn't hesitate. 'I think they look like devils, Miss Aldwych. Demons. Imps.'

Claire nodded, bit her lip. 'Me too.'

She went through to get dressed, leaving the door ajar behind her.

Chapter Six

There was never enough information on their secret website. Until now. He had missed them in Frankfurt, and again in Buenos Aires because they used e-mail and phone calls as well. But as they broadened, as they involved more people, so they had to rely more and more on the site and less on the old boy network and personal contact.

So, in Cornwall, he had them.

He knew the date and the location. It was only the time he was unsure about. And that was easily sorted – he would wait all day if necessary. They could hardly disguise the arrival of so many people, even if they staggered it over hours or even days. This time, he would be there.

In the event, he decided to wait until the evening was drawing in. Some brief and basic research at the local paper and the library in Truro was enough for Brian Goldman to know that security would be tight. The house was owned by a millionaire recluse and it was in the middle of nowhere. A stranger, someone not invited, would be obvious. And a millionaire would have the latest security equipment installed. Especially a millionaire hosting a meeting like this one.

Dusk was gathering, casting a grey gloom over the grey Cornwall landscape. Just past a solitary post box that he decided would make a useful landmark, Goldman drove his car off the narrow road and concealed it in a small area of scrub and woodland close to the edge of the estate. Across country, it was only about three miles to the house. He had a map and a compass, and he had a small holdall containing his video camera, notebook and back-up tape recorder. He took the precaution of marking where he had left the car on the map with a large pencil cross, the last thing he wanted was to get lost at night in the middle of the countryside. .

Goldman had told Linda not to expect him back until the next day, and given her the emergency number to call if he was still not back by the day after that. He had thought of everything.

Except, he discovered, for the fact that there had been heavy rain, and the fields he needed to cross were recently-ploughed. Progress was slow and messy. By the time he approached the rear of the house and his feet crunched anxiously on the gravel of the back drive, he was over an hour later than he had anticipated and his legs were caked in mud. His feet sloshed around inside the wet interior of his inadequate shoes, and he was shivering with the cold. When an owl hooted in a nearby tree, he gave an audible gasp of fright.

Even from the back of the house he could see the steady stream of traffic approaching along the main driveway. The headlights swept the grounds and the drive. Goldman ducked down behind a flower bed and hoped that none of the drivers or passengers was paying attention to the area where he was hiding. At least, he reflected, his face was dark and grimy from the mud. His problem now was how to get into the house unobserved.

The problem became more serious as Goldman saw the bobbing light of a torch cutting through the evening. Behind it he struggled to make out the silhouette of a man in uniform. A large dog strained on its lead as they passed close to Goldman. The dog turned for a moment, snarling slaverously in his direction before the man dragged it away, paying it no heed. Goldman checked his watch, and waited to see how long it would take for the guard to return.

When the guard had been back twice more, each time with an interval of just over ten minutes, Goldman decided to risk a closer look at the house. Perhaps with at least one guard on duty, the doors and windows might not all be locked. Five minutes was enough to assure him that they were. He tried to peer through the windows, but the back of the house was in darkness and he could see nothing.

Goldman checked his watch and saw that he had about five minutes before the guard returned. He could hide and wait for

49

another ten minute gap, or he could try to force a window in the remaining time. He decided that five minutes should be ample, and started work on the weakest of the windows. It was small, the frame beginning to rot. It took less than two minutes to ease his knife under the catch.

Instinctively, Goldman glanced round before he finished working the catch. And caught sight of the beam of a torch cutting across the lawn behind him. He froze, swallowing dryly. If he ran back to his hiding place he was sure to be seen. But if he stayed where he was and the guard followed his usual routine, they would practically come face to face.

That left him no option. Frantically, he worked the knife back and forth, praying under his breath that the blade would catch on the window clasp. The torch was closer every time he glanced back, and he could imagine the sound of the dog's heavy breathing, the smell of its warm breath on his face, the ripping of its teeth…

The window jumped in the frame, swinging inwards and away from him. He dropped the knife, and it clinked to the path. But Goldman did not wait to see if the torch reacted. He dived through the window, dragging his holdall after him. He could manage without the knife now that he was inside. He hoped.

It seemed to be a small storeroom. He had landed amid a pile of mops and brushes and buckets which clattered alarmingly. He lay absolutely still for what seemed like an eternity before he dared to extricate himself and tip-toe to the door. He hoped it was not locked or bolted. He certainly did not want to risk going back for his knife, even if that would help. And he had come too far to concede defeat now.

The door was closed but not locked. It opened with a creak that made him cringe, giving out on to a dimly-lit corridor that was panelled with wood and hung with dusty painting. In the distance he could hear chanting – an old mantra.

'*Ein Volk.*'

One that still made his flesh crawl.

'*Ein Reich.*'

It would be easy to follow the sound to find where the action was.

'Ein Fuhrer!'

And then somewhere to hide and watch and record.

Light spilled into the corridor between double doors at the end. He could hear the chanting, the ranting, the speeches more loudly now. From behind the doors. Was this as close as he could get?

Goldman paused by the doors, tried to see through the crack between them but could make out nothing other than light and indistinct shapes moving through it.

Then he noticed an opening to the side of the doors, a flight of steps leading upwards into darkness. He hoisted his holdall over his shoulder and made his careful way up the steps, emerging onto a gallery from where he could look down into the ballroom below where the rally was taking place. At the opposite end of the room, a similar gallery was in darkness. Behind him, a large picture window gave out into the night.

A spotlight had been mounted on the balustrades, although it was not lit. Standing beside it afforded him an excellent view down at a dais in the centre of the room. If anyone looked up, he would be a shadow, a ghost. He unzipped the holdall, and pulled out a small camcorder.

The room was full of people, mostly men but a few women as well. He was surprised and sickened by how many young people there were. The older ones, the survivors and those who were steeped in the blood of history he could understand if not condone. But the next generation, and the one after that?

The small LCD screen of the camera showed him that there was more than enough light for its digital capture of the scene below. The people, on their feet as they shouted, chanted, ranted. The seats arranged in concentric circles round the central point of the room – the dais.

On the platform stood a man, tall, blond, immaculate in a dark suit. He might be a lawyer or a stockbroker except for the passion in his voice and the madness in his eyes as he waved his fist, and whipped up the emotions of the crowd. He was speaking – declaiming – without notes. The table on the dais in front of him was bare, covered with a simple green cloth. Bare save for… Goldman zoomed the camera in on the table. It looked like a crystal ball, on a simple gold stand in the middle of the round table that stood in the middle of the concentric circles of chairs that surrounded the circular platform.

He zoomed in further, right into the heart of the glass sphere. It was as much to test the camera's abilities as anything. But there, clear in the glass, was a distorted reflection of the tall man as he shouted and waved and jerked his head emphatically. And behind that, as if deep within the glass itself, two pinpricks of red. Like eyes.

'The time is coming,' the man was shouting. 'Coming soon! While we mourn our departed brother – our mentor and guide these years in the wilderness – while we mourn him, we know that now is the time for us to forge ahead. Now is the time to prepare for the coming people. The coming Reich. The coming man.'

The room erupted again into applause and shouting. Spontaneously, it seemed, they were extending their arms, shouting. In the viewfinder, the man on the podium allowed himself a slight digital smile and waited for the sound to die down again.

'Let me show you the future,' he said quietly when they were still once more. 'Let us see the approaching firestorm, the coming war and victory.' He nodded, as if to let them know that he already knew all about it – what would happen, what they would see, and how they would react. 'And then…' he added even more quietly, so quietly that Goldman had to strain to hear and hoped that the camera's microphone would capture his words, 'and then we shall meet the architect, founder and leader of our brave new world.'

The image on the camera screen was close on the man's face as he spoke. Suddenly the face slipped sideways and disappeared. Goldman blinked in surprise. Then he realised that the man had stepped away from the table and was climbing down from the dais. Goldman zoomed out, determined to capture whatever was happening now. The people seemed to be waiting expectantly. Several, mainly the older ones, had sat down.

The man who had been speaking took a seat in the second row of chairs, nodding to the men either side and shaking their hands. A young woman, strikingly blonde, also leaned across and murmured something to him. Goldman stayed on the woman for a moment. She looked to be in her late twenties or early thirties, her hair tied up severely on her head. Like the man she was dressed in a sombre dark suit, but hers seemed to cling to the curves of her body, accentuating rather than hiding her shape.

Then the lights dimmed, and the figures in the front row of seat stood up, forming a circle round the dais. There were seven of them, all dressed in what looked like dark monks' habits. One of them stepped up on to the podium, reaching out towards the crystal ball with gloved hands.

On the camera screen, Goldman could see that the gloves were as green as the cloth that covered the table. Around the circle, the six robed figures also reached out towards the table. There was silence, the spotlight next to Goldman illuminating the table and the figure behind it. Goldman leaned forward, over the balustrade, adjusting the camera settings to compensate for the change in the light.

'The future is revealed within the Scrying Glass.' The robed man's voice was accented. Chinese perhaps? Japanese? His face was shrouded beneath the hood of his robes, lost in shadows. So Goldman zoomed in on the crystal ball – the Scrying Glass. He had enough shots of the audience, enough to pick out many of the faces from the video.

'I see the coming war.'

Was it a trick of the light? As the robed figures chanted quietly, rhythmically, it seemed as if the sphere was glowing with its own light, rather than the reflection of the spotlight. Goldman could see the green hands of the man reaching towards the glass, their reflection curved around it and distorted, elongated. But behind that was something else. Another reflection. An image.

'I see the triumph of the Reich.'

Closer still. It was difficult to hold the image still, despite the digital judder control's attempts to fix it on the screen. There was… something. Like firecracker explosions. Ruined buildings. A blood-red sky over a devastated landscape. The reflection of a painting, perhaps. Hieronymous Bosch meets Canaletto.

'I see the coming man!'

And a face. Emerging, triumphant, from the fog of the misty glass.

Goldman gasped, and stepped back, the camera waving wildly, the image pitching and yawing across the scene below. It settled on the gallery at the opposite end of the room. At the same moment, the spotlight beside him came on. It was pointing directly at the gallery opposite, a carefully stage-managed moment to illuminate and reveal the figure standing there – his grand entrance.

With a sea-sick spasm of horror, Goldman realised his foot was caught. Caught in a cable. Caught in a cable that pulled free from its socket in the back of the spotlight as he moved.

But he had no time to worry, no time to wonder if he should replace it. Already there were shouts from below. Everyone had turned towards the light that was no longer there. Everyone had seen his dark shadowy figure on the gallery where no figure should be. The faint glow of the LCD screen illuminated Goldman's face, transfixing him like a rabbit in the headlights. The blonde woman was on her feet screaming, pointing, shouting instructions to the men who were running towards the double doors. Towards the gallery stairs.

But Goldman took in little of this. His attention was fixed on the camera screen. The camera had come to rest pointing across the ballroom, aimed directly at the opposite gallery. Even with the spotlight extinguished it could make out the figure standing there, like a reflection of Goldman. Mirror image.

Except that this figure was confident, determined, not terrified and shaking. It stood leaning on the balustrade, looking across intently at the camera, at Goldman. The figure's zoomed face filled the screen, seeming to stare accusingly from the camera itself. The man's eyes were ice-blue and hard as flint. His black eyebrows were heavy with concentration. The hair was slicked across the forehead, as black as the small moustache.

'My God,' Goldman breathed. 'Oh my God in heaven.'

He could hear the running feet now, hear them coming up the stairs for him.

Goldman clutched the camera close to his chest, desperate to protect it, as he ran full tilt towards the window. And as he ran, he saw only the haunting face at it continued to stare at him.

The face filled his thoughts as he struck the glass. It filled his mind as he crashed to the gravel driveway below, his bones creaking and protesting as he rolled, scrabbled to his feet, staggered away. It filled his soul as he limped desperately towards the back of the house hoping and praying they would expect him to make for the main gates.

It blinded him to the lights that came on behind him. It deafened him to the barking of the dogs and the shouts of the men. It drove him forwards into the night, clutching the camera like a talisman against the darkness.

The face of Adolf Hitler.

Chapter Seven

'Nor is there any sign of the village being demilitarised. Still, each night and day, an army platoon patrols these deserted, decaying streets, keeping the outside world in the dark...'

'Good grief,' muttered Alistair Lethbridge-Stewart, as a squat, shadowy shape came running up behind this journalist woman on the TV screen. Another of the imp-like creatures came into shot, scuttling round the girl's legs as she continued talking, oblivious. 'Pause it, could you, Palmer?'

Palmer raised the remote and the image flickered to a halt. The girl – Claire, was it, Claire Aldwych? He was getting to be dreadful with names – was caught mid-blink on the screen.

'Very flattering,' she remarked sourly from the back of the viewing room.

The eyes of the gremlin at her feet were ghostly and red, looking straight at the camera. As he studied the almost transparent creatures on the tape, Lethbridge-Stewart forgot all about the nagging pain in his back from overdoing the gardening, his annoyance at having to cancel arrangements for his last day with Doris before her week away to be here in UNIT HQ for Palmer. He felt a familiar thrill at the sight of the unknown, to be facing up to something unearthly – soon followed by mixed feelings of guilt and regret. He was retired. His days of heading up UNIT's British forces were far behind him; now he was just a happily married man living out his last days in a big house with a fine garden. A garden he should be getting back to.

Palmer shouldn't have troubled him with this. It stirred up all the old feelings inside him. What was he supposed to do? Old Lethbridge-Stewart had retired from the fray, but he'd always known the monsters, the terrors, would never give up their designs on the Earth. The struggle would never be over; that was why UNIT existed.

That was why Brigadier Lethbridge-Stewart had existed, for such a long time.

He didn't like to think of it all going on without him.

Palmer leaned forward. 'Have you ever seen anything like it, Brigadier?'

'Eh?' Lethbridge-Stewart jerked back to the present from glory days of the past. The imp thing was staring out at him, frozen on the screen. But it was like it wasn't quite there, as if he were seeing only the reflection of the thing in the monitor screen, and that in fact, it was sitting beside him.

'Ah... No, Palmer, I haven't. Not quite like that.' He paused. 'Remind me, were you with me at Devil's End? Mid-1970s?'

Palmer shook his head. 'No sir, I was seconded to UNIT during...' He glanced anxiously at Claire in the corner. 'That time-bending business. With the Master.'

Lethbridge-Stewart smiled to himself fondly. 'Ah, yes, a while later... Well, at Devil's End we came up against a little chap with wings a bit like that. Nasty bit of work. But he was stone, Palmer, and there was only one of him. Solid. We all saw him. And we all saw him die.' He turned to Claire. 'And yet *you* claim to have seen nothing at all, Miss Aldwych?'

The girl rolled her eyes. 'Do you think I'd have stood there reporting if I'd seen those things running about the place?'

'It's like... like they're keeping an eye on you,' Palmer ventured.

'They're linked to whatever's in the bottom of that crater,' Claire said bluntly. 'Whatever those troops are guarding. It's obvious.' She looked at the two of them pointedly. 'Well, obvious to those with access to information on whatever it was that came down...'

Lethbridge-Stewart nodded thoughtfully. Palmer had given him a quick briefing once the apologies and the that's-quite-alrights were out of the way. Some kind of unidentified object had come down over this little Dorset village, and resisted all attempts to relocate it elsewhere – nothing could shift it from the bottom of this crater, as if it were anchored there in some way. So the mountain had come to Mohammed, and a military presence had remained ever since while the secrets of the craft were teased out. Teased out slowly, it seemed – nothing much had been yielded so far after half a century of effort.

Lethbridge-Stewart expressed some surprise that he hadn't come across this before. Surely such an object came under UNIT's sphere of influence – what were regular army troops doing running the show? Then, Palmer had awkwardly confided his concerns. His new CO had stumbled on the Turelhampton files and asked similar questions of the operation's head man, chap called Henderson. He'd been there a long time, the son, apparently, of the officer originally assigned to watch over the UFO back in 1944. The MOD men joked he'd come with the building. And a more secretive, obstructive type you'd never come across.

'And there was nothing in the files about sightings of these… creatures?' asked Lethbridge-Stewart.

'Nothing,' Palmer confirmed.

'And yet Henderson was ordering the tape destroyed without even seeing it,' Claire piped up. 'Why? What's he trying to cover up?'

Lethbridge-Stewart swapped a glance with Palmer and cleared his throat. 'Miss Aldwych… I suggest you forget all about this incident.'

Her green eyes widened in outrage. 'Forget all about it?' She pointed to the screen. 'All about *them*?'

'You saw nothing at the time,' Lethbridge-Stewart reasoned with practised indifference. 'Perhaps the tape is faulty?'

Claire snorted, wrinkling her long upturned nose. 'Oh, sure, we're always finding blank tapes full of devils and demons.'

A change of tack. He cleared his throat again, meaningfully. 'Miss Aldwych, you do realise you were trespassing on Ministry of Defence property?'

She stood up in outrage. 'I was *trespassing* on an ordinary rural village whose inhabitants were kicked out in 1944 and offered little or nothing in the way of compensation or explanation.'

Lethbridge-Stewart sighed. 'Miss Aldwych –'

But she was in full flight now. 'Those *troops* are the ones trespassing. Maybe you can get away with seizing a village in wartime but in 2001, I reckon it's not *too* unreasonable for people to finally get some answers –'

A terse beeping started up, and Claire's tirade died on her lips. She pulled out her mobile phone and glared at them both.

'You are *so* saved by the bell,' she informed them, before flouncing out of the room in her dark trouser-suit and slamming the door behind her.

Lethbridge-Stewart sighed. Handling women didn't get any easier with age. 'Should you go after her?'

'Sergeant Hansing will make sure she doesn't go far,' Palmer said. He looked appealingly at Lethbridge-Stewart. 'Brigadier Fernfather says he's fought his battles with Henderson. Wants nothing more to do with the man. If I refer this up it's going nowhere, but I can't help thinking...' He shrugged. 'What should I do, sir?'

Lethbridge-Stewart considered. 'First of all, I'd tell this Henderson you've done as he's asked – say the tape has been destroyed. You gave it a cursory glance and all was in order.'

'And then?'

The imp creature was still staring out at them from the TV monitor. Then, discomfortingly, the pause period reached its end and the tape turned off with a noisy whirring of clicks. A wild snowstorm of static held the screen, but the red eyes seemed to glare at them still from the screen.

'And then, Captain Palmer, I think I would do just as you have done.'

'Sir?'

'Call for help.' The Brigadier smiled. 'Back at home, I've just the thing.'

Glaring at the sergeant eyeing her in the office outside, Claire stood as far away from him as possible. That left her in the corner, facing the wall like the class dunce; rich considering the mighty intellects battling for supremacy round here. She didn't recognise the number that was flashed up on her Nokia screen, but hit the accept key anyway.

'Claire Aldwych?'

'Claire, it's Brian.' The voice sounded strained, almost stammering. 'Brian Goldman.'

Claire wracked her brains to put a face to the name – then wished she hadn't. Drunken images from a press party for some new news channel swum into her mind, with bald, charming Goldman trying to stick his tongue down her throat, and her going along with it to try making her boyfriend jealous. Her *ex*-boyfriend. Then Goldman's wife coming in, and not being too impressed either. But all that was over a year ago…

'Brian, hi, listen, can I –'

'Claire, I've just seen… Hitler. Seen Hitler.'

'What? Brian, where are you?'

'A crystal ball. It glowed… like it was burning inside.' He swallowed hard. 'Nazis. Nazis in Cornwall, they…'

She shut her eyes wearily. 'Brian, this might – *might just* – be funny at any other time, but –'

'Listen to me, for God's sake. I've got it on tape. Hitler was there. I *saw* him.'

'You saw him on a tape?'

Still the voice crackled on. From the acoustics he must be on a mobile himself. '*My* tape. I'm parked off the A39. Oakhope Manor. Near Kilkhampton.'

'Well, I'm very happy for you. Brian –'

'There was a – a ceremony. *Nazi* ceremony.'

She glanced round at the sergeant, who was still watching her. 'Brian, this really isn't a good time.'

'Check it out. Something might happen… Look I know you've done Nazis, you must check it out for me.'

'I've done Nazis? What the hell are you talking about?'

'Promise me. Promise me you'll check it out.'

She conspicuously crossed her fingers and waved them at the phone. 'Oh for God's sake, all right, I promise. I'll check it out.' *Yeah right.*

'Claire… Claire, your *Last Days of Hitler* doc…'

'The Con Channel one? What about it?'

'The skull fragments, the skull fragments from the Russians, did they match? Was he really dead? Really *dead*?'

'Brian, I have to go.' *You drunken muppet.* 'Like I say, it's not a good –'

'But you'll look into it for me? Call me when you know?'

'Sure. 'Course. I'll look into it.' *Easy on the sauce next time, right?* 'Bye now.'

She ended the call, turned ready to wade back in to the viewing room and pick up where she left off, when she saw Palmer and Brigadier Whatshisname were both out here staring at her.

'We'd both be grateful, Miss Aldwych, if you'd try to forget about all this.' The Brigadier spoke more softly now, his voice low and rich. He'd be perfect for voiceovers. 'Keep it quiet. At least for now.'

She found she couldn't be bothered to rail on at them again. Brian had sapped her strength. 'At least for ever,' she said.

'I think that's safest,' added Palmer. Some kind of threat? No, she didn't think so. And the thought made her shiver.

'If you recall anything you think may help us further, Claire,' Palmer said, offering her what looked like a business card, 'you can contact me on this number.'

'Does that put me through to your hush-hush messaging service?' Claire offered it back to him, shaking her head. 'Got that number, thanks. From the Nunton doc.'

Palmer smiled wryly and placed the card back in his breast pocket. Then he motioned to the sergeant to escort her from the building.

'*We'll* be in touch if we think you can help us again, at any rate,' the Brigadier assured her.

'I won't wait up,' said Claire.

There was a note waiting for Lethbridge-Stewart when he got back to the darkened house. He'd missed Doris going, and she'd had to get a cab to the airport. But the note was jolly, teasing him about forgetting the difference between Queen-and-country and his own queen and country house. He smiled. She was in holiday spirit, ready for a happy hen week of sun and sangria with her niece. She'd left him a meal to heat up together with instructions on how to work the microwave in her absence.

He felt, suddenly, terribly lonely without her, as empty as the house was.

After a drop of port, Lethbridge-Stewart trudged up the stairs and manhandled out the ladder to the loft. He knew exactly where he'd placed the item he was looking for. Technically, he supposed, he should never have removed it from HQ – but it had been presented to him, not to UNIT. He pictured himself as a slim, fit young man with dark hair and neat moustache, dubiously taking ownership of the thing. Now his hair was grey and smoothed back, his skin loosened and liver-spotted, the bristles of his thick moustache like fuse-wire.

Wouldn't it be wonderful, he thought, if we didn't grow old. If we could all change into younger people and just go on living.

Clambering up into the dry attic, he blew dust from the box lid and carried it carefully back downstairs.

It was only for use in the direst emergencies. Did some invisible imps near the Dorset coast count as a crisis?

The week stretched emptily ahead.

The Brigadier decided they did.

Once it was unpacked from the protective polystyrene, the Brigadier stared at the magic box. It was about the size and shape of an old cash register with a small circular antenna protruding from the featureless base. Nothing to plug in as he recalled. You just had to speak into it.

He felt self-conscious, stupid, like a child too old to believe in magic asked to accept a conjuring trick.

But then, there had never been a magician like the Doctor.

'Doctor?' he whispered, glancing about as if someone might be overhearing him. Then, more loudly: 'Doctor, I've no idea if you can hear me but... But something's come up.' He paused. 'Something I think could be right up your street.'

A noise started up, loud and trumpeting, and the Brigadier scrambled away from the machine in alarm. Then he realised the noise was coming from the hall downstairs, grinding, rasping, grating. An impossible, but very familiar noise.

By the time the Brigadier had made it half-way down the stairs he could see that the battered, blue police box had come together in his hallway.

'Wonder which one I'll get,' he murmured happily.

A moment later, with the box barely solid in the room, the TARDIS door opened. A very tall, very burly man with curly blond hair charged out into the room in a fair temper. The Brigadier found this incarnation of his old friend something of an unknown quantity – the Doctor he knew least well.

'That's what I call good service, Doctor.'

The blond man looked up, and a slow smile spread over his face. There was such spirit in his rounded face, in his glittering blue eyes – he looked the kind of man who had taken some knocks from the universe and was more than ready to give a few back in return. A knee-length coat as garish and randomly-patterned as the old testcard on television clashed horribly with the yellow-humbug trousers, orange spats and green shoes. A hastily tied blue cravat hung messily over a checked waistcoat, all but obscuring the white shirt – typically the one patch of sanity in his wardrobe – beneath it.

'I've not kept you waiting long?' the Doctor inquired with exaggerated concern.

'Barely a moment.'

'Pity,' the Doctor said, frowning, hands on hips. 'I'd hate for you to imagine I was still at your beck and call. Why I ever gave you that space-time telegraphy set...'

Perhaps something of the Brigadier's hurt had showed on his face, because in a trice the Doctor's scowl turned into a wicked smile. He crossed the hallway in an instant and was suddenly bounding up the stairs, hands outstretched to clasp the Brigadier's own.

'It's been a long time, Doctor,' the Brigadier said.

'I'm sure it will be,' agreed the Doctor.

'Travelling alone?'

The Doctor's brash front seemed to slip for a second. 'Afraid so, yes.' Then the moment was gone. Slipping an arm round the Brigadier's back, the Doctor steered him down the stairs. 'I, er, take it I'm not here on a social call?'

Lethbridge-Stewart's face clouded. 'Afraid not, Doctor.'

'What's the trouble? I take it that trouble *is* up that street of mine you mentioned?'

The Brigadier considered, picked up the videotape Palmer had dubbed off for him from the hall table. 'I've been briefed on the situation, Doctor... it's all rather unofficial I'm afraid –'

'Don't be afraid, Brigadier, I'm here now.' The Doctor smiled broadly. 'So, why not start your story at the beginning, and end at the end.'

Lethbridge-Stewart tapped the tape in his hand thoughtfully, remembered with a shudder what it depicted. 'I'll tell you what,' he said. 'I think perhaps we should start it with a pint.'

Chapter Eight

He knew that he should get away as quickly as he could. It had been a risk to call Claire from the car rather than just driving away. But he needed to tell someone. And he needed time to get himself back together before driving. He needed fresh air, needed to breathe.

Goldman was sweating and shivering. His legs felt like jelly, and he leaned against the post box for support, staring up into the cold night sky. It was incredibly clear and he could make out the stars like pin-pricks of light in the velvet darkness above him.

They would be watching for a car, he knew. And the dogs would find his trail across the fields. Would the slushy wet mud conceal the scent like a stream would? He had no idea, but he wasn't about to assume it would. He staggered back towards the car.

Goldman pulled open the door and fell inside. He reached for the keys, which he had left in the ignition. But they weren't there. He leaned forward, fumbling on the floor.

And something dropped heavily on to the passenger seat beside him. He froze, turning his head slowly to see.

It was his holdall. The holdall he realised with a shudder he had left on the gallery in the house. The holdall containing the map showing where the car was. Showing where they could come and find him. And suddenly he felt calm and at ease. He sat up and turned to face the two figures sitting veiled in darkness in the back of the car.

'You left this behind,' the man said. 'In your hurry to leave us.' His teeth glinted in the darkness. It was the man who had stood and shouted from the dais.

'I do hope it isn't important,' the woman – the blonde woman with the severe hair – added. Her voice was honeyed steel. Her accent was harsh, lowland German probably. 'It's a good job we found your car before you got here. Good job for us, that is.'

She reached forwards, and for a brief moment he thought she was about to embrace him. Until he felt the cold blade of the knife close against his throat. He was still clutching the camera, he realised. The man slid into the passenger seat, pushing the holdall down on to the floor. He took the camera from Goldman's unprotesting hands.

Goldman watched him as he examined the camera, then twisted slightly so that he could reach into his coat pocket.

The knife pressed close against his throat and he felt the warm sticky run of blood as it nicked the skin. 'Careful,' she warned.

'Tape,' he managed to grunt past the knife. 'You want the tape.' He pulled the miniature cassette from his pocket, holding it up so she could see before passing it to the man.

'How kind,' he breathed. 'And we shall want more than that.'

'More?' he croaked.

'Oh, much more,' the woman breathed in his ear. 'Names, contacts. How you found us. What you intended to do.'

'Everything,' the man said with a thin smile. 'And we shall get it. Eventually.'

They would, too. Goldman knew that. And because he knew who and what they were he had several unpleasant ideas of how they would go about it, and what they would do with him after they had it. What they would do to the people he knew, the people he would betray.

The knife was hard against his throat. Reassuringly tight. He braced himself, then lunged forwards, jerking his head back so that the soft, flabby skin of his neck was tight against it. Even in the moonlight he could see the mist of red that showered the dashboard. Even through the gathering smog and cotton-wool fuzz he could hear the man's cry of surprise and annoyance, the woman's sharp intake of breath.

Then he was falling forwards, into the steering wheel. Into oblivion.

Hanne Neumann watched as Klaus Venkel drove the car into a tree. The bonnet crumpled and he was thrown forward against the seat belt. When he got out, his dark coat was glistening in the moonlight where he had been sitting in the man's blood.

Between them they manoeuvred the dead man's body back into the driver's seat and leaned his head down over the steering wheel. Hanne had found an emergency can of petrol in the boot of the car, and she shook half the contents over the body, sprinkling the rest over the back seats and the chassis.

They stood well clear as Klaus lit his petrol-soaked handkerchief, let it burn brightly for a moment, then tossed it through the open window of the car.

The fire took hold immediately, wreathing the body with its oily orange fingers and eating into the material of the seats, the instrument panel, his clothing. They stood and watched for several minutes as the black smoke rose into the blacker sky and the shadows of the flames flickered in the trees and across the scrubland.

Klaus looked at Hanne impassively. 'The police will know this was no accident.'

'Of course they will.' She smiled. 'But it will take them a while to work out what might have happened.' She shrugged. 'What does it matter to us? Soon, we shall be gone from this miserable country.'

Venkel produced Goldman's mobile phone from his pocket, and called up something from the menu. 'He called someone. Before taking his final little stroll in the country air.' He showed her the soft-glowing display. 'A woman.'

'Claire A-Mobile.'

'A collaborator, perhaps? Should we deal with her too?'

Hanne considered. 'You're alarmist, Venkel. We do not wish to arouse undue suspicion. Let us inform the Fuhrer. We can track this woman, arrange that our agents watch her — and deal with her if necessary.'

Klaus made a note of the woman's number, and of the personal details stored on the phone. He gave a grunt of annoyance. 'Goldman,' he murmured. 'A Jew, of course.'

He advanced on the flames and threw the mobile phone into

the burning car. Then he turned and started along the short cut back to the main road.

Hanne watched the curling flames for a moment longer, then she too turned and walked into the night.

The message service cut in after a dozen rings. Claire frowned in frustration. Brian had sounded pretty distraught earlier. Whatever he had really seen, it had obviously shaken him. She'd been too fired up herself to really pay much notice at the time, but now, back home at the end of such a shattering day, she found his words, his stammering speech, preying on her mind. She'd been really off with him, and right now she quite understood the idea of needing someone to talk to.

'It's Claire,' she said in response to the terse prompt. 'Claire Aldwych, we spoke earlier. Sorry if I sounded a bit dubious,' she went on quickly, unsure how much time she had. 'I was with someone. He might be able to help actually. If there's anything in this, I mean.'

She cursed silently – she sounded sceptical again. 'He's with UNIT,' she added quickly. Goldman would know about UNIT. That might impress him. 'Anyway, I'd like to follow this up. Call me back when you can, will you?' She reeled off her number.

'Let's have that drink, Brian,' she added lamely. Mercenary or what? Still he was a journalist, he would understand. And he had called her, after all.

And there would be nothing in it anyway. Probably.

Claire decided she would go to sleep that night with the lights on.

He was shorter than both Hanne and Venkel, but there would have been no doubt to an observer who was in charge, who held the power. His blue eyes narrowed as the tape played across the television screen. A dull grey mass of nothing, the fire burning in the grate reflected together with their faces in the glass.

'Perhaps he got it wrong,' Klaus Venkel suggested. 'It is easily done. He didn't press record.'

The other man turned and looked at him, just for a moment. It was enough.

'He went to great risk,' Hanne said slowly. 'He gave his life. He did not forget to record it.' She turned to the shorter man. 'But perhaps we found this Goldman before he could begin.'

'Perhaps,' the man said quietly. 'But I received the impression he had been there for a while.' He clicked his tongue, then sucked in his lower lip as he considered. The moustache bristled as his jaw worked. 'More likely there is another tape.'

'Then it is ashes,' Venkel pointed out.

'I hope so,' the man said. 'We are close, very close. But I am not yet ready to announce my presence to the world.' He drew himself up to his full height and turned to face them directly. 'And when I do, it will be on my own terms, to gain the maximum effect and the best advantage. To bring the people along and show them the time has indeed come. Not in the stolen images of a gutter-press Jewish journalist.'

They were silent as he paced the room for a full minute. 'I should get back,' he said eventually. 'They will expect more from me. To see me again, to rekindle their flame of pride and honour. To speak of plans and the future.'

'What shall we do?' Venkel asked.

'Hanne, you will come with me. And you, Klaus – find out everything about Brian Goldman. Everything you can. We need to be sure he acted alone. We need to search his house, his office, even his garden shed.'

Klaus smiled grimly. 'Of course, my Fuhrer.'

'But discreetly. I want no unnecessary attention drawn.'

'And if we find he was not alone? That others, like this girl, know what he knew or suspected to be the case?' Hanne asked.

The Fuhrer's eyes were wide, the pupils wells of darkness as he stared at her unblinking. 'That would be unfortunate too,' he said quietly. 'For them.'

Chapter Nine

The Brigadier only lived an hour or so from Dorset. He and Doris had holidayed there many times, and the mere mention of the name brought back happy images of blue skies, cold beer and beautiful, rugged scenery.

Now he had to add shadow-demons to that list of associations. And that, combined with the Doctor's tuneless whistling as they drove along deserted B-roads in the Land Rover at crack of dawn, and the uncomfortable realisation he'd put on a few pounds since last wearing full uniform, had conspired to dull Lethbridge-Stewart's holiday spirit.

'Really, Doctor,' he grumbled. 'I don't see why we have to get there so quickly. If they came down with the ship, these creatures have probably been running around for over fifty years.'

The Doctor broke off his whistling. 'But that's exactly it! Fifty years? There's not a moment to lose!' He unwound the window and stuck out his head, striking a heroic pose against the freezing wind, his hair blowing out behind him. He smiled at Lethbridge-Stewart. 'Such a primitive, but strangely rewarding way to travel.'

'Thank you, Doctor,' the Brigadier muttered.

He supposed he'd wanted this, hadn't he? Action, drama? Something to spice up his life, to stop him vegetating in his retirement? When the Doctor had seemed so concerned once they'd watched the video, the Brigadier had found himself oddly gratified, glad he'd sent the telegraph after all. That was before he'd remembered that this particular Doctor had a boundless energy to match his intelligence, wanting to be off to investigate the second they were able. Stifling a yawn and thinking wistfully of his cosy bed, Lethbridge-Stewart wondered if he was really too old for this sort of thing after all.

'Tell me Doctor,' the Brigadier asked, deciding any conversation, however incomprehensible, would be preferable to the whistling, 'if these creatures are invisible to the eye, how come they were picked up on the tape?'

The Doctor shrugged. 'Perhaps it's the medium.'

'What, like someone at a séance? Picking up messages of the dead?'

'No, Brigadier, as in the medium of television, for example, or photography.' The Doctor pushed his seat back as far as it would go, tetchily trying to straighten his long legs in the Land Rover's footwell. 'You've heard of ghosts captured on film, haven't you? Of spectral figures in the background of photographs when eye-witnesses swore there was no one there?'

The Brigadier turned up his nose. 'Ghosts? Really, Doctor…'

'I'm not talking about the restless dead under a white sheet, clanking chains… But suppose certain beings exist as a form of energy, one that can only be interpreted correctly by specific light-sensitive receptors.'

'Do talk English, Doctor.'

'Well, while the eye is admittedly a fairly sophisticated device for picking up light, humans do have a knack for seeing only what they want to see…' he broke off. 'Left here, isn't it?'

'Thank you, Doctor,' said the Brigadier dryly, who had already flicked on his indicator to take the turn towards Wareham.

'Yes, well, in contrast to the eye, a camera lens is more impartial, but less sophisticated. Perhaps these things have been concentrating on staying out of reflexive human sight, not expecting to be captured through the stolid drudge of a glass lens.'

'They sound like vampires in reverse,' the Brigadier suggested tentatively. 'You can see their image, but not themselves.'

'Hmm.' The Doctor seemed dubious. 'In any case, I think the point that should concern us is not why we can't see them… but what are they really doing here?'

'They were shot down, Doctor,' the Brigadier reminded him. 'They may not be here through choice. And given they've been about since 1944 with no ill-effects, must we assume they're hostile?'

The Doctor looked impressed. 'What a very enlightened attitude, Brigadier.' Then he grinned wickedly. 'All you need now is to cultivate a sense of scale!' He threw open his arms, causing the Brigadier to swerve slightly as he flinched. 'Fifty years may seem a long time to you but it's a handful of heartbeats to some races. And if this Henderson and his family have really been watching over the site at Turelhampton so carefully and for so long…'

The Brigadier got what he was driving at. 'It would suggest he has some kind of agenda even if the creatures don't.'

'Right!'

Lethbridge-Stewart smiled, pleased with himself.

'No, *turn* right!' the Doctor commanded. 'It's the A352 we want!'

The Land Rover skidded round the tight corner, and the Brigadier cleared his throat. 'All a bit early for me, Doctor.'

'Better too early than too late,' the Doctor muttered. 'I'll know more once we're inside the village.'

'A comforting optimism you have, Doctor,' commented the Brigadier.

There was only a few more miles to go.

'Well, is he coming back?' Claire asked.

'Said he'd be gone for a couple of weeks,' the unhelpful idiot on the other end of the line told her.

'Look, he's got a load of my gear. Do you have a number I can reach him on?'

'You Claire?'

'Yes.'

'No.'

The phone clicked and went dead. Claire swore and ended the call. Then she went back into her bedroom, chucked the mobile on her springy bed and launched herself after it. She gazed up at the cracked ceiling, and blew a lock of hair from out of her face.

'Wonderful,' she muttered aloud. 'A whole doc written off, a brand new one to put together in two weeks and no crew whatsoever. 'Claire Aldwych, one woman show, this is your life.'

What the hell was she going to do? Things had seemed bad yesterday when she was spooked out of her head, but now the ability to think straight was creeping back into her skull, and the ability to recognise impending doom when she saw it...

She picked up the mobile, and flicked across to Last Caller. Brian's mobile number was still displayed. Another man she'd probably made too scared to return her calls. She wondered who he'd been working for on this Oakhope Manor thing. The Hitler stuff sounded really mad, but he'd been doing a fair bit for *Underbelly*, that American rag. What was their tagline? *Taking the sensational seriously.* Swap 'sensational' for 'piss', Claire reckoned, and you'd have a better summary. Yeah, rubbish. There was *nothing* in Brian's message... Probably. But hey, the Nazi thing had more appeal. *Fourth Reich in Cornish manor house.* That was the sort of thing the *Mail on Sunday* would cream themselves over.

The Big One.

Well, he had asked her to check it out for him...

Claire rolled off the bed and bounced over to her dog-eared travel atlas.

The Brigadier couldn't believe the old 'inspection ruse' actually seemed to be working.

'Of course you didn't know I was coming,' he bellowed to the white-faced Corporal Jessop at the checkpoint. 'Otherwise there'd hardly be much point! Check with your CO, who is it, Sergeant...?'

'Sergeant Dow, sir. He's seeing Under-Secretary Henderson, sir.'

'Ah, Henderson. The man at the ministry, hmm? The man in charge.'

Jessop nodded like his neck was rubber.

'Yes,' said the Brigadier, 'I know old Henderson. He called us at UNIT in the first place, to do the job you failed to do!' Lethbridge-Stewart's voice raised still higher, the tone he reserved for real roastings. 'Yes, I know why Sergeant Dow is seeing Henderson this morning, Corporal! You'll be telling me next there were no intruders here last night!' He decided he should terrorise the young soldier beside him next. 'How did they get in, Private?'

'Cut through the fence, sir,' the private barked uncomfortably.

'Where, man?' bellowed the Brigadier.

'Two hundred metres along the track there.'

'Two hundred metres along the track?' he repeated loudly for the benefit of ears he knew were hidden somewhere in the foliage beyond. 'Down from the Trowhaven turn? For God's sake man, that's an obvious spot, well placed for a getaway.' Back to Jessop, aghast. 'You didn't have men watching it?'

'No, sir,' the corporal barked. 'We –'

'I'm not interested in excuses, man!'

'We're fixing up the damage this afternoon.'

'This afternoon?' The Brigadier did his best to appear utterly scandalised. 'Have you no idea of the importance of keeping this village secure at all times?'

'Yes sir – I mean, no, sir –'

'Your squad's a disgrace, Corporal Jessop!' he roared, and thrusted his special UNIT pass in the man's reddening face. After that business in Cornwall with the nuclear warhead, the Brigadier had been satisfied to see the UN had renewed it for him even though he'd officially retired. 'Check my credentials at once. Tell Henderson that Brigadier Fernfather sent me! And you –' he gestured with his swagger stick at the young private. 'You can accompany me. Show me what's what with the rest of your security. And what we're protecting, of course, the crater. Come on, man, at the double.'

The private checked with the corporal, who nodded – but the Brigadier smiled to see Jessop discreetly mouth, 'Keep an eye on him.'

'This way is it?' demanded the Brigadier, setting off up the main road into the village.

It really was extraordinary, he decided. He'd heard of ghost towns in the wild west, but to find a village this size so completely empty, preserved practically as it was half a century ago, was extraordinary, like being on a film set.

As they moved further from the sentries standing guard, the absolute silence, the absence of any passers-by, began to make him feel ill-at-ease. The cottage gardens they passed were all overgrown. The village green looked more like Korea. There were cracks and fissures in the roads and pavements, and creeping ivy had overtaken many of the stone walls. The Brigadier kept up a brisk pace though it was giving him a stitch. He didn't know how long he had, but with one of the men watching him they wouldn't be so concerned at his movements... and he was banking on Henderson giving poor old ignorant Fernfather a lengthy grilling once the corporal had explained the way old Lethbridge-Stewart had charged in here...

'I suppose you get used to it here, do you?' the Brigadier commented to the private. 'There being no people I mean.'

'Get used to anything after a time, sir. Even the ghosts.'

The Brigadier stopped his march. 'Ghosts, Private?'

'Well, that's what we call them. You catch glimpses of them. In the shadows, sometimes. In the glass of the windows.'

'Do you indeed,' mused the Brigadier, starting up his stride again. 'And what do these ghosts look like?'

The Private looked slightly surprised, perhaps because his bizarre statement had been accepted so readily. 'Couldn't really tell you sir,' he said bashfully. 'Just little flashes in the corner of your eye. Trick of the light, sir, that's all.' He indicated a twisting road to their right. 'Crater's this way, sir.'

'Lead on, Private. I'm in a hurry.'

The private did so, quickening his step. Just as he came level with a large, gnarled oak tree, a salmon-pink arm with gaudy yellow and black pinstripe cuff swung out from behind it and pinched him on the back of the neck. The private collapsed soundlessly, and the eerie calm over Turelhampton remained undisturbed.

'You've not hurt him, Doctor?' the Brigadier inquired.

The Doctor shot him a wounded look as he dragged the soldier into a brambly passageway, keeping him out of sight. 'I've merely taken him off shift a little early.' He dusted off his hands and straightened up. 'He deserves a treat – he was spot on with the location of that hole in the fence.'

'You heard me all right, then.'

The Doctor winced. 'I imagine they heard you all the way to the coast.'

The Brigadier checked around for signs of other troops, or a red-faced corporal approaching. 'We'd better hurry, Doctor.'

'Indeed. Come on, Brigadier.'

Lethbridge-Stewart was dismayed to see the Doctor immediately charge off down the road. Kneading his aching side, the Brigadier jogged along after him.

The crater straddled the boundary of the village and an overgrown field; an old, crumbling mill house lay ruined at its lip, and its grounds were churned up and barren. The Brigadier observed that only here had any attempt been made to check the relentless advance of the undergrowth – nettles and weeds had been roughly hacked back, leaving only bald earth around the rim of the cylindrical crater. Its muddy banks stretched down quite steeply some twenty-five feet to a site covered by a dull green tarpaulin. As he watched, the plastic sheeting's edges were rustled by the chilly April wind, and Lethbridge-Stewart glimpsed something smooth and metallic beneath.

The Doctor stared down at the tarpaulin accusingly, hands on hips. 'What are you obscuring I wonder?' he said. Then he was off, scrambling down the muddy slope like an eager schoolboy. Arriving at the bottom, he started tugging the tarpaulin free.

He'd crawled underneath by the time the Brigadier had joined him. Lethbridge-Stewart sighed. 'At my age, Doctor, I should be preserving my dignity.'

'Rot!' retorted the Doctor. 'Wait till you've lived as long as I have... dignity indeed.'

The Brigadier found himself smiling as he shuffled under the green plastic and dropped down into a small holding area roughly hollowed out from the soil. Facing him was a large metal circle, like the end of an enormous tin can. They must be at the end of

the giant cylinder Palmer said had been shot down in the war
– they'd actually made it.

His smile soon faded as a soft, eerie wail started up.

'It's all right,' the Doctor told him, as he crouched over a laptop
on a folding table, which seemed connected somehow to the
metal of the cannister. 'Just the door opening.'

As the Brigadier watched the door seemed to dissolve away,
giving on to a heavy blackness barely illuminated by dim red
bulbs.

'Interesting,' the Doctor said, ignoring the noise and
concentrating on the laptop display. 'There's an enormous
localised gravitational field in the vicinity.'

'Gravity? Coming from the ship? That's why it hasn't been
removed for study?'

'That's right. You'd have more luck digging up a dwarf star. Very
clever.'

The Brigadier considered. 'If it's been like this since the
crashlanding, it suggests they were well prepared.'

'Mmm.' The Doctor glanced at him. 'Perhaps they were alien
boy scouts after their primitive aircraft combat badge.'

The Doctor went casually inside the ship without another
word, but the Brigadier felt less certain, pausing on the threshold.
The shadows were thick over the glassy smooth surfaces of the
vessel. It felt a little like being inside a submarine, deep in the
ocean. Something in the atmosphere here was disquieting,
besides the stale air. A tension, a sense of anticipation. As if the
submarine was at war, its crew readying themselves for the attack.

'What is this place, Doctor?' he whispered.

'An alien space ship,' came the obvious reply. 'This way.'

'Do you know where you're going?'

'No. I'm just following the lights. Presumably they've been set
up to lead people to where things get… A-ha! Interesting.'

The Brigadier, following the Doctor's ridiculous coat-tails, saw a
brighter light spilling from somewhere up ahead.

The corridor gave on to a large, cylindrical chamber, lit a fierce
red, the sort of intense glow a computer screen gives off in the

dark – though the Brigadier didn't notice any obvious light-sources. Five huge caskets, each a cross between a coffin and a deep-freeze, lay in a line at the rear of the room. The one nearest him had a small, ridged, glowing hemisphere attached to its side, like a glassy limpet. So did the casket next to it. There was a large space in between that one and the other three, where it seemed another should go.

'Looks like they've taken one of these things away for study,' the Brigadier observed. 'What do you make of them, Doctor?'

The Doctor didn't answer, moving ahead into what appeared to be some kind of cabin area. The curved walls and ceiling seemed to be fashioned from a cloudy, inky-coloured glass, obscuring and distorting what were presumably banks of instrumentation. Two tiers of high-backed seats like stone thrones, in rows of three, were ranged facing the focal point of the room – a complicated crystalline lattice. The convoluted strips and tubes of the opaque glassy material reached up to the high ceiling like a demented home brewing kit, but there were clear gaps in the overall structure.

The Doctor studied it closely, tracing his finger along the configuration and muttering under his breath. 'There must've been a good deal of damage done in the crash, Brigadier. See here? Clear signs of fracturing and crystalline regeneration.'

'Mmm,' The Brigadier nodded as if he knew what he was looking at. 'They don't seem to have made much progress stripping out the place, do they? And all this glass,' he said. 'How on Earth did the crew get to the controls?'

'Perhaps they didn't have to.' The Doctor looked up at him gravely from the labyrinthine mess of tubing. 'You know, I've seen this sort of thing before, I know it, I know it... come on, brain, think...' Then something else caught his butterfly attention. 'The ship may've been damaged, but it seems the autorepair systems remained operational.' Now he straightened, clicked his fingers. 'But look here. They've been unable to recreate a replacement for the ocular celluprime, or for the navi-links.'

'Ocular what, Doctor?' asked the Brigadier, wearily.

'Yes… yes, it's coming back to me, now! *The Eye-Spy Book of Alien Spaceships*… This is a Vvormak ship.'

'Vvormak?'

'Vvormak, I'm sure of it. And an ocular celluprime? Vital navigational tool. I'll explain later.' The Doctor gestured to a hole in the lattice and mimed a vaguely circular shape, preoccupied with ordering his own thoughts. 'Fits in there, medium-sized glassy thing…' He broke off, suddenly rapt. 'Interesting word, medium.'

The Brigadier felt his patience with his friend ebbing away in familiar fashion. 'Yes, Doctor, you've used it before.'

'And as you demonstrated, Brigadier, it has many meanings: an intervening material or agency for transmitting or yielding an effect… or, indeed, the substance in which living specimens are preserved or displayed.'

'What on Earth are you babbling about, Doctor?'

The Doctor gestured grandiosely to the empty thrones. 'The owners of this vessel are conspicuous by their absence, you'll agree?'

'Well that's obvious.'

'Just as its obvious from the footage taken by that young woman that *something* is still very present.' The Doctor nodded gravely. 'The witches may be dead and gone, but their familiars remain.'

'Just for once, Doctor, could you try uttering a sentence that made some kind of sense?'

The Doctor strode over to the deep freezers at the back of the room. 'The crew of this vessel had physical form –'

'Hence the chairs.'

'And hence those tanks over there, nurturing the bodies during long haulage. They didn't have to be up and about to manage the more menial tasks in life… say, for instance, the operation of their craft's controls.'

'Bless my soul…' The Brigadier remembered the insubstantial creatures clustering around the crater on the tape, scuttling like shadows around Claire. 'They had the imps to do it for them?'

The Doctor nodded as he began to examine the freezers. 'Extensions of the Vvormak's own psyches. Personal attendants, a part of them. Able to move around in the immediate vicinity, but travelling in a plane beyond the purely physical.'

'You've come across these creatures before?'

'I don't believe so. Not directly.'

With the Doctor's words something clicked into place. 'Not directly… That's just it, Doctor, isn't it! Glimpses, the private said. They must only be visible if you're looking in the right places,' the Brigadier reasoned. 'Or not looking for them at all. Reflections in glass, movement in the shadows…'

The Doctor tapped a finger against the inky opacity of the wall beside him. 'Reaching through this to operate the controls would hardly be an obstacle for them.'

'But Doctor – if you say they're a part of the crew, an extension of them…'

'Yes…' The Doctor turned his attention back to one of the freezer-like cabinets, speaking now in a hushed, reverent whisper. 'It would seem to suggest that some of the crewmembers at least are still alive.' He detached one of the limpets from the casket. The glass, cracked and dull in his hand, seemed more like stone. 'Not this one, I'm afraid.'

'There are bodies in there?' the Brigadier asked, incredulously.

'These are hibernation tanks.' He tossed the limpet from hand to hand. 'I think this thing is imbued with some kind of energy to extend the lifespan if necessary, should hibernation go on too long. But I would imagine the poor fellow in this tank is beyond such considerations.'

'So that thing's just given up on him…' The Brigadier wondered what manner of being was lying waiting in the tank, and shuddered. The harsh glow of the lighting seemed to have grown a little grainier, and was casting all sorts of macabre shadow-shapes. Were the imps running about him, even now? He kept his eyes firmly on the Doctor's round face. 'Doctor, this simply doesn't add up. If the ship has been grounded for fifty-six years with a continuous military presence in the vicinity, this control room should be stripped down to all but the metal floorboards. But instead –'

The Doctor finished his sentence for him. 'Instead, it looks as if someone's been doing the opposite. Repairing the ship. *Preparing* the ship...'

'Yes. All that's missing is...' The Brigadier trailed off. 'One of those tanks. One of the crew.'

'That and the longevity device from the casket beside you.'

The graveness of the Doctor's expression was making the Brigadier more than a little apprehensive. He coughed. He felt a little woozy suddenly. 'Hadn't we better be moving along, Doctor? They'll be on to us soon...'

'Yes. I think we've seen enough for now.' The Doctor started to cough too.

The eerie wailing noise started up again in the Brigadier's ears. 'What's that?'

'The door! Quickly, Brigadier!'

The Doctor bounded across the room but it was too late. A solid covering like ice was smothering the exit from the room. Then the Brigadier realised the light was getting grainier in the room because it was being diffused by an almost invisible mist. His eyes began to water. 'Doctor, look...'

'Gas,' he cried, tugging off his cravat and handing it to the Brigadier to breathe through. 'Some kind of booby trap, a defence mechanism.'

The gas was acrid and burning in the brigadier's throat. 'Set off when we got too near the bodies?'

'Very possibly.' The Doctor started hammering on the frosted partition.

'Surely there must be a switch that controls the doors in here?'

The Doctor gestured frantically at the walls around them. 'Hidden behind the glass!'

The Brigadier pulled his service revolver from his holster and beat its handle against the frosted surface obscuring the control panels. It didn't even scratch the surface. He aimed, ready to fire, but his sight was blurring, the gun too heavy in his hand.

The Doctor was still beating his fists against the door. 'I can't get it open! Brigadier, help me!'

But Lethbridge-Stewart had sunk to his knees, clutching at his throat, consciousness slipping away. It sounded as if the Doctor was calling to him from the end of a long dark tunnel.

'Quickly, man! We have to get out of here! We *have* to!'

The Brigadier watched helplessly as the mist grew heavier about the Doctor, swathing his colourful form in shades of grey. But before it took away his view of the door completely, he saw glowing red eyes staring coldly, unblinkingly out at him from the glass.

Chapter Ten

It had stopped snowing when they got back, though the wind was icy. The Fuhrer seemed in his element, marching through the lying snow with his hands clasped behind his back. Hanne struggled to keep up with him.

He was silent until they were in the main corridor. The rest of his entourage stamped and blew and tried to get the warmth back into their bodies. But the Fuhrer and Hanne stood still. He seemed not to notice the cold. She clenched her teeth together in an effort to ignore it.

'Ten minutes,' he told her. 'Then I wish to discuss progress.'

Hanne nodded. 'We shall miss the old man,' she said quietly.

He nodded, suddenly in a sombre mood at the thought. 'Herr Bormann had an excellent grasp of the big picture. An incisive and analytical way of looking at things.' He looked her directly in the face. 'But he was also cautious. If Martin Bormann were still alive, we should still be waiting and planning. It is time to get things moving now. Like in 1933.' The Fuhrer nodded again. 'Yes,' he said quietly, 'we shall miss him. There was a glitter of humour in his eyes as he added: 'But he was an old man. And we all have to die some time.'

The tepid shower scorched her frozen skin. She stood under it for as long as she could afford before towelling herself dry. She took her time pulling on her uniform, smoothing it down, flicking dust from the front of the jacket. Then she clicked her heels violently together and saluted the full-length mirror.

The Fuhrer was waiting for her. He was sitting on the sofa in his office. In front of him was a low table on which was a silver tray with tea things on it. He waved aside her apology, motioning instead for her to help herself to tea.

'The meeting was well attended,' she ventured.

The Fuhrer sipped at the tea, his little finger crooked away from the handle of the cup. He put the cup back on the saucer and placed it carefully on the table, then wiped his moustache. 'Yes,' he agreed. 'And despite the unfortunate interruption, everyone seemed committed and enthusiastic.' He leaned back in the sofa and tapped the ends of his fingers together. 'This is how it begins,' he said. 'We establish our network, reawaken the sleepers who have waited for our return to power. They will work with us to show the world, the Aryan world, the problem. Point out where and why action is needed.' He leaped to his feet, eyes flashing with excitement. 'And then, once the problem is apparent and undeniable and acute, then we shall provide the solution!'

There was a map of the world on the wall. He walked swiftly over to it and stood, hands behind his back, surveying the land masses. He reached out and gently tapped each of the coloured stickers in turn, each one representing a Nazi cell or focus group that was poised and ready for action.

'Soon,' he said, and Hanne got the impression he was speaking to himself, 'soon we shall begin our final power-play.' He swung round to face her. 'And the world will be ready for us, as we are ready for it.' He flicked his hair back from his forehead. 'We have waited long enough, hidden away here, watching as the so-called super-powers fritter away their strength and allow their races to degenerate and become impure. We have watched from the sidelines while the elite dwindles and is diluted and the inferior breed and multiply and pollute.' His fist was raised, thumping the air. 'But no longer can we be silent. The world needs a new order, needs a firm hand. It needs a powerful leader who will not shirk his responsibilities.'

The single ceiling light cast the Fuhrer's shadow across the map, a dark stain over the centre of Europe. For a moment Hanne thought she saw something else there, another shadow at the Fuhrer's shoulder. A trick of the light? Her imagination? Or was it the ghost? Just as suddenly as she had seen it, the impression was gone.

Not that it mattered. They had all learned to live with the shadows.

As he turned back from the wall map, the Fuhrer was calm again. 'Any news from Venkel?' he asked as he returned to the sofa.

Hanne shook her head. 'Not yet. Do you think we have a problem?'

'No,' he snapped. 'No problem at all. We merely need to move to limit any possible damage.' He reached out and poured himself more tea. 'Venkel is reliable. We will soon know if the man acted alone or if he had comrades.'

'And if he did?'

Hitler waved his hand dismissively and sipped his tea. After a moment he lowered the cup, looking into it appreciatively. Then he looked up at Hanne. 'Don't worry,' he told her with a slight smile. 'Who can possibly stop us now?'

Chapter Eleven

The Doctor's hands tingled every time he brought them down on the pulsing glass blocking their way out. Soon, his strength failing, he found he was not so much battering at the door but leaning against it for support, the gas making his eyes stream with tears.

Dark shapes shifted over the doorway, and phantom eyes bored crimson into his own.

'We mean you no harm,' the Doctor croaked. 'Do you understand me? No harm!'

Then suddenly the eerie moan started up again. For a moment the Doctor thought the familiars had understood him, but then, as the glass began to melt away he saw a soldier before him, staring in confusion and alarm. The squad had come looking.

The Doctor toppled forward, leaning on the young soldier for support. 'Thank goodness you're here,' he gasped.

'Hold it!' came a slightly shaky voice, another soldier. For now there seemed to be just the two of them.

'I *am* holding it,' the Doctor protested, gripping the private by the scruff of the neck and then hurling him into the smoky room. 'Come on, Brigadier!'

The Doctor lunged for the other soldier, grabbing for the end of his rifle. But his senses had been dulled by the gas, he wasn't fast enough. The rifle butt swung up and caught him a glancing blow behind the ear, enough to send him sprawling back against the wall.

'Don't move,' the soldier shouted at him, pointing the rifle his way with shaking hands, keeping the Doctor covered but unable to stop glancing back into the thick mist that was seeping out into the corridor, suffused with a hellfire tinge of deep red. 'Bill? Bill, are you all right?'

A heavy fist swung from out of the mist and crashed into the soldier's chin. The blow sent the soldier reeling backwards before he collapsed in a heap.

The Brigadier emerged spluttering from the smoke, dragging the other soldier along the smooth floor by his gunbelt. 'You'll have to teach me that special pinch of yours,' he announced, shaking his bruised knuckles. 'My fingers are not quite as sensitive as your own, I'm afraid.'

The Doctor grinned up at him. 'Pinch, punch, there's a first for this month.' He shook his head to try and clear it as he scrambled to his feet. 'Won't you get into trouble for knocking unconscious a member of Her Majesty's armed forces?'

'Very probably,' agreed the Brigadier, a look on his face somewhere between stoic and cheerful, before stifling another coughing fit. He was older now, the Doctor could see that, but his spirit was still indefatigable, still young.

The Doctor backed away from the encroaching mist and the Brigadier hurriedly joined him.

'Is the gas fatal?' he asked warily, handing the Doctor's cravat back to him.

'I don't think so,' answered the Doctor. 'But I imagine it would incapacitate us for some time.'

'No gas masks,' the Brigadier noted. 'These fellows were as ill-prepared for a gas attack as we were. Why leave a trap for intruders that your own men didn't know about?'

'Unless you wanted to keep that alien crew entirely safe from *all* humans, even the ones that are ostensibly there to protect.'

'Look,' whispered the Brigadier hoarsely.

In the low smoky glow spilling from the control room, the Doctor could see just the palest suggestions of the misshapen imp-like creatures, running around furiously as if in silent celebration.

'Let's get these two clear with us, shall we?' suggested the Brigadier. 'And then out of here as quickly as possible.'

'Agreed.' The Doctor started dragging the other soldier back towards the main entrance by his feet.

Once he'd left the private sleeping outside the main door, the Doctor scrambled back out of the trench beside the alien ship. He ducked his head back under the tarpaulin. 'Hurry, Brigadier!' Then he scanned the rim of the crater ahead of him while his old friend caught him up. They were lucky – no more troops. Not yet.

The tarpaulin twitched at his feet. He extended a hand to the Brigadier, who ignored it and hauled himself back up. 'Right-o, Doctor,' he puffed. 'How about we find that hole in the fence.'

'And then, perhaps, a trip to the Ministry of Defence is in order?' The Brigadier nodded gravely. 'I think this man Henderson has a good deal of explaining to do.'

Alone in his office again, staring out of the window, Henderson wearily tried to make sense of recent events. He could discern vaguely his reflection in the glass panes, a reminder that he was still a young man, despite feeling so terribly old today.

Since Captain Palmer had reported last night that the incriminating tape had been impounded and destroyed, he'd rested a little easier. To ensure nothing similar happened he'd summoned Sergeant Dow for a debrief and sent him away again with his tail between his legs, with strict instructions to improve the efficiency of his platoon. And yet the second Dow had walked through the exit, Corporal Jessop had telephoned to report this unscheduled visit from a UNIT bigwig. That old idiot Fernfather had protested he'd known nothing about it... and that the dignitary in question, a Lethbridge-Stewart, was actually retired from the organisation.

Who was this Brigadier, some kind of maverick, contacted by Palmer? Henderson ground his teeth, poured himself some water and downed it in a single gulp.

Just for a moment a grey shade seemed to slosh about in the bottom of the glass.

'I've ordered he be detained,' Henderson muttered aloud. 'What more can I do? I need more to go on.'

A shadow seemed to flit across the sturdy old mahogany dresser that had stood in the corner of his office for over fifty years. A squat shape seemed to shimmer in the rich wood, phantom fingers clawing silently at the doors.

'It is too soon,' said Henderson. 'Surely it is too soon.'

The shape continued its horrible dance in front of the old cupboard.

Claire couldn't believe she was putting another five hundred mile round trip on her battered old Nova so soon after the Dorset debacle. Cornwall, for God's sake. Her meagre expenses were vanishing, like her career chances, into thin air.

Since the petrol gauge was registering that the car was running on much the same, she decided to pull in at a small service station on the A30. No supermarket and burger bar here, it looked to be a crappy little place where you'd be lucky to pick up a Pepperami with your petrol from the yokel behind the counter. She sighed. As she was about to get out, her phone went.

'Hello, Claire Aldwych?'

There was no answer. Then the line went dead.

Claire shrugged, put the phone back in her bag, and set about filling up.

The unleaded nozzle kept pumping, the flickering digits displaying the cost a graphic demonstration of the way she seemed to be haemorrhaging cash at the moment. Miserably she looked away to the front of the service station, where a small stand daubed with big ink capitals was screaming the headline of the local rag.

KILKHAMPTON CAR CRASH – FOUL PLAY SUSPECTED

Claire stared at it, suddenly, stupidly, concerned. She tried to shrug off the feeling. There was no reason to assume –

The petrol pump cut off in her hand as the tank reached nearly full, and she almost jumped in the air. She glanced about, embarrassed.

She saw a blue car had pulled up behind her. The two men inside it seemed in no hurry to fill up. They were just watching her. Perhaps they were waiting until she moved, to get to the diesel nozzle.

She looked away, hung up the pump, and picked up a paper on her way to pay.

She felt her heart twist as she read details of the accident, which had happened in a small track just off the A39. The deceased – found with a gash in his neck which it seemed was an injury not concomitant with the circumstances of the crash – had been named as Brian Goldman.

'Is that it, then, love?' asked the man behind the counter, cheerily.

Claire looked outside. The men in the car still hadn't moved, they were still watching her.

The Brigadier could still hear the distant cries of the troops. One of them was calling for fire-fighting equipment; the gas must be seeping out now into the crater itself. Well, that would hopefully keep them busy. With the pair sent to find them still inside the ship, the others in the squad should assume their visitor on inspection was in there too. Hopefully. Even so, the Brigadier was aware just how much he was sweating, despite the cold. It irked him to think this might all be getting too much for him.

'Don't you think we'd stand a better chance of getting out of here unspotted if you'd worn something a little less garish, Doctor?' the Brigadier grumbled. He was tiring too of following such a bright backside through the overgrown bracken and gorse.

'Garish?' echoed the Doctor. 'Nonsense. Of course I won't be spotted.' He fondly stroked a badge on his lapel as he crashed through the undergrowth. 'I move as lithely as a cat.'

'If you say so, Doctor.'

'Not much further now. We should be there in a few minutes.'

The time crawled by just as they did. Lethbridge-Stewart was more uncomfortable than ever now he was forced to move at a half-crouch and his gunbelt was biting savagely into his waistline.

The idea of minutes seeming like hours suggested something to him.

'That ship's been lying dormant for half a century,' he remarked. 'And yet there's still power there in the systems?'

The Doctor paused for a moment, getting his bearings. 'It's run on something a little more advanced than a car battery, Brigadier.'

'Only I was wondering… You said something about fifty years not seeming like long to certain life forms.' He hesitated, afraid he would sound foolish. 'Well, it only takes a few hours to charge a car battery, but a spaceship…?'

The Doctor stopped dead, and the Brigadier braced himself for a caustic response. 'Of course! It's so obvious!'

'Thank you, Doctor,' said the Brigadier wryly.

'The ship's systems are powered by potential energy.'

'Like those limpet things, with the potential to increase the longevity of the crew, you mean?'

'In a way, yes. It's perfectly possible the ship's been gathering energy from the rotation of the Earth, for example. Pity they didn't crash over Jupiter, the ship would charge in half the time.' He looked pointedly at the Brigadier. 'Less chance of them being *shot down* over Jupiter, I suppose.'

The Brigadier found he was defensive. 'Tricky patch, Doctor. D-Day and all that.'

'In any case. The ship could well have been charged for years now. But without the ocular celluprime…'

'Oh dear,' sighed the Brigadier, 'here we go.'

'Well, in language you'd understand, Brigadier, it's a little like looking into a crystal ball – whoops!'

The Brigadier found himself almost bumping into the Doctor, who came up short at the end of a covering bush. Ahead of them was a guard, peering this way and that as he patrolled along a well-beaten path. They waited, breath held tight, until the soldier was out of sight.

'Don't be ridiculous, Doctor. How on Earth can a pilot navigate by looking into the future?'

'The ship can travel faster than light, so a peek into the future is not out of the question. Indeed, it's the whole point. The systems are designed to be forward thinking; the familiar sees what's coming up through the celluprime, and works with the hibernating Vvormak to construct a navigational path through that area of space. It's a kind of cruise control.'

The Brigadier struggled to take it in. 'So basically, it only shows the pilot what he knows is the case, through his sub-conscious projection-thing, the imp, which is able to look into the future.'

'More or less.'

The Brigadier sniffed. 'Couldn't they just use a map?'

'The Hurricanes that shot the ship down relied on a steersman telling them where to head for, didn't they? And the steersman relied on radar, and a working knowledge of where and when an object travelling at a set speed would arrive, to guide the planes. It's not such a dissimilar arrangement, is it?'

The Brigadier harrumphed quietly.

'If we all did things the same the universe over,' the Doctor said, with a look at the Brigadier just short of withering, 'where *would* we end up.'

The Brigadier smiled. 'But where have this ocular thing and the other bits ended up?'

'I don't know,' the Doctor confessed. 'But they seem to have been removed deliberately. Could Henderson be holding on to them to exploit the aliens in some way? Or did they go missing when this thing first came down, along with that longevity device?'

'Good grief,' said the Brigadier. 'Do you think someone could've got hold of that thing and given themselves a longer life? How long *could* they live?'

The Doctor paused, did some calculations. 'At a conservative estimate, I'd have thought such a person could last for a thousand years. Ah! There's our fence now, unless I'm very much mistaken.'

As usual, he wasn't. Gratefully, the Brigadier trailed after the Doctor through the long grass on the last dash for freedom.

Chapter Twelve

Henderson didn't bother to shout at Jessop. Not this time. He was too concerned that the Turelhampton site had been breached once again, less than 24 hours since the last intrusion. And this time it wasn't merely nosy journalists but a military presence. And someone else – someone unknown. He closed his eyes, concentrated hard, and summoned back to mind the shadowy impressions he'd been given: a tall, burly man, studying the equipment in the ship as if he might possibly understand it. Perhaps that explained the sense he had that there was something oddly familiar about the man; perhaps the Vvormak had crossed his path before.

In any case they had considered their ship in jeopardy – and now Jessop was asking awkward questions about the deployment of gas weapons in the cylinder. Henderson put the blame on the intruders, terrorists, but he knew when Sergeant Dow returned he would doubtless order a proper inspection.

Henderson knew that time, that long-cherished luxury, was finally running out. The ship needed not just its missing components in order to escape this world, but energy. And if it could not absorb what it needed in the natural way from the environment it found itself in, it must power up in a more robust fashion.

He turned slowly to the old, mahogany wardrobe.

It had always been recognised that their plans might have to change, but nothing had brought this home more than the Russian unveiling of Arzamas-16, five years ago. Arzamas-16 was the Soviets' own Turelhampton from 1946 to 1996, a closed city that literally disappeared from Russian maps, its location a state secret. Even today, it was still the premier Russian nuclear design lab. Henderson had been there himself in 1974, as part of a top secret nuclear exchange programme organised covertly by the

KGB. And in return for supplying state secrets, Henderson had been granted possession of a most unusual weapon. One that had been frighteningly easy to smuggle back home.

He took the key to the wardrobe from his desk and opened the creaking, lead-lined doors. There was nothing in the cupboard except for a large, tan leather suitcase. When Arzamas-16 had been uncovered, Henderson had been given proof that nothing could be kept hidden forever. Secrecy had a half-life, like the plutonium in the case. As the fissile material had decayed like his careful cover, so he'd acquired a fresh supply from a contact in the Russians' nuclear installation at Krasnoyarsk-26.

There was nothing more he could do to keep his secrets now.

Henderson gripped the suitcase carefully by its near-pristine handle. It was just as heavy as he remembered. But he could manage.

He strode back to his desk and buzzed for his secretary. 'Thompson, get me a car organised. To Turelhampton.'

Claire felt sick as she rounded the corner of the tiny track road and stopped the car. Ahead of her, stretches of blue-and-white hazard tape were being whipped by the wind around the charred and blackened verge ahead of her. An accident notice had been stuck round a red post box, requesting witnesses. She glanced about her. Some chance out here. It was just mud and fields, out of sight of the main road.

She was glad the blue car had driven on when she'd made the stop at Kilkhampton, and glad now for the vodka and lime she'd had at the pub. She'd asked around the locals for any gossip on recent comings and goings, and they'd all been moaning at the number of planes flying over the village. It seemed that the owner of Oakhope Manor, upper-crust businessman Jeremy Maskell, had his own airfield, and was prone to holding parties from time to time. Yesterday the village roads had been half-choked with posh traffic on its way out again. But this reclusive millionaire gave a lot to the community – or a lot of cash at any rate – so no one stayed cross with him for long.

Not a high price to pay for a quiet life, Claire decided. To be left alone, and have his international jet-setter friends about him, all goose-stepping and sieg-heiling in their armbands as they scoffed the Ferrero Rocher...

She looked at the burned undergrowth, the scorched earth. *Christ, Brian...*

He must have parked here and crossed the fields to the manor on foot. The convention would be over now, which would presumably mean that security around the place would be less tight. If she could have a snoop, she might find something... To bring Brian's killers to book? Or to get the scoop he'd missed out on?

Claire found she wasn't a hundred per cent sure herself. There was nothing wrong with a bit of both, was there?

But before she could get out of the car and put her wellies on, Claire was alerted by the sound of another car approaching.

The blue car.

She swore and restarted the engine, driving forward slowly. The men in the blue car matched her for speed. Claire realised she had no idea where this track led to, but had a hunch it wouldn't be to a nice stretch of dual carriageway with a friendly police station round the bend. She only nodded mournfully when a chained wooden fence appeared at the end of the trail, barring access to a churned up muddy field.

She unbuckled her seatbelt, ready to run if necessary, then pulled out her phone. Her heart was thudding in her chest. Who could she call, and what could she tell them? Was this how Brian had felt? Who did she hate enough to get involved in this? Of course, she could call the police, this was harassment...

She reined in her thoughts, manoeuvred the Nova into a three-point turn until she was facing the other car. The two men watching her seemed perfectly ordinary. She was letting herself become paranoid. Perhaps these people, whoever they were, just wanted to talk. Even if they were Nazis, they'd hardly murder someone else on their doorstep so soon after, would they? Maybe she could find out something here.

She speed-dialled her answerphone, then dropped the mobile on the passenger seat and wound down the window.

'What do you want?' she called to the blue car, speaking loudly and clearly as much for the phone as for the car's occupants. 'You have been trailing me since the Meldon services this morning, and now you are blocking my way out of here. Please move out of the way.'

'They're staying just where they are,' she told the phone. 'They're in a blue Audi, registration number. Just watching me. Staring. It's... it's intimidating. I'm going to drive closer to them and sound the horn.'

She did so, wondering how long her answerphone allocated for each call.

Then the blue car lunged forward and smashed into her own.

'They've just rammed me,' Claire reported for the benefit of the phone, struggling to keep calm. 'I think they're going to –' Again the car crunched into her bonnet. Her body bounced in her seat like she was being twitched on wires. 'I'm putting the car into reverse,' she shouted. 'I'm going to try and smash through the fence behind me and into the field.'

This only works in movies an unhelpful voice in her head told her as she revved the engine. The blue car paused, the driver unsure if she was going to come at him. As he revved his own engine and pushed forward once more, Claire pulled her foot off the clutch. The Nova shot backwards some twenty metres, the engine grinding and shrieking, until it smashed heavily into the fence. Claire gasped as her head jerked back, her neck prickling with pain.

'No good,' she shouted. 'The wood was too solid. It's cracked, is all.' She turned the ignition key. 'Car's stalled. Wait, the other car is reversing! It's...' She broke off, swallowed. 'No it's stopped. It's revving its engine. I think it means to run into me again. I think this is an intimidation tactic of some kind, and that after they've softened me up...' Her voice died to a croak, mouth too dry to keep talking.

The blue car switched on its headlights to main beam,

dazzlingly bright in the grey afternoon. Then the engine roared as it sped straight for her.

Claire turned the key again, swearing and shouting, and the engine finally took. She twisted the wheel round and round to her right, tyres spinning on wet grass as the Nova slid clear of the advancing car. She was jolted again as they clipped her rear, but they were travelling too fast to stop. This time the fence splintered and the car ploughed through it into the thick, clay-like mud. She saw the white reverse light flick instantly on, but it was soon hidden in a thick spray of mud as the wheels spun hopelessly, trying to get a purchase.

Claire didn't bother updating her silent audience over the phone, she just cheered with relief, tears coursing down her face. She flustered at the wheel, lurching forward, revving the engine too hard, the dead calm she'd felt from the shock slipping away to confused euphoria.

The sound of a gunshot focused her again. Clutching the wheel tight, Claire rocked and rattled away. In the mirror, the two figures flanking the stranded car were pointing after her, dwindling to the size of toy soldiers before she rounded the bend and they were lost from sight.

Claire kept driving for two hours straight, not stopping until she was physically shaking too much to carry on any further and pulled on to the hard shoulder to try to collect her thoughts.

They *knew* her. They must've found out who she was from Brian. She was involved, now, whatever else she did. Well, she wanted the Big One, didn't she?

No. She wanted out of this. She wanted police protection.

Or one better.

Sticking the heater on full, Claire's trembling fingers scrolled through her mobile's phone book for the UNIT helpline number.

Chapter Thirteen

The Brigadier was in a filthy temper as he and the Doctor finally came back in sight of the Land Rover. He felt like he'd been yomping for miles with full kit through muddy terrain. The fact that the Doctor was still as boundlessly energetic as a mountain goat wasn't helping matters.

His mood didn't improve when he found the car phone, Doris's concession to technology, not his own, was beeping irritatingly at him.

'Hadn't you better answer that?' the Doctor inquired.

The Brigadier looked grumpily at it. The Doctor lifted it from its cradle, pressed a couple of buttons and handed it to him.

'Lethbridge-Stewart,' the Brigadier rumbled.

'Palmer here, Brigadier.'

'What d'you want, Palmer, we're at Turelhampton. Bit of a flap on down here.'

'So I understand,' said Palmer. 'Fernfather's been going ballistic.'

The Brigadier smiled despite himself. 'Has he now.'

'And Henderson's on his way down there personally.'

'Is he indeed. Well that's good, we want to talk to him. Saves us a journey.'

'We, sir?'

'That's right, Captain Palmer. The Doctor and me.'

The Brigadier, as he had so many times before with awestruck junior officers, counted the seconds until Palmer found his voice again at the mention of UNIT's now almost mythical scientific advisor. He reached only three, and his estimation of the captain grew further.

'There's one more thing, sir, that you might be interested in. The journalist, Claire Aldwych? She's made contact. Sounds pretty upset, and she's seeking UNIT protection. Claims she's remembered something vital, but that her life's in danger. Sounds a bit far-fetched, I know, but –'

The Brigadier glanced at the Doctor. 'Believe me, Palmer, after what I've heard and seen here today, nothing could seem far-fetched. Take her in, see what she wants. I'll report in to you once we've had words with Henderson. Over.'

'Er… Yes, sir. Over and out.' Palmer awkwardly broke contact. Then the Brigadier realised he'd automatically treated the phone on its curly cable like an army radio, like he was back in service proper, and that Palmer had been humouring him. He put the thing back in its cradle, annoyed with himself.

'Old habits die hard?' the Doctor said softly, climbing into the passenger seat.

'Like old soldiers,' replied the Brigadier, 'they don't die at all.'

The Doctor smiled, and placed a hand on his shoulder. 'Now then – can we tell from which way Henderson will be approaching?'

'Same way as us, I'd imagine.'

'Splendid. We'd better keep a watch for him, try to make contact before he can reach the village. We don't want to go through all that palava at the main gate again.'

'His car will be unmarked, Doctor. He'll be tricky to spot.'

'Tricky to some,' said the Doctor a touch smugly. 'All we need's a good vantage point.'

The Brigadier nodded. 'I think I recall a layby close to where we came in.'

'Splendid.' The Doctor gave him a wicked smile. 'A *lay-in-wait* by…'

The Brigadier looked at him stony-faced for a few moments before shaking his head wearily. 'Quite, Doctor.' Then he started the Land Rover and pulled away.

As they drove out of the immediate area of Turelhampton, they noticed a number of Army vehicles speed past them.

'Looking for us?' wondered the Brigadier.

'Not very thoroughly, from the looks of things,' the Doctor answered.

Lethbridge-Stewart looked at him, grimly. 'Perhaps they're

setting up a cordon of some kind, hoping to appease old Henderson.'

'Perhaps,' conceded the Doctor, frowning as an uncaring troop carrier overtook them. 'Perhaps.'

'Let's turn around,' the Brigadier suggested, 'be on the safe side.'

'Yes,' agreed the Doctor, his tone growing excitable again. 'Back to the village!'

'Remarkable,' muttered the Brigadier, passing his field glasses to the Doctor. 'They look like they're –'

'– evacuating,' concluded the Doctor. 'Yes, don't they? Just like that.'

They'd parked half a mile or so away and, much to the Brigadier's dismay, had proceeded back towards Turelhampton on foot. Now they were observing the main gate from a nearby field, safely out of sight. A half-full jeep pulled up from out of the village, to the checkpoint, and behind it came a funny little vehicle, a bit like a golf-buggy with Corporal Jessop at the wheel. Lethbridge-Stewart watched as the man was met by his sergeant – Dow, was it? Jessop parked the buggy by the wall, then joined the other soldiers in the Jeep. From the look of Dow's hand-signals, it seemed he was telling Jessop to park further to the side of the entrance so as not to obstruct it.

'It makes no kind of sense, Doctor. The village has been occupied since 1944. They've had intruders and a full-scale flap just this morning. Why order all personnel out of the village?'

The Doctor shrugged. 'Down to Henderson, it must be.'

'Henderson's a civilian for heaven's sake. What powers can he have over a Regular Army platoon?'

'Given the nature of the project he's presided over for so long, he may have had certain special powers at his disposal...' The Doctor trailed off, looking worried. 'And a wider range of emergency powers.'

'Speak of the devil,' murmured the Brigadier. 'This must be him now.'

A black Mercedes pulled up to the main gate. Dow saluted as a wiry figure got out, dressed in a smart grey overcoat and bowler hat. The man went over some paperwork with Dow, signed a few things, then shook his hand and directed he join the others in the Jeep.

'All of them, just clearing out,' the Brigadier muttered in disbelief.

'Or perhaps they've been ordered to get themselves clear,' suggested the Doctor.

The Jeep pulled away, leaving Henderson on his own.

'But you said the ship wasn't going anywhere without those... those things.'

'Perhaps they've found them. Or perhaps it's time to keep the engine running for a quick getaway.'

'What about its power supply, this... potential thing?'

The Doctor had no answer.

While they'd been talking, Henderson had gone to the boot of his car. Now he struggled with a large, tan leather suitcase.

'What the devil does he think he's doing. They've moved out so now he's moving in?'

Henderson lifted the suitcase from the car and carried it carefully across to the buggy.

'Oh no,' breathed the Doctor getting to his feet and heading back to the Land Rover. 'Brigadier, I have a truly unpleasant suspicion as to the contents of that suitcase.'

Lethbridge-Stewart found himself trailing along behind like an obedient old hound as usual. 'Well?'

'A nuclear bomb!'

The Brigadier scoffed. 'Really, Doctor... Man Portable Nuclear Devices are just relics of the Cold War, surely? Apocrypha.'

'Apoc*alyptic*, certainly. I helped old Yablokov, counsellor to the Russian President, investigate their whereabouts. We found there were 84 unaccounted for. Who knows how many times they've changed hands since the 1970s?'

'But the chances of one of them finding its way to a sleepy Dorset village –'

'Are about as likely as an alien spaceship finding its way here.'

The Doctor quickened his pace. 'If Henderson's got one, it would be the perfect way to speed along the re-enabling process. But the side-effects could be deadly. Come on!'

'But, Doctor, I really can't –'

The Doctor stopped and flung his arms in the air, unable to contain his frustration. 'If that suitcase turns out to hold nothing more sinister than Henderson's pyjamas and a good book, I shall of course apologise to you for needless haste. But if I'm right…'

The Brigadier considered. 'A device of that size could still have a yield of as much as 10 kilotons. The whole surrounding area could go sky-high.'

'And the fall-out will kill many more,' cried the Doctor, running for the Land Rover. 'So come *on*!'

The Doctor brought the Land Rover to a noisy, screeching halt beside Henderson's Mercedes.

'He'll be heading for the crater,' the Doctor said. 'That buggy's small enough to get him where he needs to go in that wilderness through there.'

The Brigadier patted the Land Rover's dash. 'This isn't a Merc, Doctor. It was designed for rough terrain.'

The Doctor's answer was to stamp on the accelerator. The Land Rover smashed through the sentry gate and roared through the silent village.

'Why do you suppose Henderson would evacuate the place of troops first?' said the Brigadier.

'Perhaps he still has a use for them,' the Doctor observed. 'Perhaps you can ask him.'

The Brigadier caught a glimpse of white movement amid the brambles to their right. 'There he is!' he pointed. 'Over there!'

The Doctor spun the wheel and they left the road to plough through the forbidding tangle of foliage that had once been the village green.

The buggy would be no match for the Land Rover's speed but it was so much more manoeuvrable. The Brigadier gripped on to the door handles to stop himself bashing about all over the interior. 'What are you planning, Doctor?'

'I'm going to pull up alongside,' the Doctor shouted. 'See if we can't persuade him to stop his little golf cart.'

'Before he puts a hole in one?' ventured the Brigadier.

The speeding Land Rover worked its way over the wasteland to the buggy, in the back of which the improbable suitcase was securely strapped.

'That's enough, Henderson,' Lethbridge-Stewart shouted at the man in the grey overcoat. 'Stop the car. We know that's a bomb. Give it up man, you've some explaining to do.'

Henderson was glaring at him, hatred twisting his youthful face – no, past him, at the Doctor.

'You!' Henderson yelled.

The Brigadier wasn't fazed. 'I shan't ask again, Henderson –' But he broke off as the Doctor shouted out in pain and the Land Rover lurched away from the buggy. He turned in surprise.

The Doctor was writhing in pain, clutching at his neck, arms flailing as if he were trying to grasp something that wasn't there.

'Doctor?' shouted the Brigadier as he registered that the vehicle was out of control. Then he found himself looking harder.

There was... the *shadow* of something there on the Doctor's reddening throat.

Two red lights were glowing out of the windscreen, like the reflection of fierce flames.

The Brigadier lunged for the wheel but it was too late. A thicket of trees curled into view –

The Land Rover smashed into the thicket, sending them both flying forward. A huge, blackened branch smashed through the windscreen.

Dazed, the Brigadier heard the Doctor taking in huge gulps of air, and turned to see him massaging his throat. 'Henderson's mind can't be on his job,' he gasped. 'Familiar... distracted by the impact. Heavens to Betsy, I'm a good driver.'

Even as the Brigadier gingerly shook his head in disbelief, the Doctor was pushing at his buckled door, but it was jammed. Lethbridge-Stewart had more luck. 'We'd better not stick around here, Doctor,' he said, and staggered out into the long grass. 'It may still be here.'

'Come on, then, Brigadier,' the Doctor said as he jumped out to join him, and they set off again together.

'Henderson seemed to know you,' the Brigadier observed.

'Perhaps he sees through those little red eyes,' said the Doctor. Together, a little shakily, they ran for the crater.

Henderson had parked his buggy at the lip of the slope down to the ship.

'Surely,' panted the Brigadier, 'if it really is a bomb, he'll blow himself and that ship sky high?'

'Perhaps he doesn't care,' said the Doctor. 'He must know what he's doing.'

'I only wish we did,' the Brigadier grumbled.

They reached the rim and looked down to see Henderson lowering the suitcase down into the pit beside the ship, under the tarpaulin.

'Get away from here,' Henderson yelled at them. 'You'll be killed.'

'By the bomb, or by your alien familiars?' asked the Doctor. 'I suggest that *you* get away from here. You can't set that thing off. You mustn't.'

'I have no choice,' Henderson shouted back.

'Then neither do I,' announced the Doctor, and took an almighty leap recklessly down into the crater.

He landed practically on top of Henderson, but the man used the Doctor's momentum against him, spinning him round and throwing him on to the tarpaulin covering the alien ship.

'I'm wise to your tricks, your meddling,' Henderson said, a sneer in his voice. There was a dull clang as the back of the Doctor's head smacked against the metal beneath. 'You allowed us to be diminished. But you won't stop us this time.'

'This time?' the Doctor queried, eyes screwed up in pain. Then he brought up both legs and kicked Henderson back against the muddy slope of the crater.

'The suitcase,' muttered the Brigadier, and began scrabbling down the slope to join the fray.

The Doctor had got back to his feet, but Henderson punched him hard in the stomach and, as the Doctor doubled up, grabbed him in a necklock. The Brigadier launched himself at Henderson from behind, gripping the man in a bearhug. With a shout, the Doctor pulled himself free, but Henderson kicked him viciously in the small of his back and he sprawled forwards. The Brigadier tightened his grip but Henderson fought back furiously, elbowing Lethbridge-Stewart in the ribs to break his hold, then delivering a roundhouse punch that sent him sprawling on to the tarpaulin covering the pit.

First it sagged beneath his weight as he tried to rise. Then he fell through it to the ground eight feet below.

Winded, he looked up.

He was lying beside the suitcase.

Above him, through the tear in the tarpaulin, he saw Henderson flit across his vision, holding something in his hand; a small black box with an aerial.

'Doctor,' gasped the Brigadier, still struggling for breath.'Doctor, quickly.'

The Doctor's shaggy head leaned into view. 'Brigadier! Are you all right?'

'Stop Henderson,' gasped Lethbridge-Stewart. 'Detonator... He's going to set it off.'

'If only I knew how the absorption process operated...' The Doctor looked up the slope leading out of the crater after Henderson, then back down into the pit, his face anguished. 'No time.' He dropped himself down next to the Brigadier and started poring over the suitcase. 'We'll just have to hope I can defuse this thing.' He struggled with the clasps. 'It's locked!'

'Even if you could open it,' croaked the Brigadier. 'The arming mechanism must be booby trapped.'

'I must do something!' The Doctor kept pulling at the clasps, staring at the case in horror. '*Something!*' He dived for the laptop on the folding table and started hitting buttons.

'What are you doing?' asked the Brigadier.

The ghostly wail of the ship's door sounded as the glassy

barrier melted away. 'Getting it inside,' the Doctor said breathlessly.'It might provide some kind of shielding from the fall-out. Help me, Brigadier!'

Getting up painfully, Lethbridge-Stewart lent his strength to lifting the suitcase until they were holding it between them.

There was a quiet click from the case's innards.

'Throw it in!' cried the Doctor.

They did so, and then time seemed to slow.

The suitcase landed on its side, slithering into the shadows of the alien ship.

The Doctor's fingers rattled over the laptop's keys to close the door. The glassy seal started to reform.

Then the Doctor sprinted to the pit edge and cupped his hands ready to give the Brigadier a bunk up.

The Brigadier was moving towards him when he saw the Doctor's face twist into helpless terror at something behind him. A split-second later an incandescent brightness burnt away his friend's features all together, and a split-second after that came the darkness.

Chapter Fourteen

They were all there for the ceremony. Renchan, the Tibetan High Elder, had assured the Fuhrer that the images conjured in the Scrying Glass at this ceremony would remove all doubt as to future events.

'The future is in your hands,' he had told him. Hanne watched the Fuhrer's expression closely, had seen that it did not change as the Tibetan spoke. 'The image in the glass will show what will happen, but it is up to us – to you – to make it happen. When all things are in alignment, when the stars are set in their courses, then the image becomes reality, the future becomes the present.' He spread his hands, stretching the material of the gloves that he wore to ensure he did not physically touch the glass, did not taint its surface.

Now the robed figures of the image-callers gathered in a circle round the table where the Scrying Glass stood. Renchan stood over the Glass, hands stretched out in supplication, calling forth the image within. And behind him was the Fuhrer, watching, gazing into the future.

Even from across the chamber, Hanne could see the determination mixed with the anticipation on the Fuhrer's face. With her stood Hitler's closest advisers and confidants. Gottfried and Krenz, Hartmut and Schenk. All still, all silent. Watching.

'We call on you,' Renchan chanted, echoed by his fellows. 'We call you forth. We conjure you. The spectre in the glass.'

'The spectre in the glass,' the other Tibetans answered, and Hanne found herself mouthing the familiar litany with them.

'Show us the future. Show us the world as it will be, as we shall make it. Conjure for us the images and impressions. Be our window on the world that will come.'

The next section of the ceremony was in Tibetan. The words were guttural and strange. Strange, yet familiar – Hanne had heard them so often since that first furtive, hidden view. She allowed her attention to wander, let it play over the guttering candle flames and the flickering shadows. Unbidden, her attention turned to where she had first seen the shadow on the wall, by the door. And of course, there was nothing there.

The Scrying Glass was a swirl of mist. Hitler was leaning closer, eager. His pale tongue whipped out and over his lips in a rapid and abrupt gesture. Hanne found that she too was leaning forwards, and was aware that either side of her others were also straining to see the images as they emerged from the clearing fog.

Her first impression was of a melee of arms – swinging, turning. Hands clutched out of the swirling smoke of the glass before sinking again below the surface. Then a face, as if pressed to the glass. A round, face topped with a straggly mass of curling fair hair. Then the face swung away again and Hanne could see that the man was in a headlock. She was watching two men fighting. They turned and twisted deeper into the smoky interior, until they were lost to view.

A breeze riffled the candle flames so that the light danced. Then suddenly the whole room was filled with the light from inside the Scrying Glass. An abrupt, violent explosion that seemed to shatter out of the glass and scatter across the room, blindingly intense for the briefest moment. Then the smoke was back, billowing upwards, forming a mushroom cloud captured within the sphere as it rose and spread.

'We see the coming time,' Renchan cried, arms spread wide as if to welcome it. 'We see the images brought forth for us here. Give us a sign, a sign that you are here, among us.'

'A sign.' Hanne was shouting as loud as the others, struggling to be heard over the silent explosion within the glass, to be included in the supplication.

'We welcome your power, your force among us. Come forth from the Glass and show us that what we see is truly an image of the future, of the world as it will be – as it should be.'

Renchan paused, glanced back as if to gain the Fuhrer's approval. But Hitler was staring deep into the glass. He reached out, pointing, his mouth opening slightly in surprise and wonder. Renchan turned back to the table, Hanne's attention mirroring his, returning to the Glass.

Where a face was forming, looming over the fog and the smoke, emerging from the mushroom cloud of the future war and coming apocalypse.

A face from hell.

A face that fitted the shadows and half-seen glimmers of reality that Hanne knew so well.

It was grey, pitted like stone. The glowing, red eyes were slanted and oval, running down rather than across the face. The forehead rose up and over the hairless head, broken only by the stubby horns that erupted from it. The nose was a cruel beak jutting out over a lipless mouth. It seemed to stare out of the glass at them, the mouth twitching in what might have been an approximation of a smile.

Silence.

For several seconds nobody moved. Nobody breathed. The chanting died away. Then the face faded back into the smoke and the room breathed out again, scattering the candle flames and breaking the spell.

For a moment there was a relieved silence. Hitler was smiling, nodding his head as if to show he believed this was indeed the sign they needed. All attention was on him. The Tibetans continued with the ceremony, resuming their chant, but nobody was paying attention.

'Show us your presence among us.' The words seemed irrelevant, insubstantial now.

Until Renchan froze, his arms half-lifted, poised in salute. And the Fuhrer stopped nodding, his attention fixed on the darkness behind Hanne and the others.

Slowly, so slowly, she turned towards the shadowy blackness behind her. And saw the burning eyes.

They were so red, so bright that it hurt to look at them. So bright that it took her a while to realise what they were. Lights, they were lights, glowing from inside the cabinet that stood at the back of the room. Shining through the opaque glass that encased the cabinet, illuminating the dull silver that she had never before seen within.

All attention was now on the cabinet as the lights continued to burn, putting the candles to shame. The area that had been in shadows was now glowing a dull red that illuminated the cabinet and the wall behind. And the thing inside, behind the glass, moving through the silver interior like an image in smoke.

As her eyes adjusted to the red glow, Hanne could see the form, the shape that moved within. She could see that it was a figure – misshapen, elongated, as if made of bones without the flesh or muscle on them. A thin finger pressed forward and tapped on the glass shell. The tiny sound it made echoed in the cold silence. Several people flinched visibly. Hanne hoped she was not one of them.

Then the hand drew back, before flying again at the glass, harder this time. With a crack like lightning the glass split across. The skeletal hand drew back again, and the entire figure seemed to lunge forwards, smashing into the front of the cabinet.

The dark glass exploded in a storm of sound and flying fragments. The lights died, and the disjointed, inhuman figure stumbled forwards out of the shadows. Its lidless eyes seemed to fix on Hanne as it crumpled to its knees, one bony arm stretched out. A sickly sweet smell seemed to pervade the whole room as the creature pitched forwards on to the stone floor, a single arm outstretched towards the watchers.

On the central table, the mist in the Scrying Glass faded to clarity.

Broken across the shards of glass around the prone figure, Hanne could see the fragmented reflection of the spectre from within the glass – the creature of shadows. Hesitantly, she took a step forwards.

Then, one by one, the candles were snuffed out.

Darkness.

And out of the darkness, the Fuhrer's voice, level and confident: 'The sign is made. The time is now. The Fourth Reich is upon us.'

Chapter Fifteen

Quickly, Brigadier, on your feet.'

Lethbridge-Stewart could hear the Doctor talking to him as if he were underwater. Gradually, sensation returned to his limbs, and he realised he ached all over. Typical. Absolutely typical.

'Why did I call on you, anyway?' he grumbled sleepily.

Then he remembered all that had happened.

His eyes snapped open as he started in horror, and pushed himself up on his elbows. He looked frantically round, and realised he was lying on long grass at the crater's edge. His uniform was covered in mud, and the Doctor was looking down at him in concern, presumably red-faced from manhandling the Brigadier up the slope.

'The bomb... what happened?'

'It exploded.'

The Brigadier blinked stupidly around at their surroundings. 'But we're still alive, this place is untouched –'

'The bomb went off but there was no real explosion. Seems Henderson did know exactly what he was doing – and why the imps didn't try to stop us down there. The potential of the atomic blast must have been absorbed.'

'Then...' the Brigadier's head was throbbing, and he struggled to think straight. 'Then that's good, isn't it?'

'It's only good,' the Doctor informed him loudly, 'while that thing remains on the ground. When it takes off again, the full destructive force of a nuclear blast will be released over Dorset – with a good deal more energy thrown in for good measure.'

'And Henderson?'

'He's long gone. And goodness knows where.'

'We can start with his office at the Ministry of Defence,' suggested the Brigadier.

'I have a feeling he's too clever to have left us clues as to his whereabouts.' The Doctor clenched his large fists in frustration. '*Why* is he doing this?'

'Doing what?' Lethbridge-Stewart protested. 'We don't even know what he's really up to – nor who's in it with him.'

The Doctor nodded, frowning. 'We have to get hold of the ocular celluprime. The ship won't get far without a means of navigation. If we have that, at least we'll have something to barter with.'

'Barter with?'

'That's right. "Do please leave us in peace without destroying the Earth in retaliation for shooting you down."'

'Ah,' said the Brigadier heavily.

The Doctor started to pace back and forth. 'It's hardly going to make them sympathetic to working with me to find a way of dissipating the nuclear energy our friend Henderson has so sweetly obliged them with in a less destructive manner…'

The Brigadier got slowly back up. 'But we're talking about a nuclear explosion. How can so much energy just have been absorbed without… well, leakage of any kind.'

He realised the Doctor was looking grimly over his shoulder at something. 'How indeed. It seems the answer is, it can't.'

The Brigadier turned and saw what looked like a swarm of fireflies, a kind of twinkling in the grey afternoon sky over the crater. 'What's that?'

'Some kind of localised force emission, I'd imagine. The ship has the means to convert energy into fuel, but perhaps its enforced idleness means that mechanism is running at less than full capacity –'

The Brigadier waved him into silence, his head hurting enough already. 'You mean it's… *belching* nuclear energy?'

'If fusion or fission were still taking place we'd know about it, believe me. Or rather we wouldn't.' The Doctor threw a broken twig towards the flickering lights in the air. It burst into flame and fell to the earth that was already crackling, starting to smoke. The Doctor let out a short breath in amazement. 'No, this has resulted in some kind of powerfield being generated, as a waste product of the absorption process.'

'Like exhaust you mean,' said the Brigadier, trying another analogy. 'Or smoke out of a chimney.'

'If you like.' The Doctor slapped his fist against his palm. 'Henderson must've known this might be the result.'

'That's why he evacuated the area?'

'Very responsible of him,' the Doctor said, his voice dripping with sarcasm. 'But the powerfield will spread, and go on spreading. There's no way of knowing how far. You must get this place properly isolated, Brigadier.'

'I told Palmer UNIT should be looking after this village,' said Lethbridge-Stewart wryly.

'Well tell him to get his finger out now,' the Doctor snapped.

'You can tell him yourself, Doctor,' the Brigadier told him. 'I suggest we decamp to UNIT HQ and plan our next actions.' He considered. 'I'll arrange for Sergeant Dow and Corporal Jessop to be interviewed, find out more about what's been going on here... maybe even get a lead on where Henderson might be headed. Oh, and that journalist woman, seems she's turned up there with something vital to say on the subject of those imps...'

'Has she now,' the Doctor said petulantly, heading off back to the Land Rover. 'Well, all right. But we must hurry. I don't know how long we have, or in what direction the field will spread, but all villages nearby should be evacuated too, whatever happens.'

'That's going to be difficult to explain, Doctor.'

'Well, Brigadier, practise makes perfect,' the Doctor said pointedly. 'I think I've done enough explaining for one day.'

Claire decided that, thoughtful though Captain Palmer was, she was just about sick of the supposed comfort of hot, sweet Army tea. She pushed her mug away miserably, and tossed a half-eaten custard cream after it. She ran her hands through her unkempt red hair and then pushed it back into a scruffy ponytail and yawned. It was nine o'clock at night, she'd had only biscuits to eat all day, and her teeth now felt like they'd grown fur. Still, at least she felt a little more secure here in the empty conference room with a guard outside the door.

The thought of going out all alone into the big, dangerous world outside right now was too much to bear. This was the second day running she'd been scared half to death. First shadowy imp things, then Nazi thugs. She couldn't wait to see what good news tomorrow would bring.

Just then the doors flew open, and Claire jumped, spilling her mug of cold tea.

'Whoops,' cried a bizarre, multi-coloured figure sweeping into the room like the mutant offspring of Joe Bugner and Ronald McDonald. He mopped at the spreading brown puddle with a spotted handkerchief before smiling reassuringly at her.

'Hello. Miss Claire Aldwych, I presume. Please don't be alarmed. You can call me the Doctor.'

'The Doctor,' Claire repeated. Not the patient? But then she looked at him again, and decided that the clown about him was more grand theatrical Pierrot than cheap gaudy showman. She felt instinctively there was... a kind of sorrow about him. With her bargain basement psychology hat on she decided anyone dressing like that, so blatantly scorning conformity, secretly hoped that one day they'd find somewhere they'd fit in. Or perhaps he was just crazy, and actually thought he looked good in that get-up.

Either way, she grinned back. She decided she liked him already.

Behind him, more sombre in both appearance and manner, was the old Brigadier. Despite his obvious chauvinism, and his being, presumably, of retirement age, she realised there was a real warmth about him that she found appealing. 'Well, Miss Aldwych? Captain Palmer informs me you've something you wish to say, but only to me as one of the "old school" – whatever that might mean. Well?'

He looked at her expectantly, and Claire squirmed. She certainly *had* told that to Palmer, but only to buy herself time to think of something she could make up about the imps. She had no fresh information at all, but knew that a lot of talk about Cornish Nazis would've got her laughed off the phone instead of access to a military safehouse.

'I...' She looked between him and the Doctor, who had already

114

consumed the two biscuits remaining on the plate and who was coyly eyeing the half-eaten custard cream. 'Some people tried to kill me today.'

At this, the Doctor tore his attention away from the biscuit. 'There's a lot of it about,' he said, deadpan.

The Brigadier, in contrast, seemed gravely concerned. 'In conjunction with what you took away with you from Turelhampton?'

'Possibly,' Claire said, realising she didn't really have to lie after all. 'I don't know.'

She told them what had happened to her, leaving out the business with Brian. When she'd finished, the Brigadier and the Doctor exchanged glances.

'And you've not done anything that would encourage such...' The Doctor groped for the right word. '...Such attentions?'

Claire shrugged and shoved the bit of biscuit into her mouth to hide her embarrassment. The Doctor looked vaguely crestfallen.

'It's clear you've had something of an ordeal, Miss Aldwych,' the Brigadier said patiently, 'but you contacted Captain Palmer about what happened at Turelhampton?'

'Well, I just thought that...' Claire thought hard as she crunched her biscuit. 'I just thought that whoever tried to kill me might have done so because of the tape. I mean this man in charge of the whole Turelhampton thing, he went to great lengths to have the thing destroyed...'

'I have a feeling there are more important things on his mind right now than that tape,' the Doctor said. He turned to the Brigadier in sudden irritation. 'Why aren't there hordes of aides swarming round you inundating you with updates and progress reports?' he demanded. 'Where's Palmer with the latest on the Dorset evacuation?'

'Doctor!' protested the Brigadier in some embarrassment, pointing at Claire and shaking his head. 'I'm not in charge anymore, Doctor, remember?' There was no denying the rankle in the old boy's voice. 'Palmer's deployed a hazard squad down there to get things rolling but I really don't think –'

'Oh, for goodness' sake,' the Doctor retorted. 'Action's what we need here, not prevarication.' He flashed a smile at Claire. 'You won't breathe a word of this to anyone, will you?'

'Upon my soul,' said Claire, beaming back at him.

'There,' he said, 'you see?'

'What evacuation? What's been happening?'

The Brigadier groaned. 'She's a journalist, Doctor,' he protested.

'A noble profession.' The Doctor turned to her. 'Young lady, have you heard of Sarah Jane Smith?'

'The Metropolitan woman?' Claire nodded. 'She's done some amazing stuff. You know her?'

'Oh, to nod to in the street.' The Doctor smiled smugly at the Brigadier, then his face clouded again. 'Now what's being done to find Henderson?'

The old boy had – doubtless not for the first time – clearly given up arguing with him. 'A raid's being arranged on his rooms at Horseguards. There's been a big hoo-hah over Dow and Jessop with the Regular Army, seems Henderson's traditionally had certain powers over their division for many years, as you thought. Anyway, they're coming in for questioning. These things *do* take time, you know, Doctor.'

'Well they shouldn't. You should tell your men –'

'Not *my* men, Doctor. And it would help if they knew what they were looking for. What exactly does this ocular celluprime thing look like anyway? Could you be a little more forthcoming than a medium sized…' He mimed a vaguely circular shape in the air.

The Doctor sighed. 'When I mentioned a crystal ball earlier I wasn't speaking entirely figuratively. I think your men will know it when they find it. There's something about it… it's not just clear glass. It will have that oily, cloudy look about it, like we found back at the ship –'

'Ship?' Claire queried, to a look on the Brigadier's face that spoke of almost physical pain.

' – and there'll be a glow about it…' The Doctor seemed quite enraptured with his description. 'As if lit from within with the dying ember of a fading dream…'

'But… but that's what Brian said!' Claire blurted out.

The Doctor took a little umbrage at this. 'All that was said… by *Brian*?'

'Brian who?' demanded the Brigadier.

'Brian Goldman. A journalist. As of last night, a dead journalist. He called me yesterday, on my mobile, when I was here, remember. And he saw a crystal ball thing, and he said how it glowed, sort of from inside…'

'Where did he see it?' demanded the Doctor.

'In Cornwall. At a secret Nazi rally in a millionaire's mansion outside of Kilkhampton. I went there today to follow up his leads, like he asked me to. The sod.' She swallowed. Perhaps she'd best not mention now just whose face Brian said he'd seen in the crystal ball – it had to be just a reflection of a photograph or something. Probably. 'He was going to expose them and they killed him for it. And I think the people who killed him want to kill me too.'

'Nazis?' echoed the Brigadier in disbelief. 'My dear woman, don't be so absurd.'

'Absurd?' she yelled at him. 'Tell that to Goldman's widow! I'm telling you, they killed him.'

The Brigadier fell silent. 'I'm sorry, Miss Aldwych', he murmured.

'Remember, Brigadier,' the Doctor said quietly, 'the alien ship came down in 1944. The war was still on, and the Nazis still very much in existence.'

'But Doctor…'

'What other leads do we have?' He forced a smile. 'And since you're *not* in charge of the UNIT operation, it'll give us all something to follow up while we wait for news.'

The Brigadier sighed. 'Do you know Goldman's address, Miss Aldwych?'

Claire tapped her bag. 'In my diary. It's somewhere in Lewisham I think.'

'Well,' the Brigadier declared, 'it's too late to go tonight, and it seems it's been a trying day for us all. I suppose, Miss Aldwych, I had better put you up for the night.'

'Oh, had you?' Claire began, presumptuous old sod, before remembering that the last place she wanted to be right now was anywhere alone.

'Yes, I had!' the Brigadier said, brooking no argument. 'Where I can keep an eye on the pair of you. We'll all see Goldman's widow tomorrow.'

'At first light,' the Doctor qualified.

The Brigadier nodded weakly, and Claire groaned at the prospect. But her mind was awash with alien ships, evacuations of Dorset, Hitler alive, crystal balls...

It was all frightening as hell, sure – but a gift.

This could *really* be the Big One.

Chapter Sixteen

Claire slept well in the Brigadier's spare room, snug in one of his shirts that came down almost to her knees. Out in the country, the only sound to disturb her during the night had been the Doctor pacing about. Several times she'd heard him call UNIT HQ, demanding updates on the spread of this powerfield over Turelhampton, offering gobbledy-gook advice and insisting they keep him informed. She wondered if he'd had a wink of sleep, but on the long journey through the sleepy streets to Lewisham this morning he seemed perfectly refreshed.

Jammy swine.

It was decided that the Brigadier should approach Goldman's wife first, as the only one of them with even semi-official status. Claire also suspected that Mrs Goldman was unlikely to take kindly to being accosted on her doorstep by a burly clown and the girl she'd once caught with a tongue down her husband's throat. She ushered the Brigadier up the garden path while she and the Doctor hung back. It was a quite nice semi on a quiet street. Brian had done all right for himself.

She thought again of that cordoned-off patch of blackened grass down the muddy little track, and shuddered.

Alarm bells started ringing when the Brigadier knocked on the front door and it creaked open. 'Mrs Goldman?' he called.

'Are you the police?' came a fraught woman's voice.

The Brigadier glanced behind him and Claire and the Doctor, as if unable to make up his mind *what* they were. 'Please don't be afraid,' he said, producing his pass and holding it out to her so she could see it for herself. 'We're with UNIT... Military Intelligence. We've come regarding your husband.'

The door was opened and a small, haggard-looking blonde woman came to the door. She didn't look like she'd seen daylight for a week, watery-eyed and pale in shapeless, baggy clothes.

Quite a change from the last time they'd met, when Mrs Goldman had been all tarted up and screaming in her face.

'I'm waiting for the police. They said they'd be round this morning. We… I had a break-in last night.'

The Doctor bounded forward. Claire had the impression he wasn't accustomed to waiting around on the sidelines. 'Did they take anything?'

Mrs Goldman shook her head. 'Not really… a few bits of jewellery I'd left lying about, but mainly…' Her voice shook, and she took a deep shuddering breath. 'Mainly they just went through Brian's things.'

'His work things?' the Doctor asked urgently. 'Tapes? Papers?'

The woman nodded, eyes welling up. The Doctor tried awkwardly to pat her shoulder, but she shrunk away from him. The Doctor looked meaningfully at Claire, and jerked his head as if to say she was needed.

Claire braced herself and walked forward. The mousy little woman narrowed her tearful eyes. 'Claire Aldwych? What are you doing here?'

'I'm… I suppose I'm on the story. Hello, er…'

Mrs Goldman looked at her like she'd just crawled from under the proverbial stone. 'Linda.'

'Linda, of course. Hello… again.'

'I'm not surprised you've forgotten my name. You forgot about me altogether at the party.'

'Perhaps we could go inside and talk there?' the Brigadier suggested, ever the diplomat.

The Doctor didn't wait for an answer, just bustled the poor woman inside. 'Now, Mrs Goldman, how much did you know about your husband's work…'

The Brigadier lingered on the doorstep with Claire for a moment, and looked at her enquiringly. 'You don't get along?'

'Long story going nowhere,' Claire answered, and busied herself removing a jiffy bag that had been wedged in the mailbox mounted on the wall. She raised it above her head. 'Peace offering,' she said weakly, and they both walked inside.

Mrs Goldman – Linda – didn't offer them any tea. She just slumped down on the sofa, a horrid floral thing. Her taste or Brian's? Claire wondered vaguely.

'I doubt I can help you. Brian always kept me in the dark about what he was working on.' Linda gave a brittle laugh. 'He used to joke that if he ever told me, he'd have to kill me.'

Ouch.

'And he never mentioned anything about a kind of crystal ball? Or a village, Turelhampton, in Dorset?'

Linda looked blankly at the Brigadier. Claire sighed, and sat down heavily in an armchair. She tossed the package on the coffee table.

Linda just glared first at her, then at the padded envelope. 'Postman came with that this morning. Would you believe it? Postage to be paid. I say, "My husband's dead, I've just been burgled, and you want me to pay the postage on some bloody junk for Brian…"'

The Doctor picked up the package thoughtfully, turning it over in his hands. Suddenly Linda snatched it from him and studied it herself.

The Brigadier swapped a baffled glance with Claire. 'Mrs Goldman?'

'It's Brian's writing,' she whispered, fresh tears welling. 'It's from *Brian*.'

'There was a postbox right next to the place…' Claire checked herself. 'The place where it happened.'

'You were there?' Linda hissed.

She started to explain about Brian's call, painfully aware his wife would hardly be cheered to learn Claire Aldwych was one of the last people her husband ever spoke to, but was grateful when the Doctor interrupted her by taking back the package and noisily ripping it open.

A mini DV cassette fell out into the Doctor's hand. Everyone looked at everyone else for a moment. Then the Doctor jumped to his feet. 'We need to watch this. Quickly. Now!'

Claire wondered what the police would make of the scene if they called round to investigate the burglary right now – four very different figures all glued to the screen in Brian's ransacked office, watching some kind of Nazi occult ceremony.

'Oh my God,' whispered Linda, transfixed, repeating the words over and over again. 'Oh my God, oh my God…'

Watching it sent a chill along Claire's spine. Not just because Brian must've been discovered and killed by these people, nor even because they'd tried to kill her too, just for having talked to him. It was the way they were all so desperately serious about what they were doing. The mad-eyed man whipping up the crowd with talk of Der Fuhrer, all of them so focused, gathered round the dais, so into something that should objectively have been so ridiculous. Then the orientals, all robes and green gloves and chanting in the dark, gathered around some –

'That's it!' the Doctor announced, clapping his hands together and making them all jump half a mile. 'The ocular celluprime! "Scrying Glass" indeed…'

'I told you the two were linked!' Claire said, amazed herself but never one to miss a trick.

'And where was all this taking place?' the Doctor asked her.

'Oakhope Manor, Kilkhampton,' said Claire. 'But it's no good, they've all cleared out. Left the country, there's an airfield in the grounds –'

'I see the coming man!' came the voice from the TV.

'Good grief,' muttered the Brigadier, still transfixed by what was on the screen. They all turned to see.

'Oh, Jesus,' said Claire.

There was a white-faced figure in a spotlight's glare, leaning on the balustrade.

'That's…' Linda croaked.

The Doctor took a step closer to the screen. 'Adolf *Hitler*?'

'A lookalike,' the Brigadier said. 'It must be.'

'Must it?' The Doctor stared, aghast, shaking his head. 'There's something about him…'

It should, objectively, have been so ridiculous.

Claire turned away and bit her lip so hard she drew blood.

* * *

The police finally arrived, just as Claire and the others were leaving. The Brigadier had a few 'Official Secrets Act' type words about his presence here with the constable, announcing that UNIT needed to know if clues as to the intruder's identity were discovered.

Claire felt a pang of guilt as she just walked away, leaving Mrs Goldman alone and dazed to cope with all this. Not that the little woman would appreciate her sympathy, she supposed. Thank God Linda had let them keep the tape. The Brigadier had told her he'd make sure police high-ups saw it and acted on it; it would be a big help in tracking down Brian's killers. Claire had decided not to mention it would be a big help in putting together the documentary of the century too. She kept feeling in her pocket to check it was still there.

'What do you reckon, then?' she asked the Brigadier as they got back into his Jag. She slid along the back seat till she was in the middle, grateful that the black leather had absorbed some small heat from the cool morning sunshine.

'I don't think they'll find anything,' he answered, mis-understanding her question. 'I'd imagine these neo-Nazi types are scrupulous in clearing up after themselves. I must say, I believe you're very lucky to be alive after your own run-in with them, Miss Aldwych.'

'Seems History is saving me for better things,' she said archly, furtively tapping the cassette in her pocket once again. 'Anyway, I didn't mean the police, I meant, what do you reckon to the tape? *Could* that have been Hitler?'

'Nazis being such fanatical sorts,' reflected the Brigadier, 'seems a little disrespectful to dress someone up as him, give him a big build-up and put him on parade.'

'But that man looked young. If that really *was* Hitler, he'd be…'

'…Well over a hundred years old,' the Doctor chipped in, getting himself comfortable in the passenger seat. 'Unless, of course…'

'Unless that longevity thing got into German hands as well as the Scrying Glass?' The Brigadier looked grim. 'Could that have happened? Could Hitler have been saved somehow?'

'Hitler was killed, he took his own life in his Berlin bunker,' said the Doctor.

'*Believed* killed.' Claire felt the hairs on the back of her neck prickling. 'I did a doc a few years ago on his last days. Some weird stuff was going on. Lots of contradictions.' She paused, cast her mind back. 'There were questions asked about the remains, and the bones too. Big power-plays in the Kremlin. The Russians only came out and admitted Hitler was dead for definite in 1967, and there were these skull fragments, see...'

'Yes, thank you, Miss Aldwych,' said the Brigadier, raising his hands in protest at fact overload. 'I'm sure your researches have been most conscientious.'

'Well, we can't afford not to take this seriously. A new breed of Nazis is bad enough, but if that really is...' The Doctor trailed off. 'We need to do some research of our own. Find out what really happened in Turelhampton when the ship came down.'

'Where do you suggest we start,' the Brigadier scoffed. 'Put a notice in the *Dorset Echo*?'

'You can start with me, if you like,' Claire said, pretending to be only vaguely interested and giving the Brigadier a mock-snooty look. 'Me and my most conscientious researches.'

'Well, Claire?' the Doctor looked at her, bright-eyed.

Claire reverted to her usual tone, bubbling with enthusiasm. 'I managed to track down this Army guy, one of the men assigned to guarding the village when it was first evacuated. God knows, it wasn't easy. Friend of a friend of a friend of a friend had to pull some serious strings at some loony bin to get his details.'

'And what is the name of this expert witness?' wondered the Brigadier dourly.

'Peter Spinney. He wasn't keen on talking, had some kind of breakdown after the war...'

The Doctor seemed urgent. 'Where is he now?'

The Brigadier shifted uncomfortably in his own seat. 'Please don't say he's in Newcastle.'

'Salisbury way, I think,' Claire replied. 'We'd need to go back to my place and check my files.'

'And where *is* your place?' asked the long-suffering Brigadier.

'Forest Hill. Oh, and Brigadier, do you have a PC at home, and a modem?'

'My wife has, but I fail to see –'

'Only I've got a secure server too, on-line, where a lot of my stuff's backed up. Some good stuff on Hitler and all that if you're interested. We can sort through it all together back at your place.'

'Can we indeed?' sighed the Brigadier. 'You seem to be becoming quite a fixture, Miss Aldwych. Very helpful, I'm sure.'

'Come on Brigadier, get a move on,' the Doctor urged him. 'Shall I drive?'

The Brigadier was emphatic. 'No.'

They found Claire's place had been broken into, just as Brian's had. Except with the luxury of time, since no one had been around, the intruder hadn't made much mess beyond breaking the glass in her front door. None of her stuff had been damaged; everything had clearly been gone through, but had been rearranged again quite neatly. Somehow that was almost more disturbing.

The only thing that was missing was the tape from her answerphone, the live report of her earlier encounter. It made her feel sick. Just how much of her stuff had these people gone through? Luckily there had been nothing here linking her to Brian's own researches. Even so, Claire didn't imagine she would ever feel safe in her own home again.

It hadn't taken her long to get hold of Peter Spinney's details. While the Doctor had swiftly fixed up her door, the Brigadier had contacted Captain Palmer for an update.

Then it had been back in the car and off to the speck on the map that was Winterbourne Dauntsey.

'Winterbourne Dauntsey?' Palmer queried, frowning down the phone as if the Brigadier could see him doing so at the other end of the line. 'Never heard of it, sir. Still, if this Spinney character can shed some light on the situation...' He looked across at Dow and

Jessop, seated in his office facing dead ahead, speaking when spoken to and playing everything by the book. Then he sighed. 'The 105th boys aren't much help, I'm afraid. Orders is orders, they're saying, and Henderson had every right to give them out... Yes, we'll keep talking, sir. Good luck. Bye now, sir.'

Palmer turned back to Dow and took a deep breath. 'Henderson is Under Secretary for...' he broke off, checked against a piece of paper: 'Emergency peacetime affairs. And yet there's no permanent secretary or minister heading up such a department. That never struck you as odd.'

'In that situation, sir, Mr Henderson as under-secretary gives the orders.'

'And you never...'

'Orders –'

'– is orders, Dow. Yes, I do know.' He sighed, drummed his fingers on the desk, wondered again how he was ever going to control the spread of this killer energy field down at Turelhampton. 'I *do* know.'

The room was empty save for a table covered in a tangle of old electronics, a simple chair, and a large map of the world pinned to a bare wall, long-since faded from sunlight shining through the one window.

It was old and dusty, one of the many safehouses Henderson had arranged for himself over the years, ready for the inevitable time for action.

He sat there now, weak and shivering, hunched over the radio set with a set of 'phones. He'd felt the lost familiar of the missing crewman trying to reach out to him over impossible distance in his dreams again and again over the years. When the bomb had gone off, when the energy had been released, the faint touch of the crewman's presence in his consciousness had grown warmer, brighter. And then it had faded. And a part of him, an alien part somewhere deep within, knew he would never feel that presence again.

The loss and the pain were all he felt right now.

So he sat here, listening to the crackling transmissions from the electronic bug he'd fastened to Dow's uniform when dismissing him at Turelhampton. He'd known his men would be questioned. He wished to learn more about his enemies, how much they knew, what they were planning.

The voices crackled on in his ears. Then, abruptly, Henderson sat up straight. This was more than he could've ever have hoped for. He would rest, rest and recover a little, wait for his enemies to flounder on their trail, to wind up nowhere. Then simply walk in and take what was needed, with the minimum of effort.

He put down the headphones, and crossed to the map with an HB pencil sharpened to a lethal looking point.

In neat print, he scratched across England:

PETER SPINNEY. WINTERBOURNE DAUNTSEY.

Claire daydreamed in the back of the car. It was comforting to be driven about for a change. Like when you were a kid, just left to sit and sleep on the back seat, let the grown-ups worry about the road.

She distracted herself from thoughts of home by focusing on her new documentary. *Did Hitler Survive?* With Brian's stuff, and the footage from Turelhampton, she knew she had big league material already. Who knew what was coming next, but she wasn't going to miss a thing. She slipped a hand in her bag to check she could switch her DAT walkman on to record without looking.

Anne Diamond and her TV Week could go swivel.

The M3 was pretty clear, and a couple of hours later they'd arrived in the tiny village. The Doctor was out of the Jag in seconds, dragging out Claire and propelling her up the little driveway to Spinney's cottage to act as first contact.

Spinney was a wizened old boy – the biggest thing about him were his chunky 1970s NHS glasses, his ears bent over almost at right angles under their weight. He claimed to remember Claire calling before, and led all three of them into his living room.

'This the TV crew, is it?' Spinney asked, his voice like a creaking door.

'These are my boys,' Claire said, winking at the scandalised Doctor.

'Good job he's behind the cameras wearing that get-up,' Spinney said with a chuckle. The Doctor's beatific smile in response made Claire want to laugh out loud.

While Spinney brewed a pot of tea, Claire looked round, gingerly. 'Shoot me before I get old,' she muttered. The living room doubled as his bedroom, saturated with the cloying reek of cherry tobacco. While the patterns on both carpet and wallpaper were fussy in the extreme, Spinney himself was clearly not. Ornaments and bric-a-brac were piled high on mantelpiece, dining table and even on a rickety old piano. It felt more like some old junk shop than a home.

She switched the walkman on to record and sat down on the bed, waiting for the little old man to join them.

'So, Mr Spinney,' the Doctor inquired, draining his mug as soon as it was presented to him as if to get it out of the way. 'You recall the unidentified object that fell on Turelhampton that night in 1944?'

'Doesn't muck about, does he?' Spinney said, broken teeth bared in a big smile. 'Yeah, I remember it. Spent most of me life trying to forget it, but I can see it plain as day even now. Me, Alan Watson and Gerrard Lassiter, privates we were, we found it first...'

'Both dead,' mouthed Claire to the Brigadier and the Doctor behind Spinney's back.

'Anyways, old Dogson orders us three to stand guard over it while they stand by for further orders. Funny looking thing it was, all metal and glass, shiny and dark at the same time.'

'Did you look inside?' asked the Brigadier.

'Well... I suppose we might've done.'

'You remember it "plain as day", Mr Spinney?' the Doctor asked a little heavy-handedly.

'We had a quick look round. Had to be quick. Dogson appointed an officer to take charge, he ordered us away and went for a butchers himself...' Spinney smiled. 'The Dorset Darling. Henderson, his name was.'

'And what happened then?' Claire asked.

Spinney's spindly frame seemed to shrink even smaller. 'They took me off D-Day duties. Had to stand guard in an empty village for the next year. Stand doing nothing, while all me mates...' He trailed off, eyes staring cloudily into the distance. 'All me mates...'

'I understand, Mr Spinney,' said the Brigadier quietly.

But the Doctor was like a dog with a bone. 'What I would *like* to understand is how a component from that UFO might've ended up in the hands of the Reich!'

'Well, I don't know,' said Spinney distantly, not reacting, 'Perhaps it went when the Germans raided the village in August 1944.'

Chapter Seventeen

Claire felt a shiver pass through her at Spinney's casual words.

The Brigadier's voice was low and distinct. 'Would you mind repeating yourself, Mr Spinney?'

Spinney seemed to come back to life. 'Last bit of action I saw, it was. Germans. Crack troops, they were. Knew what they were after too: that thing from the sky.'

'How did they learn about it, Doctor?' asked the Brigadier quietly.

'Perhaps it took in Western Europe on its flight path,' said the Doctor. 'And the Luftwaffe *didn't* shoot it down.'

'Hardly surprising – not a patch on our boys,' mumbled the Brigadier, until he realised the Doctor was looking at him pointedly.

Spinney was lost again with his memories. 'I'm telling you, we'd have been done for if reinforcements hadn't arrived. We were just a squad, they couldn't spare many men for that sort of duty. But then a keen old bunch turned up, nick of time job…'

'The Germans were captured?' Claire asked.

Spinney shook his head and his glasses slid down his nose. 'No, they got away… Got away with something from the ship. They came in Bibers, see, and an E-boat was waiting to take them back…'

'Mr Spinney,' boomed the Doctor, 'what did they take from the ship?'

'A box. A big box from inside.'

'A sort of casket, a bit like a freezer chest?' the Brigadier asked urgently. Claire recognised the description from the Doctor's nocturnal account of their adventures there. So the Germans had taken an alien body away with them? This was beyond *X-Files*…

'That's the one,' Spinney said agreeably. 'Took it away, they did. Right away.'

'Explains the gap there today,' noted the Brigadier.

'And was the longevity device still attached, I wonder?' muttered the Doctor. 'If it *was*...'

'So it *could* be him?' Claire said, her heart beating faster.

'Him?' asked Spinney.

'What was the date?' the Doctor asked, abruptly changing the subject. 'When in August, what time?'

'Night of the 18th, it was.'

'You're sure?'

'Does it matter?' Claire wondered.

'It could matter a very great deal,' the Doctor told her.

'It was the 18th, all right,' Spinney said sadly. 'Around eleven. I remember 'cause it was old Gerrard's birthday, see. We were the same age. Twenty-two he would've been then, if...'

Spinney's voice trailed off again, and he swallowed stickily.

'Thank you, Mr Spinney,' the Doctor said, shoving his hands deep into his colourful coat pockets. 'You've been a very great help to us.'

'Will I be on the telly, then?' Spinney asked.

'When I come back with a TV camera,' Claire told him gently, discreetly switching off her walkman, 'you can depend on it.'

Spinney closed the door after them, and dimly heard the sound of the big car's engine starting up, ready to take. He didn't often have people round to call. He would leave their tea mugs untouched to remind him of them.

There was something else that helped him remember. Something secret.

He crossed to his cluttered tallboy and picked up a small lump wrapped in a lace doily. Then he unwrapped it with clumsy fingers.

Inside the doily was a curved piece of glass. A pinprick of crimson light glowed deep within it.

Palmer stared on grimly as the wall of smoky air wafted just a little further out into the deserted streets of Turelhampton. All their scientists and all their gadgets had failed to come up with anything to check the advance of this thing. Even tips and suggestions from the Doctor had brought them no closer to even understanding it, let alone halting it. So the troops were busy now evacuating the surrounding area – the only positive action they could take. 'It's 1944 all over again,' the older residents were claiming, quite cheerily, some of them. Perhaps they were comforted, in a way, to know that some things really do stay the same.

With that thought in mind, Palmer had called in the special reserve. Someone with field experience of working with the Doctor's lunatic gadgetry, of dealing scientifically with the unknown.

Mr Osgood tutted beside him as he gazed on at the powerfield. He was a thin, wheezing man in his late fifties now, who looked like he'd have trouble dealing with a steep flight of steps. But his eyes were still sharp through his thick glasses, and he was scrawling endless equations on a battered, lined notebook.

The tattered thatch of a cottage roof ignited in flames as the powerfield inched nearer. 'Fall back!' Palmer ordered, and a pack of white-coated boffins wasted no time scrabbling to obey, even weighed down with so many useless contraptions. Osgood watched them go knowingly, and smiled sadly to himself.

A radial area of about 200 yards around the alien ship was now nothing more than blackened stubble flecking the charred ground, barely visible through the broiling air.

'Mr Osgood,' Palmer asked, 'do you have any idea how far the effect could spread?'

'None,' Osgood admitted, cheerily. 'But I do think we should try to contain it as soon as possible.'

Palmer took a deep breath and reluctantly fell back himself, glowering at the energy field, his walkie-talkie squawked into life.

'Palmer,' he snapped. Sergeant Hansing gave his report, and Palmer closed his eyes wearily at more bad news.

'So, what can we do now?' the Brigadier asked, turning on to the main road out of the little village.

'Hitler's still alive,' said Claire. 'He must be, that's what this is about. That longevity thing must've worked on him somehow.'

'Hmm. You know, it does seem a tad suspicious that Henderson was in charge of the UFO's safekeeping and a German task force just happen to find their way straight to it,' the Brigadier said. 'Could Henderson be a traitor, working for the Nazis?'

'Keeping the ship, and the crew, safe all these years just so Hitler can come along and take charge when the time is right?' Claire breathed.

The Doctor didn't speculate. 'Can we get word from Palmer on Henderson's whereabouts? And an update on the powerfield?'

The Brigadier obliged, and from both his tone and his face, it was clear the news wasn't good.

'Sergeant Hansing's boys have been on the case, but Henderson's cleaned out his office. No clues.'

'I didn't think there would be,' said the Doctor gloomily.

'And it's reported that the powerfield is spreading in a radial direction with the ship at the epicentre. Diameter of two hundred yards, and spreading, burning to ash everything it touches.'

'Two hundred yards?' the Doctor muttered. 'Then soon the entire village will be reduced to slag, and from there...'

'Old Osgood's been brought in to help out,' the Brigadier reported cheerily.

'Osgood, eh?' the Doctor said, a fond smile soon replaced with a doubtful frown. 'I'm not convinced our troubles are over.'

'So what do we do, Doctor?' asked the Brigadier. Claire found it quite surreal that he, and all UNIT it seemed, could be so dependent on this one, peculiar man.

'We have to get hold of the Ocular... of the Scrying Glass,' said the Doctor. 'It's needed by both the Nazis and the aliens.'

'You said they need it to fly by,' the Brigadier said stiffly. 'But has it occurred to you they might not want to leave the Earth at all? That they could be here to take over? That the ship in Turelhampton is just the scout craft, and both the crew *and* the Nazis have been waiting patiently all this time for a full invasion force to arrive?'

No one said anything for a couple of minutes as the possibility sank in.

'We need more information,' the Doctor conceded, keeping carefully neutral. 'You were impressed with Claire's research, Brigadier. Now's your chance to work with her on some more.'

Claire grinned, but the Brigadier seemed unconvinced. 'Doctor?'

'We need to find out more about the Nazi forces as they stand now – and about the supposed death of Hitler. Anything you can find, post-war sightings, the Russian suppression of evidence… anything that might give us an insight to where the Nazi forces might be massing.'

'Because that's where we'll find the Scrying Glass,' Claire finished. 'Understood. We could dig around in Jeremy Maskell's dealings for starters – he's the bloke who owns Nazi Manor. And like I say, I've got some good contacts from the Hitler doc…'

'I do have one or two contacts of my own, Miss Aldwych,' bristled the Brigadier.

Claire discreetly saluted, and the Doctor smiled.

'What about you, Doctor?' the Brigadier asked. 'What will *you* be doing? Shame you can't pop back in time and take the Scrying Glass before the Nazis get it.'

The Doctor seemed to take the facetious comment seriously. 'That would be breaking the rules, Brigadier. I now know they *have* the Scrying Glass, it's immutable fact.' He paused. 'But perhaps I could *join* the raid, somehow, try to find out where the Glass went… I'd imagine they'd find an expert on the occult quite handy.'

'That's possible?' the Brigadier asked, incredulous.

'You'd be amazed,' said the Doctor, eyes suddenly twinkling, 'at the one or two contacts in *my* little black book.'

Claire stared at him in puzzlement.

'And it's really worth going to such lengths?'

'Hitler sparked off the worst, the most bloody conflict in this planet's history. Imagine the outcome of such a war fought not only with today's weapons, but with the unimaginable arsenal of an alien race.' He nodded grimly. 'I think it's worth it.'

'I think you're both nutters,' Claire muttered.

The rest of the car journey back to the Brigadier's house passed in silence.

And sometime that evening, after a meeting with the Brigadier behind closed doors, the Doctor disappeared. Lethbridge-Stewart wouldn't be drawn on the subject. Claire found herself listening out for the Doctor through the night, but he didn't come back.

Chapter Eighteen

During the invasion it was like a talisman. He could feel it, heavy in his uniform jacket pocket as he waited in the landing craft, praying they would avoid the shells and that he would keep his breakfast down. It was with him on the beach as he crawled towards the tangled webs of barbed wire through the sand-stinging hail of bullets.

It kept him company as he charged the machine gun nest, as he lay exhausted at the roadside, as he climbed into the halftrack. Was driven towards the next hellish encounter with the enemy in the Normandy countryside.

And it was with him now as they made their cautious way through the ruined main street of a nameless French rural town.

Lassiter knew it had the power to show him the future. He had not known that when he took it, and been shocked and surprised and puzzled the next morning when he stared into the misty depths of the crystal. He had expected to see himself – to see Gerrard Lassiter staring back out of the rounded glass. Instead he had seen a sea peppered with landing craft. Explosions and spray. Death on the beaches and under the cliffs.

Even as he stared, aghast, he knew he was seeing the future. His future. And he saw himself charging foolhardy at the machine guns as they jammed, dragging the pin from the mills bomb with his teeth, lobbing it over the sandbags. Surviving.

Several times since then he had stared into the orb, looked into the seeds of time. It needed calm and quiet. He had to think himself into the same relaxed stillness as that first time. Otherwise, there was nothing. But when he managed it, he could see, deep within the glass sphere, images of the future.

One side of the building had been blown away. The rest of the patrol was ahead of him and off to the side, clearing the Germans

136

from the wrecked town. It was not a difficult task. The enemy seemed happy enough to leave – to retreat and regroup. There would be harder battles in the days and months ahead. But for the moment it was steady and almost routine. Routine, save for the suspicion that at any moment a bullet might rip the side of your head off. Just as a shell had ripped away the side of the building.

Lassiter stepped over the remains of the outside wall and stood in what had once been a kitchen. The building was a small house or a cottage. The kitchen floor was flagged with uneven stone. Stone that was now pitted and scarred. Chunks of masonry and piles of bricks lay strewn across the room. A wooden table had collapsed when a section of the roof fell on it. A single chair stood on sentry duty by the blocked door into the rest of the house.

Looking round, the whole landscape seemed to be made of the same broken texture. A sea of rubble and half-destroyed buildings. Constant collapse. As he looked round, Lassiter felt a pang of guilt as well and pain. He might spend the rest of his life sifting through the rubble and the dirt, looking for more people to kill rather than hunting for those in need of rescue. How long could it go on? How long could *he* go on?

Without really thinking about it, he found that he was sitting on the chair. It rocked uneasily on a the uneven floor. He laid his rifle down carefully on the ground beside him, within easy reach. His hand was in his pocket, and he drew out the glass, the crystal ball. It surprised him that it was warm to the touch. He held it up so that it caught the light, turned it slowly, checking it was not damaged. As ever, it seemed perfect, unblemished. Lassiter made to return it to his pocket. But as he did so, his eyes caught an image, deep within the glass. He froze.

Then, slowly, he lifted the glass so he could see more clearly, careful not to lose to image deep within.

It was a man.

He was a good way off, standing up behind a broken wall. Rising from concealment, looking round furtively. His field grey uniform was dusty, his black helmet dented. It was impossible to make out what rank the German soldier was, but Lassiter was transfixed, letting his mind relax into nothing as he watched the man move slowly, cat-like towards him in the glass.

What did it mean? The images seemed to be from his own point of view, so what was he now seeing? As the soldier pulled something from a leather sheaf on his thigh, Lassiter realised with a shock what it was.

The knife glinted as sunlight caught the dazzling blade.

He was seeing his own death.

The image distorted as the German seemed almost to lean out of the glass at him, knife-arm extended, blade angled.

Lassiter gasped, and too late he reached for his rifle.

As the blade was drawn sharply across his throat.

Gunther Brun stepped back abruptly to avoid the blood. Without thinking he wiped the blade across his cuff, and returned it to his sheath. Then he carefully stepped forwards and lifted the glass ball from the dead man's fingers. His grip was surprisingly tight, and Brun's own fingers slipped on the bloody surface of the sphere as he prised it free. A souvenir. A trophy.

Strange, Brun thought as he looked round, that the British soldier had not reacted. Brun had seen his own image over the man's shoulder, reflected in the surface of the glass. Why hadn't he turned, or at least cried out?

Still, who cared? Strange things happened in war. And his main concern was getting back through the allied lines and rejoining his unit. He polished the glass ball on his dusty jacket, then slipped it into his pocket without another thought.

Somehow, he could not just leave it. But he was desperate to be rid of the thing. So when he found he was losing, offering it instead of rations or marks seemed like the best option.

His opponent was Otto Klein, a Colonel in the Waffen SS. His uniform was black, and Brun reckoned his heart was blacker. But he seemed willing to accept the glass sphere as Brun's wager. Brun made sure the colonel won. And being in the SS, the colonel was arrogant and assured enough to assume that he deserved to win.

'What is it?' Colonel Klein asked as he lifted the sphere from the makeshift card table. 'It is heavy.' He peered at it. 'Misty. Strange how it catches the light and seems almost to move.'

Brun licked his dry lips, but said nothing, certainly nothing of the images he had seen inside the glass. Terrible images.

'What is it?' Klein asked again.

Brun shrugged. 'I have no idea,' he admitted. 'I... found it.'

Klein spared him a quick glance. They both knew what that meant. 'You would part with this rather than a few marks or a bar of chocolate?' He seemed surprised, and somehow that made him seem more human.

Brun leaned forward. 'I tell you,' he said quietly, 'if I never see that thing again, it will be too soon.'

Two weeks after his luck at cards, Colonel Klein was back in Berlin. He was uneasy.

He was uneasy about the strange glass sphere that he had won, and the things he saw when he stared deep into it at night. He was uneasy about the way the war was going, seeing no let up in the allied advance. And he was uneasy to the point of fear that he had been summoned back to Berlin on the express wishes of the Reichsfuhrer himself.

Klein had met Heinrich Himmler on two occasions previously, but both had been ceremonial. One was when he entered the SS, his ancestry checked for Aryan purity back to the eighteenth century. The other was at Wewelsburg, Himmler's castle, when together with five comrades he was presented with his SS dagger and ring.

Now he waited in the Reichsfuhrer's anteroom. He had killed men in cold blood, run through a hail of bullets to escape the allied advance in Normandy, picked up a grenade that came in through the window of his staff car and flung it out again - and all without more than a tremor of apprehension. But sitting, waiting for Himmler, Otto Klein found that for the first time he could remember, he was afraid.

Himmler kept him waiting for another ten minutes. Then Klein stood to attention before Himmler's desk for another two before the Reichsfuhrer so much as looked up.

'You may be seated,' he said at last. His voice was clipped and nasal. When he looked up, the light from the desklamp caught his small round glasses, reflecting off them so that they became opaque white. Himmler's face was round, his thin hair receding. His teeth glinted below a stubbly upper lip. Perhaps, Klein thought, this was a smile.

Himmler laid aside the papers he had been working on and stared unnervingly at Klein. 'You are aware, colonel,' he said, 'that any – what shall we say?' He paused to tap the ends of his fingers together as he considered. 'Confiscated? Yes, confiscated. Any confiscated material or possessions of prisoners or victims of war belong to the state.'

Klein had never heard of such a thing. But he could believe it. He nodded, not trusting his voice.

'Good. Good.' Himmler returned to his papers, apparently having finished with Klein.

The colonel cleared his throat nervously.

'Was there anything else?' Himmler asked without looking up.

'I, er... I wondered if that was all, Herr Reichsfuhrer.'

Himmler looked up, an expression of forced patience on his face. 'Unless you can think of some subject that requires our attention,' he said. 'Or,' he added, as if as an afterthought, 'you are aware of some material or possession that falls into the category I mentioned? Something you might wish to declare, perhaps?' He stared up at Klein again. 'Something of value to the Reich. In which I might have an interest? No?' He clicked his tongue in disappointment even before Klein could answer. 'That was all.'

'There...' Klein swallowed. 'There might be one object, sir. Something that chanced to come into my possession. Something in which the Reichsfuhrer might have an interest.'

'Really?' Himmler was leaning forward, elbows on the desk. 'How fortunate. For us both.'

'Indeed, sir.' Klein pulled the glass sphere from his pocket. His hand caught in the material and for a stomach-lurching moment he was afraid he would not get it out again. He set the glass down on the desk, watching for Himmler's reaction.

There was none. No change of expression. Just the hint of a nod.

'And when you look within the glass,' Himmler said slowly, 'you see, what exactly?' His voice was level, but there was an eagerness in it now.

'Images. Pictures. I don't know what they are or what they mean.' Klein shrugged. 'I'm sure they will be more relevant to the Reichsfuhrer.'

'I'm sure they will.' Without having touched the sphere, Himmler leaned back and pulled his papers towards him on the desk. 'Thank you for bringing this to me,' he said as he returned to work. 'The Fuhrer will also, I'm sure, wish me to pass on his gratitude.'

'The Fuhrer?'

'He has expressed an interest in this sphere. This, what shall we call it? This Scrying Glass.'

Himmler looked up again. This time there was no mistaking the slight smile that played on his lips. His eyes were unnaturally wide through the lenses of his glasses. 'I know you are sorry to part with it,' he said.

In a slight daze, Klein turned and left the room. As the door closed behind him he could still hear the forced bark of laughter the Reichsfuhrer had used to punctuate his parting words: 'Although, I suppose some people might actually say that if they never saw it again, it would be too soon.'

Chapter Nineteen

She had to work the computer for him. Claire thought that meant she was in charge, in the driving seat. Usually, she liked to sit at the keyboard. Usually she relished the control. But while Lethbridge-Stewart might not know a lot about computers, she soon realised he knew how to get people to work for him.

More surprising still, she found she did not resent it. Somehow it was more like a partnership than simply taking orders, and she realised why Palmer had taken him the tape. She could imagine he had been so much more than merely a commanding officer – he had been brother, father, mentor and friend to his men as well. And in an organisation with the remit of UNIT, that must have been an awesome combination.

The other thing that surprised her was his intelligence and analytical skill. Her impression of most soldiers was that they merely followed orders, carried out pre-ordained tasks without thought or insight. The higher ranking the officer, the truer it was – only the orders were 'bigger' and came from even higher. While she saw that the retired Brigadier was adept at giving orders, she somehow doubted he had been so accomplished in taking them.

But most of all, when she could not find what he wanted, or the computer did not have the necessary network clearances, he swore at the machine. Not at the person operating it.

'OK,' Claire said at last. 'I think this is the section we're after.'

Both the Brigadier and Claire had assumed that the Ministry of Defence archives and files from 1945 would be on yellowed paper in buff folders on dusty shelves in a forgotten basement. A small bespectacled man who seemed to be called 'Freddo' had led them to a small office, pointed to a PC standing idle on the desk and suggested they help themselves to whatever they wanted.

Freddo handed Claire a key to lock the door behind them if they left the room. The Brigadier put his leather briefcase down on the floor, and motioned for Claire to take the single seat at the computer.

It struck Claire that Freddo was the one contact who could make her work for the Conspiracy Channel both simple and impressive. But ten minutes later she realised that the computer's access was limited to the areas the Brigadier had requested on the phone two hours earlier. And while the information was indeed all online and digitised, it consisted almost entirely of badly-scanned images of the original documents on yellowed paper in buff folders on dusty shelves in a forgotten basement. Which meant they were difficult to read, and offered none of the advantages she might have expected. You couldn't do a text search on them, you couldn't even riffle through them. There was an index document for each folder, but even if you could find something that sounded useful, you had to try to guess what eight-character abbreviation had been used to file that particular document. Assuming it was there at all.

At the Brigadier's suggestion they started by looking at all the index documents and printing them off on a scratchy dot matrix printer. On Claire's advice, they then stuck the printed versions up on the wall so they could see them, and annotate them.

'There are two approaches here,' the Brigadier said as they stared at the plastered wall.

'Start at the beginning and do it methodically, or just pick and choose, you mean?' Claire said.

He glanced sideways at her. 'Actually,' he said almost apologetically, 'I meant we can approach the problem either by trying to ascertain what happened to Hitler at the end of the war, in the Fuhrerbunker, or by looking at alleged sightings of the man after that.'

Claire cursed under her breath. She had assumed he was talking about the files. Of course, he was talking about the problem they were trying to solve – the question to be answered. She, the seasoned researcher, had been concentrating on the medium rather than the message. It took her mind a moment to adjust. 'You mean either we can prove or disprove his death directly, or we can deduce it from whether he was really around after it was supposed to have happened.'

The Brigadier smiled. 'Exactly. The question is, which approach would the available evidence favour?'

Since the documents seemed to be prefixed by a date code, they agreed to start after the war. Whatever files related to the events in the bunker would be harder to identify individually as they all started '445' or '545' meaning they related to April or May of 1945.

'There were a few alleged sightings of Adolf Hitler just after the war,' Claire said. 'The stuff I did was mainly about the bunker so I didn't look at them.' She flicked back her hair as she admitted quietly, 'Maybe I should have.'

The Brigadier's grey moustache twitched slightly. 'Ah,' he said wryly, 'but you were out to prove a point and looking for evidence to support it. Right now, we're trying to ascertain the truth.'

Claire was not sure she liked the implication of that, so she decided to assume it was a joke, and smiled. However accurate it might be.

Actually, they discovered, there were many supposed sightings of the Fuhrer after his alleged death. At first they made notes against the document listings. But after a while they discounted the more obscure or ridiculous.

Adolf Hitler, the Brigadier neatly noted, was living in a hacienda nearly five hundred miles from Buenos Aires in July 1945. The source document for this was a photostatted copy of a letter to a newspaper in Chicago, that had been intercepted by the American Office of Censorship. Claire made a mental note to find out why the country that called itself the home of free speech had an Office of Censorship. The letter went on to give instructions on how to enter the house and what flash-light codes to use to be identified as a friend.

'Do we take this seriously?' Claire wondered.

In answer the Brigadier tapped the bottom of the scanned document on the screen in front of her. There was a scrawled handwritten note that was all but indecipherable. 'He evidently took it seriously.'

Claire peered at the signature. 'Can't quite make it out,' she murmured.

'J. Edgar Hoover,' the Brigadier said. He hesitated, obviously unsure how much she really knew and not wanting to patronise her. 'He was director of the FBI at the time.'

Next they found a clipping from a Russian newspaper that put Hitler and Eva Braun in a castle in Westphalia. Claire was keen to note it, but the Brigadier shook his head.

'Just because it was in a newspaper?' she asked. 'It's not all propaganda and sensation, you know.'

'This is,' the Brigadier told her. 'It's a Soviet newspaper. And Westphalia was in the British zone. They're implying that the British spirited Hitler away.'

'Maybe they did,' Claire suggested, not entirely seriously.

'It would be possible for that to happen and for you not to know about it,' the Brigadier admitted. 'But I'd know.'

She didn't press the point.

Neither of them took seriously suggestions that Hitler had become a hermit in Italy, or a shepherd in the Swiss Alps. He had not, they decided, gone to Ireland, or supplemented his income by working as a croupier in an Evian casino.

'All right,' Lethbridge-Stewart eventually said with a sigh, 'I'm convinced. We aren't going to find anything conclusive here one way or the other. The most we can hope for is corroborative evidence for whatever we can find out about the last days in the bunker.'

'Go to 1945?' Claire asked.

The Brigadier's moustache bristled slightly, as if for some reason he were suppressing a smile at this comment.

But he nodded and she opened one of the 1945 folders. 'This is September, judging by the date codes.' There were only two documents in the folder. 'That large one is probably Hugh Trevor-Roper's report.'

'Report about what?'

Claire smiled. It was good to be able to impart some information of her own for a change. 'He was a major, I think. But in civilian life even then he was a History don at Oxford. The allies had him put together a report into the death of Hitler. It's still the most detailed and probably the most accurate documentary evidence there is.'

The Brigadier nodded thoughtfully. 'We'll look at that after we've assessed the other stuff for ourselves then. Don't want to be led by his conclusions.' He pointed to the screen. 'What's the other file here?'

Claire shrugged and opened it. 'Seems to be translations of Russian stuff. Speeches, documents…' She gave a low whistle as she started to read.

Over her shoulder, the Brigadier was also reading. 'The Russians were the ones who took Berlin,' he said. 'So whatever they had to say is probably worth listening to.'

Claire nodded. 'Look at this – ninth of June. Marshal Zhukov, whoever he was, said: "We have not identified the body of Hitler."'

'Zhukov commanded one of the invading Russian armies.'

'Well he was talking bollocks,' Claire said. 'They knew they had Hitler. They did a post-mortem for God's sake.'

'Did they? Isn't that what we're trying to find out?'

'Yes,' Claire said. 'OK, so they did a post mortem on someone.'

The Brigadier nodded. He pointed lower down the document. 'Here's a report that Stalin told President Truman at Potsdam that he thought Hitler was in Spain or Argentina.'

'He didn't know?' Claire wondered. 'Or did they just not want to tell anyone.'

The Brigadier shrugged. 'You can bet they didn't want to be wrong about it. On the other hand…' His voice tailed off. 'What else is there?'

'Not much.' She scrolled down. 'Some official Soviet statement dated September 1945.' She was about to close the file when the final paragraph caught her eye. Her hand froze on the mouse. 'No trace of the bodies of Hitler or Eva Braun has been discovered,' she read out loud. 'What were they playing at?'

'I see it,' the Brigadier breathed. They both read in silence:

It is established that Hitler, by means of false testimony, sought to hide his traces. Irrefutable proof exists that a small airplane left the Tiergarten at dawn on 30th April 1945 flying towards Hamburg. Three men and a woman are know to have been on board. It has also been established that a large submarine left Hamburg before the arrival of the British forces. Persons unknown were aboard the submarine, among them a woman.

At the bottom was another handwritten annotation. The text was jagged and clipped by the scanning process and Claire struggled to read it. 'Hopkins says Stalin told him one of the men was Bormann.' She looked at the Brigadier. 'I wonder who Hopkins was.'

'I know who Bormann was,' he replied tightly. He was still leaning over her, and he drummed his fingers on the top of the desk for several moments. 'Turn that thing off for a minute,' he said. 'I think we need to find some coffee.'

'You're not wrong.' She switched off the screen, but left the computer running.

'No chance of anything stronger on these premises, I'm afraid,' Lethbridge-Stewart said with a smile.

He stepped away to let her out of the chair. As she moved she caught a reflection in the blank screen. A fleeting glimpse, no more. A flash of imagination.

Probably.

Just for a moment, no longer, she imagined she saw an imp-like face staring back at her, its eyes burning coals within the glass. As if it too had been watching over her shoulder as she read the files. An impression, that was all. Imagination working overtime, she decided. Imps in Dorset, she could cope with. Just about. But she could not imagine them hopping on to an inter city and scurrying about London looking for her.

'Wish I'd thought to bring a hip flask,' the Brigadier said ruefully from the door. 'I could do with a stiff drink.'

'So could I,' Claire told him. She locked the door behind her.

The coffee looked and tasted like mud. It came out of an ancient dispensing machine and arrived in plastic cups that were too thin either to contain the heat of the liquid, or to remain fully rigid when you held them. The curled lip of the cup had been designed so that it was impossible to drink without dribbles of coffee escaping down your chin.

Claire and the Brigadier took their coffee back to the room, where each elected to leave it half drunk at the back of the desk.

It did not take long for Claire to realise that the documents that were filed on the computer were transcriptions of interviews, or original documents from which Trevor Roper had compiled his landmark report. There was even a copy of Hitler and Eva Braun's marriage certificate together with two handwritten pages of background notes.

But if there was significant new evidence, it was not on the network. They sifted through it anyway, but Claire pointed out that they might as well read Trevor Roper's version which was more accessible and meticulously cross-referenced.

'It will be something small. Something that seems insignificant or inconsequential,' Lethbridge-Stewart said.

'What will?'

'Whatever the clue is – if indeed there is a clue – to what really happened.'

'And why do you think that?' she asked.

'Because otherwise someone would already have picked up on it.'

Claire nodded. 'Makes sense.'

The only other document they eventually found, mis-filed, was a copy of the Russian autopsy report. 'They sat on it,' Claire said as she scrolled through the dense text.

'I beg your pardon?'

'Kept it secret. You know.' She yawned. 'You sure you want to look through this lot? I mean, if he was dead…'

The Brigadier considered. 'Can you print it off?' he asked. 'Easier to look through it on paper than on that screen. But I think it might be worth the effort.'

'But if he was dead.'

'*If*,' he reminded her. 'That is what we need to establish. If, as you say, the Soviets kept this post mortem under wraps for over twenty years, maybe they weren't sure it was really Hitler whose body they cut up.'

She paused, letting the blurred page on the screen settle into a slightly sharper image as it stopped moving. 'It's a thought. After all, they didn't even admit they knew he was dead until 1950. Maybe they had some doubt.'

'You saw the reports of aircraft leaving Berlin with mysterious passengers, Stalin's comments, all that. I think they had very grave doubts.' The Brigadier sighed and reached for his coffee. Then he seemed to change his mind, perhaps remembering what it tasted like. 'Why did they get married?' he asked abruptly.

'What?'

'Hitler and Eva Braun. You saw the marriage certificate just now. Why did he bother to marry her?'

'Perhaps,' she offered, only half joking, 'they were in love.'

'You know,' he agreed, 'I think they were. But even so. She had been his mistress, secretly, for years. Why then, as his world fell apart, did he marry her?'

'On a whim? They knew they were going to die.'

'True. But quite a whim. According to the notes with the marriage certificate, they sent Goebbels out into the war in Berlin to find a civic official to perform the ceremony.'

Claire set the autopsy printing. 'Is it important?' she asked over the harsh rasp of the printer.

The Brigadier shrugged. 'It might give us an insight into his state of mind those last days.'

'And hers,' Claire added. 'She came to Berlin to be with him, after all. Left the safety of Munich to come to her death. He told her to leave, and she refused.'

The Brigadier stared at the printer as a page of A4 paper

crawled noisily out of it. 'I'd like to read Trevor Roper's report. But my eyes won't cope with that screen for much longer, and my ears are offended by this thing.'

Claire smiled. 'I've got a copy at home,' she said. 'From that documentary we did. It's in a box in the spare bedroom, I think. How about we finish printing this, then go back to my place for some decent coffee and you can read it there?' She shuddered as she remembered that her flat had been broken into – violated. But at least she would not be alone there. She'd cope.

The Brigadier's moustache twitched again. 'I think we're about done here,' he admitted. 'And at the risk of sounding forward, that's the best offer I've had in a long time.'

They took each page from the printer as it was finished. It seemed to take a painfully long time, and the ribbon was wearing thin.

'The bodies were very badly burned,' Claire remarked as she handed the Brigadier yet another page of fading text. 'Eva Braun's even more than Hitler's, and they only identified him in the end by his teeth. If it was him,' she added.

While they waited for the kettle to come to the boil, Claire started to sort through the mass of cardboard boxes and piles of paper in the spare bedroom.

After a while, Lethbridge-Stewart appeared in the doorway. 'You need a filing clerk,' he said.

'I need an archaeologist,' she retorted as she lifted the lid of another box and peered dubiously inside. 'Ah, this is the one!' She carried the box through to the living room before making the coffee.

Because it was now dark outside, and not at all out of any feeling of paranoia, she drew the curtains before opening the box and pulling out the copy of Trevor Roper's 'The Last Days of Hitler.'

'It's a book,' he said in surprise as he took it from her.

'Published by Macmillan in 1947,' she said. 'That's open government for you.'

The Brigadier snorted. 'No such thing. Mind you, the MOD are pretty meticulous. I think we saw everything they had to offer.' He set the book down and sipped at his coffee. 'This is much better, you know.'

'Thanks.'

'Now the Russians, different kettle of fish.' He jabbed a finger at the pages of the autopsy report lying on the arm of the chair beside him. 'They could have all sorts of other evidence in their archives and not even know it themselves.' He set down the mug. 'Might be worth popping over to see.'

'You think we should go to Russia?' This was more than she had bargained for.

'I have a few contacts over there from... the old days. Did a couple of joint missions actually. Rather hush-hush. And before you ask, no I can't tell you anything about them.' He paused, as if choosing his next words carefully. 'That's one reason of course why, if I do go, you won't be coming with me.'

She was about to protest, to give him a piece of her mind. But as he had been speaking, she had been going through the other documents and papers in her box. Her eyes alighted on a black and white photograph just as she opened her mouth. There was a page of handwritten notes attached to the photo by a paperclip. Her mouth remained open.

Then she swore.

'What is it? What have you found?'

'I'd forgotten,' she said. Her voice betrayed her surprise at how this could be possible. 'Hitler had a double.'

'I don't know much more than this,' she said in response to his rapid fire questions, and handed him the black and white photo and the sheet of notes. The photograph was of a body, lying on its back. A framed picture had been propped against an arm that was across the stomach, so that the picture was angled on the body's chest. Even on close examination, the face seemed to be that of Adolf Hitler. The hair was a similar shade and cut. The toothbrush moustache was immediately recognisable. And there was a neat, dark hole drilled through the centre of the man's forehead.

'The body was found in the water tower in the Reichschancellery grounds. The picture they've put there is Hitler's mother,' Claire explained. She took back her notes and scanned them rapidly. 'When the Russians found the body, they thought it was Hitler. Not surprisingly, looking at him. Some of the senior Nazis they captured even identified it. But others said it wasn't. Nobody knows who it really is. As you can see in the picture, the poor bugger had been shot through the head. We mentioned him in the show, but there isn't much you can make of it really.' She looked over the Brigadier's shoulder. 'Probably not important anyway.'

'On the contrary,' he said. 'I skimmed through this autopsy thing while you were hunting out your crate there. A double for Hitler might explain a lot.'

'But this double didn't fool anyone. At least, not for long. And anyway, it doesn't alter the fact that they found Hitler's body with Eva Braun's in a bomb crater. Even burned to a crisp he was more convincing than this bloke.'

'They found a body with Eva Braun's, true. And yes, he was more convincing as you say than this bloke.' He leaned forward, his eyes shining. 'But if you were going to use a double and try to fool everyone into thinking you were dead, you'd use the most convincing one you could find.'

She took a deep breath as she followed the trail of his logic. 'You're saying that they didn't try to fool anyone that this was Hitler, because it wouldn't have worked.'

'Evidently.'

'But that doesn't mean there wasn't a better, more convincing double available. And maybe he got burned, and Hitler never died at all. So this guy,' she tapped the photo, 'he failed the audition.'

'You have to admit, it's an intriguing possibility. The presence – and it cannot be accidental – of one look-alike suggests there may have been others.' He was on a roll now, talking quickly as he thought it through. 'You told me that the Russians had to identify Hitler by his teeth. This,' he said grabbing the autopsy report and brandishing it, 'says that Hitler's lower jaw was not attached to the body. It wasn't necessarily even from the same corpse!'

'And that's why the Russians were so cagey about it?'

He nodded. 'There's more. The body only had one testicle.'

'The other one burned?'

'Apparently not. And while we all know that "Hitler has only got one ball"…'

'Do we?' she asked, confused.

'I thought we did. But a childish rhyme is not historical evidence, and there is, the autopsy notes, no reason to suppose it was true.'

'But maybe it was,' she said. 'And anyway, aren't you doing what you accused me of earlier? Aren't you looking for evidence to support a theory you already have?'

He smiled. 'Touché, Miss Aldwych. All right then, try this – bodies shrink slightly when they are exposed to intense heat. Sometimes by as much as an inch.'

'I haven't had much experience of charred bodies I'm afraid,' she quipped.

But her smile was wiped away by the way he blinked quickly and looked away. 'Lucky you,' he murmured.

'Sorry. So, what's the point.'

He passed her the report. 'I marked that section while you were looking for Trevor Roper's book. You'll see that it notes that the height of the corpse they examined, the corpse officially identified as Adolf Hitler, was shorter than we know the Fuhrer to have been.' Their eyes locked. She had already read the sentence he had underlined, but he said it anyway: 'Shorter by ten full centimetres.'

In the bottom of the box was a videotape of Claire's documentary. Despite her protestations, the Brigadier insisted that they watch it. She thought she would cringe all the way through while he made sarcastic comments. But they watched in silence, nodding to each other as points were made that they had rediscovered, or when there was something that could be take as further evidence to support the Brigadier's fantastic hypothesis.

Other inconsistencies, like the blood on Hitler's bed that was never explained, they decided they could ignore as well as anyone else.

Afterwards, Claire made more coffee while the Brigadier flicked through the autopsy report yet again. They drank their coffee in near-silence as they thought it through. Claire read the sections of the autopsy that the Brigadier had marked.

She read about how the body had been identified – on the word of a dental assistant examining the charred remains of a lower jaw that had been detached from the skull and comparing what she saw to her memory of Hitler's teeth. She tried to find a hole in the Brigadier's theory. There was only one.

'But if Hitler survived, escaped – why hasn't he turned up again?'

'Why indeed?' the Brigadier replied. His expression was as unreadable as his tone.

Claire thought it through. 'You'll go to Russia then?'

'It seems like the best move.'

'And I can't come?'

'I'm sorry. I… I should be going. Things to arrange, you know.'

She gave him a half-smile. 'That's all right. I won't push it. I know I wouldn't win the argument anyway.' She stood up. 'Let me get you some more coffee.'

'May I borrow this?' He was holding Trevor Roper's book.

'Of course. It'll give you something to read on the plane.'

She carried the empty mugs through to her study and collected another from beside the computer. He was reading the book, and did not seem to notice how long it took her. Then she took all three out to the kitchen.

Once there she pushed the door closed behind her, pausing only to peep back and see that he was still sitting in the armchair, flicking through the book. Beside him, on the wall, his shadow made the same motions – turning pages, leaning forward to read sections more closely. Except that the angle of the table lamp made it look as if his form was misshapen. As if, perched on the arm of the chair beside him, was another tiny figure. Watching.

Nerves, she told herself. Tiredness, and nerves, and imagination. And sure enough, when she wiped her eyes and looked back, there seemed to be nothing out of the ordinary. She put the kettle on.

Lethbridge-Stewart's leather briefcase was still where he had left it when they came in, on the kitchen table.

Chapter Twenty

Winston Churchill signed into the War Rooms and set off for his private study, his mood as gloomy as the corridors he trudged along. He always felt the same dreary déjà vu coming here to this fortress for civil servants; his vitality dulled as if buried deep in the reinforced concrete that kept them safe from attack. All he knew was a weary, festering resentment of Hitler, the man who had made it necessary to live, and work and plan like this skulking in the ground while, up above, London burned. It was something of an irony that coming here, to the one place the bombs could never reach, should place him so bitterly in mind of the carnage wreaked above.

He remembered being here years back, in 1940, insisting his aides and staff accompany him up above to the rooftop, so that they could watch the bombs fall on the city's back. To witness helplessly each explosion, each senseless ruination of the skyline, the snuffing out of so many lives, so that in the morning when the death statistics found their way to in-trays each man there could marry the numbers to a meaning.

His footsteps echoed disconsolately on the tiled floor. Could it really be four years since the Blitz this coming September? And in June, only a month ago, the new terror had begun, when the first V1s had been launched at London. Churchill had been forced to come here more often again since then. The destruction of life surrounded him still, but the British *way* of life would never be destroyed. Churchill had pledged that to the people of Great Britain. And the war *would* be won, and decisively so. One day.

He rounded a corner. In the dim light he perceived the usual dog-eared sign on the wall: a bare light bulb glowing fiercely with a red line through it, big black capitals demanding HAVE YOU SWITCHED OFF?

'If only I could,' grumbled Churchill, fishing in his pocket for the heavy iron key as he finally reached his office door.

But the door was unlocked.

Churchill was about to charge off and find a secretary to bully about security when the door opened abruptly.

Churchill should have been angry, outraged, or at the very least surprised. But when he saw who it was waiting for him inside, dressed in a dark, expensive-looking suit and sitting nonchalantly behind the oak desk as if he'd been casually ruling the roost in Churchill's absence, he wasn't surprised in the least. He wasn't even surprised that the man looked just the same as when last they'd met, back when the King had abdicated, fully eight years ago.* His straggly-curled hair was perhaps a little longer but it was still blond, and his full, proud face was barely lined.

'Doctor,' said Churchill, a slow smile spreading across his face.

'It's been a while, Winston.'

'I'm surprised our paths haven't crossed sooner in this wretched war.'

'So am I. The timing of my arrivals has hardly improved.'

Churchill chuckled to hear that warm, familiar voice; that of a born orator. 'How on Earth did you get in here?'

The Doctor tapped his nose. 'Careless talk costs lives,' he said innocently.

Churchill roared with laughter and shook the Doctor heartily by the hand. 'It's good to see you, my friend. Though I trust your arrival won't herald a further appearance from that troublesome countess?'

'I've come to you because I need your help.'

'My help?' Churchill said vaguely, as he weighed appreciatively a heavy crystal decanter, half-filled with brandy, from the desk, and hunted about for a second glass.

'I need you to get me into France.'

Churchill was glad he'd not found the glass, for fear of dropping it.

The Doctor looked idly about the war room for the hundredth

* See *Doctor Who – Players*

157

time, barely stifling an enormous yawn. Every feature of the room had been carefully prepared with obsessive military fastidiousness, though the air was thick now with wreaths of cigar smoke and disgruntled conversation. Heavy trestle tables were arranged in a large square ring, with desk blotters perfectly in place in the middle of each. Seated in pride of place was Churchill, and beside him was a man the Doctor thought he recognised, the Prime Minister's trusted advisor Professor Lindemann – or would he be Lord Cherwell by now? The Doctor hadn't paid too much attention at the introductions, having taken an instant and consuming dislike to the elderly Air Marshall Anthony Forbes-Bennett, a chinless wonder with the personality of a wet fish and something of the appearance. He'd looked down his long nose at the Doctor and muttered something to the effect that Churchill's summons today was a waste of time better spent winning the war. The wretched pomposity of the man had obfuscated a whole host of double-barrelled Generals and bewhiskered Admirals and heaven knew who else, as they'd filed solemnly into the room and shaken hands.

There were four clocks, one on each wall, so each VIP present knew precisely how long they had before reporting to their next engagements. The Doctor was using his to count off the tedious minutes spent trying to prise open so many firmly closed military minds. He wondered what the collective noun for so many military high-ups was, and his gaze fell again on Forbes-Bennett.

'A dunderhead?' he mused. The room fell silent as grave faces turned to him. The Doctor smiled in apology. 'I'm so sorry, did I say that aloud?'

Air Marshall Forbes-Bennett raised an eyebrow and smiled thinly. 'Were we all to be so candid with our private thoughts on your enterprise, Doctor, I fear you would be sorry indeed.'

The Doctor matched his smile for enthusiasm. 'I fear you don't know me very well, Air Marshall.'

Churchill turned to Forbes-Bennett. 'Anthony,' he rumbled, 'I know the Doctor of old. His credentials are impeccable, and his mission may be of the most vital importance.'

'Or it may be a capricious waste of our resources,' scoffed Forbes-Watson. 'And as for this preposterous rot about a planned German incursion…'

'I trust the Doctor's sources,' Churchill said gravely.

'But what *are* his sources?' Forbes-Bennett turned to the Doctor. 'Frankly, sir, I suspect your intelligence is most dubious.'

'Your own is practically non-existent!' the Doctor countered furiously. '*Sir!*'

There was a scandalised outbreak of muttering until Churchill roared, 'Gentlemen!' Hush fell heavily. 'May I remind you this is a council of war? We are not in a kindergarten.'

'More an old folk's home,' the Doctor muttered under his breath, smiling sweetly at Forbes-Bennett.

Churchill turned to his aide. 'Strike all that from the minutes.' He straightened in his seat, puffed on his fat cigar and knitted together his fat fingers, gathering himself to speak. An air of expectancy was immediate in the smoky room.

'Gentlemen, we can consider at length the implications of the Doctor's most valued information as regards a German military presence on these shores. But his request that he be smuggled into France, however outlandish it may initially seem to you, must surely be granted swiftly. I have already said that I will vouchsafe for the Doctor absolutely. In the past he has been a great friend to both our country and sovereign.'

Forbes-Bennett looked beadily at the Doctor, but his expression had softened a little. 'You place a good deal of trust in him.'

Churchill nodded. 'I do.'

The Doctor kept his face carefully neutral but sank back in his chair, relieved, sensing the Air Marshall's resistance weakening in the face of Winston's show of support.

'Our agents can concoct a cover story and provide documents that will serve the Doctor's planned covert activities in Germany,' Churchill continued. 'The apparatus already exists for taking him behind enemy lines. I suggest we employ it without further tarry.'

One of the generals piped up, eager to please: 'Our sources in the Maquis can be notified tonight… The good weather should hold. We're dropping an agent over Clermont-Ferrand tomorrow. Reckon you can tag along, Doctor.'

'In a Halifax?' The Doctor gleefully rubbed his hands together. 'A mark VII? Splendid, I've not been up in one of those...' he checked the clock. '...until next March.'

Ringed by confused faces, the Doctor cleared his throat and moved swiftly on. 'No. 148 squadron, I wonder?'

'624 operate over France,' Forbes-Bennett corrected him automatically.

The Doctor smiled indulgently and gestured grandiosely at the general. 'You'll forgive me, Air Marshall, but I think it's no. 148 squadron that work with MI6 on covert duties?'

Forbes-Bennett's thin face reddened.

Churchill turned to him, amusement on his craggy features. 'You were questioning the veracity of the Doctor's intelligence, Anthony...?'

The night roared past outside as the Doctor readied himself for the jump. He idly checked his parachute rig, patted his skinny secret agent companion heartily on the back and leapt enthusiastically from the Halifax.

Flashes of torch light below gave him something to aim for, Maquis agents hiding out in the hills. They would shelter him and disguise him before sending him on the first leg of his perilous journey cross-country to the German heartland. Meanwhile, British Intelligence experts would be conjuring a wealth of papers and documents, creating a suitably impressive lifetime of pseudo-scientific achievements on his behalf. All he could do then was hope that Himmler would consider his services indispensable as occult advisor for the Turelhampton raid next month.

He pondered. The next few days would be filled with risk and danger, and adventure.

And he could think of nowhere he would rather be.

Relishing the trials ahead, the Doctor kicked his legs and gave himself up happily to the descent through the warm night air.

Chapter Twenty-one

The Fuhrer, as always, was sceptical. But he watched in silence as they prepared.

Himmler, by contrast, was shaking with nervous energy. He checked constantly that the table was exactly aligned, that the cloth on it was pulled straight, that the circle marked on the floor in chalk was unblemished. Between these checks and hurried, officious conversations snatched with the people setting up, he returned to Hitler to provide a running commentary, as if he were afraid that the Fuhrer might get bored and leave unless he was kept appraised of the situation.

'The cloth on the table, and indeed the gloves the officiating lama will wear are suffused with copper oxide,' he confided in a low voice.

Hitler nodded as if that made perfect sense. In fact, it made no matter to him whatsoever.

But Heinrich Himmler was keen to explain. 'We have found that the substance enhances the effect. Just as the lamas my people persuaded to join us from Tibet are the most adept at achieving the perfect state of mind. The stillness of being that is essential for clarity.'

'I thought you said that one of your own colonels could do it,' Hitler remarked.

'Indeed. And I believe several others have shown an aptitude. But the Tibetans, their abilities are far in excess. As we shall shortly see.'

'I hope so, Heinrich,' the Fuhrer said quietly. 'I certainly hope so.'

But Himmler had already gone, scurried away to supervise the positioning of the film camera.

Klein had imagined that he would be posted back to his unit immediately. Or possibly, sent to the Eastern front. Instead he was informed that he had an office in the Reichschancellery and a staff of researchers. He was given no further information, just a roll of film together with a projector and screen.

He watched the film three times. By the end of it he was little wiser. He watched as six grainy people in near-darkness formed a circle around a seventh who stood at a table. All were wearing long monastic robes.

Then the camera closed in on the table, and Klein could see the Scrying Glass – his Scrying Glass – set upon it, and he started to understand. He watched the images that seemed to form within the glass. Even on the film they were clearer than anything he had seen. But somehow, divorced from reality on to celluloid they were less intense, less unsettling.

Himmler came to see him the next day. The presence of the Reichsfuhrer in his own office was even more unnerving than Klein's interview with him several days earlier. Klein leaped to his feet as Himmler entered unannounced, clicking his heels together smartly.

Without a word, Himmler handed Klein a plain white envelope. Then he sat down, motioning Klein to do the same.

The envelope was not sealed. Klein pulled the flap from inside, and extracted a single piece of paper. It was thick, white, and headed with a stylised eagle holding a swastika in its claws.

'Aloud, if you would be so kind,' Himmler murmured.

Klein read. 'To whom it may concern. Colonel Otto Klein of the SS is acting on my direct instructions. He is to be accorded every facility and his urgent work for the Reich has the utmost priority. All personnel of whatever rank and station will provide him with whatever he wishes with the greatest expedition.'

Klein looked up in amazement.

Himmler was nodding slowly, a slight smile on his lips. 'And is it signed?' he inquired, though Klein was sure that he already knew the answer.

'Adolf Hitler,' he read, trying to keep his voice level.

'May I?' Himmler reached out, and Klein immediately handed him the letter. Himmler scanned it as if he had never seen it before, which Klein was certain was not the case. Then he handed it back and gave his curious half-bark of laughter. 'It would appear,' he said with amusement, 'that even I should have to consider myself at your disposal.' The sparkle of amusement in his eyes died. 'If you so desired.'

Klein had no illusions about that either. 'The Reichsfuhrer is too kind,' he muttered. 'Though,' he added, surprising himself, 'I would ask one thing.'

Himmler's eyes were flint, though the vague traces of the smile lingered on his lips as he waved a hand.

'Perhaps the Reichsfuhrer would be good enough to explain what is expected of me. What is my urgent work of the utmost priority?'

'Ah. You have seen the film?'

'Several times.'

'Good. And..?'

Klein shrugged. 'It shows a ceremony of some kind. Involving the Scrying Glass that you –' He caught himself. 'Er, that I delivered to you.'

'Indeed. And that ceremony, the details of which need not bother us here and now, achieved uncommon effects, I think you would agree.'

Klein nodded.

'The Fuhrer was most impressed.' Himmler leaned forward. 'And it takes a lot to impress the Fuhrer these days. Especially in such arcane matters.' He leaned back again. 'The images, within the Glass. What did you make of them?'

Klein chose his words carefully. He had thought through what answer he might give to this question many times since he had seen the film. 'There is a succession of images. Almost a narrative. It is unlike anything I saw within the Glass.'

'And what did you see?'

'What I took to be the future.'

Himmler nodded. 'Why so?'

'Partly because of what Brun told me he had seen. Partly because it seemed that what I saw often came to pass.'

'Go on.'

'But, as I say, Reichsfuhrer, this was different. Almost like a narrative, a movie. It starts with what seems to be a camera mounted on a plane. A plane that is approaching land from high altitude, down through the clouds. That aircraft is then engaged by British fighters and brought down. There is a confusion of images – the land growing closer, larger. The sky as the craft twists and turns. Smoke, flame, confusion. And then, the rapid approach of the site where the craft crashed.'

The Reichsfuhrer was leaning forward eagerly. 'And the final images, what did you make of those?'

Klein shrugged. 'A cave perhaps? Dark, anyway. Or smoky. The walls seemed curved, the ceiling vaulted. Strange caskets, or cabinets, arranged in a circle. And then, in the centre of that circle, the final image...'

'Yes, Colonel Klein?'

'The Scrying Glass. An image of itself.'

'You are right,' Himmler told him. 'It was smoky, that place. A red, misty image within the glass.' He stared of into space for a moment. 'Perhaps we should have used colour film. No matter.'

'I am still not – ' Klein began.

But Himmler cut him off. 'And you are right that the images were different. At other ceremonies we have held to conjure forth the images in the glass, we too have seen the future – the glorious future of the Reich. But this ceremony was different. This time we wanted to try to learn the mysteries of the Glass itself. Its origins perhaps.'

'You can do that? Ask it?'

'Not easily. But you saw the result.'

'Whatever it was,' Klein murmured.

'It was the origin of the Scrying Glass. And your mission, Colonel Klein, is to discover what other artefacts of occult and arcane power came with it.'

Klein just stared at him.

'The coastline is distinctive. It should be possible to identify the village where the, what shall we say? The craft came down.'

'And then what?' Klein asked, his mouth suddenly dry.

'And then you will plan an operation to go to this place, find the craft and learn its mysteries.' Himmler stood up. 'You have five days.'

The Fuhrer listened as he leafed through the thick file. Himmler stood beside him, reaching down to point out pages and sections of interest as he spoke.

'You will see from this frame of the film that the coastline is clearly visible, and distinctive.' His finger moved across to a section of a map. It showed the southern coast of the English county of Dorset. 'On the seventeenth of May this year, our tracking stations observed an unidentified contact that was intercepted and shot down by a group of RAF Hurricanes from their 482 squadron. We assumed it was a training exercise of some sort. But perhaps not. While the interception was over the Channel, the images in the Glass seemed to show that the craft drifted for a while before it finally came down.'

The Fuhrer nodded and turned several pages. 'And it came down... here?' he asked as he found another map – a large scale map of an English village. 'In Turelhampton?'

'So Colonel Klein assures me. There is a frame from the film, just before the apparent impact. I am told that the church that is plainly visible towards the upper left corner – here – has a distinctive tower, detached from the main part of the church.'

'That is rare,' the Fuhrer agreed.

Himmler laughed. 'There is a local story that the devil moved the tower to spite the saintly villagers. Apparently if you were to walk backwards around the tower thirteen times, the Devil would appear.'

Slowly, Adolf Hitler turned to look at Himmler. His bright blue eyes bored into the Reichsfuhrer's smile. Himmler coughed, the smile died. 'There are other indications as well,' he went on quickly. 'The formation of the cliffs, the short distance from the coast, the treeline...'

Hitler turned the page, not waiting for Himmler to finish. 'What is this?'

The next page was taken up with a photostatted copy of an official document. It was headed 'Southern Command' and it was in English.

'Ah, this is the letter sent to the villagers of Turelhampton. There is a translation overleaf, but it says in short that their property is required for training purposes.'

Hitler turned the page, and Himmler read out loud sections from the translation. 'In order to give our troops the fullest opportunity to perfect their training... The most careful search has been made to find an area suitable for the Army's purposes, etcetera... You will realise that the chosen area must be cleared of all civilians...'

'And was it?' Hitler interrupted.

Himmler nodded. 'That same night. The letters were sent several days later. If you will turn to the proposed details of the raid, we have several aerial photographs of the village taken this week. Although we lost four spotter planes getting them. Allow me.' He reached out and turned to the appropriate section of the report. 'You will notice that there is a conspicuous absence of troops perfecting their training, or anything else, in that area. Unlike most of the South Coast of Britain at the moment as they try to consolidate their expedition into France.'

'You think a raid is feasible?' Again Hitler's piercing stare was turned on Himmler. 'If there are more artefacts there, potential weapons even, then we must have them.'

'To prevent the allies from using them,' Himmler said.

The Fuhrer shook his head. 'To turn the tide of the war,' he said. He waved Himmler to a seat opposite him. 'Tell me the plan.'

'A raid is certainly feasible. A small incursion, perhaps a dozen men. Colonel Klein proposes the use of Bibers.'

'The mini submarines?' The Fuhrer considered. 'They are ready?'

'Speer tells me that we are planning to use them operationally in the next month. They are proven in trials. The results are encouraging. They would obviate the problems of getting a plane over the area and making a clandestine parachute drop.'

'Very well. Go on.'

'Klein has suggested a man to lead the raiding party. Captain Voss, a most reliable man. But we still need to identify an expert officer to make decisions relating to whatever we find. Someone who has knowledge of these matters and can determine the priorities and relative importance of material to be retrieved.'

'Is there such a person?' the Fuhrer asked.

'I have several such people on my staff,' Himmler announced. 'And Klein's team has identified another two possibilities from staff files and service records.' Himmler leaned forwards, pointing to the report now lying closed on the desk. 'There is a brief list of the seven possible candidates at the back of the proposal, my Fuhrer.'

Hitler turned to it, and scanned the names. There were no details or explanations beside them. His eyes stopped at the penultimate name on the list. His finger tapped it several times. 'This is the man,' he said. 'He will lead the expedition.'

Himmler craned to see which name the Fuhrer had picked. 'May I ask..?' He let the question hang.

'I know the man. He is supremely able and inspires confidence.' Hitler nodded as he looked down at the name again. He smiled. 'Major Johann Schmidt, of the Fifth Medical Corps here in Berlin, if I remember correctly,' he said. 'Yes, he is the perfect choice.' He looked up at Himmler. 'Give him my regards.'

Himmler blinked. This man must indeed be able and talented to inspire such appreciation from the Fuhrer. 'Very well.'

'An excellent plan,' Hitler said as he closed the file. 'Oh and, by the way, about Major Schmidt – he prefers to be known simply as *the Doctor.*'

Chapter Twenty-two

Whatever the true economic situation in the former Soviet Union, Lethbridge-Stewart found himself experiencing a healthy dash of déjà vu when he got off the plane at Moscow airport. He was met by an official car, and just as every other time he had been to Russia for secret negotiations about UNIT operations behind the Iron Curtain, or more recently to advise the Russian Special Operations Forces, as they called their own version of UNIT, the car was black. Just like every other time, it smelled of cigarette smoke, and the heating did not work.

So, just as every other time he had stayed in a Moscow hotel, the Brigadier automatically assumed the room, the phone, and probably even the shaving mirror were bugged. The fact that there was no hot water, no plug in the sink, and the telephone crackled like a chip pan only added to his feeling that despite what he had heard and read, little had changed here.

He was still having a meagre breakfast in the hotel restaurant when the woman arrived. She was a short woman, in her late sixties at least. Her white hair was tied in a bun on her head and she regarded the Brigadier through small round spectacles as he spread oily butter on his black bread. Eventually he could ignore her shadow over his plate no longer and looked up.

'Brigadier?' she demanded as soon as she had his attention.

He nodded, not wanting to risk trying to talk through the crumbly dry bread.

'I am Irina Kobulov. From the State Special Trophy Archive.' She thrust out her hand so violently that the Brigadier flinched.

He swallowed the bread and quickly washed it down with a mouthful of black coffee so strong and viscous you could stand the spoon up in it. 'Delighted,' he lied. 'I was led to believe that while I was welcome to visit, it was entirely unofficial. I was expecting to have to make my own way there. Lethbridge-Stewart, at your service.' Her grip, he noted, was as firm as his own.

'No,' she barked in her heavily accented English. 'It is I who am at your service. Special assignment, very short notice. We go now, yes?' But if it was intended as a question, she did not wait for a reply. She spun rapidly on her Rosa Klebb heels and clacked across the wooden floor towards the door.

The Brigadier hurriedly dropped his napkin on his side plate and followed her. His guess was that she had a car outside – a black car with no heating that stank of cigarettes.

Irina Kobulov turned out to be rather more helpful than the Brigadier had expected from their initial meeting. She explained that she did not actually work at the Archive, but had been drafted in to help after retiring from the Diplomatic Service. The Brigadier raised an eyebrow and said nothing.

But she had a way of getting what the Brigadier wanted, and getting it quickly. Whatever rank or position within the Diplomatic service she had actually held, assuming she wasn't actually ex-KGB, the Archivists jumped at her command.

She also proved to be well aware of the material that was available, and had already produced a list, in English, from which the Brigadier could choose.

'I've read the autopsy report,' the Brigadier began.

'Which one?' she snapped. 'There were two.'

'Er, the official one,' the Brigadier hazarded.

Irina Kobulov sniffed emphatically. 'I will get you copy of the second autopsy,' she promised. 'You will also want to see the file on Operation Myth.'

The file consisted of six buff-coloured folders tied with faded red ribbon. An archivist dumped them on the small, plain wooden table in the small, plain wood-panelled room where the Brigadier and Irina were sitting.

When they were alone again, the Brigadier moved his briefcase from the table and set it down on top of a plain wooden filing cabinet behind them so he had room to examine the folders. 'Tell me,' he said slowly, 'what exactly is Operation Myth?'

She seemed to soften slightly at this. Perhaps, he thought she was pleased to be asked a question so she could demonstrate her expertise, or perhaps she was pleased that he would admit he did not know everything. 'Perhaps I translate badly,' she said. 'The official title is *IG-23 – Hitler and his Entourage*, but everyone knows it as the Operation Myth file. It is what you have been calling The Hitler Archive. It is everything about Hitler from his last days in the Reichschancellery Bunker, through to Magdeburg in 1970.'

The Brigadier caught his breath. '1970?'

She frowned. 'You do not know what happened to Hitler, and to Eva Braun, after their deaths?'

He leaned forward, facing her across the table. 'Perhaps, to save me ploughing through this lot in its entirety, you could tell me?'

At this, she actually smiled.

There was a kettle on a low table in the corner of the room. On a tray beside it were coffee sachets, powdered milk, sugar, and a stack of plastic cups together with several lids to keep the coffee hot. Remembering the coffee at the hotel, the Brigadier decided perhaps he would not risk it. He offered Irina Kobulov a cup as she started to speak, but she shook her head with a vehemence that suggested he had made the right decision.

Her story turned out to be interesting, but probably not relevant the Brigadier decided as he listened. However, he knew from experience that where the Doctor was involved you could never be certain what made sense or mattered. So he made notes as she spoke, and if nothing else he decided he was making diplomatic progress.

The autopsies were done in Buch, and afterwards the bodies of the Hitlers and the Goebbels family – including their six dead children – were buried there together with the remains of General Krebs and two dogs exhumed from the Reichschancellery garden. Except for the jaws and teeth from Hitler and his wife, which were sent to Moscow.

When the Russians left Buch, all the bodies were dug up again, this time to be reburied at Finow, about thirty miles away.

Irina leafed through the loose papers in one of the folders to find what she needed before she continued. 'Ah, yes. On June 3rd 1945, that was when the bodies were again moved.'

'Again?' This was taking on the appearance of a Whitehall Farce, the Brigadier decided. But he was silenced by her glare.

'Again,' she insisted. 'They were buried at Ratenow.' She consulted the papers again. 'At a depth of one point seven metres, laid out East to West in the following order.' She cleared her throat. The Brigadier breathed deeply. 'Adolf Hitler, Eva Braun, Herr Goebbels, Magda Goebbels, General Krebs, the Goebbels children. Then pine trees were planted.'

He was tempted to ask about the dogs. But he restrained himself. 'So that is Hitler's final resting place,' he mused. 'A pine forest.'

'No,' she told him flatly. She was sifting through papers again. 'In February 1946 the bodies were removed to Magdeburg and buried in the courtyard of number 36 Westerndstrasse at a depth of two metres.'

'Why was that address chosen?' He felt he was losing the plot a little here.

'Headquarters of Smersh in that region,' she said simply.

'And what happened in 1970?'

She gave another little sniff. 'Building was returned to DDR, to East Germany, and Smersh moved out. So head of the KGB, Yuri Andropov, ordered the bodies destroyed.'

That made sense, the Brigadier decided. The Russians were nothing if not methodical. They would want to take no chances, and even the very slight risk that someone might stumble across and identify the secret grave of Adolf Hitler would be avoided if at all possible. 'And they *were* destroyed?'

'Incinerated. Utterly. It was called Operation Archive.'

'Strange name.' Usually, the Brigadier knew, code names bore some tangential relevance to the operation itself.

She shrugged. 'Cover story was that Counter Intelligence had discovered there were secret Nazi documents buried in the courtyard. That explained the digging. Then the bodies, the bones, were mixed up including the dogs'. They were incinerated on 5th April 1970 on waste ground at Schonebeck. The ground on which they were burned was dug out and thrown into the river.' She sat back and regarded him for several moments. 'You have not told me why you are here,' she said at last. 'But if you are looking for evidence that Hitler survived, there is none. He is dead, and his remains are almost all destroyed.'

He nodded. It certainly seemed that way. 'So, just the teeth and jaw bone survived,' he said.

She smiled thinly. 'And the skull fragments, of course. You wish to see them?'

The picture was grainy and small. The bandwidth wasn't great, so the movement was jerky and frames seemed to overlap. But the sound was quite good, Claire decided. It was pumped up to full volume through the twin speakers attached to her PC, and she was probably running up a huge bill in connect time even though the call was a freephone number. She hoped she was recording the sound on her tape deck, and filling her hard disk with stored frames from the webcam.

After a while she got bored with the overlapping images, and slowed the frame rate to just one image a minute. If nothing else, it would prolong the life of the camera's battery and the storage on her disc.

She was amazed, actually, that it worked. Even if the technology held up and the batteries didn't die on her, any number of things could have gone wrong. They might have found the tiny camera and its transmitter and power source at the airport. Or the building might be shielded in some way so that it couldn't connect and broadcast its pictures and sound to the website she had set up. Or the Brigadier might himself have found the camera concealed within his briefcase, or left his briefcase behind or in the hotel. Or even just stuck it in a corner of the room so that the camera saw nothing and the sound was muffled.

But Claire's luck had held at every stage. And now she had a good view over the Brigadier's shoulder, and listened as the little old lady ordered up Hitler's skull fragments. She watched as the Brigadier drew one of the folders across the table and began to look through it. The documents within were all in Russian of course, and he had to ask the woman to translate. That suited Claire fine – another piece of luck.

The tape in the cassette captured her reedy voice as she read the Brigadier extracts from the second autopsy performed on Hitler as they waited for his skull. Then she read him, rather more reluctantly it seemed to Claire, parts of the initial post mortem performed on Eva Braun.

'The condition of the body made immediate identification impossible, as with Hitler,' she said thinly. 'Braun's body was even more badly burned. But it was a female aged between thirty and forty. She was identified by the remains of her teeth. There were fragments of glass in the mouth, assumed to be from a poison ampoule. Despite her other injuries, the commission concluded that she had died from cyanide poisoning, like Hitler.'

A still frame caught her in the act of closing the folder. Over the image, the Brigadier's voice was strong and firm. 'What other injuries?'

'I am sorry?'

'You said despite other injuries.'

'The body was… damaged.'

'In what way?'

Claire could hear the shrug in her voice. 'A splinter injury to the thorax and hemothorax, also to one lung. Metal fragments – what do you say? Shrapnel? Shrapnel was found in the body. Shell splinters.' There was a pause. Then: 'The bodies were found in a shell crater after all.'

There was a confused noise after that, which as the next frame came up, Claire realised was the door opening and a space being cleared on the table so that an old, discoloured cardboard box could be set down. She had a good view from above of the contents of the box. It looked like old bones.

* * *

173

'May I?'

She nodded, and the Brigadier carefully lifted the fragments of skull from the ancient box. There were four of them. The largest had a hole in it.

'The box was used for ball point pens,' she said apologetically as the Brigadier laid out the pieces of skull on the table. He had expected to feel some awe, some sense of history. But he felt nothing at all. Just a professional detachment.

'That's a bullet hole,' he said, pointing to it.

She nodded. 'Second autopsy suggests the bullet entered through the roof of the mouth and exited there.'

'But the first autopsy says he took cyanide.'

'These fragments were found later, when the crater was re-excavated for the second investigation. It seems he took poison and shot himself at the same time.'

'I don't believe that was made public,' the Brigadier observed dryly.

'In Russia,' she told him, 'many things are not made public. It suited Stalin that Hitler took poison – the death of a coward.'

'A bullet is more honourable, is it?' the Brigadier asked. He did not expect an answer from her, though he had one of his own. He picked up the largest fragment and examined it closely. The edges were ragged and crumbling under his touch. 'Have these been DNA tested?' he asked her.

'Why? We have nothing to compare the results to. It would tell us nothing.'

He sucked in his cheeks. 'Yes, good point.'

She pressed home her argument. 'We could perhaps also test the bodily fluids, but that would only tell us it is the same body, not whose body it is.'

'Mmm.' He set down the piece of skull beside the others. She had gone very quiet, and he looked up. There was something in her face. He could not read it, but her eyes were slightly wide as if she was aware she had said something she should not have. He replayed her words in his mind.

'What bodily fluids would those be?' he asked innocently.

* * *

174

Claire leaned forward. She had caught the significance too. Maybe there was nothing to it, but the woman had definitely misspoken. Perhaps it was simply that she was not supposed to know.

'After the autopsies, the bodily fluids from Hitler and the others were taken to Cellar 291. I believe they are still archived here. Somewhere.'

'Could I see them?'

'Why?' she asked, just too quickly it seemed to Claire.

The Brigadier's tone was light by comparison. 'Oh, just morbid curiosity I suppose.'

While the Brigadier waited for Irina to return, Claire made herself coffee. The Brigadier seemed content, according to the webcam shots to leaf through each of the six folders, one by one. He seemed to examine each sheet of paper in each file in turn. She wondered what he was hoping to find. Probably he did not know.

There was movement in the background of the frame. She caught it out of the corner of her eye as the Brigadier remained unmoved between the two frames. Probably the door beginning to open, she decided. The next frame would probably show Irina again at the table a minute later with two flasks, or bottle or jars. In what did the Russians preserve the bodily fluids of dead dictators, she wondered.

But the next frame showed no change. And it struck her that in any case she would have heard the door open before the frame appeared. Irritated, Claire recalled the previous couple of frames to see what the difference was. Had she imagined it? Not that it mattered, she thought. But it was something to do while she waited.

There it was – in the background. Something had moved. Close to the table with the kettle. The stack of plastic cups had been visible, but in the second of the frames it was obscured. She moved the live webcam window to the corner of her screen, and concentrated on the single frame. She enlarged the area close to the kettle, peering at the dim, grainy image. She could see nothing.

But it was intriguing and worrying her. So she called up the webcam properties window and adjusted the resolution. The next frame would take longer to download, and eat up space on her disc. But it would be high enough resolution to make out whatever was beside the kettle in the shadows in the corner of the room.

She heard the door creak open as the image appeared, line by line. She heard the glass jars being set down carefully on the table, and the shuffle of papers as the Brigadier moved them out of the way.

She heard him demand: 'What's this? Why didn't you tell me about this?'

And the woman's startled bluster of a reply: 'It is in English. I thought you would know...'

She heard the Brigadier's low grunt in response.

But all she saw, still grainy, still shadowed, still more of an outline in the window than a clear image, was the squat shape of the imp-like creature crouching in the corner of the room. Its eyes were alive with inner intensity as it watched events unfold.

Chapter Twenty-three

Churchill's agents had only been able to do so much. They had kitted out the Doctor with the necessary personal papers, and suggested how and where he might be able to get faked records into the German system. The Doctor had had almost a month of free time in which to do this, though he was conscious that the earlier would be the better.

He had little trouble getting employment in the records office, his papers and – ironically – doctor's certificate attesting to his terrible wounds sustained on the Russian front during Barbarossa in 1941. He enjoyed wearing the eye patch, found no difficulty preparing and filing a complete fake identity, and spent the evenings making an in-depth survey of the Berlin restaurants.

In fact, it was almost childishly simple, he thought to himself one evening as he sampled a fine wine and decided that the next day he should get himself attached to the military unit his records said he was posted to. The entire system was methodical to the point of obsession. But it was entirely geared to ensuring that no records went astray and that all were accounted for at every stage of every process. Adding new records was, he decided in retrospect, a doddle. And he smiled benignly at the waiter as if to prove his own point.

No, he decided, the hardest part, aside from remembering which leg he had been wounded in and limping accordingly, was yet to come. He now had to place his faith in the system he had so easily subverted, cross his fingers and hope that Heinrich Himmler had the good sense to recruit him for the forthcoming Turelhampton mission.

The next morning, Major Johann Schmidt reported for duty at the Fifth Medical Corps headquarters in Friedrichstrasse. This happened to coincide with the departure of Colonel Johann

Schmidt from the Reich Records Department. And while neither group recalled that they were expecting either to lose or to gain a member of staff, each discovered on checking that the paperwork was in order and had actually been on file for months.

For five days the new Major acted as an advisor to the Medical corps. He helped with the filing, outlined ways of streamlining procedures, and even suggested improved procedures to several of the surgeons. Within that time he became hugely respected and soon everyone knew the large immaculately uniformed, if rather ample, figure by sight. They smiled at the way his uncommonly long curly blond hair poked out from under his uniform cap, and were flattered by the way he greeted them all by name.

So they were sorry when he was called away. Rumours that his expertise and experience had been requested by none other than Reichsfuhrer Himmler himself did not surprise them.

Wewelsburg, Himmler's huge stone-built castle in Westphalia, was large and square. As he was driven in through the main entrance, the Doctor was impressed by the work that had gone into the restoration and rebuilding of it. He was also saddened at the cost and lack of historical appreciation. He was almost overcome by a sense of foreboding and lurking malevolence.

He was led through to the massive dining hall. In the centre of the huge room stood a large, round oak table. There were twelve high-backed chairs positioned around it. On the far side of the table, dwarfed by the other elements of the theatrical tableau, sat Heinrich Himmler.

'I am told that you like to be called "The Doctor", Major Schmidt.' His voice was almost lost in the vastness of the room.

'And I see that you like to play at King Arthur and the Knights of the Round Table.'

Himmler blinked. 'The Fuhrer thinks very highly of you,' he said slowly, making it clear that he would not otherwise countenance such a quip.

The Doctor frowned. He had not been expecting that. Had Hitler himself seen his records? No, from Himmler's tone it was more than that. 'Well,' he said seating himself opposite Himmler, 'I have lots of thoughts about the Fuhrer too.'

'He did not, however, mention how unconventional you seem to be.'

The Doctor smiled. 'You must mean the length of my hair. Finding a decent barber in these benighted days is so difficult, don't you find?' He glanced at Himmler's receding hairline. 'Or perhaps you don't.'

'I meant your manner,' the Reichsfuhrer said levelly.

'Ah. Well. Yes.' The Doctor struggled to seem contrite. 'Well,' he offered, 'I can always get my hair cut.'

Himmler tapped the tips of his fingers together as he considered how to respond to this. 'The Fuhrer is convinced that you are the man for the task I have,' he said at last.

'But you are not convinced?'

Himmler did not reply.

So the Doctor continued. 'I don't know what this task you mention might be,' he said, keeping his fingers crossed beneath the table, 'but I assume given the location of our meeting that you are at least interested in my occult skills and knowledge.' He grinned. 'Perhaps that's what impresses the Fuhrer.'

'I have yet to be impressed,' Himmler replied.

'Oh but I am,' the Doctor said at once. 'With this castle,' he added. 'A monumental task, restoring it like this. Did you know that just a few miles...' He paused and swung in his seat searching for the direction he wanted. '...That way,' he decided, 'Arminius battled the Romans?' He turned back to face Himmler. 'But of course you did. I imagine that is partly why you chose this place.' He shook his head as he remembered. 'So many died that day,' he said sadly. 'And here at this round table,' he went on enthusiastically, 'you can seat your chosen Gruppenfuhrers. I imagine their coats of arms will be hung on the walls.' He just managed to stop himself from adding: 'Those who have them.' Himmler's own coat of arms had been designed by Professor Diebitsch only recently.

Himmler was watching him closely. His eyes had narrowed

behind the glasses. His hands were folded on the table in front of him.

Still not convinced, the Doctor decided. So he said, 'Tell me, does King Heinrich's ghost still haunt this place?'

Himmler did react to this. He flinched with surprise, then rose to his feet. 'You know of that?' he asked, his voice slightly husky.

The Doctor beamed at him. 'I'm an expert in these matters. It is my business to know.'

Himmler regarded him closely for a moment. 'Come with me, Doctor,' he said. 'I wish to show you something.'

'Guided tour,' the Doctor muttered as he followed Himmler across the room to the door. 'Can't wait.' He yawned discreetly.

The room that Himmler led him to was directly beneath the dining room, though it was rather small. It was circular, the floor formed into a shallow bowl. Three steps led down into it, but Himmler stood in the doorway, the Doctor beside him.

'You know where we are?' Himmler asked.

The Doctor did indeed. 'The place of the dead,' he said, and was rewarded with Himmler's look of surprise and interest. 'Here,' the Doctor went on, 'the coat of arms of a deceased knight of the SS is ceremonially burned.'

'And the steps?' Himmler asked quietly.

'Three steps,' the Doctor replied. 'that symbolise the three Reichs.'

Himmler nodded slowly. 'I do believe, Doctor,' he said quietly, 'that you are the man that I need.'

The Doctor smiled back. 'Good-oh,' he said.

As they ascended the steps back towards the dining room, Himmler said: 'The Fuhrer told me that he would willingly shed his blood for you, Doctor. It seemed to be a kind of joke. I was wondering if you can explain it.'

The Doctor paused on the stairs, his frown lost in the shadows. 'No,' he said, utterly serious for the first time since he had arrived at the castle. 'No, I'm afraid I can't.'

He was dropped into Southern Ireland by parachute, close to the

Ulster border, and left to make his own way to mainland Britain. He had a week in all. It took almost that to get to Dorset and find his way to Turelhampton.

It was not until the night before he was due to meet the German raiding party as they came ashore that the Doctor was able to get to the village. But one night was enough, he knew. He could get to the alien craft and perhaps – just perhaps – he might decide to thumb his nose at the First Law of Time and remove the Scrying Glass before the Germans arrived. He smiled as he thought of how he might have viewed such a suggestion in previous incarnations. The tall one with the teeth and the dark mass of curly hair would have been up for it, he reckoned. But the ruffle-shirted toff with the big nose would have had a fit at the merest suggestion. He was more pragmatic now, he thought. More experienced. He'd see how he felt at the time.

And with these thoughts in his mind, he slipped through the barbed wire and vanished like a shadow across the village green.

He found the entrance to the ship easily enough, and made his way inside. The atmosphere, the smell, the heaviness of the air was all as he remembered. Could it be déjà vu, given he had already been here in the future, he wondered. And as he wondered he stopped abruptly and stared into the red gloom.

There was a hibernation tank filling the gap that would be there in 2001 when he was here with the Brigadier – he had been right about that.

But the Scrying Glass was already gone. And suddenly things that had been gnawing at the back of the Doctor's mind made sense. He should have wondered, should have asked how Himmler knew where to come and what to look for. He should have been more contrite and willing to listen rather than demonstrating his arcane knowledge at every opportunity to try to impress the little man to ensure he was given a place on the raid. Himmler already had the Glass. Now the Doctor was committed to helping the Germans remove the hibernation tank as well, and in return he was no further forward, had learned nothing new. Absolutely nothing.

'I hope you're doing better than I am, Alistair,' he said to himself as he made his way through the graveyard, between the church and its detached tower. Through the shadowy creatures that he could almost feel but could not see as they watched him go.

Chapter Twenty-four

The glass jars were dusty with sealed lids. The contents were murky and discoloured. But the Brigadier hardly noticed. He brandished the sheet of paper he had discovered. It was brittle with age, and blackened by smoke. The edges had been burned and the lower half of the paper was missing.

'I know it's in English,' he said. 'Did you know it was here?'

'I…' She floundered. 'I do not know what it is,' she confessed.

'Really? Well let me show it to you.' He cleared his throat. 'This is a sworn testimony taken by Lieutenant George Simmonds of the US Air Force on July 14th 1945 from Hans Baur, personal pilot to Adolf Hitler. As you can see, most of it is missing, but the first part is substantially intact. Look at it.' He laid it down on the table so she could see.

SIMMONDS: Tell us what happened on April 30th.

BAUR: After the business with the doubles, I flew them out of the Tiergarten to rendezvous with the submarine at Hamburg.

SIMMONDS: Them?

BAUR: Bormann went too. As protector.

SIMMONDS: Tell me about the doubles.

BAUR: I told you already.

SIMMONDS: For the record.

BAUR: I told you. A double of the Fuhrer turned up. And I told you about the body, about how Linge and I set the tableau while Rattenhuber kept the others outside. About the substitution before the bodies were burned.

SIMMONDS: And who exactly –

The rest of the paper was charred and unreadable. Irina's face was a contrasting white.

'I have not seen this before,' she said. 'I will check the index for the file.' She leafed through the papers, and eventually found what she was looking for.

The Brigadier was silent as he waited, his mind reeling from the implications. After all this, buried in amongst the so-called Operation Myth file was a single piece of paper that proved – no, hold on, he told himself, that suggested – Hitler had not died. All the rigmarole after his death, all the exhumations and reburials and speculation about how he had died counted for nothing. Perhaps.

'Here.' She thrust another sheet of paper at him.

This one was unblemished, though old. It was handwritten in Russian. He glanced at it and handed it back. 'Well?'

'The index pairs the two documents. This one is the report of the officer who examined the burned sheet. In his opinion it is a deception.'

'A deception?'

She nodded. 'There is no corroborative evidence. It was found by chance in the Russian sector of Berlin in 1947. As you can see, it is incomplete. Who knows what else it may have said. Baur was bargaining with the Americans for his life. It may even be a forgery,' she concluded.

'Oh?'

'Baur was captured by our own forces, badly wounded, in 1945.'

The Brigadier frowned; yes, he recalled reading Trevor-Roper's mention of Baur on the plane on the way over now he came to think about it. 'I take it he did not repeat whatever allegations he was making, then.'

'He did not,' she said forcefully.

The Brigadier sighed. Another dead end? Or a cover-up? He was sure it was significant. And even if the Russians had believed the interrogation report was faked, they had kept a copy of it together with the report. A single charred sheet of paper had been deemed important enough to make its way to Moscow and get included in the file. There was something in this, he was sure.

'Is there a photocopier I can use?' he asked.

Her mouth dropped open. 'I cannot allow – ' she began.

But he interrupted her. 'I was told I would be accorded every facility. And I wish to make a copy of this second autopsy report.' He lifted the sheaf of papers from the table, watching her expression relax as he discarded the interrogation transcript.

'Oh,' she said. 'I am sure that will be permitted. There is a copier along the corridor. May I help?'

'No, I'm sure I can manage, thank you.' He smiled at her, reaching for the transcript again and the report that 'proved' it was of no importance. 'And while I'm at it, I'll just make a copy of these too.'

Claire almost laughed at the frozen look on Irina Kobulov's face. Almost.

But visible behind the woman was the imp-like shape of the demon, still crouched in the corner of the room. She could imagine its fiery, invisible eyes darting back and forth as like her it watched the conversation. For the last few minutes, Claire had been trying to decide whether she should contact the Brigadier somehow, and tell him he was being watched.

But the irony that she knew this because she was herself spying on him was not lost on her. It was not so much a wrestle with her conscience as a worry about being caught.

What happened next dispelled all such worries, and decided her. The frame changed just as Irina Kobulov's voice came through the speakers. The image of the little old woman holding a small mobile phone to her ear was somehow bizarre. But the way her voice had hardened, was more worrying. Even to Claire's less than expert ear, she was speaking not in Russian, but German. Before Irina had finished the brief call, Claire was on her own phone, thankful she had a second line for the internet connection. She had no idea how to find out the telephone number of the State Special Trophy Archive, but the Russian equivalent of directory enquiries had to be a good place to start.

It turned out to be rather easier than she had expected. She managed to persuade someone in Moscow who spoke no English to put her through to another operator who could just about understand what she wanted. Claire realised to her horror that when she had trouble explaining, she raised her voice like a clichéd English tourist. She made a conscious effort to lower it. As she waited for the operator to put her through, she changed the cassette tape and hunted out a battered portable player, winding the tape back and hoping it had recorded OK.

The woman who answered the phone at the Archive seemed to speak passable English, and understood immediately that she wished to speak urgently with their distinguished British visitor. A single frame captured on the computer screen showed a woman – perhaps the woman she had spoken to, perhaps not – asking Lethbridge-Stewart if he could spare a few moments to take an urgent call. The next showed her leading the bemused Brigadier from the room. Claire was pleased to see that he took the sheets he had just photocopied with him. She also noted that the demon in the corner stayed in the room. Watching Irina Kobulov.

'Lethbridge-Stewart speaking.'

She had rehearsed what she intended to say while she waited for him to come on the phone. She had tried to imagine how angry he would be. She wasn't even close.

'It's Claire,' she said. 'Claire Aldwych.'

'How did you know where I was?' he asked before she could go on. 'I mean, *exactly* where I was?'

She swallowed, her throat dry.

But before she could say anything, he was speaking again. 'It's in my briefcase, isn't it?' he said calmly.

'Er, well yes actually,' she admitted, surprised.

The phone seemed to explode in her ear, and she pulled it away rapidly.

'I didn't call you to confess and say sorry,' she said as soon as there was a break in the tirade. 'Though I am sorry, I suppose. And I know it was silly and dangerous and could have got you into trouble. But I had to warn you...'

He listened. He was calm. It was as if he needed to vent his spleen and now that was done he was quite willing to put the anger behind him and move on again. She played him the tape of Irina's call, and he listened without comment.

'Do you understand what she's saying?' Claire asked when it was done.

'Enough to tell she's leaving a message for someone called Hanne Neumann. She seems to think I may be able to lead them to some other artefacts they need, whatever that's all about. She also seems to think that I'm getting close to something, some clue to whatever it is she's trying to keep secret.'

'That burned interrogation report?'

'Perhaps,' he admitted. 'She did seem a bit precious about it, didn't she. So,' he went on thoughtfully, 'I'm being watched by at least three sets of undesirables.'

'Hey,' she told him, 'I said sorry. And if I hadn't been – '

'I didn't mean you. There's kindly little Irina Kobulov, this imp-thing, and the Kremlin. What is it the KGB call themselves these days?'

'The Kremlin?' she said. 'How do you know they – '

Again he cut her off. 'You don't really think you can smuggle a camera, microphone and transmitter into a secret Russian government establishment without them knowing, do you?' he demanded.

'Oh,' she said.

'Any more,' he said with forced deliberation, 'than you can ring it up on the telephone and not expect them to be listening to your conversation.'

'Oh,' she said again. 'So what do we do?'

'Not a lot we can do about our imp friend, I think,' he replied. 'The Russians will have enough sense and know enough about me to be sure that I won't cause them embarrassment.' She sensed that he was not saying this for her benefit, but rather speaking directly to the secret listeners also on the line. 'They'll leave it to myself and the Doctor to sort things out.' He emphasised 'the Doctor', and she sensed that this might actually carry even more weight than the Brigadier's own standing in Russia.

'And Grandma Irina?' she asked.

'Oh I think you can leave me to deal with her.' She could almost hear the smile of anticipation in his voice.

'Ah, there it is.' There was a clear expression of relief on Lethbridge-Stewart's face as he came into the room. He went straight over to the filing cabinet where his briefcase was, and patted it gently. 'Good,' he said.

Irina watched him impassively. 'Important call?' she enquired.

'What? Oh yes. Absolutely. Another clue, you know.'

'Another clue?' She did not really expect him to be forthcoming, but provided she was careful she could try to learn more.

'Oh yes. Lots of things going on. Most extraordinary.' He shook his head as if unable to believe them himself. 'But I think I have all the evidence now.' He lifted down the briefcase and set it on the table. 'Yes, I do believe that the key to it all is in here,' and he patted it again.

'Really?' She tried not to sound too interested.

The Brigadier glanced at his watch. 'Better just give Doris a call, actually,' he said. He was about to lift the briefcase from the table when he seemed to change his mind. 'Would you keep an eye on this for me?' he asked. 'I shan't be long, I hope. And then I think we're almost done here.' He leaned forward and said quietly, 'Rather not carry it about too much. You know how it is.' Then he straightened up again. 'Back in a tick.'

She waited until he had been gone for a full minute, then checked the corridor was clear. Then Irina Kobulov took the Brigadier's briefcase from the table, and left the room.

The office opposite the room they had been using was empty. The door was open just enough for the Brigadier to watch Irina as she walked purposefully down the corridor. He smiled as he saw she was carrying his briefcase. There was nothing in it he really needed. The photocopied autopsy report and page of interrogation were folded away in his jacket pocket.

He waited until she was out of sight, then returned to the room.

'I know you're still here,' he said to the shadows in the corner of the room as he went over and took two plastic cups from beside the kettle. 'I hope you've been enjoying the show,' he added as he took two lids.

He snapped off a tiny, crumbling corner from the largest of the skull fragments, neatly folded a clean handkerchief around it, and put it in his pocket. Then he turned his attention to the glass jars. They were labelled, but he could not read the Russian. One he knew was Adolf Hitler's fluid remains. The other was Eva Braun's. But he had no way of telling which was which. So he copied the labels as best he could on to a sheet of paper, and marked one 'A' and the other 'B'. Then he marked one of the plastic cups as 'A' with a felt pen, hoping it would not smear. The other he marked 'B'.

He double-checked which was which, then levered up the lid of the first jar. The jar was cold, almost icy, and he guessed it had been kept refrigerated. He tried to shut out the smell that oozed from inside, gagging as he poured a small amount of the liquid into cup 'A'. Then he repeated the process with the other jar, this time pouring some of its contents into cup 'B'. He resealed the jars, then wound yellowing sellotape from an ancient dispenser round the tops of the cups to help hold the lids firmly in place.

If the woman at the reception desk in the imposing lobby was surprised that their visitor wished to take two plastic cups of coffee with him to 'keep him warm in the taxi' that eventually appeared, she gave no sign of it.

As he got carefully into the taxi, cradling the plastic cups, Brigadier Lethbridge-Stewart spared a glance back at the Archive. Well aware that the amusement this brought him was caused by nervous energy more than real humour, he murmured quietly to himself: 'Adolf Hitler has now left the building.'

Chapter Twenty-five

The Doctor watched them bobbing in on the waves, the thin moonlight catching on the metal shells of the Bibers. He signalled with his torch, giving them the all clear. Soon the German taskforce would be on English shores. It was ten o'clock. Spinney had told him the invaders had arrived at about eleven and the reinforcements not long after. Would Churchill have the British reinforcements ready and waiting? Would the raid be repulsed?

It was a strange feeling for the Doctor. He knew the raid would happen, knew the hibernation tank would be stolen, but knew nothing of his own part in the proceedings. But there was no sense agonising over what he should and shouldn't do. Like a sleeping man can cheat an alarm call by incorporating it into his dream, as a fire alarm or a ringing telephone, so Time itself could effortlessly sublimate the tampering of even the most flagrant meddlers, such as himself. There was a simple elegance to the way it responded to such stimulus; efficiently mending its torn web, unthinking, again and again like a spider.

A dark, shadowy shape splashed out of the water and approached, his low whisper barely audible above the hissing of the tide. 'Herr Doktor?'

The Doctor nodded, shook his hand. 'You must be Captain Voss.' The squad leader was a man in his early thirties, with a nose that had clearly been broken at some point and a Rhett Butler moustache. He beckoned his men, and the Doctor could see them now, rising like solid shadows from the sea, their one-man subs moored somewhere out of sight. How many times would they have performed such a landing on dry runs and exercises? Now the action was real. The Doctor found it hard to avoid being caught up in the sense of expectation in the air. Two of the men were carrying a heavy crate between them. The Doctor knew it would be full of guns.

He let them stealthily up the causeway to where an army truck was parked and waiting, just as he'd arranged with Churchill's general in the war rooms. An army truck for his own, private use. He'd not mentioned, of course, that he was going to give the Germans a lift to Turelhampton...

People were going to die. The Doctor closed his eyes. Hundreds of thousands of people died during this war. He could hardly go back and save them all.

'You know what you're looking for?' the Doctor asked Voss in faultless German.

Voss nodded. 'Treasures. Treasures like the Glass, from within the Artefact. The means to win the war.'

'Indeed,' the Doctor said quietly, driving slowly, cautiously along the winding country lane with headlights switched off.

The gibbous moon was a help as they made their way closer to Turelhampton. The men shrugged off their wetsuits in the truck, revealing simple black jumpsuits, without markings. The Doctor wore a black jersey over his own dark outfit, his blond hair hidden under a woolly hat.

'You're to fire only if fired upon, you understand?' the Doctor told Voss and his men. 'You must avoid needless bloodshed. Get in, and get out.'

Voss looked at him, almost suspiciously. Then he nodded. 'I will act only in the interests of the success of the mission.'

Soon they were trundling up the road that led to the abandoned village. It seemed so peaceful in the dark. The Doctor tried to push from his mind what it must look like back in 2001, building after building flaring up and burning down, nothing left but an incandescent bubble of energy stretching further and further out, destroying everything within it.

'All right,' Voss called to his men, checking his machine gun, before turning to the Doctor. 'The time has come, do you agree?'

The Doctor nodded, moved a hand to rub the cat badge on his lapel – he affected to scratch his neck when he remembered his coat was back in the TARDIS – and stepped on the accelerator pedal.

He heard shouts from English soldiers, lights snap on at the main gate. At the first sound of gunfire Voss tossed a brief, disparaging glance at the Doctor, leaned out of the open window and fired his own weapon.

For the second time, the Doctor drove a vehicle smashing through the barrier blocking his way into the beleaguered village. The dull scattering of shots against the truck as they passed the checkpoint sounded like hail. The window beside the Doctor's head shattered, a fine smoke of glass particles stinging his skin. He kept going along the darkened streets, listening out for the alarm sirens that would herald fresh carnage, fervently hoping the silence would hold. The village green was still quite neatly trimmed in this time, and the truck bounced easily over it. A hundred yards or so from the crater he brought the truck skidding to a halt.

The Doctor's hearts sank as he heard running footsteps.

'Guards!' hissed Voss, flinging open his door and jumping out. 'Take them!'

Yelling and shouting, the German troops piled out of the back, weapons blazing. Lit strobe-like by the gunfire, the Doctor saw the British troops twitch and dance as bullets found their mark.

'This way,' the Doctor shouted, dashing in the direction of the crater, hoping to distract them from the killing. 'We must hurry.'

'Kelner, Horst, guard the truck,' Voss ordered. 'You four, cover the rim here. The rest, with me.'

The Doctor led them down the slopes of the crater, treacherous with scree, and down into the maw in the earth beside the alien ship. 'It's this way.'

Two more men remained in the trench to guard the entrance, while the Doctor led the remainder of the shock troops on through the shattered craft. Again he was struck by the stark comparison with the regenerated version in Claire's time. The light was dull and sickly, and the cramped confines of the ship carried a stench of infected wounds, and powdered glass crunched like a frosting of ice beneath booted feet.

At last they came to the ruined control room. Voss looked

around in wonder. 'Then it's real,' he breathed. 'Doctor, what must we take? What will make us strong.'

The Doctor looked about him, but said nothing.

Voss crossed to join him. 'Well? You are the expert?' Then he looked down and saw what the Doctor was standing beside.

'What is this?'

'A hibernation tank.'

'Something lives inside?'

The Doctor gestured at the opaque lid of the casket, and Voss bent down to look more closely. The smoky glass would grow thick and impenetrable over the sleeper by 2001, but here, in 1944 mere months after the crash, the casket's occupant was unpleasantly visible. Voss recoiled in horror but his gaze remained fixed to the lean, gargoyle-like figure frozen inside, its closed eyes like thick vertical grooves scored in clay.

'A demon,' Voss muttered.

'Sleeping,' observed the Doctor. 'And helpless in the tank.'

'It will wish to stay hibernating where we're going, that's for sure,' Voss said darkly. 'You three,' he said, picking out his burliest men. 'Help us here.'

The men struggled with the casket, but it seemed too heavy to move. 'What is this,' Voss asked, tapping on the soft-glowing longevity device.

'I…' The Doctor tailed off. What should he say?

'A lock of some kind, perhaps,' Voss muttered, and brought his rifle butt down hard on the glassy shell.

Before the Doctor could cry out in protest, the device shattered into ice-like shards, the ball of light within exhausting itself in a brief, gaseous flare of red. He stared down at the pieces in puzzlement.

'A clamp here, Captain,' hissed one of the men, grappling with some workings at the back of the casket. There was a hiss of steam and murmured congratulations as the casket rocked clear of the ground in their grip.

'To think,' whispered Voss, gazing raptly down at the creature in the tank. 'Our own *demon*. Our mastery over the forces of night shall be absolute.' He seemed to drag himself from out of his trance. 'Now, out of here!' he commanded. 'We'll see what other treasures we can loot along our way.'

The Doctor was last out, staring moodily at the empty space among the frozen sleepers, and the stubborn spatters of glowing glass on the floor.

As they approached the exit, the Doctor could hear trouble up ahead, sirens and shouting.

'What's happening, Karl?' shouted Voss, straining as he ran along supporting his corner of the hibernation tank.

'More soldiers!' The voice was punctuated with machine gunfire, not far away. 'Reinforcements!'

'Our intelligence said only a token force...' Voss glared at the Doctor.

'It may be the Home Guard,' suggested the Doctor coolly. 'I suggest we get away from here at once.'

'No more treasures,' muttered Voss. 'Very well. We go.'

The two guards at the entrance ran ahead, ensuring the way was clear for the casket bearers. Voss and his three men acted as one, lifting the casket clear of the ground and clearing the muddy rise in seconds. The Doctor began to climb after them. He could see the four men who had guarded the rim assemble in formation ready to take over the carrying of the hibernation tank for the last sprint across to the truck.

'Hold it!' The voice sounded oddly familiar. 'Put down the tank, at once!'

The Doctor cleared the top of the crater, lying low, and watched as a lone British soldier emerged from out of the night shadows, aiming a revolver. All the man's attention was on the casket. He didn't see one of Voss's entrance guards swing round his machine gun to cover him, but the Doctor did as he scrambled to his feet.

Too many people had died already.

'No!' shouted the Doctor.

The gun went off, rattling bullets into the night.

And he hurled himself at the British soldier, knocking the revolver aside as it fired.

'You fool!' he heard Voss cry. 'You've hit the Doctor, he was disarming that man!'

The Doctor was unharmed, but played along. He let his body appear to go limp, but really he was holding fast the man struggling beneath him.

'Quiet,' he hissed into the man's ear. 'They'll kill us both!'

'They'll take the casket, you fool!' The young man pushed him away, his eyes burning up at him in almost feverish hatred. 'The navigational's lost already... we are diminished. You've let them *diminish* us...'

And the Doctor realised he was looking into the youthful face of George Henderson.

For a second time seemed to shift and he was back here, at the crater site in 2001, staring up at the same face, he and the Brigadier fighting to stop the suitcase bomb from detonating.

'I'm wise to your tricks, your meddling,' Henderson said, a sneer in his voice... *'You allowed us to be diminished. But you won't stop us this time!'*

Then Henderson was twisting beneath him, pushing him away, scrambling up in pursuit of Voss and his men as they raced away with their treasure.

'It was you,' whispered the Doctor, staring after Henderson into the night. 'And it *will* be you. You remembered this day. It has *always* been you...'

Voss had destroyed the longevity device attached to the stolen hibernation tank. He remembered the dead shell he and the Brigadier had found attached to the casket in 2001. But if it was *Henderson* who had absorbed the life-extending energies... then what about Hitler?

The Doctor dimly heard the distant roar of the army truck as it started up, and the running footsteps and shouting of the reinforcements as they raced by. Then a boot nudged him in the back.

'On your feet, Kraut,' came a gruff English voice, and the Doctor obeyed, still staring worriedly after Henderson.

'Got one, Private?' inquired a languid voice the Doctor

recognised from a time more recent. 'Very well, I'll take over.'

The Doctor turned and saw Churchill's General from the War Rooms. 'Seems your intelligence was good, Doctor,' the man said. 'And your mission successfully completed?'

The Doctor turned to look again into the darkness after Henderson, and the truck racing back to the Dorset coast, lost in thought. He shook his head, just a fraction. 'No, General,' he said softly. 'It seems that for all this, my mission is far from over.'

Chapter Twenty-six

The Brigadier woke at five in the morning and lay fitfully for a while in the dark, hopeful that sleep might take him again. With Doris gone he had the whole bed in which to stretch out, of course, but that didn't seem right somehow. He stuck to his own patch.

When it became clear he was awake for the duration, he decided to go down and make himself some cocoa.

The Brigadier rubbed the back of his neck, still stiff and sore from the long journey on the plane home. 'Damned jet lag,' he grumbled, trudging wearily about the kitchen looking for the saucepan. Where on Earth was the Doctor? He could be gone for months and still pop back a minute after he'd left, wasn't that the sort of rot he was always saying?

Then he heard the wheezing and groaning of the TARDIS, and smiled with relief. Here was a pain in the neck he'd welcome any time.

He got out another mug. On the kitchen worktop, next to the mugs, stood two plastic cups, their lids sealed with tape. Beside them was a neatly folded handkerchief.

The two of them swapped their stories at the breakfast bar as the new day slowly brightened, the wan moon still hanging in the pale sky as if reluctant to leave. The Brigadier filled in the Doctor on his trip to Moscow, of all he had learned, and of the current status of Turelhampton – the powerfield had edged up to the perimeter of the village and was showing no signs of burning itself out.

When it was the Doctor's turn to speak, the Brigadier found himself both grinning and grimacing in amazement at his friend's antics, and all the casual meetings with the men who had steered the course of the war. He wondered what Claire would make of the Doctor's tale, straight out of a Boy's Own annual; for himself, he felt a twinge of jealousy at his old friend's wartime heroics.

'So the whole escapade was something of a wild goose chase,' the Brigadier surmised, draining the last of his cocoa. 'Or do I mean goose-*stepping* chase?'

The Doctor ignored the joke. 'At least we know two things for certain,' he said. 'Firstly, Spinney can't have been telling us the whole truth. The Scrying Glass had disappeared before the Germans arrived, before even Henderson could get to it – he told me himself, components from the navigational units were "lost". Spinney has to know more about what happened to it.'

'And you're certain Henderson is the one who's long-lived?'

'Oh yes. That wasn't his son we met at the crater site, but the man himself. He remembered me from 1944 as the man he thinks ruined his only chance to stop the hibernation tank leaving the country.'

'That explains the why the imp attacked you, and not us both...' said the Brigadier. 'But if Henderson's been acting for the aliens in return for immortality, what about Hitler?'

The Doctor tapped his teaspoon against his lips, deep in thought. 'Perhaps he *is* an impostor, after all?'

'I'm telling you Doctor, there is more than a suspicion that Hitler's death pact with Eva Braun was a sham. That a double was sacrificed in Hitler's place. I'd say Hitler's looking remarkably well-preserved for a cremated corpse, wouldn't you? It *fits*, Doctor. It's the only possible answer.'

He pulled a crumpled photocopied sheet of paper from his pocket and thrust it at the Doctor. 'The Russians think this is a fake of some sort. Another wild goose chase. But given the way the Nazi agent tried to keep me off it, I think there's more than a grain of truth in here.' He tapped the sheet emphatically.

'The mystery deepens,' murmured the Doctor as he scanned through it. 'I suppose the hibernation tank itself must have certain properties conducive to an extended lifespan...' Abruptly he sat up straight, fixing the Brigadier with a worried gaze. 'And you say the Nazis were on to you and your researches?'

'The Nazis, the Kremlin, an imp and heaven knows what else, Doctor!' said the Brigadier ruefully.

'One of the familiars?' the Doctor breathed.

'Captured on Claire's web camera.'

'Indeed… I wonder how far they can travel away from their host's body.'

'Well, the Nazis have the tank…' The Brigadier rubbed his stiff neck again as he considered. 'Could the imp's presence be a clue to the Scrying Glass's location? That the Nazis are based somewhere in Russia?'

'Not necessarily. While the aliens are sleeping, I doubt the imps can wander too far – but if one was wide awake, I'd imagine the astral projection could travel a good deal further… And since it seems the original occupant of that tank has been turfed out a long time ago…'

'We've no clue at all as to where they might be,' the Brigadier concluded. 'But if Claire's web-camera thing in my stolen briefcase is still working, perhaps we can find some kind of lead as to where they're based?'

'Excellent.' The Doctor jumped up. 'Can we review the footage?'

'Er, more Claire's field I think, Doctor,' the Brigadier said apologetically. 'And she's asleep upstairs. Like most right-minded people.'

The Doctor picked up the empty cocoa-pan and a wooden spoon and marched out of the room, heading upstairs. 'Not for much longer she isn't…'

'Yeah, it's still running,' Claire reported, stifling a jaw-cracking yawn as she logged on to the secure site.

They saw a blur of white wall and out of focus portraits standing on their sides. The case had clearly been left on a table somewhere.

'Well, that's not telling us much,' the Brigadier said unnecessarily.

'Don't panic,' said Claire. 'I've set it to download frames every two minutes. We can whizz through them, get a sense of where they've been, what they're up to, where they are now…'

She accessed the frame stores and waited for the images to start loading in a new window. The atmosphere was electric in the Brigadier's old study as they watched the bleary rectangle parade an endless array of abstract views. A building, a corridor. The old woman was on a mission. Sky. A straight track – an airfield? Meeting someone… A man in a long black leather coat and – no, it was a woman. In black uniform and a tight white… Jesus, *definitely* a woman.

'I imagine that when it comes to Nazi fetish movies, she can name her price,' Claire murmured. She shivered as glacier blue eyes and a smug smile loaded up, as the woman examined the stolen briefcase.

'You don't know what we know,' Claire said in a sing-song voice.

'When was this?' the Doctor asked.

'This is soon after he left Moscow.' She patted Lethbridge-Stewart on the bum, and smiled to see him flinch. 'Fifteen hours ago.'

The images kept on coming as the old woman and her Nazi consort boarded the private jet, but then the case was stowed in a locker, and all they could see was grey mesh and defocused light.

'Stowed for take off,' announced Claire. 'Let's pop forward an hour.'

The image was the same. She tried skipping ahead to four hours later.

The picture hadn't changed. 'Long flight,' she announced.

Travelling through another few hours in a matter of seconds, the image finally changed. The case was being removed from the plane, and carried somewhere…

'Look at all that snow,' Claire remarked.

'Snow and ice…' said the Brigadier. The image cut and was replaced with the sight of dark double doors, presumably closing shut on the frozen landscape. Then a concrete corridor, a flash of red carpet. Paintings on the wall.

'Like a bunker of some kind,' the Brigadier went on.

'Wait!' The Doctor leaned in. 'Look, the real time image!'

The window showed a blur of movement. 'Come on, come on,' said the Doctor impatiently.

'Can you enlarge it?' the Brigadier grumbled, straining to see.

Claire nodded. 'We'll lose a bit of resolution, but...'

As she widened the window, right on cue, the next image loaded.

A face now filled the screen, a sour face with ice-blue eyes full of hate. It was a man with dark hair slicked in a side parting, pockmarked skin, and a neat block of hair bristling beneath his nose.

Claire recoiled automatically from the image.

Then the window filled with blackness.

'They've found the camera,' murmured Claire.

The Brigadier nodded gravely. 'And if their agents have been trailing you, they'll know where to find me... all of us.'

'Then we must find out the truth from Spinney,' the Doctor announced. 'Get some proper answers, before it's too late!'

Palmer drummed his fingers impatiently on the table in the portacabin. Under the slightly scatty supervision of old Osgood, Sergeant Yeowell of the Science Corps had spent hours working with a load more white-coated sorts from some government lab or other. But the results of this pooling of intellect and resources seemed singularly unimpressive. It was basically a rack of black boxes sprouting cables like tresses of hair. Palmer decided it looked as if a gibbon had decided to rewire a hi-fi.

'And this will solve all our problems?' he demanded of Osgood.

'Knowing the Doctor, it'll probably be the start of a good many others,' he said with a twinkle in his eye. 'But the theory itself is sound. It works by deadening the molecular jostling that's –'

'You can spare me the double-dutch, Mr Osgood,' said Palmer. He looked out the portacabin window at the smoking wall of fire preceding the boundary of the energy field. 'Just make it work, and make it get rid of *that*.'

* * *

Peter Spinney was surprised to hear the noise of another car pulling up outside his house. As usual he'd been expecting no visitors, and was currently still lying in bed, puffing on his pipe to while away the morning.

He strained to hear a car door being opened and steps approaching up the drive, but his hearing wasn't good enough. He waited, but no one came. Perhaps the driver was lost.

He got stiffly out of bed and crossed in his nightshirt to the window. Pulled back the heavy curtain. Squinted into the light.

There was no one outside, but still there was movement in the glass, a dark reflection of some kind, as if someone were standing behind him.

Spinney looked round, unsettled, but there was no-one with him in the room. Just the clutter of a lifetime's hoarding, and the shadows.

Then he heard the front door opening, from the inside.

He walked through to the hall in time to see a dull shape flit across the glass in the door as it swung open. A man was standing in the doorway, silhouetted against the sunlight pouring in behind him. The figure reached out an arm – not to shake Spinney's hand in greeting, but to take from him.

When he saw it was Sergeant Henderson looking just the same as he always had, Spinney knew he must really still be in his bed, that it was just a dream.

And when the silhouette of something squat, misshapen, *evil*-looking came stalking towards him across the floor, he knew it was a nightmare.

'Where is it, Spinney?'

The old man backed away, jaw flapping, transfixed by the approaching shadow. 'What… what's that thing…'

'We need it, Spinney. It's been lost for so long. Just like you.'

'What do you want?' Spinney yelped. The shadow was fading as clouds obscured the sun. Ghostly red eyes burnt in the glass panels of the front door as Henderson gently pushed it to, behind him.

'The Glass,' he said. 'The object you took from the ship.'

Spinney stared, distraught. 'How did you know?'

'We have always known. Oh, you've hidden yourself well, Spinney, you've been difficult to find. But now the time has come.'

'I didn't want to be found,' Spinney said, close to tears. 'It's only these last few years I've wanted to live at all.' He clenched his little fists. 'I wanted to die, all that time, all because of you and your orders and that stupid thing from the sky. Can you understand that, *sir*? I wanted to *die*.'

Henderson remained impassive. 'It's never too late, Spinney. We must have back what you stole... at any cost.'

Steadily, hand still outstretched, he advanced on the old man.

Chapter Twenty-seven

Moaning in terror, Spinney hobbled into his living room. He swept off teacups and bric-a-brac from his tallboy, clutching for the glass disk in its doily.

A shape formed slyly in the glass of the cupboard door, watching his frantic scrabbling with cold red eyes.

As Spinney saw it and recoiled, Henderson came slowly through the living room door.

'Take it!' yelled Spinney. 'Please, take it!'

'Not just yet, Henderson!'

As the loud voice carried like a cavalry charge, the door swung back open, cannoning into Henderson's back and knocking him to the floor.

The man who had come the day before, the big one in the strange clothes, knelt beside Henderson, gripping one of his arms in a half-nelson. 'No more killing, Henderson,' he stated. 'The war is over, remember?'

Spinney stared, hot tears in his eyes, as the older man in the army get-up came after the colourful bloke into the room, and then as the girl from the TV squeezed carefully past them both. She came over to Spinney and sat him down, trembling, on the bed. He gripped her hand and rested his old head against her warm shoulder.

'Doctor!' shouted the older man.

Spinney cried out as the blond bloke, this Doctor, suddenly smashed forwards into the table and chairs, propelled by some invisible force. He seemed to be growing hazy, indistinct, as if the air about him were turning grey. The TV girl stood up, arms flailing in panicked indecision as she tried to think what she could do.

Henderson knelt up now the Doctor was no longer keeping him down, but the old boy produced a service revolver and pressed it to the young man's head.

'How will you finish your quest,' he said calmly, 'with your brains spread all over this room?'

Henderson glared at Spinney, as if this was somehow all his fault. Then he waved his arm at the Doctor – still shaking and gasping as if suffocating in the shadows – and called, 'Enough.'

Gradually the Doctor's struggles subsided, and an uneasy calm descended on the room. The TV girl crouched beside him, helping him back up. The military man still held his gun to Henderson's head.

'Well, then,' the Doctor said shakily, getting to his feet. 'Since we're all here, how about we swap some old stories?' His voice hardened as he looked between Henderson and Spinney in turn. 'I want to know exactly what happened back in 1944 when the ship came down, and why its legacy has brought us all together here almost sixty years later.' He paused, and suddenly presented Claire with a mischievous smile. 'And while I'm in demanding mood, a cup of tea would go down very nicely, too.'

'Here we go then.'

The heat from the powerfield was intense. Palmer took a step back and motioned his men to do the same.

Osgood took a step closer, craning his neck to check up on Yeowell's progress. 'Gentle with that circuit, now!' he called warningly.

Palmer sighed and tapped him on the shoulder. 'Mr Osgood, as a civilian you should be standing well away from –'

'Oh, nonsense, Captain,' snorted Osgood. 'You wanted my experience. I'm not going to experience anything at all from back there, am I?' He squinted once more at Yeowell's nimble fingers. 'That's it. Mind out for any feedback.'

A short while later, Yeowell grinned and gave a thumbs-up.

Osgood clapped his hands together. 'We'll soon know if we stand a chance or not,' he said.

Palmer shifted uneasily. 'You mean, stand a chance of containing the powerfield.'

Osgood looked him in the eye and chuckled.

The machine shook and shuddered as it kicked into life with an angry roar. Palmer looked at the swirling mass of the wall of energy as it nudged forward just a little closer. 'When should we see it having some effect, then?' he called.

'Any time now,' Osgood said.

A waft of smoke blocked their view for a few seconds, but when it cleared it seemed to Palmer that so had the air. He could see patches of blue sky now instead of only the glowing mist.

'It's working,' Palmer breathed.

'They always do at first,' Osgood said with a sigh.

Fate, being so tempted, clearly couldn't resist. Yeowell, still crouching by the machine, gave a great cry of alarm as a bolt of blue energy crackled out of one of the black boxes. He jumped back.

The roar of the machine altered its pitch, becoming more of an angry whine.

'Oh dear,' said Osgood. 'That's never a good sound.'

It had been a long time since Claire had played tea-girl, but she actually found the simple mechanical actions of making a brew quite soothing. The Doctor had a cheek asking, but at least it got her away from the atmosphere in there for a while, which was no bad thing.

Clicking on her recordable walkman once again, she carried the tea things through.

Henderson was now sitting on one of Spinney's chairs, staring covetously down at the curved piece of glass in the Doctor's hand, about the size and shape of a paperweight. The Brigadier still had his gun drawn, but was leaning against the wall and covering Henderson more discreetly. Spinney sat, still shaking, on his bed, and the Doctor was sat cross-legged on the floor, an expectant audience.

Spinney and the Doctor both took their tea as Henderson began.

'You know that the ship was shot down in the run-up to D-Day and crashed,' he began, 'you know that the village was sealed off and the troops sent in.'

'No one knows it better than Mr Spinney, there,' said the Doctor. 'And with his friends, he went inside.' He turned to Spinney. 'But you did more than just look, didn't you? You touched?'

'Never seen nothing like it,' Spinney whispered, both hands clasping his tea. 'None of us had. There was so much lying inside, broken, we thought, where's the harm?'

He sniffed, took a noisy slurp of his drink. Claire found it hard to imagine that this pathetic, shrivelled figure had ever really been an active young man in his twenties, getting his kicks where he could in a '40s summer.

'You stole from us,' Henderson said.

'Souvenirs, that was all. I mean, it's not every day you see something like that... Souvenirs. Watson took a disk, looked a bit like a glass coin.'

'I have the component Watson took.'

Claire doubted he'd asked nicely; neither did Spinney by the look of him.

'Yes, well... I took that thing you've got, Doctor, and poor old Gerrard Lassiter...'

'*He* took the Scrying Glass,' concluded the Brigadier. 'And when the Allies pressed on through Europe...'

'...It fell into the hands of the Nazis.' Claire nodded. 'Just like the spaceman in the casket.'

'We are diminished.' Henderson looked so frustrated Claire found herself feeling almost sorry for him.

'You know nothing of what Hitler might've done to himself through any powers siphoned from the hibernation tank?' demanded the Doctor.

Henderson shook his head wearily.

'Then you're *not* allied with the Nazis?' the Brigadier asked.

'Nazis?' Henderson shook his head fiercely. 'We are allied to no man. We wish only to leave...' Were those actually tears in Henderson's eyes? 'Now one more of us is dead. I have glimpsed the ghost of his familiar at the full-stretch of my consciousness... but its location remains lost to us.' He paused. 'I have sensed too the presence of the ocular celluprime –'

'And you hoped Spinney had it,' said the Doctor, looking down at the glass, before tossing it over to Henderson – much to Claire's and the Brigadier's surprise.

Henderson grabbed for it and clutched it tight in both hands, as if it he were Superman trying to crush a piece of coal into diamonds.

'This is a focusing chip, important to us… but this Glass, as you call it, is a part of the ship's heart. As long as it exists it will be drawn back to the craft…'

'And with your own existence extended by the Vvormak and the ship stuck here recharging, you had all the time in the world to reclaim it.' The Doctor paused. 'Until the likes of us started poking around, threatening to blow wide open your covert little operation.'

'We had to protect the ship,' said Henderson simply.

'At the cost of how many human lives?' the Doctor snapped.

'The area was evacuated.'

The Doctor flew to his feet in a rage. 'The area is being devastated by unprocessed energy! The village is all but destroyed already… How far will the effect spread?'

Henderson didn't answer.

'Well?'

'The Vvormak will be safe at the heart of the effect.'

'And if it takes years to find the Scrying Glass? Decades?' He received no answer. The Doctor looked at him coldly. 'Well. So much for the Vvormak. Selfish… destructive… No better than those that shot you down.'

'Why did you do it, Henderson,' the Brigadier asked him coldly. 'Why take these aliens' shilling?'

Henderson's eyes were closed, he was holding the focusing chip to his face like it was a nosegay, and smelt as sweet. 'When Spinney and the others stole from the ship, the Pilot, already dying in his tank, was roused. The Vvormak had the measure of man then – violent aggressors, thieves and vandals. They had come to Earth on a survey mission.' He paused, his voice dropped to a whisper. 'He showed me. Showed me it all, everything that they'd seen, that they'd recorded and catalogued…'

The Brigadier looked at the Doctor. 'They played with his mind?'

'They communed with him in some way, yes. He's still touched by the Vvormak life-force.'

'He made his familiar my own. Transferred to me his life-force, from the casket.'

The Doctor nodded. 'So you could make the ship whole, no matter how long it took.'

Claire took advantage of all eyes being on Henderson to check her walkman was still going. She wanted to punch the air. Her mind had gone beyond trying to take in all the individual details right now – she just knew this would be the biggest story the world had ever seen, the story that would see Claire Aldwych going down in history.

'All we want to do is leave.' Henderson's voice was low and fierce.

'I think we'd all welcome that,' the Doctor said. 'And I'm prepared to help you find the Scrying Glass with my own transport to speed that along.'

Claire looked at him. 'Just what is this mysterious transport of yours?'

'Never mind that,' the Doctor said hastily.

'You try to trick us,' Henderson said. 'You conspired to take the casket away in 1944, you stopped me from retrieving it.'

The Doctor was indignant. 'I stopped you from being murdered by a German sniper. And where would your precious mission be then?' He leant forward so that he was looking directly into Henderson's face, 'Believe me, I'm as keen it succeeds as you are. All that bothers me is that when the ship takes off, the pool of destructive energy leaking out from around your ship will become a tidalwave that could wipe up a good deal of southern England. If I'm to help you, what do you propose to do about that?'

Henderson looked up at the Doctor, his face unreadable.

Then the sound of squealing brakes and car doors opening and heavy footsteps made them all look automatically to the windows. The curtains were still drawn against the April sunlight, so the Doctor reached across and opened them.

There was time to register a shape hurling itself at the window, and that was all; then the room was filled with the sound of breaking glass. The Doctor fell back with a shout; the dark shape coming at them was a man, dressed all in black. He had righted himself in a second.

Claire couldn't stop the scream dragging itself from her lungs as the man pulled out a knife and slashed at the Doctor's throat.

Chapter Twenty-eight

The Brigadier fired his revolver before the blade could bite into the Doctor's flesh. The assassin was thrown backwards by the impact of the bullet, the knife arcing through the air to be lost amid the bric-a-brac cluttering Spinney's chest of drawers.

A pounding started up at the cottage's front door. 'Nazis?' Claire asked as she helped the Doctor up.

'Seems so,' he gasped, pulling free to yank the heavy curtains closed again. 'Mr Spinney, is there a back way out?'

Spinney was staring dead ahead, eyes glassy, his face twisted in horror.

'Yes, in the kitchen –' Claire began, but the Doctor waved her into silence.

'Mr Spinney…?'

'I wouldn't bother, Doctor,' said the Brigadier grimly, feeling Spinney's throat for a pulse. 'He's dead. Shock, I'd imagine.'

'Come on,' the Doctor said softly, the words almost lost beneath the battering at the door.

The Brigadier fired another shot into the heavy fabric of the curtain at the broken window. The smashing of the door died down.

'Might make them more cautious,' the Brigadier said quietly, 'buy us time.'

'Can you help us?' the Doctor asked Henderson. Somehow, Claire could sense the presence of the shadowy imp-thing in the room with them. She remembered watching the things shifting round her on the Turelhampton tape and shuddered.

'Nazis, you say?' Henderson had risen to his feet. 'The people who have the Glass? Our dead crewman?'

'A force for evil.' The Doctor had clearly noted Henderson's sudden interest and was doing his best to discourage it. 'You fought against them once, as plain Sergeant George Henderson.

You fought against them because you knew that if you didn't, they would overwhelm and destroy you. These are the people using whatever powers and secrets they can steal from your people to help them take dominance over the Earth.'

'They can lead me to the Glass,' Henderson said.

'They'll kill you!' stormed the Doctor.

'We can be free…' With his slicked-back blond hair and messianic zeal Claire decided he could probably pass for a Nazi himself.

Another window shattered. Claire yelled and threw herself to the floor along with Henderson and the Doctor as bullets smashed into the little room. The Brigadier sheltered behind the tallboy. Spinney's corpse jumped and shook and spat blood at them before toppling face-down on to the old threadbare carpet.

'Quickly, Doctor!' the Brigadier called, opening the door and crawling for the kitchen. Claire scooted after him, grabbing her bag and thanking God her bag hadn't been hit. Her foot caught on Spinney's body and her stomach lurched, but she kept on going…

'Come with us,' the Doctor implored Henderson. 'They'll kill you.'

Henderson shook his head and shut his eyes.

'You must know that whatever they may say or do, you can't *trust* them.' The Doctor was trembling with frustration. 'What about the War? The friends you lost… the life you lost. Do those old loyalties *really* count for nothing now?'

'As you said, Doctor,' Henderson whispered. 'The war is over now.'

Venkel observed impassively as his three men stood poised like statues, ready to open fire again the second he commanded. The gun from the cottage had fired twice. Karl must be dead, too slow. Venkel would not underestimate his quarry again. He didn't believe the noise of the gunfire would carry to the nearest neighbour, but even if it did and an alarm was raised, they would be gone before assistance could arrive.

It must be the military man, this nosy Brigadier, who had dared open fire on them. Venkel had been instructed to capture the man and question him, to learn how much he knew – or if that proved unfeasible, simply to kill him. With the journalist girl in his company too, the opportunity to rid themselves of all the thorns in their flesh seemed too good to resist.

'All right, men,' Venkel called. 'Again. We will show those inside no quarter.'

The men cautiously advanced on the shattered windows, listening out for signs of life from inside.

But death came from outside.

Claire stared in alarm as every piece of glass in the room started to shake and glow. There was a choked scream from outside, sounds of consternation.

'Your familiar?' the Doctor questioned.

Henderson looked at him coldly. 'This time I will not allow him to be distracted. Leave now. While you can.'

'Come *on*, Doctor!' Claire begged him.

'Way's clear so far,' the Brigadier reported back, calm and professional about things. It had been his job, this sort of thing, she supposed; and she turned and looked into his craggy face with a new respect.

The Doctor had reached his decision. He scrambled across to join Claire and the Brigadier as the shouts from outside continued. 'We'll meet again,' he assured Henderson.

'Don't know where, don't know when,' Claire murmured miserably, as they ran through Spinney's overgrown back yard and for the cover of the forest beyond. 'But I hope it's no bloody time soon.'

Venkel cowered back against his car as his men shook and screamed, clawing the air as if it were alive with demons. The hairs at the back of his neck prickled like pins as he watched.

Then whatever it was, the storm that had caught only his men, seemed to pass. They fell one by one to the ground.

Now he must act. Scrambling up, Venkel rushed to the

weakened door and kicked it savagely. It flapped back on its twisted hinges and he pushed through.

There was only one man inside, a man Venkel did not recognise. There was a glass disk in his hand, and a cold, dangerous look in his pale eyes.

Venkel tried to level his gun and found he was still shaking.

The man smiled faintly and shook his head.

Whether Henderson had used his familiar to force the surviving Nazis to take him to his Vvormak buddy, or whether they had seen he possessed a miniature Scrying Glass and had taken him away to explain himself, thirty minutes later the house was deserted save for Spinney's corpse.

'Poor old man,' muttered the Brigadier. 'To think he lived his life for so many years burdened with the guilt of *not* being killed by the Nazis.'

'Someone up there has a sick sense of humour,' Claire remarked.

The Doctor stared down at Spinney's body and heaved a huge sigh. Then he looked back up at Claire and the Brigadier in turn.

'We can't stop to think,' he said slowly. 'Too many people are still at risk.'

'Think about it too long,' Claire realised, 'and it becomes downright impossible to believe. I mean, I don't know which is crazier, aliens in Dorset or Hitler coming back to take over the world – to find you're dealing with both…'

'It's a shame there was no time to learn more about the powers of this wretched hibernation tank affair,' said the Brigadier. 'After all, Hitler seemed a wreck at the end by all accounts. Suffering from Parkinson's, left arm shaking uncontrollably, on endless medication, cocaine and strychnine included… and yet the man we've seen looks more like the Hitler of old.'

'If it isn't Hitler, we're going to feel pretty stupid after all this, aren't we?' Claire suggested tactfully.

'It's a mystery, and men have died in its making,' brooded the Doctor. 'We need to know for sure,' he said, looking at the

Brigadier, 'that those fragments of skull you brought back are really Hitler's.'

'No, really? And how are you going to prove that, exactly?' Claire inquired facetiously.

But the Doctor was nodding at the Brigadier as if there were some secret understanding between them.

Lethbridge-Stewart looked at him with a slight glint in his eye. 'Is that not breaking the rules, Doctor?'

'"I am so steeped in blood…"' declaimed the Doctor, before shrugging. 'Let Time watch out for itself. Always manages to smooth things over with the minimum of fuss.'

'And him?' Claire pointed discreetly at Spinney. 'Is all this going to be smoothed over with the minimum of fuss?'

'Another little mopping up operation for UNIT, I suspect,' the Doctor said.

'As if we didn't have enough to do coping with that powerfield,' remarked the Brigadier sullenly.

The Doctor agreed with a worried look. 'And then, Brigadier, you and I have some past business to attend to.'

'All right, that's enough, Yeowell!' Palmer shouted, the powerfield so close now he could feel it on his face, making the skin prickle and burn. 'Fall back, man!'

'But the Doctor's machine,' protested Yeowell, making some kind of multicoloured cat's-cradle from the wires in its smoking innards.

'Too late,' Palmer yelled, charging forwards to grab Yeowell himself, tugging him away from the broiling wall of air.

Just as the machine exploded, the blast throwing them forward.

Palmer groaned and lifted himself up. 'When I give a direct order, Yeowell, you'll bloody well obey it in future.'

Yeowell stirred weakly beside him. 'Yes, Sir.'

Palmer saw Osgood approach to stand over him. He was chuckling to himself.

'It blew up,' he observed, almost fondly. 'The Doctor's gadgets always do that.'

Palmer shut his eyes. 'Can we build another?'

Osgood frowned. 'What for? It'll only blow up again.'

Yeowell nodded. 'The field's too big to contain now. The machine can't handle the power flow.'

The seething air before them shifted and whorled, as thick smoke from the burning foliage drove them back, choking them.

Palmer looked at both men. 'So what are our options?'

'Hope that it stops,' said Osgood simply.

'That's the best we can do?' Palmer asked in disbelief.

'That's all we can do,' Yeowell murmured.

A sudden wind drew a curtain of smoke over the angry scene, the burning earth. As if they were children, being shielded from this terrible thing they shouldn't see, that they couldn't understand. Something that would only be larger, fiercer, closer when the curtain pulled back once more.

Chapter Twenty-nine

The centre of the ballroom was given over to the dancing. Couples waltzed magnificently – the men in crisp military uniform, the women in gorgeous evening dress. Around the edge of the dance floor there were tables where food was being served. Guests were talking, eating, laughing. The huge chandeliers glistened frostily over the celebrations below. It was August 1942, and the Third Reich was at its glorious height.

The only guest who did not seem impressed as he descended the central staircase of the hotel from the rooms above was Brigadier Lethbridge-Stewart. He glowered, pulling at the hem of his uniform jacket in an effort to make it fit. Beside him, the Doctor spared an amused glance, adjusted his monocle, straightened his own uniform jacket, and led the way to the celebrations below.

'Do try to look as if you're enjoying these festivities,' the Doctor said quietly as he lifted two glasses of champagne from a passing waiter's tray and handed one to the Brigadier.

Lethbridge-Stewart inspected the glass doubtfully. 'I know what's paying for it,' he replied. 'And so do you.'

'Mmm,' the Doctor agreed. 'And that's what may very well happen again if we don't get what we need.'

The Brigadier considered this. He sipped his champagne. He found it was actually rather good. And he hated himself for liking it. But he put on a smile, and nodded politely at people.

'Not quite where I was aiming for,' the Doctor admitted as he looked round. 'But it's often better to trust to the old girl's judgement and go with the flow, as it were.'

But the Brigadier was hardly listening. 'Doctor,' he said after a few moments, his face a mask of surprise, 'I don't speak German. At least, a smattering, but not that well. And yet...'

The Doctor grinned at him. 'Must be the champagne,' he said.

'Don't worry about it, Brigadier. Don't worry about it.' As he spoke, he looked around the room, his face split into an ecstatic grin of pantomime proportions. He nudged the Brigadier, sending champagne sloshing, and nodded towards the far end of the room.

'Good God,' the Brigadier said tightly.

'I don't think so.'

Standing at the end of the room, visible over the people crowding round him only because he was standing on a raised platform, stood the Fuhrer of the Third Reich himself, Adolf Hitler. Despite the fact he was smiling thinly, he looked bored.

'See the woman over his left shoulder?' the Doctor said quietly.

The Brigadier looked. There was a tall slim woman with blond curly hair standing discreetly behind the Fuhrer. 'Eva Braun?' he asked.

The Doctor nodded. 'The best kept secret of the Reich. The Fuhrer would remain aloof, untouchable. To the rest of the world, even to allied intelligence services, she is just a secretary. Nobody. Insignificant.'

'Yet in his last hours he marries her.' The Brigadier shook his head in disbelief. He was having trouble believing he was here at all.

'So what do we do?' he asked as the Doctor took a plate and queued for food. 'Apart from take advantage of the hospitality?' He took the next plate from the pile together with a linen napkin. 'Hope that a hair drops out of his moustache and into the soup?'

'I'll think of something,' the Doctor said indistinctly. But he seemed more interested in the sausage roll he was munching as he motioned for the waiter to pile on more potato salad.

The Brigadier was not really hungry, he decided. But he stood beside the Doctor as they ambled slowly after other people along the side of the dance floor. One of the dancers, a beautiful woman with long dark hair smiled at him as she spun past. The Brigadier caught himself smiling back, and hastily looked ahead.

As he did so, he realised that they were standing in another queue, albeit a long one. He craned his head to see where it was leading.

'You not eating?' the Doctor rumbled beside him.

'Oh, er, no. Not really hungry actually.'

'Can't let it go to waste.' The Doctor lifted the plate from the Brigadier's hands and swapped it for his own plate. There was a half-eaten sausage roll left on it, and a smear of pickle that looked suspiciously as though it had been somehow crafted into a question mark, with the remains of the sausage roll as the dot. The Doctor belched loudly. 'Ooh, manners,' he exclaimed happily, and tucked into the Brigadier's ham rolls.

Returning his attention to the queue he was standing in, the Brigadier noticed with a start that it led to the podium at the end of the room where he had seen Adolf Hitler standing. He felt his blood run cold as he realised what was happening, and looked round urgently, wondering what he could do. They could not just leave, not be seen to walk away from an imminent audience with the Fuhrer himself.

And imminent was about right. The small crowd in front was thinning out rapidly. In just a couple of minutes they'd be standing in front of the man.

'Doctor,' he hissed. 'Doctor, do you know what we're queuing for?'

'What?' The Doctor looked up. 'Nearly there,' he said breezily. 'We're queuing to see the Fuhrer.'

The Brigadier glared.

But the Doctor merely grinned back, apparently oblivious. 'Some people ask for his autograph you know,' he said airily. 'But I think we shall need a bit more than that, don't you?'

But before he could reply, the people in front moved on, and they found themselves standing next to a tall thin man in a black uniform. His nose was a beak, and his neck was as long as a turkey's. 'Names,' he barked.

'Certainly,' the Doctor said, somehow managing to lose his plate and napkin on a side table as he spoke. 'I am Major Johann Schmidt, and this is Brigadier General...' He faltered, and turned to the Brigadier. 'I'm so sorry, I have no idea what your name is.'

The Brigadier was aware that his mouth had dropped open.

'Oh, er, neither have I,' he said. 'That is, Brigadier General Braun.' He blinked. 'No relation,' he added quickly.

The man with the beak was looking at him as if he were mad. The Doctor leaned forward and murmured, just loud enough for the Brigadier to hear: 'I'm so sorry, he's just come from the Russian front.'

This seemed to satisfy beak-nose, and he stepped towards the Fuhrer to announce them. 'Major Johann Schmidt, and Brigadier General Braun,' he said quickly, then stepped away.

The Brigadier knew from watching the people immediately ahead of them that the protocol now was to nod, mutter something appropriate and leave quickly. This was not, however, the way that the Doctor did things.

Instead he stepped forward, clicked his heels smartly together and held out his hand. 'Delighted!' he exclaimed.

The Fuhrer was taken aback. So surprised, in fact that he reached out instinctively and the Doctor immediately grabbed the proffered hand and shook it enthusiastically. Then he stepped slightly aside so that the Brigadier could take his place.

The Brigadier was also surprised by this, and he also held out his hand. But even as he did so, even as he caught sight of the Fuhrer's puzzled expression, the outraged exchanged glances of the other officials and Eva Braun's stifled smile, he realised this was the most embarrassing moment of his life. Not only was he meeting a man he firmly believed was among the most monstrous and evil who had ever walked the planet at the very height of his power, he was holding out to him a dirty plate on which was a half-eaten sausage roll.

The Doctor recovered from the incident before anyone else. 'I'm sorry,' said quickly, 'perhaps I should say that I'm usually referred to as the Doctor.'

'Doctor?' Hitler returned his attention to the Doctor.

'Sometimes attached to the Fifth Medical Corps here in Berlin. We haven't had time to eat,' he added, as if this explained the Brigadier's behaviour.

The Fuhrer's face seemed to clear at this. 'Indeed,' he said. 'Perhaps in about half an hour then, Doctor.' He turned and beckoned to a large man in uniform that the Brigadier thought he recognised. 'Martin, show the Doctor and his associate to my room. They will wait for us there.'

The man saluted and led the way back along the ballroom.

'Doctor,' the Brigadier hissed, 'what's going on? Who is this man? Where are we going?'

'He's Martin Bormann, Hitler's personal secretary as well as Nazi party secretary,' the Doctor replied quietly. 'Other than that, I have no idea. Good distraction with the sausage roll though. That had them flummoxed.'

Bormann took them up the stairs and to a room not very distant from where the TARDIS had landed. He unlocked the door and led them inside.

They found themselves in a small sitting room, another door presumably leading to a larger bedroom at the side. There was an antique writing desk and several chairs. The walls were panelled with wood, and there were several paintings hanging in gilt frames on the walls.

'You understand what is required?' Bormann asked them.

'Absolutely,' the Doctor said at once.

'Not a clue,' the Brigadier started to say. But he managed to turn it into a cough.

'But perhaps just a quick refresher, from your own perspective? How do you see things?' the Doctor asked. 'What would you say is the Fuhrer's priority here?'

'To find a personal physician he can put his trust in,' Bormann said with a smile that seemed to be approaching a sneer.

'Ah,' both the Doctor and the Brigadier said as light began to dawn.

'And to get the blood samples taken as quickly and unobtrusively as possible so they can be tested for compatibility. Why you had to turn up here rather than keeping the appointment agreed for tomorrow I can't imagine. But no doubt you will have a suitable explanation for the Fuhrer when he asks. A reason for disrupting events. Your discretion is essential and must be absolute,' he added, as if that was self-evident.

'Of course.' The Doctor beamed hugely. 'I'll let you get back to the party then. Ta-ta.'

As soon as the door closed behind Bormann, the Brigadier rounded on the Doctor. 'You can't take a blood sample from Hitler!'

'Why not? I'd have thought that was exactly what we should do. It's ideal.'

'It's lunacy. He'll know you're not his physician as soon as he stops to think about it. Anyway, how will you do it? Where's your syringe?'

The Doctor smiled. 'I think I have a bag of tricks in the TARDIS somewhere. Tell you what, you hold the fort here for a minute and I'll pop along and get it.' He was at the door before the Brigadier had recovered. 'Shan't be long.'

'Hang on, Doctor – what do I do if he gets here before you're back?'

'Keep him talking,' the Doctor's voice floated back along the corridor. 'Or you could offer him another sausage roll.'

In the event, the Doctor was back well before Hitler arrived. He was carrying a Gladstone bag, and spent the time they waited rummaging through it.

'Sure I had a syringe in here somewhere,' he muttered. 'Got to be in keeping with the period, of course. Or close enough for him not to notice.'

'Do you actually have the expertise to take a blood sample, Doctor?' The Brigadier was not sure he really wanted to know the answer. He was saved from finding out as the door opened at that moment, and they both leaped to their feet.

Hitler came in first, behind him was Martin Bormann. And Eva Braun.

'As quickly as you can please,' Bormann snapped as the Fuhrer seated himself in a small armchair. 'This is extremely inconvenient as you well know.' He shot a glance at Hitler, and the Brigadier guessed he had already taken the opportunity of making that point to the Fuhrer.

But Hitler seemed in a forgiving mood. 'The Brigadier General shares your name, my dear,' he said to Eva, ignoring the scowling Bormann. The Fuhrer started to roll up his sleeve – his right sleeve, the Brigadier noted, and remembered that Hitler had been left-handed. 'I gather you were at the Eastern Front.'

'It took a moment for Lethbridge-Stewart to realise that he was being spoken to. 'Oh, er, yes... My Fuhrer,' he said.

The Fuhrer looked up, ignoring the Doctor who was tapping his arm to try to locate a vein. His eyes, the Brigadier saw, were a pale, piercing blue. He was reminded both of the photograph of the dead doppelganger, a hole through his forehead, and of the video image of the same man – if it was indeed the same man – hardly looking older than he did now, staring out of a television screen.

'And what is your opinion?' the Fuhrer demanded.

'About what?' the Brigadier asked, confused and suddenly frightened by the intense scrutiny.

'I imagine he thinks as I do,' the Doctor said without looking up, 'that Stalingrad is key.' He straightened up, holding a glass syringe full of red liquid. 'There we are, all done. Whoever wins Stalingrad will win the war.'

Hitler was watching him carefully. 'You have followed the Russian campaign?'

'Oh I'm not just a medical doctor. I have various fields of expertise.' He smiled. 'Bear that in mind if, for instance, you ever need an occult specialist.' Then he winked, actually winked at the Fuhrer. 'All bunk of course, despite what good old Heinrich might say. Well, most of it. But it is a useful tool don't you think?'

The Fuhrer stood up, rubbing his arm, and then rolling down his sleeve. 'You are a perceptive man, Doctor,' he said. He nodded to Eva Braun and she took his place in the chair, slipping off her jacket. 'Have you ever been to Wewelsburg Castle?'

The Doctor exchanged an astonished look with the Brigadier. 'Not yet,' he said hurriedly. 'But I do anticipate an invitation in the future.'

Eva was rolling up her sleeve too. The Fuhrer had fixed the

Doctor with an intense stare, looking up at the larger man yet equal to him, the Brigadier saw. As they spoke, the Doctor held out the full syringe and the Brigadier took it carefully from him. He eventually interpreted the Doctor's gestures as a request for another syringe, and started to look through the bag.

Behind him he could hear the conversation between the Fuhrer and the Doctor.

'I make a point of not going,' Hitler said. 'Such folly.'

'But it is not what is actually true, of course that's important,' the Doctor said. 'It is what the people believe to be true. As no doubt Joseph would agree.'

'Indeed he would.'

In amongst the apple cores, yo-yos, electronic instruments, spare keys and discarded sweet papers, the Brigadier at last found a syringe. He hoped it would do, it looked similar to the one the Doctor had used. He passed it to the Doctor, wondering briefly how sterile it could be. Then he wondered if he cared.

'So a blood sample from each of you,' the Doctor said as he tapped at Eva Braun's arm.

'Of course,' Bormann said with ill-disguised impatience.

'Yes, well, we'll get this all sorted out just as quickly as we can then,' the Doctor assured the Fuhrer as he handed the second syringe to the Brigadier. 'Don't get them mixed up,' he cautioned as he handed Eva a strip of sticking plaster.

'Thank you, Doctor,' Eva said as she put her jacket back on and followed Bormann from the room.

The Fuhrer paused before following. 'Why did Doktor Eckhardt not attend us today?' he asked.

'Indisposed,' the Doctor said at once. 'You know how it is.'

The Fuhrer's eyes narrowed, but he did not push the point. Instead he said, 'We shall meet again I am sure, Major-Doctor.'

'Indeed we shall,' the Doctor said. He saluted.

The Brigadier also managed a half-hearted salute as the Fuhrer left. They followed him out and Bormann locked the door behind them.

* * *

'You took your time,' Claire told them. 'How long does it take two fully grown men to boil a kettle, for God's sake?'

'Less of the fully grown if you don't mind,' the Doctor said as he followed the Brigadier through to his living room. The Brigadier was carrying a tray of coffee.

'You've been gone for ages. Nearly quarter of an hour. You weren't in the kitchen, because I looked when I heard that awful noise the first time.' She helped herself to one of the mugs of coffee, and almost spilled it as she saw what the Doctor was holding. 'What the hell is that?'

'Well,' said the Doctor helpfully, 'in this syringe is a sample of Adolf Hitler's blood. And in this one, superfluous to requirements I grant you but nonetheless impressive for that, is a sample of Eva Braun's.'

Claire put her coffee down again. Very, very carefully.

Chapter Thirty

Henderson sat on the bed, unmoving. He was leaning forward, chin resting on his hands, elbows supported on his knees. He stared at the heavy metal door to the small room. Events had been set in motion. The door would open, he knew it would.

All the time in the back of his mind he listened to the tiny whispering voice of his familiar as it explored the redoubt, as it made its way through the dimly lit corridors. He shared its joy and surprise when it met its fellow, caught something of the overwhelming relief and release of the other familiar as it learned it was no longer alone, no longer cut off. No longer abandoned.

Through his familiar's eyes he saw the people working in their various rooms, and heard their conversations. He caught the tone of excitement, the sense that a new era was beginning. He had learned German years ago, there were no secrets from him here. He stared at the door, but he saw the Nazis as they prepared for the ceremony ahead. The stupid fools.

The woman, the blonde woman who delighted in pain and in power, was talking with the leader in the room with the maps on the wall. The familiar scurried over to examine the maps, listened acutely to their conversation, hid in the shadows at the edges of their consciousness.

'Bormann's strength was in planning,' the leader was saying. A part of Henderson recognised him as Hitler, a part of him was even surprised. 'He set this up all those years ago when he got me away.'

'Anyone loyal could have done that,' the woman said.

'But the financial arrangements,' Hitler chided her, 'that took genius.'

'Yes, my Fuhrer,' she said contritely. But the familiar could sense the burning in her heart and soul.

'In August 1944, as early as that,' Hitler said, 'Bormann set up a meeting in Strasbourg. A secret meeting with the leaders of German business. A meeting to decide how the struggle could continue even after the war was lost. And then he set up Operation Eagle Flight, and spirited away money, gold, bonds. Even copyrights and patents, from under the noses of the allies and into over seven hundred front corporations he set up. Oh yes,' Hitler concluded, 'do not doubt that he was a genius. And that we shall miss his expertise and experience in the days ahead.'

'But we shall win,' she told him fervently. 'Now we have these new... artefacts, these discs, we shall win.'

'Did you ever doubt it, my dear?' he asked. And she looked away.

'Prepare the final ceremony,' Hitler told her. 'See that everything is ready. With the forces and powers of darkness on our side, we cannot fail.'

The familiars followed Hanne Neumann as she went from room to room, as she bullied and cajoled and ordered the Tibetans and the Germans and the others. She gave orders in the Fuhrer's name and revelled in the power that gave her. She believed absolutely in him and in victory.

And Henderson continued to stare at the door, knowing it would open and release him.

He knew because his familiar had found the Scrying Glass, found it standing on a green-covered table at the centre of a circular chamber. Found it close to the ruins of a hibernation tank and its dead occupant. The Vvormak to which the other familiar had belonged had died as it struggled out of the tank when the potential energy of the explosion at Turelhampton remained unrealised. And Henderson's familiar had looked into the Glass and had seen the future unfold.

It – and through it Henderson too – had seen the door open. He had seen the Doctor standing there, in the doorway, waiting.

Chapter Thirty-one

Keeping Claire out of the TARDIS would probably not have been possible, the Brigadier realised. Once she believed that the Doctor was not joking and that he had actually acquired a sample of Hitler's blood somehow, there was no way she was going to leave his side.

He made her promise that she had no hidden video cameras or microphones about her person before he consented to open the TARDIS and let her in.

The Brigadier shot the Doctor a wary look. But the Doctor smiled. 'We need to use the lab if we're to learn anything.'

'This is your lab?' she asked as she pushed past them. 'Bit small isn't it?' Then a moment later, from inside the TARDIS came her exclamation as she discovered how wrong that assessment was.

'You mustn't always judge by appearances,' the Doctor told her. 'Which I suppose is why we're here, after all. Come on.'

He led them through the Console Room and down a long roundelled corridor, hesitating outside several doors before deciding on one.

'My God, this place is massive,' Claire said, not for the first time as she stared round in a state of continual amazement.

'You said,' the Brigadier reminded her.

'Wish I'd brought a camera.'

'You promised,' he reminded her again.

'I can still wish, though can't I?' She kept her fingers crossed in her pocket. She had not really lied, though. She really didn't have a hidden microphone or a video camera with her. Just a small, digital stills camera that she always carried in her pocket. Obviously, that didn't count. After all she wouldn't use it. Would she?

They followed the Doctor through the door, and the Brigadier was not at all surprised to find himself inside a huge laboratory. It seemed to be a mixture of styles and eras. In one corner was a basin with a pestle and mortar standing on the worktop beside it, together with a pile of what looked like dried leaves. Further along was a Victorian entanglement of glass tubes and flasks held in place by retorts and stands. The Doctor was at another part of the workbench, beside a collection of clinically white boxes with electronic read-outs set in them and stainless steel handles on their doors.

In front of him on the workbench the Doctor had arranged the tiny fragment of bone from Hitler's skull – from whoever's skull – beside one of the plastic cups of liquid. Beside these he placed a glass syringe. Further away, he had put the other cup and the other syringe.

The Brigadier stood with Claire as they watched the Doctor at work. Claire maintained a respectful silence for a change.

'Soon we shall know,' the Doctor mused as he chipped off an even smaller fragment of bone from the piece of skull and placed it inside one of the white devices. There was a whirring sound, barely more than a background hum, and the read-out screen lit up. A trail of numbers moved swiftly across it, and, just as rapidly, the Doctor noted them down on a jotter with a well-chewed stump of pencil.

'I had no idea DNA testing was that simple,' the Brigadier said as the Doctor removed the fragment of bone from the machine.

'It isn't,' the Doctor told him. 'At least, not yet.' He removed the lid from the cup marked 'A' and carefully lowered a pipette into it, squeezing the bulb gently. 'Niffs a bit, doesn't he!' He replaced the lid, and dripped a drop of the liquid onto a microscope slide. That too went into the device, and again the Doctor jotted down the numbers and letters that the readout displayed.

'Yes, you see – they match.' The Doctor held up the notepad like a music hall magician.

The Brigadier was less impressed. 'Yes, well that's hardly surprising.'

'What does that tell us?' Claire asked.

'It tells us that the skull fragments and the bodily fluids come from the same person,' the Doctor explained. 'Which means that at least we're only dealing with one body.' He reached for the syringe and allowed a drop of blood to fall from the tip on to another slide. 'Now for the clincher.'

'We know from the document I found that there was a substitution,' the Brigadier said. 'We already know these won't match. That the body wasn't Hitler.'

The Doctor started to copy down the readout display. 'We know nothing of the sort. Until now we only suspect.' He finished writing and looked up, his face split by a smile. '*Now* we know,' he said and brandished the pad.

Claire peered at it while the Brigadier and the Doctor grinned at each other triumphantly. 'Hang on a minute,' she said. 'I mean, I hate to break up the party, but you've just written down the same DNA sequence again.'

'What?' the Doctor squeaked uncharacteristically.

'All three match.'

They stared at the pad. The Doctor ran his finger along character by character. For once, he seemed at a loss for words.

'Is it possible we got the samples muddled?' the Brigadier asked.

'Then they wouldn't match at all,' Claire told him.

'Or maybe this equipment isn't working.'

'It's working fine,' the Doctor told him in a huff. 'You were wrong, that's all.'

'I was wrong, Doctor?' The Brigadier was bristling now. 'Hold on a moment, just now you yourself were saying – '

Claire held her hands up for silence. 'It doesn't matter!' she shouted over them. 'It doesn't matter at all who said what to whom or what the consequence was.'

'You're right of course,' the Brigadier agreed. 'But I was so sure,' he said with evident disappointment.

'Not enough, I'm afraid,' the Doctor said. 'Hitler is dead. He died in the Berlin bunker on April 30th 1945, just as everyone knows. And this proves it.'

'So where does that leave us?' Claire asked.

'Goodness only knows,' the Brigadier said.

The Doctor said nothing. He was removing the lid from the other plastic cup, and dipping in a fresh pipette. 'I like to be tidy, and I like to be thorough,' he told them as they watched him put the slide into the machine. Again he jotted down the numbers and letters. Then he reached for the second syringe.

'I suppose it changes nothing,' he said as he started the machine one last time, waiting for the readout to light up. 'The problem is the same, only the players have changed. In fact, discrediting our fake Hitler should be pretty straightforward which will speed things up.' He finished writing and looked at the pad thoughtfully.

'Assuming you can persuade people that you just happen to have genuine blood samples from Adolf Hitler and Eva Braun,' the Brigadier said.

'And assuming I have,' the Doctor replied. His voice was low, but there was an edge of excitement in it. 'That document you copied, Brigadier.'

'What about it?'

'What's-his-name, Baur, said that the body was substituted, isn't that right? That a different body was burned so nobody would spot the substitution.'

'Yes, but now we know he lied.'

The Doctor was shaking his head. 'No he didn't. Because he wasn't talking about Adolf Hitler being replaced by a double at all.'

The Doctor passed the pad to the Brigadier and he looked down at the last two lines written on it. Beside him, Claire craned to see it too. 'My God,' he murmured. 'He meant Eva Braun. It was Eva Braun who had a double.'

They had returned to the Brigadier's sitting room for drinks. Claire was nursing a large brandy, her brain repeating time after time in her head: 'This is the Big One, this is the Big One,' as she wondered how she could ever prove anything, or come to that what it meant.

The Brigadier had an even larger brandy and was trying to calm the Doctor who was pacing the room muttering excitedly. His brandy was long gone – lost in a single gigantic gulp. It appeared to have had no effect whatsoever.

'Where's that autopsy report?' the Doctor demanded. 'The Russian one.'

'It's in Russian,' the Brigadier said apologetically, producing it from his desk in the corner of the room.

'Well of course it is.' The Doctor raised his eyes momentarily heavenwards.

'No don't tell me, you learned Russian years ago so as to read Tolstoy in the original,' the Brigadier said, voice dripping with sarcasm.

'Don't be absurd,' the Doctor said as he looked through the photocopied pages. 'It was Chekov. Often you know,' he went on as he flicked through the pages, 'it's what is omitted rather than what is said that is enlightening.'

'Such as?' Claire asked.

'Such as the fact that while there were fragments of glass in Eva Braun's mouth – well, whoever's mouth – there is no mention that cyanide or any other strong poison was found in her body.' He slumped into a chair and started going through the report again. 'Don't you think that's interesting?'

'So she wasn't poisoned,' Claire said quietly.

The Brigadier looked across at her, excited. 'Of course, don't you remember, there were shrapnel wounds.'

'Yes, here we are,' the Doctor said waving a page. 'Upper lobe of the left lung showed two large perforations… six steel fragments removed from the body measuring…' He looked up in surprise. 'Measuring up to half a square centimetre. That's rather big. And here, there's a description of a "clearly discernible haemorrhage."'

'Is that important?' Claire asked.

'Vital. If there was sufficient blood pressure actually to haemorrhage, it would suggest, very strongly suggest, that the poor unfortunate woman was alive when she was hit by the shrapnel.'

'She was hit by shell fragments?' the Brigadier mused. 'Berlin was a battle zone at the time, after all.'

'Then they made it look like she was Eva Braun and she'd taken poison.' The Doctor blew out a long breath that made the papers shiver. 'Her teeth were in a pretty parlous state after the burning. Hard to think they could ever believe they'd got an accurate identification from those.'

'But why?' the Brigadier asked. 'It all seems to fit, even the report of Bormann taking a woman to Hamburg and on to that submarine. But why go to such lengths to save Eva Braun, but not the Fuhrer?'

'Yes, what could she possibly have that they wanted to preserve that he couldn't?' Claire asked.

'Come to that,' the Brigadier went on, 'why go to Berlin at all if only to escape again. With the Russians knocking at the gate, why not just keep well away?'

Suddenly the Doctor was on his feet again. Pages of autopsy went flying in a blizzard of paper. 'Oh come on!' he roared. 'It's staring us in the face – can't you see it?'

'To be frank, Doctor, no I can't,' the Brigadier said.

'You're right. You're both right,' he said excitedly.

'Oh good,' Claire said.

But the Doctor ignored her. 'She went to Berlin to see Hitler. And what else did she do while she was there?' He pointed at the Brigadier and snapped his fingers like a Victorian school master. 'Come on, come on,' he urged.

'Well, she got married to him.'

'Exactly!' He stared at their blank faces. 'Still not there, are you?' He shook his head in disappointment at his star pupils' failure to catch on. 'Why was it important that she talk to him?' the Doctor asked. 'Why was it important that they be married? Why, back in August 1942, were both Hitler and Eva Braun having blood tests?' He looked at Claire, his eyes alive and intense. 'You said yourself, it had to be something she could do that he couldn't, that was why she was saved. What were they really preserving?'

Then she saw it. And it all made perfect sense. 'Oh my God,' she said, her blood running cold in her veins. 'Eva Braun was pregnant.'

Chapter Thirty-two

Once the shock had worn off, they spent some time reconstructing the events of 1945. Claire made notes, scribbling down their conclusions over more brandy. It was beginning to go to her head and she felt slightly unreal. Her handwriting was all over the place.

'They found a body somewhere, a woman who was already dead which is I suppose a mercy.'

'No shortage,' the Doctor said. 'As the Brigadier points out, Berlin was being blown apart. There was enough death on the streets even for the Nazis.'

'Do you think they were all in on it? Everyone in the bunker?' she asked.

'Doubt it,' the Brigadier said. 'Baur talked about a tableau in that fragment of interrogation. Like any clandestine operation, the fewer people who know the better.' He paused to sip at his brandy. 'I'd say that Baur the pilot and Linge the valet were in on it. And Rattenhuber – Baur mentioned him keeping the others out. He was Hitler's chief bodyguard. Bormann too of course. But the others, the secretaries, even Goebbels and his wife, probably not.'

'So Hitler and Eva say their goodbyes and retire to their room,' the Doctor went on. 'Hitler takes poison and as he bites into the capsule he shoots himself, probably under the chin. That would force his mouth to close on the ampoule too.'

Claire grimaced. 'Ugh!'

'As you so aptly say, "ugh." Then Linge says he heard a shot – maybe he did, but the others don't remember. He goes in first, maybe with Baur, to check everything's all right. Hitler is dead, and Eva is curled up on the sofa pretending. But the doctor, Stumpfegger presumably, pronounced them dead.'

'So he had to be in on it too,' Claire pointed out.

'Very likely,' the Brigadier agreed. 'Or else they just told him what to say and kept him away from Eva. He'd be more interested in Hitler anyway.'

'The bodies are wrapped in blankets,' the Doctor continued, 'and carried out of the Bunker.'

'There are witnesses who saw Eva's face, though they didn't know who she was,' the Brigadier said. 'So the substitution was made outside. Perhaps the other body was waiting there to be burned.'

The Doctor nodded. 'They burn the bodies, and then Bormann takes Eva away. Baur flies them out of the Tiergarten and down to Hamburg where they join a submarine and they're away to... where, I wonder?'

'Argentina?' Claire suggested. 'That seems a traditional haunt of escaping Nazis.'

'A stopping off point perhaps, but hardly a long term base. No,' the Doctor tapped his chin thoughtfully. 'No, they'd want somewhere secure, secret, isolated. But wherever it was, the child is born. It's a boy. A boy who is now fifty-five or fifty-six years old.'

'Hitler celebrated his fifty-sixth birthday in the Bunker, days before he died,' Claire reminded them. 'If celebrated is the right word.'

'The boy is brought up to revere the memory of his father, imbued with his ideals, given his vision.' The Doctor shook his head sadly. 'The poor, poor child.' He took a deep breath. 'But with one difference. Unlike his father, this Hitler – Hitler Junior if you like – is taught from birth that the occult, the dark arts, the arcana is not half-baked nonsense only useful to drive the propaganda machine, but is actually real and useful to him in its own right.'

'The question is, Doctor, what are they doing?'

'We know what they're doing, Brigadier,' the Doctor snapped back. 'They already have huge economic influences, most of them secret. They are gaining credibility for their hateful philosophy and ideals. They are building support both at the grass roots level and amongst leaders in industry, finance and politics. They are using the Scrying Glass to see their own future, and they are planning the right moment simultaneously to unleash the forces of darkness.'

'Whatever that means,' Claire murmured.

'Whatever that means?' the Doctor echoed incredulously. 'Whatever that means?! It means an explosion of power that will make the nuclear blast at Turelhampton look like a damp firecracker if they can focus enough potential energy into the Glass itself.'

'Another nuclear bomb?' the Brigadier asked.

'Nothing so crude. They've been pouring in hate and emotion and fear at every one of their nonsensical ceremonies around the world for decades. Imagine the power within that Glass now, the power waiting to be unleashed if and when they hit on the right way to do it.'

'Which is?'

'I don't know, Claire. And I hope they don't either. No, the question is, to get back to the Brigadier's earlier point, the question is – where are they now? Where is their secret base of operations?'

Claire put down her brandy glass. She had drunk quite enough she decided. 'You know, after my death of Hitler documentary, which I have to say is looking slightly jaded now, Gordon at the Conspiracy Channel had me research a follow-up about how UFOs are really secret Nazi-designed flying discs, and the Fourth Reich is actually in existence inside the Earth's crust. But all that hollow Earth stuff, and the notion of Nazis abducting people for experimental surgery while pretending to be aliens... Well, it was too far-fetched even for Gordon.'

The Doctor was looking at her through narrowed eyes. 'Tell me,' he said tightly, 'is there a point to this? At all?'

Claire shrugged. 'I was just wondering if this secret base thing could be in Antarctica. That's all.' When they just stared at her, she felt perhaps she ought to elaborate. 'You see, never mind the hollow Earth theory, the Nazis were very interested in Antarctica. Just before the war, like 1938 or 1939, they sent expeditions and claimed the territory. Even dropped Swastika flags all over the place. They renamed it Neu Schwabenland, or something. Did loads of surveys.'

'Scientific or geographical interest perhaps?' the Brigadier wondered.

'Maybe. But the conspiracy people were hot on the idea that the German expeditions were really to set up a secret base under the ice.' She trailed off, seeing their blank expressions. 'OK, so it was just a thought. What with the ice and snow and stuff we saw on the camera in the Brig's briefcase, I just wondered... Right,' she decided. 'Forget it. Next?'

The Doctor's expression was unchanged as he leaped out of his chair and grabbed Claire's unsuspecting hand. He pumped it up and down and a broad grin finally broke across his face. 'Brilliant,' he exclaimed. 'An excellent example of deductive reasoning under the influence of pressure.' He wrinkled his nose, evidently catching the brandy on her breath. 'Not to mention, other influences.'

The Brigadier however remained dubious. 'You really think so, Doctor?'

'I do, I do,' he maintained emphatically.

'So what do we do about it?' Claire asked, retrieving her aching hand.

'We go and look, of course. Come along, come along. Don't dawdle.'

He was out of the room before either Claire or the Brigadier had recovered sufficiently to follow.

'But Doctor,' the Brigadier called after him as they hurried out, 'isn't Antarctica a trifle too large to just go there and see?'

The Doctor was standing by the open TARDIS door. 'Not at all,' he cried. He shooed them inside, his expression set to 'smug.'

Once inside the Doctor was immediately at the TARDIS controls. 'We'll just hover about a bit and look for heat traces. If they are there, the old girl will sniff them out. Won't you,' he added, patting the console affectionately.

'But surely someone else would have seen heat traces,' Claire said. 'I mean, satellites, or planes, or scientific surveys or something.'

'She's got a point, Doctor.'

'Possibly. But there aren't many satellites looking at the south pole you know, and people don't holiday there often.'

'Even so,' she grumbled.

'Even so, I fancy the TARDIS sensors are considerably more sensitive than anything else that's been up and peeked.' He flicked a switch, watching in satisfaction as the central column rose and fell. 'We shall soon know.'

The scanner showed an unbroken expanse of white.

'Nothing,' the Brigadier said, disappointed.

'I haven't set the parameters for the sensors yet, you know. Give it a chance.' The Doctor busied himself at the controls. 'I'll just set it for heat sensitivity, and get the old girl to home in on whatever source she finds. There we are.' He straightened up and clapped his hands together. 'That should do it.'

'Still nothing,' Claire pointed out. But even as she said it she could see a faint image forming over the ice and snow below them. A shape was creeping out of the whiteness, formed out of shades of blue and orange and red.

'I would think that's it, wouldn't you?' the Doctor said quietly.

'They're nothing if not arrogant, are they?' the Brigadier agreed. 'Let's go in a bit closer and see if we can make out that landing strip, shall we?'

Claire said nothing. She was still staring at the image on the scanner. At the rainbow-coloured shape standing proud of the icy wastes of Antarctica, showing the heat signature of an underground base. An underground base that had been built in the shape of a Swastika.

Chapter Thirty-three

It was cold and it was damp, and Claire felt that she had kept to the spirit of her agreement if not to the letter. The camera she had in her pocket was a tiny digital stills camera, but she had been true to her promise and taken no photos inside the TARDIS. That was partly why she was so indignant when both the Doctor and the Brigadier suggested she might like to stay inside the TARDIS while they went out to see what was happening.

Actually, indignant was a slight understatement. She had explained at high speed and high volume what she thought of this suggestion, and despite some muttered comments from the Doctor and a grim look from the Brigadier, they had agreed.

However it worked, the TARDIS had somehow landed inside the Nazi base. Probably that was no more impressive than the fact that it had taken off from inside a building. But it unsettled Claire nonetheless. She kept close to her two companions as they made their furtive way along the damp stone-walled corridor.

They paused at an intersection with another, wider corridor and the Doctor gestured for them to huddle close together so he could whisper. 'I don't think there's anyone about,' he said in his normal voice and Claire was pleased to see that the Brigadier flinched as well.

The Doctor seemed oblivious. 'The TARDIS set us down in what showed on the scanner as the coldest part of the complex.'

'We can tell,' Claire told him, shivering.

He spared her a quick look of annoyance, then went on: 'I'm hoping that the reason this area is so much colder than the rest is because they don't use it. Or at least, not much. So we can sneak into the more populated part rather than draw attention to ourselves by materialising in front of everyone.'

'Or wearing particularly garish clothes,' Claire said through chattering teeth.

The Doctor regarded her closely. 'If anyone sees you sneaking about,' he said loftily, 'they might well conclude that you have no business here. Whereas my own rather sartorial attire will immediately mark me out as a person of status who has every reason to be here and knows it.' He nodded abruptly, point made.

'So are we just going to stand around here freezing our...' The Brigadier glanced at Claire before he went on, 'freezing our toes off, or do you have some sort of plan, Doctor?'

'You won't have to freeze your toes off for long,' the Doctor replied. 'Because we're heading for the hottest part of the base. The main generators.'

'Good,' Claire told him.

'And we're going to sabotage the generators, so that everybody's toes are equally frozen. Then while they're all trying to keep warm and get the generators repaired, we can use the confusion to cover our search for the Scrying Glass.'

'And what then?'

'Then we take it back to the TARDIS and away we go. Job done. No problem.'

'That'll be a first,' the Brigadier said with a sniff.

They were walking along the wider corridor now, and Claire was sure it was getting slightly warmer. There were doors set at regular intervals along both sides.

'But before all that,' the Doctor said as he stopped abruptly in front of a door, 'I want to know why this door is bolted when all the others are not.'

'Idle curiosity?' the Brigadier wondered as the Doctor reached for the bolt.

He turned his head as he struggled to pull the bolt back. 'Not entirely. Look at the shadow on the wall opposite.'

The doors were staggered on each side of the corridor, so that each door faced blank wall on the other side. There were lights hanging from the ceiling, casting stark yellowish light on to the walls and doors and floor. On the wall opposite the door the Doctor was opening there was indeed a shadow, though Claire could see nothing between the wall and the light that might be casting it.

It was a figure, short and squat with a smooth head. And protruding from the head were two stumpy horns. As she watched, the shadow moved, the head turning so that it seemed to be watching her. She shivered again, and turned quickly away.

The Doctor had the bolt undone now, and opened the door. The room beyond seemed to be a cell. It was devoid of furniture apart from a low metal-framed bed with a thin mattress on it. Sitting on the bed was Henderson, his chin resting on his hands, his elbows on his knees as he watched the door swing open.

Claire gave a sharp intake of breath. 'You're alive,' she said in some surprise.

But Henderson ignored her. 'Doctor,' he said quietly, 'we've been waiting for you.'

Without further explanation, Henderson rose from the bed and pushed past them into the corridor. He set off in the direction they had been going before. The shadow he cast as he walked showed two of the imp-like figures keeping pace with him, one on either side.

'Would you mind telling us where we're going?' the Doctor asked. He had to run to catch up.

'To retrieve the Scrying Glass.'

'You know where it is?'

'My familiars have found it. We know the way.'

The Doctor nodded. 'Picked up a friend have you? The familiar who was with the Vvormak in the hibernation tank the Germans took in 1944, I assume. What happened to him?'

'He is dead,' Henderson said simply. 'The potential energy I stored up at Turelhampton was sufficient to wake him, bring him out of the casket. But it was never realised, and so it could not sustain life outside the tank. There was only enough for the familiar to survive. Afraid and alone.'

'I'm sorry,' the Doctor told him.

'Oh don't worry about us,' Claire muttered. 'Or Goldman, or Spinney.'

'So far so good,' the Brigadier said. 'But we're bound to run into someone soon if we aren't careful. What do we do then?'

Henderson paused, and they all waited. Claire took the opportunity to turn away from them and snap a quick shot of the corridor. Not very exciting, she thought. It could be anywhere, after all.

She turned back in time to see Henderson make a gesture with his hands, as if shooing an animal away. In response there was a blur of motion along the corridor walls. Shadows darted, scuttled along them. She realised that he had sent the familiars, the imps, on ahead to warn them if anyone was coming.

But there was nobody. Nobody at all. The whole place seemed to be deserted. They crossed a large dining area where the four main corridors that formed the cross of the Swastika met. They turned down one of the corridors, and followed it almost to the end, almost to the knee-bend.

As they made their way along the corridor, it seemed to Claire that she could hear something. Quiet, faint at first, the sounds grew louder as they proceeded. It was a regular, rhythmic sound that she only recognised when the Brigadier murmured.

'I can hear chanting.'

'Yes,' the Doctor said. His voice was low. 'I rather think we've arrived during one of their occult ceremonies.'

'The final ceremony,' Henderson said, still leading them onwards. 'The ceremony during which they believe they will conjure the forces that will shape their future.'

'And will they?' Claire asked, breathless.

'In a sense, yes.' He had to speak loudly to be heard above the chants and cries now. 'Here!' He stopped outside a large wooden door braced with steel. 'This is the place. The Scrying Glass is through here.'

'So by the sound of it is everyone else,' the Brigadier pointed out. 'I'd suggest we wait until they've finished this nonsense, then try to sneak in and get hold of the thing.'

'I think discretion is called for, don't you?' the Doctor said to Henderson.

He returned the Doctor's level gaze. 'No,' he said. 'We go in now.'

'But we can't possibly succeed,' the Doctor objected. 'There is no way we can get in there, steal the Scrying Glass and get out again without being stopped. If we're lucky, they may just kill us.'

'Now,' Henderson repeated with determination, turning to the door, reaching for the handle.

'Why?' the Doctor cried with exasperation as the Brigadier moved quickly to catch his hand, to stop him opening the door.

But Henderson was stronger, his eyes burning with determination. Shadows swirled round him and the Brigadier seemed to be shoved suddenly aside.

'Because I have seen it happen,' Henderson said. And he threw open the door.

The chamber facing them was tiny – an anteroom of some kind. There was a door in the opposite wall that might lead through to another room. Maybe that was where the Scrying Glass was, as Claire could see that it wasn't in here.

But the room was not empty. Two figures emerged from either side of the door. A man and a woman. Claire recognised both.

One was the blonde woman they had seen on the briefcase camera. And she was holding a gun. She motioned for them to step into the small room, and Claire followed the example of Henderson, the Doctor and the Brigadier and obeyed.

The man watched them carefully, the candlelight flickering in his brilliant blue eyes. She knew the face only too well.

Beside Claire, the Doctor leaned forward. His tone was at once somehow mocking and deadly serious. 'Adolf Hitler, I presume.'

The man smiled as he surveyed the little group of them standing in the cramped space.

'Actually, you are right,' he said at last in slightly accented English. 'Named after my father. Welcome to the future. Welcome to the Fourth Reich.'

'And what do you know of the future?' the Doctor asked.

'I have seen it,' he replied simply. 'Although, sadly, you shall not.' He turned to the woman with the gun. 'Hanne…?'

But at that moment, the outer door opened and another man,

an Oriental, came into the room. He was dressed in a dark robe, and he was carrying the Scrying Glass. Henderson immediately stepped forward, but the woman – Hanne – prodded him back with the gun.

'Thank you, Renchan,' Hitler said to the robed figure. 'We shall continue shortly. My apologies for this slight delay.'

The robed man nodded, and placed the Scrying Glass carefully on a low table by the inner door.

Hitler spread his hands either side of the ball of crystal so that the reflections of his fingers seemed to stretch round it, as if holding it. 'My window on to the future,' he said. 'From here we conjure the forces that will help us. We summon the night. We bring forth the darkness.'

The Doctor whistled through his teeth. 'Sounds to me like a lot of euphemisms for not very much. Once summoned and brought forth, what will all this obliging blackness do for you?'

'I have seen it all, here in the Glass,' said Hitler softly. 'How the world falls. The sky burning red over levelled buildings. A sign that soon there shall be a single flag planted in all the Earth.' He looked the Doctor unflinchingly in the eye. 'The world moves too quickly now to sustain a war that could last years. With the weapons at our disposal… with the forces of the abyss we are harnessing… our *blitzkrieg* will be exactly that. Key military and industrial targets around the globe will be destroyed from the outset. With our own shadow economy geared up to take over Germany, with our political forces poised to seize control of world governments –'

'Oh, I understand,' the Doctor cut across him coldly. 'That's what all this is about. The same old stagnant ideals dredged up once again. The *old* order, stamping their feet like sulking brats, desperate to continue the stupid, idiot carnage begun over half a century ago.' The room rang with his words as his voice rose in volume and passion. 'Your philosophy is barren, Hitler. Your filthy creed is as tired and as worn out as your precious father was by the War's end, a shell of a man within the shell of a building.'

'You will be silent!' roared Hitler.

'And you know it, too, that's why you've been skulking about in the dark for so long. Why you look to the blazing red sky over a ruined landscape as some kind of victory – because there is no place in the daylit world for you or your laughable, despicable policies.' The Doctor abruptly yawned, loudly. 'Your father would not have been impressed,' he said as he stretched.

Hitler's eyes flashed with anger as he turned to the Doctor. 'What do you know of my father?' he demanded.

'Oh I knew him,' the Doctor said. 'The Brigadier here offered him a sausage roll, didn't you Alistair?'

'I'd rather not be reminded of that, thank you Doctor,' the Brigadier said in an embarrassed tone. To Claire, this was more convincing than if he had agreed enthusiastically. She shivered.

'He never believed in all that occult nonsense,' the Doctor went on. 'We chatted about it once, I recall. But then, he never had the benefit of your rather special educational background.'

'What do you know about my background?' Hitler demanded.

'Rather a lot, I fancy. I know, for instance, that your mother was smuggled out of Berlin by Reichleiter Bormann before you were born.' He stepped closer to Hitler, towering over him. He pointed to the Scrying Glass. 'And I know what this is, which is more than you do, I fancy.'

'You know nothing!' Hitler spat back at him. The blonde woman raised her gun to cover the Doctor, her face hard as granite.

'All right, smarty pants,' the Doctor shouted back with equal vehemence. 'If you're so clever, what is it? Tell us that.'

Hitler controlled his anger. He was shaking with suppressed emotion, but his voice was level. 'Like I say, I have seen the forces of the abyss summoned forth within it. The shadow in the glass.'

'Really? And what form did these forces take?'

'A face in the darkness. The horned beast, its eyes shining bright.'

The Doctor glanced at Henderson. But the other man was staring at the Scrying Glass, his attention fully focused. Claire looked instinctively to where his shadow danced and flickered on the floor. But it seemed to be only a shadow of Henderson himself.

'You still have not answered my question,' the Doctor said, turning back to Hitler. 'You've told me what you think it does, not what you think it is.'

'My Fuhrer.' The blonde woman was getting impatient. The robed figure was also shuffling his feet awkwardly.

'It is all right, Hanne,' Hitler replied. 'It uses the Vril energy that surrounds us all, surrounds the whole world,' he said to the Doctor, looking again at the Scrying Glass. 'But I don't expect you to understand that.'

'Really?' The Doctor sounded bored. 'It seems to me that I'm not the one who has trouble understanding.'

'What do you mean?'

'Vril energy? What nonsense.' The Doctor gave a snort of laughter.

'You know nothing of these matters,' Hitler shot back.

'I know that Vril energy, or Astral Light as it is also called, is supposed to be a subtle energy that surrounds the whole Earth. In it is preserved a record of every thought and every action that has ever occurred.'

'So, you do know.'

'I also know that it's complete and utter nonsense. Fiction.'

'Fiction?' Hitler's eyes blazed.

'Fiction,' the Doctor repeated calmly. 'From a novel. It's actually not bad, I can recommend you read it since you obviously haven't.' Hitler was shaking now, his whole frame seemed to be about to burst as the Doctor went on: '*The Coming Race*, written by an Englishman called Edward Bulwer-Lytton. Published in 1870, I think.' He smiled hugely. Then a cloud seemed to cross his face. 'No, wait I'm wrong.'

'You admit your folly!' Hitler declaimed in triumph.

'I certainly do, how could I be so crass?' the Doctor cried, smacking his palm against his forehead. 'What was I thinking about? It was 1871.' And suddenly his grin was back.

Hitler was shaking again, so much so he had trouble speaking.

'You – you will watch the final ceremony. You will see the forces conjured forth.'

'Doubt it,' the Doctor told him, taking a pace backwards in response to Hanne's jab with the pistol.

'Then… Then you will die.' He threw open the inner door, and for a moment the background sound of the chanting was louder.

Then the chanting stopped abruptly.

The immediate impression Claire got was that the room was huge – bigger even than the dining area they had passed through. It was circular, the edges of it lost in darkness. The only illumination came from the hundreds, if not thousands, of black candles that stood in concentric circles.

And the room was full of people. At first she thought there was only the robed man at the central podium, his hand frozen, upraised. But then she saw the robed figures standing in a circle round him. And finally, as they turned towards the door, she saw the others – perhaps fifty people, men and women, in dark uniforms.

The Doctor seemed interested, looking round with animation and nodding politely to the people standing in concentric circles. The Brigadier held his head high, proud and almost aristocratic under pressure. Henderson seemed unperturbed, his attention focused, Claire saw, on the robed figure who now carried the Scrying Glass to the podium. He set it on a stand on the green-covered table set there.

A large man with a broken nose joined Hanne and led them all to the back of the room. He too had a pistol. Hanne followed, keeping her own gun aimed squarely at the Doctor's back. At the podium, Hitler joined the front row of observers.

As they were ushered into the outermost circle, Claire looked round. Apart from Hanne and the man with the gun, everyone else was concentrating on the podium, watching as the man raised his gloved hands over the Scrying Glass. Was it her imagination, Claire wondered, or were the shadows behind him somehow deeper than they had been before?

The Brigadier was standing next to her, but she had no time to ask his opinion, as the chanting started. The final ceremony to conjure forth the dark forces had begun.

Chapter Thirty-four

It was almost funny. Almost.

Under different circumstances, Claire might have laughed out loud. The room was quiet. Not a soul moved. The robed figures round the podium stood with their arms upraised. The master of ceremonies or whatever he was looked round anxiously.

Further along the row where Claire was standing, the Doctor cleared his throat noisily into the silence. His voice was clear and unrepentant. 'Well, I did tell you.'

The ceremony had lasted perhaps half an hour. If it weren't for the incentive of people with guns standing watching, Claire would have left halfway through out of boredom. Lots of chanting, some audience response and participation. Most of it in German, some of it in what the Doctor stage-whispered was a Tibetan dialect. And then, as the whole thing reached its impassioned climax... Nothing happened.

Hitler stepped on to the podium, elbowing the robed figure aside. 'I don't understand.' He did not speak especially loudly, and his words were directed at the Tibetan, Renchan. But his voice carried easily to the back of the room.

'Then you should,' the Doctor called back. Hanne jabbed him in the small of the back with her gun and he turned to glare at her indignantly. 'You'd rather not know what the problem is then?' he demanded. 'What a many-splendoured thing ignorance can be.'

Hitler was staring down at the table, at the inert Scrying Glass. But he had heard the Doctor's words. 'Explain!' he roared without looking up.

'Ah!' The Doctor immediately brightened. 'A man with aspirations to learn, how refreshing.' He pushed aside Hanne's gun with his fingertip. 'Excuse me, would you?' he asked sweetly, and made his way towards the podium. As he passed behind Henderson, the Brigadier and Claire he murmured: 'See you back at the TARDIS. After Mr Henderson's diversion.'

Claire had no idea what he meant. But she could feel the adrenaline. She was ready to run as soon as she could do so without fear of being shot. She fingered the slim shape of the digital camera through the material of her jacket, but she did not dare to try to use it. An exclusive like this was all very well, but it wasn't worth dying for. Probably.

'Now then,' the Doctor said as he joined Hitler on the podium and looked down at the Scrying Glass and the discs. 'What appears to be the problem?'

There was a general shuffling of feet now, Murmured conversations were starting amongst the onlookers.

On the podium, Hitler was shaking his head. 'Why didn't it work?' he demanded. 'All the signs have been there.'

'Perhaps you've not been reading them correctly,' the Doctor suggested.

'Each and every ceremony has built on the last. Every image, every vision has suggested that the forces will be conjured forth.' He looked up at the Doctor, face pale and drawn. 'When the war was coming to an end, Himmler ordered ceremonies to be held all across Berlin, echoing this ceremony. Those specially trained to find the still point within themselves died – took their own lives – to enhance the images I have seen since. And I tell you, I have seen the face of the darkness, here within the crystal.'

The Doctor's reply was barely more than a whisper. 'I don't think so.'

'I tell you I have!' Hitler screamed back at him. He was shaking his head in rage and exasperation. The onlookers were quiet again now, stilled by his temper. 'My father used the Glass,' he said, slightly calmer now. 'I know he did.'

'I think you're right,' the Doctor said. 'In fact I think Himmler and your father used it many times, and foresaw this moment. Adolf Hitler spoke of the "coming man". He meant his son. He meant you.'

'If it worked for him, why won't it work for me. Now?'

All attention was on the two men on the podium. Slowly, as

quietly as she could, Claire stepped out into the aisle and started towards them.

The Doctor was shaking his head. 'I think it has shown you all it needs to. Its only purpose is to be reunited with the ship it came from. It showed your father where that ship was in the hope he would bring the whole craft to Berlin and put the Glass back inside. Since then it has shown you only images that will bring you to the same point – the ship to the Glass, or the Glass to the ship.'

Claire was level with the front row now. She hoped that Hanne and the man with the gun were too preoccupied watching the podium to have noticed her, hoped they were aware only of Henderson and the Brigadier.

'You are talking nonsense. I have seen the sky blood red over the decimation. I have seen the explosions in the night that herald the coming blitzkrieg.' He reached up and grabbed the Doctor's lapels, pulling him down to stare right into his eyes. 'I have seen the face of the darkness.'

The Doctor knocked his hands away, and there was an audible gasp from the others there. But before anyone could react further, the Doctor had grabbed Hitler's shoulders, turning him back to face the table, pointing at the Scrying glass with a steady index finger. 'Is that what you saw?' he demanded.

Claire craned forward, trying to make out the shape in the Glass.

'Yes,' Hitler breathed. 'Yes. Do you see it? In the Glass?'

'Yes and no,' the Doctor replied.

Claire could see it. The face of one of the imp-like familiars seeming to stare out of the Glass at them, its eyes glowing as it looked from Hitler to the Doctor.

'Is that what you have seen before?' the Doctor asked quietly.

Hitler nodded, his attention fixed on the glass.

'I'm sorry to disillusion you,' the Doctor said, 'but that isn't an image in the Scrying Glass at all, you know. That is not the future.'

'It is there,' Hitler told him.

'No it isn't. It's over there, actually. Look.' He pointed to the floor beside the podium. 'You can see its shadow.'

Slowly Hitler turned to look where the Doctor pointed. Claire was staring at the ground too, as, she sensed, were most of the other people in the room. And there, cast in flickering darkness across the floor, was the stark shadow of one of the familiars. Its hunched form turned slowly as if looking round at the assembled crowd. In the Glass, the face swung slowly from side to side, the eyes darting back and forth. There was a collective gasp of surprise.

'What are you saying?' Hitler's voice was a dry croak.

'That you saw nothing in the Glass. At least, not any sort of face of darkness. What you saw was right beside you, watching with you. A reflection. A shadow. No more.'

'No. It isn't true! I do not believe it.'

The Doctor opened his mouth to reply. But it was Henderson's voice that cut through from the back of the room. 'Believe it. Could an image do this?'

And at that moment, despite what the Doctor had said, it seemed to her that all the forces of hell broke loose.

The black candles swayed despite the lack of breeze, and one by one they were snuffed out. At first it was a slow process, drawing gasps first of surprise, then of apprehension. The process was speeding up, candle after candle was snuffed out, sending smoky trails of darkness lazily into the air, adding to the encroaching shadows. There was no other light in the room apart from the candles. The darkness was growing.

And then the breeze came. It was a sudden impossible inrush of air, a great wind that blew through the room, guttering the remaining candles and extinguishing many of them. It was accompanied by a roaring sound, a growing rumble of noise that seemed to emanate from the stone of the walls, from the floor, even from the ceiling. It echoed around and within the place, joined almost at once by the screams and shouts of the people trapped in there with it.

Hitler seemed not to notice. He was leaning on the table, his head level with the Scrying Glass as he stared into it. Claire could see his mouth working, could just make out his words:

'Not true... Not true. I did see. I did!'

The door was open now, casting a skewed oblong of light across the concentric circles and the snuffed out candles. Providing a point of focus other than the podium and the few candles that still burned. An escape. People were rushing, pushing, climbing, hurling themselves towards the door as the rush of wind continued to increase, hurling candle-holders across the room and whipping at people's hair and clothes.

Claire struggled to stay upright, struggled not to be swept off her feet by the rushing air or the rushing people. Illuminated in the light from the doorway, just for a moment before it was all but blotted out by the dark mass of people that surged and poured through it, Claire saw Hanne standing at the back of the room. The gun was still in her hand and she turned, swinging the run round, looking for a target. Beside her the armed man was doing the same. But they could see nothing to shoot at. As Claire watched, she saw Hanne caught in a rush of people, swept away and towards the door. She was still waving the gun, shouting, struggling, yelling at the man who was left behind.

At the podium, the Doctor had mirrored Hitler's action, bending down so his head was level with the Scrying Glass. He was looking through it – straight at Hitler.

Claire still struggled towards them. 'The Glass, Doctor!' she shouted. 'Get the Glass.' There was someone beside her, helping her, taking her arm and pushing her forwards. She saw with surprise that it was the Brigadier.

'She's right, Doctor,' he yelled. 'Grab the thing and let's get out of here while we can!'

But the Doctor seemed as transfixed as Hitler. Both of them were staring into the Glass. And as they approached, Claire and the Brigadier could also see the image within it.

It was clear within the misty crystal. The TARDIS, where they had left it at the end of a corridor. The Doctor was opening the door, his motion slowed and drawn out. He was pushing the door open now. And he was ushering Hitler inside. The image faded, to be replaced by another. Claire recognised the place. She had seen

254

so many photographs. She had even been there, although now it was a grassy open space with apartment blocks around it. A single low brick-built ventilation stack was all that remained today to show what had once been underneath this place. The garden of the Reichschancellery – the entrance to Hitler's Fuhrerbunker.

Hitler and the Doctor were looking through the Glass now, at each other. Claire and the Brigadier had almost reached them through the storm. The Doctor's hair was blowing madly.

'You can take me there!' Hitler cried. 'That is your future.'

'Never!' the Doctor shouted back.

'You can take me back to complete the ceremony. My father can unlock the secrets of the Glass.' He straightened up, and reached for the Glass. 'You have seen it happen.'

The Doctor too was reaching for the Glass. Claire lunged forwards, the Brigadier slightly ahead of her.

But none of them reached it. Another hand plucked it from the stand, raising it above them in exaltation.

'At last!' Henderson cried above the noise. 'At last we shall be complete!' His eyes were glowing a fierce red as he turned in triumph towards the Doctor, the Scrying Glass resting on the palm of his outstretched hand. Without a word, the Doctor scooped up the two flat discs and slipped them into his coat pocket.

The wind died. Henderson's shadow was cast grotesquely across the podium by the light from the door. They could all see the two hunched figures, one on each side of him. The doorway was clear now. The room was empty – apart from Hitler and the Doctor looking up powerlessly at Henderson; apart from Claire and the Brigadier, frozen in tableau. Apart from the man with the gun.

With the sound of the storm dying away, the shot was deafening. It echoed and re-echoed round the room. It caught Henderson full in the chest, punching him backwards and knocking him off his feet. As he fell, the Scrying Glass tumbled from his hand.

The Doctor reacted quickest. He dived after Henderson,

catching the Scrying Glass one-handed at full stretch. He landed and rolled, coming up almost at once. 'Howzat?!' he shouted.

The Brigadier was at Henderson's side almost as quickly. He had landed face up, and over the Brigadier's shoulder, Claire could see that he was dead. A trickle of blood escaped from the side of his gaping mouth and ran down his cheek before dripping to the floor. In the dim light from the doorway she could see that his face was lined, his skin wrinkled. His fair hair had turned white in a moment, and his whole body seemed to have shrunk and wasted away within his blood-stained suit.

But she had no time to wonder at it. The Brigadier was standing again, running, grabbing her hand and pulling her after him. After the Doctor who was leaping across a fallen candle-holder and sprinting towards the door, the Scrying Glass flashing in his hand as it caught the light.

Hitler was screaming after them, shouting at the man to shoot again. Then he was running too, chasing after them.

The shadows along the aisle seemed to darken beside Claire as she ran. She was watching the man with the gun, watching him raise it again, watching him aim at the Doctor as he approached the man on his way to the doorway. So she was watching him as the shadows seemed to gather themselves and leap.

With an ear-splitting howling screech, a dark mass engulfed the man, knocking him sideways. The gun went off, the bullet ricocheting off the ceiling. Then the gun was itself spinning away towards the back wall. An arm lashed out of the shadows where the man lay, the shadows that seemed to tear and claw at his screaming body. The arm convulsed, the fingers clutching on thick air, before it was ripped from the body.

But then, mercifully, Claire had reached the door. She ran from the room, following the Brigadier and the Doctor down the corridor, hearing their shouts to her to hurry, and knowing that Hitler was close behind her.

She had not gone far when she realised that she was not alone. There was a blackness, a shadow running along the wall beside her, alongside her own shadow. As she watched, it seemed to separate into two discrete forms – the imps. Then the shapes dissolved into an amorphous smudge of darkness on the wall, sliding across the floor in front of her as she ran.

'Doctor!' she called.

Ahead of her, he turned in response to her shout, saw the darkness on the floor gather itself, spring towards him. It was as if the air had for a brief moment become solid. A lighting bolt of blackness cracked into the Doctor's outstretched palm.

The Scrying Glass in his hand was suddenly a smoky black. For a moment, as she drew level with him, Claire could see two faces staring back at her from the Glass in the Doctor's hand. Then it was clear again, and he stuffed it into his pocket.

'I think they want to go home,' the Doctor said as he ran.

'For once,' the Brigadier replied, 'I know exactly how they feel.'

Where everyone else had gone they neither knew nor cared. The corridors were as empty as when they had first arrived. Perhaps everyone had fled the base and were huddled outside in the icy wastes of Antarctica. Or perhaps they were barricaded in their rooms, waiting for the courage to emerge and see what was happening.

But as they hurried through the base, they saw nobody except the man chasing after them, screaming and shouting that he had seen the future and about his destiny and the Fourth Reich.

Claire was out of breath, rasping painfully long before they got back to the TARDIS. The Brigadier was in similar shape. The Doctor slowed so they could keep up, but despite his ample form he seemed to regard the procedure as light exercise rather than a sprint for their lives. The only thing that made Claire feel better was that Hitler was flagging too, falling further and further behind them.

They struggled to catch their breath outside the TARDIS as the Doctor fumbled through his pockets for the key. Claire leaned against the corridor wall, winded, vaguely aware that the door in the wall beside her was slightly ajar.

'What was that business in the Glass, then Doctor?' the

Brigadier managed to say. 'You and Hitler. And the TARDIS.'

The Doctor was upbeat. He brandished the TARDIS key, and tossed the Scrying Glass casually into the air before catching it again. 'I was never very hot on destiny,' he said. But as he finished speaking, the wide grin across his face became a sudden mask of shock and anger.

Claire had no time to ask him why. The cold muzzle of a gun jabbed painfully into her cheek and a black-uniformed arm wound tight round her throat.

'Her first. Then you,' Hanne Neumann said silkily. She nodded at the Doctor.

From further down the corridor came the sound of heavy breathing and rapid footsteps.

'Well done, Hanne,' Hitler said as he joined them. He walked up to the Doctor and stared him close in the face. 'Our destinies,' he said quietly, 'will be fulfilled.'

The Doctor looked from Claire, still held tight by Hanne, to the Brigadier. 'I've always been very keen on destiny,' he said with a tight, humourless smile.

He unlocked the TARDIS door and pushed it open. He ushered Hitler inside.

Chapter Thirty-five

They had never finished plastering the corridor walls. They were brown and they sweated, dank and dripping. The ceilings were low and the air was heavy. It was, Adolf Hitler often thought, like being dead and buried already. It was like being in a crypt. Cramped and crowded. Yet despite the people living on top of each other in the restricted space he was alone. Utterly alone. Apart from Eva.

As he walked through the central corridor, Bormann a few steps behind him, Hitler was aware of the mass of earth above him. The bunker was fifty feet below the ground. Above the ceiling was fifteen feet of reinforced concrete, earth and soil above that.

There was the muffled crump of an explosion as a shell landed somewhere above them, in the Reichschancellery or Foreign Office garden. A fragment of plaster fell from the ceiling. The lights were swaying and suddenly there was dust everywhere.

The Fuhrer coughed and waved his hand in an effort to clear the air. Fifty feet, he mused, and it still was not enough. But he had known that for weeks. And he would not have to endure it for very much longer. The Russians were within the city limits now. Soon, Berlin would fall. He was determined that he would not see that happen.

The noise of the TARDIS landing was lost in the sounds of war. The dull thump of its final materialisation might have been a shell landing half a mile away. Moments later, a small group emerged from the blue box – a smudge of colour in a desolated grey landscape drained of life.

At Hitler's son's insistence, the Doctor had substituted a huge dark greatcoat for his more usual multi-coloured one. Hitler would be the one to decide where and when they got people's attention. He led the way across the remains of the garden towards the emergency exit from the bunker. Hanne Neumann stood at the back, her pistol ready, urging the Doctor, Brigadier and Claire to follow her Fuhrer.

There was a guard at the door. He gaped when he saw Hitler approaching, evidently believing this to be his own Fuhrer and wondering why after so many days he had decided to leave the bunker. Perhaps he also wondered who the others were – the man in the massive great coat; the older man with a military bearing but dressed in a plain suit; the woman in unsuitably casual dress; and the woman in a variation of SS uniform holding a pistol. Perhaps he pondered on how well the Fuhrer was looking compared with his last public appearance on his birthday. But he said nothing.

The guard clicked his heels and saluted as he let them through the doorway. He watched them turn the corner, heard the sound of their feet on the steps, fading into the background noise of the Russian bombardment.

The Brigadier had a keen interest in military history. He had actually quite enjoyed researching what had happened and not happened in the Fuhrerbunker in 1945. But this was rather closer to events than he had ever hoped or wanted to get.

As they made their way down the steep, narrow staircase, he noticed that the Doctor was hanging back slightly, edging Claire ahead of him. As the Brigadier also passed him, the Doctor muttered, barely loud enough for him to hear:

'I'll distract her. You try to get Claire back to the TARDIS. I'll join you there when I can. No arguments.'

The Doctor's last instruction was redundant; there was obviously no time or opportunity to argue or debate the matter. So the Brigadier nodded slightly to show he had heard, and allowed the Doctor to fall behind him. As he did so, the Brigadier felt something slip into his jacket pocket – the TARDIS key.

A few years ago, he thought, it would have been him planning the heroics. A few – all right, quite a few – years ago he would have been up to disarming the woman with the gun and done it automatically as quickly as thinking about it. But his senses and his reactions were older and slower now. His strength was reduced and his confidence in his abilities was perhaps tempered both by the mitigation of those abilities and by an increasing sense of realism. And of mortality.

At the bottom of the stairs Hitler's son hesitated. There was a corridor leading onwards, badly lit and with a low ceiling. To the left there was a doorway giving on to another, wider passageway.

Hanne's attention was on Hitler as he decided which corridor to take. He turned at last towards the wider, better lit passageway to the left. And as he turned, so the Doctor moved.

It was an electric-fast movement: his hand and arm smashing upwards into Hanne Neumann's wrist, sending the pistol flying backwards so that it clattered on the concrete steps.

In the same moment, the Brigadier grabbed Claire. He had been hoping to drag or push her back up the steps, to run past the sentry before anyone realised what was happening or tried to stop them. But Hanne had fallen backwards across the stairway, scrabbling for the gun. And the Doctor in his efforts to stop her getting it was blocking the way. It would take forever to force their way past. So instead he pushed the young woman forwards, shoving Hitler aside and into the passageway.

The Brigadier ran, pulled the surprised Claire after him, along the dimly-lit corridor towards... who knew what. There was a door standing open a short way along. The Brigadier turned and made to slam it shut behind them.

As the door closed, he caught a glimpse of the scene at the foot of stairs. Hitler's son now held a gun too, had it jammed in the small of the Doctor's back. The Doctor had his hands raised, a resigned look on his face. Behind him, Hanne was picking herself up, and staring murderously after the Brigadier.

'Get after them,' Hitler shouted at her. 'Kill them both.'

Then the door closed and they were lost to view.

'Where are we going?' Claire asked

'Back to the TARDIS. I hope.'

'What about the Doctor?'

'It was his idea,' the Brigadier pointed out. 'He knows what he's doing. Usually,' he added under his breath.

The Brigadier pulled Claire after him as he hurried along, through yet another set of doors. There was an area caged off to their right, in which several large Alsatian dogs were lying bored. One looked up as they passed, but otherwise they seemed uninterested. Opposite this was a door. It was standing open, and the Brigadier could see that it was a large walk-in cupboard or small store room, various boxes arranged on shelves. Further along the passageway was another door, and then a flight of steps.

'Do you think we can get out this way?' Claire asked, breathless with hope and anticipation.

'It's a thought,' the Brigadier told her.

The steps led into a circular area structure. The base of an observation tower of some sort, the Brigadier decided. But it was unfinished. There was a rough concrete ceiling and the steps ended abruptly. Dead end. From below and behind them came the sound of a door slamming shut.

Hanne Neumann moved cautiously, like a cat. The gun felt natural in her hand, an extension of her very being. This was what she lived for – the hunter closing in on the prey. And when she found them...

Her senses seemed to move up a gear. The frail old man and the feeble young woman had made a fool of her back there. They had shown her up in front of the man she respected most in the world. And they would pay for it. She licked her lips.

There was a door across the corridor. She opened it, making no effort to hide the noise. Let them come. They were unarmed, and she knew from studying the Bunker that this corridor was a dead end. Dead. The old man first, she decided. He had been a soldier, she could tell. He would know how to deal with death. But the woman was a very different prospect. Her suffering would be exquisite.

The uniform hugged her close and warm as she tightened her grip on the gun.

* * *

The Brigadier's mind was racing. 'Stay here,' he snapped to Claire.

'Where are you going?'

'To try to stop her. Or at least lead her away.'

'Can I...' Claire gulped. 'Can I help?'

'Yes,' he told her. 'You can go back to the TARDIS and wait for us there.'

'What?'

He thrust the key into her hand. 'That will give me one less thing to worry about, and believe you me, Miss Aldwych, I have more than enough to concern me right now.'

He did not wait for her reaction or reply, but turned and ran back the way they had come. The only thing he could think to do was to get back to the small storeroom. Maybe there was something in there that he could use to slow her down.

Hanne entered the area at the same time as the Brigadier. He knew there was no escape back the way he had come. So instead he dived into the storeroom and slammed the door shut behind him. Mercifully, there was a light inside. He reached for the bolt on the door, but there was none.

Outside he could hear the dogs barking.

The handle of the door started to turn.

The gun was poking hard into the Doctor's back as he was pushed along the corridor. They saw nobody in the few yards to the door to Hitler's personal rooms.

'Sure this is the right room?' the Doctor asked.

'You think I wouldn't have studied the layout of my father's final resting place?'

'You didn't seem so sure earlier. Getting your bearings were you?'

Hitler's son did not reply. He leaned past the Doctor and opened the door, pushing it open. Then he shoved the Doctor inside.

'What now?'

They were in a small sitting room. There was a low table in

front of a long sofa. Several other small armchairs were arranged close by. The walls were panelled, lit by a single hanging bulb under a simple shade. There was a map of Europe on one wall. At the back of the room was another doorway, through which the Doctor could see a small dressing room, with a bedroom attached.

Hitler's son sat in one of the armchairs, the gun trained on the Doctor as he in turn seated himself on the sofa. He could feel the weight of the Scrying Glass and the two discs in his coat pocket as he arranged himself comfortably.

'Now,' Hitler said, 'we wait.'

One of the boxes was labelled 'Blondi.' Without really knowing why, the Brigadier lifted it quickly down before stepping behind the door. His guess – his hope – was that Hanne had rarely if ever come up against an enemy who knew what they were doing. Her operational experience might be limited to shooting people in cold blood or waving a gun about threateningly. That was all he had to rely on.

That and the box.

Blondi was a word he had recognised, clung to like a drowning man. Now, as the door swung slowly open towards him, he remembered what it was – Hitler's dog was called Blondi. In a moment he recalled how they had tested the cyanide on the dog, buried it with him, dug it up and moved it... Eventually burned it with its master's final remains and thrown the ashes in the river.

The door was still opening. He was looking quickly and quietly at the contents of the box – lead, collar, syringe, a tube of cream, a smaller box lined with cotton wool... After Hitler had discovered that Himmler was negotiating secretly with the allies, he had tested one of the poison ampoules on his dog. Himmler had provided the poison and Hitler had been worried that Himmler might have tricked him – might have substituted a sleeping potion meaning to dope Hitler then surrender him to the allies.

And as the door reached its full extent and Hanne's gun arm appeared in the Brigadier's line of sight, he gently lifted the tiny glass ampoule from the cotton wool. A spare poison capsule? Only one way to find out.

The dogs were still barking outside. She stepped into the room, swinging the gun in an arc, finding nobody there. He saw her whole body tense with realisation as she started to turn, to look behind her. Now. Now was the moment.

He stepped forward, dropping the box. It crumpled on the concrete floor, the contents spilling out. Her mouth was open in surprise and annoyance, which made it easier. He clamped one hand over her mouth, desperately reaching for the gun with the other, struggling to deflect the inevitable shot.

An explosion of sound. Falling plaster and masonry. Her breath hot on his palm as he forced the glass capsule inside her mouth. Smashing the gun against the edge of the open door. And again. Grip weakening, gun falling. Her eyes wide in anger and surprise, and perhaps fear. Then the gun hit the floor and he let go of her arm, moving his hand to her chin and forcing her mouth closed.

He held his breath as he heard the crunch of teeth on glass. Whipped his hand away as the foaming, screaming mass exploded from her mouth – spitting, retching, coughing. Falling.

Her body convulsed once. A massive, wrenching spasm. A final rasping exhalation. Then she was still. Curled and foetal.

The Brigadier stepped over Hanne Neumann's body, scooped up the gun and put it in his pocket. He paused to look down at her jack-knifed body. What a waste, he thought. But while he felt a deep, deep sadness he had no illusions about who was really responsible. Well, he thought ruefully, the monsters down here that looked like ordinary men needed a substitute body for Eva Braun. And here was a woman who might have made the sacrifice willingly.

He made his way back to the unfinished observation tower, his heart and his feet heavy. He called cautiously for Claire.

But she was gone.

The sound of Hanne's retching scream had confirmed to Claire that the Brigadier was more than capable of looking after himself.

She tiptoed past the door to the store room. She knew that if he was aware what she doing, the Brigadier would stop her.

But she just wanted a few shots, that was all. Some unique, exclusive still pictures. What was a story without pictures? A quick look round, then she would meet them back at the TARDIS as arranged. Surely there was no harm in that. But even as she thought this, a part of her mind was telling her that she should do as the Brigadier had said and get back to the TARDIS right now.

He had two choices, the Brigadier decided. He could return to the TARDIS as the Doctor had told him. Or he could try to find the Doctor and help him. No doubt the Doctor believed he could take care of himself. And no doubt he was wrong, the Brigadier thought wryly.

He made his way cautiously back to the steps where they had come in, and turned down the wide passageway that Hitler's son and the Doctor must have taken. Provided nobody questioned who he was or why he was here, there should be no problems. And in his pocket he had Hanne's gun.

He was perhaps halfway along the passage when he saw two people walking towards him from the other direction. One was short, stooping slightly. Beside him was a larger, broad-built man. The shorter man passed under a light, and the Brigadier recognised him at once. So the other man must be the Doctor. He prepared to draw the gun, to call to Hitler's son that the game was up, the die was cast, it was all over now.

But then, the other man also emerged from the shadows and the Brigadier found himself looking into the face of Reichsleiter Martin Bormann.

Hitler, he now saw as they stood close to each other, was a shell of his former self. He was barely recognisable as the same man the Brigadier had met three years previously. His eyes were no longer a startling iceberg blue, but hazy and faded. He held his left arm with his right as he walked, to stop it shaking. He was stooped. He looked old. For a moment the Brigadier was reminded of the empty shell of a village that Turelhampton had become – a vestige of its former self, but emptied of life. Of soul.

Turelhampton was burning. Hitler would go the same way. Wouldn't he?

'What are you doing here?' Bormann demanded.

But Hitler spoke before the Brigadier could answer. 'Brigadier General Braun.' His eyes flickered with recognition. 'Come to pay your last respects to your Fuhrer?' He did not wait for an answer. 'Is the Doctor here too? He lives?' His voice was a husky croak, but there was a hint of enthusiasm behind the question. 'I should like to meet him again. Just once more.'

'Er, yes.' The Brigadier cleared his throat, feeling embarrassment more than anything else. 'He's here somewhere.'

The Fuhrer nodded. 'Excellent. That is excellent news. I shall await him in my rooms. You may come too,' he told the Brigadier. It was obviously not an invitation he was expected to turn down. 'Eva will be joining us shortly. You remember Eva?' Hitler started walking again, taking the Brigadier's arm, leaning on him for support. 'We are married now you know,' he added, almost wistfully. He seemed not to notice the Brigadier's intake of breath and the way he cringed at the Fuhrer's touch.

She saw nobody. It was as if, Claire thought, the bunker was dying along with Berlin. It had taken her only a moment to realise that the Brigadier was right. It was foolhardy to the point of stupidity to try to get pictures. Who could she show them to? Who would believe her?

And, almost against her nature, she found that she could not betray the Brigadier – her friend, she realised, with a half-smile – by abusing his trust. So she made her way cautiously back to the stairway, and started to climb.

For several moments they just stared at each other. Bormann stood in the doorway, his mouth hanging open in astonishment. Then he seemed to gather himself and shut the door.

The Brigadier glanced uneasily at the Doctor who seemed comfortable on the sofa. He grinned back.

'Father!' breathed the younger Hitler. He stood up slowly, and took a step towards the Fuhrer, the gun still in his hand, shaking with emotion. 'Father, I cannot believe that I am meeting you now.'

The Fuhrer stared back at him, his face white but expressionless. 'Who are you?' he demanded. Then he turned towards the sofa. 'Doctor, my friend – who is this man?'

Hitler's son stopped, incredulous. He gaped, turned to the Doctor, his face a mask of astonishment.

'I did warn you,' the Doctor said quietly. Then he too stood up. He clicked his heels and gave a short bow. 'My Fuhrer,' he said, 'I am delighted to renew your acquaintance. And this man,' he nodded apologetically at the younger Hitler, 'tells me that his name is Adolf Hitler.'

Claire felt better for the air. April 30th, the Doctor had said when they arrived. There was a clock tower behind the blue incongruity of the TARDIS, just visible in the smoky distance. She could see that the clock said it was ten minutes to three. Assuming it was working.

A cloud of smoke rose noisily beside the clock tower. The air stank of cordite.

Bormann reacted quickest. With four brisk strides, he was across the room. He wrenched the gun from Hitler's son's grasp and held it for the Fuhrer to see.

'What is the meaning of this?' he demanded, looking at each of them in turn. 'However faithfully you have served the Fuhrer, there is no excuse for breaking into his private rooms uninvited in these last days.'

'The door was unlocked,' the Doctor murmured.

The Brigadier said nothing. He at least had been invited inside.

The younger Hitler was still staring at the husk of a man that had been his father. Whatever he had expected, whatever anticipation of this historic meeting he might have had, it seemed he was disappointed in what he had found. But he gathered himself, blinked, and started to speak.

To the Brigadier, who knew the story he was telling, it made sense. But even so, it was hard work keeping up with the changes of location and time, the dislocated images and the man's half-remembered upbringing. To Hitler and to Bormann he could tell it would sound like gibberish. The way the Doctor spread his hands, shrugged, smiled sympathetically and raised his eyebrows heavenwards only added to the picture that the younger Hitler was painting of himself.

Before he was even halfway through his story, Hitler senior interrupted. 'What is he talking about?' he demanded of the Doctor.

'I'm sorry,' the Doctor said. 'He forced me in here at gunpoint.'

'You must have some idea.'

The Doctor smiled. 'It is a tale told by an idiot,' he said. The younger Hitler started to object, but the Doctor shouted over him. 'Full of sound and fury,' he cried. 'Signifying nothing!'

The younger Hitler was shaking with rage now. But the Doctor ignored him and turned to the Fuhrer, his voice calmer. 'I'm sorry, I had no intention of troubling you with these things at such a time as this.'

'You know?' Hitler asked. 'You know what I intend to do this afternoon? But of course you do.' He nodded as if this were confirmation of his plan.

'No, you must listen to me,' the younger Hitler said through gritted teeth.

'Why?' Bormann demanded.

'What can you possibly tell me that will help now?' the older Hitler asked him. 'You who have stolen my face and it seems my name. Who are you to break in here and talk to us in such a way?'

'Have you heard nothing I've said?' He took a step towards his father, ignoring the gun in Bormann's hand. 'I am your son!' he shouted. His blue eyes were wide with anger and pleading. 'I am the Coming Man.'

Hitler stared at him dumbstruck.

'See what I mean,' the Doctor said apologetically. 'He's really not himself, you know.'

'Ask – ask the Scrying Glass,' the younger Hitler said, his voice calmer now. In control. He ignored the Doctor.

This the Fuhrer could understand. 'What do you know of the Scrying Glass?' he demanded.

'Everything! The symbol of our power. The future in a crystal.'

The Fuhrer looked at the Doctor. But the Doctor shook his head. 'I have told him nothing. Well,' he added, 'nothing of consequence anyway.' He paused, and the Brigadier could see that a thought had occurred to him. 'It's a pity we can't ask Heinrich Himmler what he makes of all this,' he said levelly.

The Brigadier was not sure what the Doctor hoped to achieve by his words. But the younger Hitler latched on to them at once. 'Of course – Himmler. He understands the arcane mysteries and the instruments of darkness. He was a man of learning and wisdom in these matters. He is sure to understand.'

For a moment there was silence. The Brigadier could see from the expression on Bormann's face that this was a turning point. The Doctor raised his eyebrows, his expression edging towards the smug. 'So,' he said, stirring in the poison, 'you think we should seek the informed and informative opinion of former Reichsfuhrer Himmler?'

The effect on the older Hitler was astounding. He had been glaring at his double, as if trying to decide what to say. He seemed to draw himself up. His eyes were clear now, focused and sharp. 'Himmler?' he cried. 'The Bavarian peasant – we reach an age where we have finally left mysticism behind and he wants to reinvent it. Even in these last days he sends out his Oriental lackeys to commit suicide in the hope of raising some supernatural help. And when that fails, he goes to the allies...' The anger seemed to boil out of him. 'That traitor! That bastard has betrayed us all.'

The younger Hitler was backing away, uncertain now, his confidence all but broken by this tirade. His father stepped after him, Bormann close on their heels.

'But the Scrying Glass – look in the Scrying Glass,' Hitler's son said. 'It's in the Doctor's pocket.'

'Is it?' the Doctor asked innocently.

The Fuhrer halted abruptly. 'Now I know you are mad,' he said levelly. 'Reichleiter Bormann has the Scrying Glass, ready to take it to a place of safety. Along with... with other materials.'

Behind him, Bormann nodded.

The younger Hitler took another pace backwards. He was almost in the doorway through to the bedroom now. 'Please, father – listen to me. At least hear me out!'

The Fuhrer hesitated. The Brigadier held his breath. He felt the Doctor tense beside him as they watched. Let the man talk and he might yet convince Hitler of the truth. Give him time to get his thoughts together and he might present a sensible argument.

But before the Fuhrer could say anything, there was a knock at the door. They all turned to watch as the door opened.

Eva Braun stepped into the room. 'Darling,' she said, 'it is time.' Then she saw the younger Hitler over her husband's shoulder, framed in the doorway to the dressing room. She blinked in astonishment, focusing at last on the figure of the Doctor.

'Delighted to meet you again,' the Doctor said. 'And congratulations, by the way.'

'Doctor,' she acknowledged. 'And General Braun, isn't it?' The Brigadier nodded stiffly. She turned towards the figure in the other doorway, his mouth working soundlessly. 'But you...'

'You don't know him?' the Doctor asked.

She glanced at her husband, then shook her head. 'No. Indeed, no...'

The younger Hitler was staring back at her, his eyes wide and watery.

The Doctor sighed theatrically. 'Yet he seems to know you.' He turned towards the younger Hitler. 'You know who this is, don't you?'

His voice was dry and choked. He was shaking with emotion. 'Mother,' he croaked.

Eva Braun's hand flew to her mouth. She was trembling. Her other hand clutched suddenly at her stomach as if in pain.

Slowly, her husband turned away from her, back towards the man in the doorway.

The Brigadier almost gasped out loud.

Beside him, the Doctor's expression and manner was suddenly deadly serious. He looked from one Hitler to the other, and then to Eva. Finally he turned back to the younger Hitler. He was the one who seemed stooped and old now. 'How dare you?' the Doctor said.

The Fuhrer's hand – his left hand – was held out towards Bormann, the palm open. It was shaking slightly, but nothing like as much as it had in the corridor outside. 'How dare you,' he whispered hoarsely, repeating the Doctor's inflection as well as his words. Without comment, Bormann placed the gun in his outstretched hand.

Hitler's son stepped backwards again, mouth working silently. He was inside the dressing room now, shaking his head, face drained of colour.

The Fuhrer brought the gun up, single-handed. His knuckles whitened.

The Brigadier gave an inadvertent gasp of shock as the gun went off.

The shot caught the man who would have ruled over the Fourth Reich in the dead centre of the forehead. His eyes rolled upwards as if to see where he had been hit. At the same moment he was sent staggering backwards by the force of the bullet, slammed through the small dressing room to collapse on the bed in the room beyond. He sat there, seemingly dazed for a moment. Then his head fell forwards, and the blood splattered on to the covers.

'Check he is dead,' Hitler told the Doctor. 'You are a doctor, after all.' He ushered them through to his bedroom. 'Eva and I must say our farewells soon. And then... Well,' he sighed, 'then this madness will be over. And a new madness will take hold of the world.'

He turned to Bormann. 'You will attend to matters? As we discussed?'

'Of course.' Bormann looked pale. 'And...' he nodded towards the corpse bleeding on the bed.

The Brigadier looked at it too. The blood on the bed, he understood now. 'The double,' he murmured. 'In the water tower.'

'Yes,' Hitler said, standing beside him. 'A good notion.' He turned back to Bormann. 'Dump it in the water tower. And after that there is another matter that requires your attention.'

Bormann nodded. 'The woman's body. Of course.' He hefted the corpse on to his broad shoulders and carried it from the room. A single arm flopped pathetically down, fingers trailing lifelessly through the air.

Hitler turned back to the Brigadier. 'Farewell, Brigadier General Braun,' he said, and shook him by the hand. The Brigadier said nothing. Felt nothing. He just stared at Eva Braun, as if he could see the life forming within her, and then back at Hitler. Thinking where it would all end. Two evil lives, ended under the same crumbling ceiling.

'And you, Doctor.' Hitler took the Doctor's hand in both his own. 'You have been a good and faithful man.'

The Doctor's face was grave, unreadable. 'I try my best,' he said.

Hitler nodded, as if he understood. Then they left him there with his wife, closing the door behind them.

Claire stood in the shadow of the TARDIS, the key half-inserted in the lock. She paused and took in a final impression of bombed-out Berlin, staring round stupidly, aware this view would have to last her almost 60 years. From where she was standing, she had a good view of the water tower where the body of Hitler's double had been – or rather would be – found.

As she gazed across at it, wondering where she had stood – would stand years later – when she visited the site, she saw a figure making its way from the Bunker towards the water tower. It was a big man, carrying a body over his shoulders. She recognised Martin Bormann as he turned towards her for a moment, adjusting the weight of the body. This was a dream, an impossibility. She stared, transfixed.

The corpse swung slightly as Bormann continued his progress. For a moment the face was visible, and Claire felt a jolt of shock – Adolf Hitler. Then she realised it was the double. And who the double was.

* * *

'We know what happens now,' the Doctor said quietly to the Brigadier as they left the sitting room.

The Brigadier nodded. 'There's a ready-made replacement for Miss Braun – Mrs Hitler, I should say – lying in the store cupboard back there.'

The Doctor looked questioningly at him. 'Hanne…?'

'Well, what else is the woman good for?' the Brigadier said brusquely. 'Let's find Miss Aldwych and get out of here.'

The Doctor frowned. 'Claire? I thought she was with you. Where is she?'

'Well, I hope she's gone back to the TARDIS, Doctor.' He gave a hurried account of events.

'You know, Brigadier,' the Doctor said when he had finished, 'I have the greatest respect for you.'

'Why do I feel a "but" coming next, Doctor?' Lethbridge-Stewart asked.

'But,' the Doctor said deliberately, 'Claire is a journalist. And as far as she is concerned, this is the story of the century.'

The Brigadier nodded, chastened. 'I take your point. Where do we start?'

The Doctor sighed and shook his head. 'If we wait about ten minutes, she'll come here.'

'Here? But why?' The Doctor just looked at him. 'Oh, yes of course. The death of Hitler. I see.'

'And I'm not sure we'll be welcome guests at that point. Not least because history doesn't want us here.'

'Doctor, I don't want us here. So where would you recommend?'

They started at the far end of the Bunker. It was mercifully small, and the guard at the spiral staircase that led to the upper level – the servants' quarters and Goebbels' rooms – assured them that no woman had been that way in the past hour at least.

'Perhaps she really has gone back to the TARDIS?' the Brigadier hazarded as they found themselves approaching Hitler's rooms again. 'I gave her the key. And there isn't much else left.'

Outside the Fuhrer's rooms, a small group was gathered.

'We need a distraction,' the Doctor murmured. At that moment, a middle-aged woman pushed past them and rushed towards the door.

'Magda Goebbels,' the Brigadier said. 'She'll force her way in to see the Fuhrer one last time. Beg him not to go through with it.'

The Doctor nodded. 'That will do,' he said. 'She was really pleading for her own life, of course,' he said grimly. 'And her husband's. And her children's lives too.'

There was confusion outside Hitler's room now. Magda Goebbels was shouting, banging on the door. Several men were trying to hold her back. The corridor was blocked, and there was no option but to wait.

The valet, Linge, was wringing his hands, pacing to and fro, checking his watch every few seconds. His pacing brought him face to face with the Brigadier, and he frowned, puzzled. He opened his mouth to speak, but abruptly turned back towards the door to Hitler's rooms.

Linge's voice was hoarse and raw. 'Was that a shot?' he asked.

If the distant clock was correct, if this was April 30th 1945, then Hitler – the real Adolf Hitler – would soon be saying his final farewells in the corridor outside his room. Claire blew out a long breath and shuffled her feet, still taking it all in outside the doors of the magic police box. She was getting cold, but knew that an experience like this – to be back in time almost sixty years, and to be *here*, *now*...

The moment would never come again.

Just across the torn-up ground in front of her – between the TARDIS and the Bunker – that was where the photographs showed the shell crater where the bodies had been unearthed.

But there was no crater. The ground was churned up, the grass patchy and broken with mud. But there was no crater.

How could that be? Instinctively she walked across the shattered garden towards where the crater should be. She dug the toe of her shoe into a lonely, dying tuft of grass.

She looked up, startled for some reason she could not immediately place. Maybe it was the movement – Bormann was returning across the garden, making for the Bunker exit. He seemed to be hurrying, glancing back and up at the sky.

Then she heard the noise… It was a whining, whistling sound. She had not been aware of it until now. But it was growing louder and closer by the moment. From above her.

It took Claire only a split-second to connect the sound in the sky with the crater that was not yet there. Then she was running, running for all she was worth. The entrance to the Bunker was closer than the TARDIS and she sprinted towards it.

Bormann was standing in the doorway now, looking back at her, encouraging her. And with a cry of relief, she threw herself forwards, stumbling and falling into the huge man's arms.

For a moment he held her. 'Perfect,' he breathed.

Then he was dragging her outside again; even as she struggled against his short, powerful form, even as the whistling grew louder to a piercing shriek, he pushed her away from him, hurled her across the muddy remains of the garden.

Into the blast.

The explosion threw mud and debris high into the ashen sky. It caught her across the chest as she screamed, covering her face. Bormann had turned away, mud splattering across his back.

She was sinking, falling, clutching at the edge of the crater.

Alive.

The smoke was settling like mist over the newly-formed shell crater. Claire's body had been thrown against the edge of it, one hand clutching upwards as if to pull herself up and out. Through her tears and through the pain and through the drifting smoke she could see Bormann walking slowly towards her, fumbling in his jacket pocket. But already her vision was misting over.

Through a blur she saw him reach down to her, and breathed a racking, retching sigh of relief. She felt his hand under her head, lifting it slightly. Then, through the red of her tears she saw his fingers groping towards her face, saw the glass ampoule that caught the shadowy light filtering through the smoke and the blood. Felt the hard, cold glass in her mouth and the savage thrust of his fist under her jaw.

And she felt the crunch and the fire as the glass broke in her mouth.

The door to Hitler's rooms was standing open. The Doctor sighed and patted the Brigadier heavily on the shoulder. 'The weight of history,' he said quietly. 'This will only take a moment.'

He crossed to where the bodies were. Adolf Hitler first. The Doctor gave the man's neck a cursory inspection with his fingers, as if he couldn't quite bring himself to take the task seriously. It was apparent anyway, from the hole in the top of head, the blood dripping from his mouth, that Hitler was dead. Dead and gone, like his as-yet unborn legacy. The Brigadier couldn't help a slow, satisfied smile spread over his face, but was puzzled to find a tear squeezing itself from his eye at the same time. He rubbed it away, self-consciously.

Eva Braun's body was curled on the couch, her eyes closed. There was no apparent injury. A pistol lay untouched on the table in front of her. Bormann, his uniform freshly splashed with mud, pushed past the Brigadier and joined the Doctor as he reached the body. After a moment the Doctor straightened up and shook his head. 'I'm afraid she's dead too,' he said, looking directly at the Brigadier as he told the lie. Then he nodded to Bormann.

They left Bormann giving instructions to the others. He wrapped Eva's body in a blanket himself, then carried it from the room.

They paused outside the TARDIS and looked back, across the garden. Bormann was carefully putting down the blanket he was carrying on the side of the crater further from the Bunker exit. From where they were, the Brigadier and the Doctor saw him check quickly that he was ahead of the others, then nod.

A figure, a young woman, got up cautiously from the blanket. She ran quickly to a group of trees by the wall, hiding in the shadows. Then Bormann rearranged the blanket, just as the soldiers arrived with Hitler's body.

The Brigadier felt suddenly cold. 'Doctor,' he said slowly. 'Doctor, don't you think we should check?'

Without a word, they both walked slowly back towards the crater.

There were two bodies on the ground as expected, both covered by blankets. As they watched, the blankets erupted into fire. Flames curled and licked out of the burning mass. The blankets seemed to peel back, away from the bodies.

There was a gust of wind, enough to blow the flames sideways for a moment. For that instant, Hitler's face was once again revealed, staring sightlessly at the sky.

'Well,' the Brigadier reflected, 'at least we know it really was him after all.'

'Something of a relief,' the Doctor agreed.

'As for the woman...' The Brigadier's voice trailed off. The blanket had burned away from the second body too, revealing the face of a girl in her late-twenties through the smoky, oily flames. Her eyes were also open, also sightless. A shock of red hair frazzled suddenly in the heat.

'No,' the Brigadier breathed.

'Claire,' the Doctor murmured. 'Oh Claire.'

'Why, Doctor?' The Brigadier's voice was hoarse. 'Why, when that Nazi bitch is lying dead in that bunker? Why someone good, someone –'

The Brigadier broke off when he realised the Doctor wasn't listening. He was just staring at Claire as her body burned and blackened, became one with the lengthening shadows stretching over the ruined city.

Then he turned and walked back to the TARDIS without a word.

In the distance the shells were still dropping and the guns still firing, edging ever nearer. Acrid smoke blew into the Brigadier's face, stinging his eyes to tears. Then he turned and followed after the Doctor, to where the Police Box stood waiting to depart.

Waffenstillstand

'It ends now.'

The Doctor stood at the broiling edge of the powerfield. Behind him, a few metres away, the Brigadier and Captain Palmer were standing at the head of the UNIT force beaten back by its relentless advance. And before him were the spectral shapes of the Vvormak familiars, four of them, their grotesque silhouettes standing as thick and dark as shadows at high noon, unharmed in the maelstrom.

He held out the Scrying Glass and the two discs to them, his fingers mere inches away from the poisonous energy. The impish creatures shimmered and danced.

One spoke; there was a noise like someone blowing into the neck of a bottle, but the words themselves seemed to sound in the Doctor's mind. 'You bring our survivors.'

'Yes, they're here. Held safely in the Glass.'

'Then, the ship is complete.'

The Doctor nodded wearily. He ached as if his soul were sick. He wanted nothing better than to throw this wretched crystal ball as far as he could with the little strength he had left and just walk away from the monsters, from the burning land that was being devoured around him. But he wouldn't of course. He *couldn't*. He'd see the trial through.

'Your long wait is over at last,' he said. 'But just as I come to you voluntarily, and in the spirit of peace, so I would ask that you leave the Earth without reprisal.'

The shadows said nothing. The Doctor took a half-step back as the crackling of the powerfield seemed to intensify a little, held the components back to his chest. The tarmac he stood on was starting to bubble and crack, all around a thin, foul-smelling smoke blew as further field and hedgerow went up in orange flame.

The Doctor tried again. 'You must know that the energy with

which Henderson provided you will devastate this place when you leave. You can see that leakage has already done irreparable damage to the environment. Please…' His voice shook, and he paused for a moment. 'Let me work with you to find a way to let you depart with no further loss of life.'

Again, the eerie melodic whistling. 'The Vvormak shall depart on low power only, converting the leakage into fuel, and realising the full energy potential from this place and from the tainted Glass safely in space.'

The Doctor realised he'd been holding his breath. He released it slowly. 'Thank you,' he said simply, offering them the Glass and the focusing chips, the ghost of a smile on his lips.

His palms tickled as if a feather brushed across them, and then the components, and the shadows, were gone.

'Well, Doctor?' he heard the Brigadier call tentatively from behind him.

The Doctor just stared into the heat-haze, felt the energies crackling in front of his face. How many times had he tempted fate, cheated death?

'Doctor?'

There was no sense agonising over what he should and shouldn't do, he'd thought

'Doctor, is everything all right now?'

But when it all went wrong… when he warred with Time and others were caught in the crossfire…

There was a simple elegance to the way it responded to such stimulus

The Doctor closed his eyes, felt fierce heat on his skin. Thought of Claire, her body charred black, long ago.

When he looked again, the powerfield had gone. Vanished, just like that. Like a shadow will vanish when a cloud pushes over the sun.

The Brigadier walked over to join him by his side. Ahead of them in a mighty arc was barren land, scorched featureless and dead, stretching ahead of them as far as they could see.

'Have they gone?' he asked.

Overhead, in the sky, a bright red stain was spreading. A few seconds later a sound like muted thunder rumbled around the crumbling, deserted remains of Turelhampton. And still there was the bright light, leaving just an impression printed on the retina: like a firecracker explosion. Ruined buildings. A blood-red sky over a devastated landscape.

'They've gone,' affirmed the Doctor. 'The nuclear energy has been converted into fuel.' He paused. 'Along with all the hate and the fear and the potential of the Fourth Reich.'

'I'll arrange for a clean-up squad to go to that Antarctic base. There should be all the information we need there to uncover these secret Nazi cells. To smash them.'

The Doctor sighed sullenly. 'It's over.'

'Thanks to you,' the Brigadier said quietly.

'Oh yes,' the Doctor said bitterly. 'Well done me. Always me, whipping up the storm and waiting at its epicentre, watching as others are swept up around me... but only watching *out* for myself.'

'The Vvormak ship was at the epicentre of this particular storm, I believe, Doctor,' said the Brigadier gruffly. 'And watching from here you have a choice of views.' He pointed before them with his swagger stick. 'The dead past on one side...'

He gently steered the Doctor round to face the opposite way, where the fields stretched out serenely as if nothing had happened.

'And on this side, the present. The living present, that will lead to a future.'

The Doctor wouldn't look up, hands thrust deep in his pockets. He stared down at the grey tarmac of the narrow road that he knew fizzled to a stop behind him.

The Brigadier cleared his throat. 'Doctor, I know that you're compelled to walk between the two... always will be. But don't ever forget the differences you make. Even if the battle seems lost... the war's won.'

He placed a hand on the Doctor's shoulder.

And then he was gone, shouting to Palmer, ordering the men,

taking the first steps to sweep all this under a carpet somewhere in Whitehall.

As the last of the UNIT soldiers trickled away about him, the Doctor finally looked up, took in the fine Dorset countryside stretching out to a thick blue wedge of sea under the strengthening sun. He wanted to take a deep breath, but the air here still carried the taint of the burning fumes. He would find somewhere closer to the sea, watch it rise and fall, feel the salt spray on his skin, perhaps. Breathe clean air again.

He would do that soon.

Historical Note

Obviously *The Shadow in the Glass* is a work of fiction. However, just as obviously, it does overlap with historical events. Part of the fun and the challenge has been to produce the fiction without disturbing the truth.

So, for those who are interested, we have tried not to contradict anything that actually happened. Of course, so far as those last days in Hitler's Bunker are concerned, there is plenty of room even now for speculation. But the characters are real, and everything the Brigadier discovers in his researches is established historical fact, with one exception (which we shall come to in a moment). Whether or not that also is true, is still a matter of debate, but the reported sightings of Hitler and others after the war are well documented, the autopsy reports are now available. And yes – Hitler and Eva Braun's bodies really were identified by a dental nurse's recollection of the state of their teeth. (Hitler's dentist was captured by the Americans, and the Russians did not want to ask for his help and thereby admit they had a corpse that might be Hitler's.)

Have we cheated? Of course we have. And it's only fair to own up. But the extent to which we have manipulated things, apart of course from having the TARDIS and its occupants arrive in the Reichschancellery garden on April 30th 1945, is actually very small.

We have ignored evidence that doesn't support our story, though actually there isn't much. If you want to know more, seek out Hugh Trevor-Roper's *The Last Days of Hitler*, or the latest and, to our minds most complete account and explanation – *The Death of Hitler*, by Ada Petrova and Peter Watson (W.W. Norton and Company, 1995).

Hitler's pilot, Hans Baur, was never reported to be captured by the Americans before the Russians took him, and the transcript of his interrogation by the USAF is entirely fictional. In any case, the Russians found him to be at best an 'unreliable' witness.

Most documentaries and written works on the subject will tell you that the corpse of Hitler's doppelganger found in the water tower has never been identified. Actually, it seems likely it was one Gustave Weler who was employed in the Reichschancellery and did actually work as a double for Hitler on occasion.

Reichsleiter Martin Bormann almost certainly died trying to escape from Berlin. He did indeed set up secret funding in 1944 for the continuation of the Reich, calling on help from German industry as well as 'friendly' industrialists and businessmen in Europe and the USA. The amount he raised was huge – in today's terms, allowing for compound interest and inflation, it would be in the region of a trillion dollars. For many years, Bormann was thought to have escaped. But what is almost certainly his body was discovered on waste ground in West Berlin in 1972. There were in fact two bodies, the other has been identified as (again probably) Doctor Ludwig Stumpfegger – the man who actually certified Hitler dead in the Bunker.

And, of course, Turelhampton does not exist any more than what fell on it in May 1944. That said, in November 1943, ten square miles of Dorset including the village of Tyneham was evacuated at very short notice to make way for D-Day training manoeuvres. Despite promises made at the time, the village has never been returned to its former inhabitants. The 'ghost village' of Tyneham remains as it was following the evacuation and subsequent manoeuvres. It is now demilitarised and owned by the National Trust.

Strange as it may seem, the fact that our theory (born out of desperation when for reasons that need not concern us here, we had just two days in which to come up with a detailed outline for this novel) seems to stand up has been a serious worry. Have we missed something obvious?

Almost certainly the basic elements of the theory we put forward for what happened, and why, are speculative nonsense. But even so, we've found ourselves looking over our shoulders these last few weeks, half-expecting to catch sight of the fleeting shadow of someone who doesn't want the truth to come out.

Maybe writing about conspiracies does that to you.

Justin Richards & Stephen Cole
17 January 2001

About the Authors

JUSTIN RICHARDS is a writer and editor. Amongst other misdemeanours he acts as Doctor Who Range Consultant to BBC Worldwide, which means that if you don't like the books, basically it's all his fault. That's doubly true for this one.

One of Justin's goals for 2001 was to avoid having to write a Doctor Who novel. So here it is.

STEPHEN COLE is a writer and editor. Amongst other misdemeanours he acted for three years as Doctor Who Range Consultant to BBC Worldwide, which means that if you used to dislike the books, basically it was all his fault. That's doubly true for this one.

One of Stephen's goals for 2001 was to write a Doctor Who novel – so here's his second in a month.